# PASSAGE OAK

*Other books in the Silent Grove collection*

*Whitebeam*

*Willow Oak*

# PASSAGE OAK

by K.M. Del Mara

Printed in the United States of America, First Printing, 2015

Characters, establishments, and events related herein exist solely in the minds of the author and readers.


ISBN 978-0-9883967-5-3 *Passage Oak* Paperback

ISBN 978-0-9883967-6-0 *Passage Oak* E-book

Library of Congress Control Number: 2015913176


Contact K.M. del Mara at

kmdelmara@hotmail.com

www.kmdelmara.com




*Cover design by K.M. del Mara*
*Photos used with permission*

*Front cover photo by Henry Zielinski, reworked by the author*

*Back cover photo by Baz Richardson, reworked by the author*

*IN MEMORY*

*of my grandparents,*

*Ward and Florence Beckwith Smith,*

*and*

*of Margaret, my mother,*

*the little waif they cherished.*

*When the oak is felled the whole forest echoes with its fall,*

*but a hundred acorns are sown in silence*

*by an unnoticed breeze*

-Thomas Carlyle (1795 – 1881)

\*\*

*A noiseless patient spider,*

*I marked where on a little promontory it stood isolated,*

*Marked how to explore the vacant vast surrounding,*

*It launched forth filament, filament, filament, out of itself,*

*Ever unreeling them, ever tirelessly speeding them.*

*And you O my soul where you stand,*

*Surrounded, detached, in measureless oceans of space,*

*Ceaselessly musing, venturing, throwing, seeking the spheres to*

*connect them,*

*Till the bridge you will need be formed, till the ductile anchor hold,*

*Till the gossamer thread you fling catch somewhere, O my soul.*

-Walt Whitman (1819-1892) *Leaves of Grass*

# NOTE

*T*here is a type of oak tree known as a Cornish oak. It is a sessile oak, which means its acorns grow without stalks. Its Latin name, *petraea*, indicates its preference for rocky places. Since prehistoric times, Cornish oaks were plentiful in the British Isles. They grow to great heights and can be of immense age. The famous Pontfadog Oak in North Wales was thought to be over twelve hundred years old before it blew down in high winds in 2013. Its trunk measured over forty-two feet in girth.

The people of Porthcoombe, Cornwall have their own version of a historic tree. They have used a certain Cornish oak as a landmark for generations. In their tight, tradition-bound community, where anything unique or remarkable is looked upon with suspicion, this old tree is an exception. They used to call it the Tremen Oak, the Cornish word 'tremen' meaning passage, though only a few villagers knew the reason why it was given this name.

A vast variety of creatures make homes in the Passage Oak, and such a number of ferns, mosses and lichens co-exist there that its trunk is clothed in green. Ages from now, when it falls, even as it decays on the forest floor, the old oak will continue to sustain, in great variety, a multitude of life forms.

$W$e wrestle constantly with the problem of which bridges to burn and which bridges to cross.

Where do we find the conviction to make a choice? "Measureless oceans of space", spanned by a bridge -- should we cross or not? We make a decision with a flutter of fear, and that bridge falls behind, forever behind us. Try as we might, we can never circle back there again. Not to that same bridge, over that same space.

Caroline Sydney burned a bridge when she decided that she and her daughter must part. Emilia was four days old. This separation broke open an abyss that could never be bridged. The mother struggled with it. The daughter struggled with it. It was a ghost that walked beside them all their days, a persistent wondering about the other. How could such an emptiness weigh so heavily? By a wonderful coincidence, they did finally come together, but their meeting was cruelly interrupted. Death issued that decree. Their time together had to be short. So short that months passed before Emilia even realized it had happened, though we must hope that Caroline knew before she closed her eyes for the last time.

When Caroline Sydney died, the people at her bedside did not even know her name. But her death was not entirely unmarked by an impassive universe. If nothing else, her passing left a gap.

Where Caroline had been, now there was a void, and that void needed to be filled. Because the universe does not allow emptiness. Whatever is available, whether anticipated or unexpected, desired or undesirable, whatever is at hand, that is what comes flooding in.

When that happens, something begins. Maybe no one notices at first. The pendulum of Time, like a spider's bound prey, swings back and forth above the void. But far, far down in that dark emptiness, something new begins to grow.

London, England
November 1818
The *Crocodile*

*O*n a gray morning in early November, there was only one passenger, a woman, waving from the deck of the merchant ship *Crocodile* as it pulled away from the dock. After months of indecision about this trip, the woman had recklessly made a choice. Since her mother in London was not expected to live much longer, the woman wanted to complete a rather singular search for her sake. Therefore, quite suddenly, she decided she needed to go to Cornwall, and she didn't care what vessel took her there. The *Crocodile* had scheduled a stop at Penzance, to load tin. They would also discharge the woman, their only passenger, before sailing straight south to the port of Gijon, Spain.

By terrible coincidence, an early winter storm of mythic intensity came barreling out of the North Sea, heading in the same direction. The woman passenger had sailed through storms before, but this time she was frightened. She knew she would not rest easy until she was standing on Cornish soil. She simply had to get to Penzance.

She heard the captain call for all hands. She could sense uneasiness among the crew. But the captain insisted they could stay ahead of the storm, so they ran before the wind under full sail. The woman pulled her cloak close about her. But when the freezing rain started, the heaving deck became so slippery she could barely find a footing. She retreated to her cabin and left the frantic sailors to battle the storm.

The angry wind was gorged with wintry cold. It beat about the *Crocodile* until every spar, every shroud and cable became encased with ice. The crew fought to maintain their heading but the struggle was exhausting.

The stubborn captain finally relented. He shouted to the crew to lower everything but a staysail.

But by then the pulleys had frozen and nothing would move.

The weight of the ice-covered canvas made the *Crocodile* top-heavy and they lost two good men trying to bring her into Plymouth. They battled to keep control of her and prayed that they would find some sliver of sand along the coast where they could run her aground. But she broached off Cawsands and three more worthy crewmen slid into the icy sea. The ship tossed and drifted helplessly until somehow, by sheer good luck, the north wind heaved her into the tiny harbor at Porthcoombe. She careened between the headlands and through the narrow harbor entrance without too much damage. The remaining crew didn't even have time to count their blessings, though, when they saw before them, right in the middle of the harbor, a menacingly tall slab of rock. At full speed, the *Crocodile* collided with it, smashed right up against it. And half her hull was torn asunder.

It was feared that all hands were lost.

As always when there was a ship in distress along this treacherous coast, villagers from miles around wasted no time.

They had already begun to gather, to watch the sad sight, to help in any way they could. Or to plunder, as circumstances allowed. The raging wind carried back no answer to their shouted halloos. There seemed to be no one left alive.

It was a tragedy. And, it cannot be denied, a windfall for the villagers. They set to work. By evening, anyone searching the harbor would be hard-pressed to find a board, even so much as a button, belonging to the *Crocodile* or her crew.

*M*eanwhile, high above Porthcoombe harbor, in the oakwood at the top of the coombe, Emilia Mesola, aged fifteen, paused to catch her breath. She fumbled a handkerchief from a pocket and wiped tears and rain, in equal amounts, from her face. She had been running, almost blinded by the pouring rain, and was soaking wet. She leaned against the ancient oak they called the Passage Oak. It was a huge tree, an enormous tree, the only oak of its kind left in that forest. It had been a landmark down the ages, for lovers and outlaws, tradesmen and smugglers. Under the Passage Oak, Emilia huddled to collect her scattered wits, and for shelter from the wind and icy rain, before attempting the descent through the woods to the village.

The clap of thunder startled her. She had heard tales of oak trees drawing lightning to themselves. Then Emilia realized this was not thunder she was hearing, but the boom of a cannon. A signal. Shipwreck! As curious as anyone when disasters occur, she crossed the bridge over tumultuous Gwill Brook and slipped and slid down the steep path to the village.

She stumbled through their back gate and into the garden. Their house, at the top of Narrow Lane, had a bird's-eye view of the harbor. And there she saw it, the wounded ship lying on its side, brutal waves bashing it against the great fang of rock, Karrek Fekyl. The deceitful two-faced rock: a dangerous obstacle and yet a protective breakwater that calmed the surf in Porthcoombe pool. Beyond Karrek Fekyl, beyond the headlands that formed a lopsided horseshoe around their harbor, the heartless sea still beat against the high granite cliffs.

Emilia, half walking and half sliding, made it all the way down to Chapel Street before she thought of blankets. The shipwrecked crew in their wet clothing would need blankets desperately. She considered turning back but seeing the size of the crowds along the harbor, she figured that by now the survivors were probably enjoying the welcome warmth of cottage fires. If there were any survivors.

The slipway was jammed with people, despite the storm. Men held fast to their hats and women's skirts billowed in the wind. Small children huddled against older sisters, mothers clutched babies under their shawls.

Emilia squeezed past the batsmen. Their faces grim, they hardly noticed her, every particle of their concentration focused on the cliff tops, watching for greedy customs officers. The batsmen guarded a line of wagons ranged along the uphill path to the road. The oxen and horses waited, heads hanging, wondering what madness required all this standing about in nasty wind and icy rain.

Emilia shouldered her way silently through the crowd, down to the water's edge, almost the only person not caught up in the frenzy. Men splashed into the water to haul barrels and crates ashore. They quickly crowbarred them open and then sorted them onto wagons.

The vicar and a local squire were shouting at each other, arguing about whether the contraband should be hidden in the vaults under the church floor or in the squire's barns. Wherever the loot ended up, it had to be stowed away quickly or it would be confiscated by the customs men.

Children ran about, bent nearly to the ground looking for small treasure, squabbling like seagulls over broken shoe buckles or giddy with the prize of a silver coin. There were even people hanging precariously on the rock cliffs, making a grab for any booty floating in Porthcoombe pool. Gaggles of women were sorting through piles of clothing, distributing jackets and boots according to strict local custom that only they could interpret. Emilia ducked out of the way to avoid two matrons, life-long neighbors and both of them spitting-mad, yanking fistfuls of hair and tearing at each other's shawls in a dispute over some choice pair of trousers.

Emilia almost tripped over the former occupant of the trousers. Dead, he and his fellows lay on the cold wet ground, heaped rather carelessly and completely naked. It wasn't lack of respect, really. Now that the villagers knew there were no survivors of the tragedy, they regarded this shipwreck as their possession. A cornucopia of loot. The booty must be secured before the customs officers showed up. The dead had no say in the matter. They would have to wait.

Everyone wanted a share of the hoard. They would pick the *Crocodile's* bones clean, right down to the last rib. This was allowed, not exactly by law, but by an old code of maritime conduct that took effect only if all hands had been lost. If there were survivors, that would change everything. Rather, it was supposed to make a difference. Would a lone survivor or two be safe from avaricious villagers? Truth be told, wicked threats, even murders, had been known to make true the claim of "no survivors", but the people of Porthcoombe were never tempted to go quite that far. They prided themselves on that. Why, had not two of their own young men lost their lives just last year, attempting to reach a wreck that had hung up on the Gazelles to the north of here? Yes, the people of Porthcoombe had paid their dues to English law many times over. And the voracious sea very often took from them what little was left. Sons, husbands and fathers lost. What more could England ask? If the devil himself snatched away those corrupt English customs officers, hardly a soul in Cornwall would care.

As for the tales of ships lured by pirate lights onto dangerous reefs so they could be stripped clean, well, that had certainly never happened here. Not as far as anyone was willing to remember. Even Emilia, who saved very little room in her heart for these villagers, even she could not imagine such a thing happening in Porthcoombe.

She had seen enough of tragedy for one day. She was about to turn away when her eye was caught by a movement over at the far edge of the pool, beyond the Karrek Fekyl rock, out beneath the sheer granite cliff.

"Look!" she cried. Hardly anyone heard her, much less paid her any mind. "Out there! A woman!" Emilia stumbled into the churning waves, arms held wide for balance. She searched for footholds, trying to work her way along the steep cliffs at the edge of the cove. The rocks were treacherously slippery. She waded deeper.

"Ooo! Mind you don't get that dress wet there, Emma!" cawed one of the fishermen's wives.

"Or those bee-oo-ti-fool boots!" jeered another.

"What's out there?"

"Yeah, what's she after, anyway?"

"Who?"

"That brown one. That Emma."

"It's Eh-MEE-lee-ah, if ya please."

"Stupid name. Foreigner's name. I call her Emma."

"Will someone tell me why she's out there scramblin' for bits of things?"

"Aye, ain't we the ones what need them bitses? It's us what are the ones in real need, ain't that so?"

"She surely don't need fer nothin', that one. Miss Fancy Pants."

"Hey, lookit! She's right, though. There is a survivor."

"Crimey!"

"What's that woman out there got hold of? A spar or something?"

"There's some bad luck. Now she's going to ruin everything for the rest of us."

"Ain't it just like that Emma to find trouble? I hate that brown witch."

The women watched, disgusted, pairs of hands on sturdy hips.

"Well, there goes a whole entire day of hard work."

"Can't ya just leave things be?" one woman called to Emilia.

"Well, hold up here, old dolls. You think maybe we should oughta do somethin' to help?"

"Naa. Should we?"

"It is only right. Poor woman, out there freezing."

"Naw, it's too late."

"Don't bother. That woman's gonna be half dead anyways."

"Aye, she's been too long in that cold water, most likely."

Emilia heard many of their remarks but, for once, did not bother with a retort. She was up to her waist in freezing water, bracing against the waves. The woman splashed clumsily out there against the rocks, the sea now sucking, now pulling around her.

"Wait! I'm coming!" Emilia shouted to her. "Help me, someone! There's a woman out there!"

Finally all activity quieted. All eyes watched Emilia the way a crowd, holding its breath, gawks at a tightrope walker. A low growl began among the young men and more than one hand went to the hilt of a knife. If any were inspired to help Emilia, they looked nervously to their fellows and dared not move. Turn your heads away, gents. A lone survivor might be better left to drown.

Emilia, stiffening with cold, sloshed along the edge of the pool. The waves had heaved the woman, clinging to the spar, closer to the granite wall. She saw Emilia now. She stretched a desperate hand to her. Emilia stumbled, lost her footing and slid underwater. She came up thrashing and choking bitter cold sea water. Now they were close enough for Emilia to grab hold of the spar. She clung to it and they both rode a swell that pushed them closer to the cliff. Emilia found a foothold, a place where she could climb up. She felt the urgency to be quick but nothing would force her chilled arms and legs to move faster. Shaking uncontrollably, she knelt and reached a hand down to the woman.

Then Emilia heard a scrambling behind her. Strong hands pulled her aside. Sébastien Roland waded onto the ledge and grasped the woman's arms. Her skirts were heavy, sodden with seawater. She was so exhausted and confused that she could do little to help herself. Sébastien managed to reach under her arms. Linking his hands across her back, he dragged her, only half conscious, onto the ledge. Emilia wept with relief. By now, others were sliding down to help. Roddy Campion took hold of Emilia. It took several men to carry the woman up to safe footing.

Someone brought blankets and a stretcher. The woman could barely stand. As her muscles lost functionality, they allowed a surge of warm blood to pass from her core to her extremities. This new warmth convinced her that she was overheating. She tore at her clothes. She fought at the men who tried to wrap her in blankets. Sébastien had to hold her arms so they could tie her onto the stretcher. Then slowly they inched their way down the path to the street.

Emilia huddled on the sidelines with her teeth chattering uncontrollably. She pulled a blanket tight around herself. She was shaking so violently she had to pick her way very slowly down the steep path. But a little cloud of satisfaction buoyed her. She, Emilia, had helped to save the lady! They say that if you save someone's life, it creates a bond of friendship. That would be nice, very nice for a change. She would like that. Given her present troubles, and given the horrible things that had happened today, yes, it certainly would feel good to be able to bond with somebody. She hoped fervently that the lady would be all right. She looked up to see Sébastien Roland gesturing to her.

"You'd better get some dry clothes on," he yelled over the wind. "You look frozen."

She stumbled toward him. "You helped that lady. Thank you." Emilia realized she hadn't spoken civilly to Sébastien in a long time. She should make it a point to speak to him later. At the moment, though, she could hardly form her words. Shivering, she pulled the blanket up around her blue lips.

"You'll get on home then?" he called over his shoulder as he headed back to help with the stretcher. "Get some dry clothes on."

"Where?" Emilia shouted after him. She was too muddled to think of the right words. "Where are you taking her?"

He turned with a show of minor impatience. "Mr. Campion's, I should think." He paused and took a step back toward her. "I must say, you surprised everyone." Emilia felt a small smile bubbling to the surface. "You, of all people. Our Emilia, acting the hero."

Her smile sank. Disintegrated. "I wasn't acting the hero. That's not why I did it."

"Don't get huffy. I just meant that you showed more spunk than most people give you credit for."

"You thought I'd let her drown? Thanks so much, Sébastien." This was a horrible day.

"I didn't say that."

"You could give me a little credit for trying to save her life, you know."

"Stop bristling like a sea urchin, Emilia. I was only trying to be funny."

"It didn't sound like that to me." Her mind was too thick to cope with what he was saying. "You're as bad as all the rest."

Sébastien laughed. "There we go. There's that old chip on the shoulder. Come on, I'll walk you up the hill."

"I'll walk myself up the hill." Crushed, weary, Emilia was too tired to keep hot tears from welling up. She bundled the blanket close to cover her face and pushed past him.

He stood for a moment, looking after her, his own feelings a welter of confusion.

No one else paid any attention to Emilia. She squeezed her way through the crowd just as the batsmen were forming their double row. The wagons trundled between them, loaded and overloaded, finally on their way to the manor house. The guards smacked their bats against the palms of their hands, grim as a school of sharks. If there were customs men hiding along the path, waiting until everything was loaded to make their move, they would have to fight half the village to get their hands on anything.

Meanwhile, many smaller battles had played themselves out and hardly anyone went home empty-handed. The vicar, though, had lost his argument with the squire. The barrels were not going to be hidden under the church floor. They were heading for the squire's barns after all. The Reverend Vingout, a staunch Methodist, nevertheless gestured with surprising rudeness to the squire and jumped aboard one of the wagons. He was going to keep a close eye on those barrels. Slippery as a dew snail, that squire was.

As empty carts took the place of those full of contraband, the bodies of the dead crewmen drew some guilty looks. Something had to be done with them. A few men grudgingly lifted them by arms and legs and placed them on a cart so small that the naked bodies had to be piled on top of each other. But what choice did they have? All the large wagons were needed for more important cargo. Since no evidence had been found that any of the dead were Christian, they would not risk burying them in the churchyard. A couple of the old men would have to haul them down to some small cove and bury them, eventually, in a mass grave.

Emilia, a little sickened at the sight, hurried past. In her foggy-headed haste, she stumbled against a woman.

"Hey, watch yourself!" snapped one sturdy fishwife.

"Brown witch!" muttered another.

Emilia slipped in the muck along the shoreline and just caught herself from falling.

"Excuse me," she said.

"You got a problem? We in your way?" one of the women challenged.

"Yes, it happens that you are!" Emilia spit back. She glared, pulled her wet skirts close and shoved on past them.

The ice had gone out of the rain but the road was slippery with mud. She was slow making her way up the hill and along Narrow

Lane to the surgeon's house, across the street from her own. Bess Campion opened the door to her knock.

"The lady?" Emilia blurted. "Is she here?"

"Yes, they brought her in a little while ago. Come inside."

"Is she going to be all right?"

"Come in, my dear. Out of the rain. Hurry! Look at you, soaked to the skin. Yes, Mr. Campion is examining her right now and I'm filling a pan of coals for her bed. Why don't you go put on some dry clothes and then come back? I'll have a nice pot of tea ready for you."

"I would like to see her, Mrs. Campion, to talk to her for a minute."

"When you're dry, love. I don't want you catching your death, now, do I?"

"I'll be fine."

"No, it's important to get out of those wet things, Emilia. Besides, there's hardly any sense in trying to talk to her yet. She doesn't even know what she's saying at the moment. We can't make any sense out of her. Be quick, now! Go home and change clothes. I'll put the kettle on."

In a short time, Emilia was back. She knocked several times and then let herself in.

"Mrs. Campion?" Emilia tapped lightly on the bedroom door. "Mrs. Campion?"

Bess came to the door. "Come in, come in. It's all right, isn't it, Rafe?" she asked her husband. "Can Emilia come in for just a minute?"

"Yes, yes. Emilia, pull those rocks out of the fire and bring them in here. Give her something to wrap them in, Bess."

They nestled warm rocks along the lady's sides. They had managed to get her wet clothes off her. She wore one of Bess's white nightgowns.

Emilia leaned over her. The lady's eyes were vague, unfocused.

Emilia tried to put herself in the lady's view. "How are you feeling?"

The lady's eyes widened and she blinked rapidly, trying to focus.

"Are you nice and warm now?" Emilia smiled at her and now the eyes seemed glued to her as she sat down beside the bed.

Mr. Rafe Campion stood watching his patient. "I've done all I can for her, I'm afraid," he said.

"She'll live, won't she?" whispered Emilia.

The surgeon looked meaningfully at Emilia. How could he speak negative words in front of a patient? He touched the lady's arm. "You rest for now. I'll come to see you in a little while."

Bess Campion left to make tea. Mr. Campion had to go down to the harbor to set a broken arm for one of the treasure hunters who had slipped on the rocks. Emilia sat alone by the bed.

She touched the lady's hand. It was ice cold, and no wonder. Emilia hadn't been immersed in seawater nearly as long and she was still shivering. She slipped off her boots and crawled under the quilt. She put her arm around the woman and held her tight. Their heads on the same pillow, their eyes still locked, Emilia thought the lady smiled at her before she closed her eyes.

Bess Campion came in with a tray. "You should drink some hot tea, Emilia. You must have caught quite a chill yourself."

"In a minute."

The tea was stone cold by the time Emilia rose from the bed. The lady was alarmingly still. Emilia felt for a pulse. Nothing. She ran to the bedroom door.

"Mrs. Campion?" she hollered. "Can you come in here? Something's gone wrong. Quick! I don't think she's breathing!"

They tried what they could to rouse her, Emilia becoming more frantic as each attempt failed. Bess even tried slapping her. No response. She lowered the lady gently back to the bed.

"This must be her time to go." Bess took Emilia's arm and spoke quietly. "Let her be, Emilia. Come on. Come sit by the fire. There is nothing you can do for her now."

"No! We can't let her go! Try giving her some tea!" She struggled to lift the woman to a sitting position. "Help me! She needs warm tea!"

"She's gone, sweetcake, can't you see?"

"No! No!" Emilia shook the lady. "Do something for her! What can we do?"

"There is nothing we can do. She is beyond our help." Mrs. Campion pulled gently on Emilia's shoulders.

"Wait! Don't give up! Please, please!" Emilia chafed the lady's hand. "Get more warm rocks. Is she breathing now? Did you see that? I saw her take a breath." She started to cry. "Help her, Mrs. Campion. Can't you do something? Please!" she sobbed.

Bess Campion pried Emilia away. She crossed the lady's bluish hands over her breast and pulled the sheet over her still face.

"Noo!" wailed Emilia.

"It's no use." She turned Emilia's wet face toward her and made her listen. "She is gone from this life. You cannot hold her here."

"I'll go get Mr. Campion." She struggled with her boots. "He will help her!"

"Emilia, listen to me. She is beyond our help." She pulled Emilia's head to her shoulder and rocked her like a baby.

When Emilia's tears finally quieted, Bess Campion led her to a seat by the fire. "You did your best. Sébastien was here when they brought the lady in. He said you did your best for her." She laid a gentle hand on Emilia's head. "Don't trouble yourself so."

Emilia looked unseeing into the flames, consumed by the strangest feeling of loss.

"She must have been a gentlewoman," Mrs. Campion continued. "Look, her clothes are lovely, aren't they?" She shook the garments where they dripped beside the fire, heavy with seawater. "She was wearing this little gold cross. I wondered if you would like to have it?"

Emilia shrugged and shook her head. "No." She paused. "Wait. Yes. Yes, I would like to have it." She studied the fine gold chain Bess dropped onto her palm. "Thank you."

"I hope you don't blame yourself, my girl. That water is deadly cold. It's a wonder she stayed conscious for as long as she did." She rose and filled Emilia's teacup. "Were there any children among the dead?"

"I don't think so."

"Because she was calling for her daughter. What foul weather to be out in. I wonder where she was going."

Seeing as how the lady was a Christian, they buried her in the churchyard at St. Buryan's. They found no article on her person with a name on it. Nothing at all to identify her. So only a rock marked the spot where she lay. A rock and a little clump of wild rose that Emilia planted for her.

$A$s it turned out, all the happenings of that day lay at the center of a web of events. Many filaments, some short, some long, led to the tiny village of Porthcoombe, Cornwall. One strand of this tale began sixteen years earlier, in the fall of 1802, twelve miles off the coast of Jamaica. It was a turning point in the life of a young woman. She crossed a metaphorical bridge and everything changed.

*Bridge to Nowhere*

*A bridge where one or both ends are broken or incomplete, it stands as a monument to possibility, but does not lead anywhere.*

CAROLINE SYDNEY

1802

The *Punch*

*T*he tropical sun fingered the distant island for a few moments, turning it to a lump of molten gold floating between the gray sea and the high black clouds. Caroline Sydney turned away and faced into the wind coming across the cold Atlantic. She dabbed at her forehead with her handkerchief and again retched over the rail of the HMS *Sapphire*. When she had come out from London a year ago, the six-week voyage had seemed magical. But then, a year ago, she had been only a girl. This visit to her aunt and uncle, the governor of Jamaica, had been mandated by her parents. They would have done anything to separate her from her reckless London friends. They were desperate to convince her to give up her wild behavior, and faraway Jamaica seemed the perfect answer. But they had not figured on Jack Punch. Caroline's parents intended Jamaica to be a penalty, or a rebuke, or at least a calming influence. What a joke!

Yes, a year ago she had known, without a shred of doubt, all there was to know of the world. The mysteries of love read like an open book to her. After all, had anyone been in love more often than Caroline Sydney? So a year ago, her ship had barely passed the Scilly Isles before she was smitten again. Really smitten this time. She loved to laugh, to dance and party. So did Jack Punch, and that is how they began. So flippant, and so naive. So knowing, one short year ago.

His real name was John Perkins. Tall, ambitious, self-possessed, with green eyes and skin the color of amber. Heart-stoppingly handsome. He was everything her London beaus were not. A very successful privateer, he was going back to Jamaica to take command of a ship of His Majesty's Navy. He was being made Master and Commander. For a Jamaican mulatto, even one with his distinguished naval record, this was a high honor indeed. Too high, according to some in the Admiralty. The office they had promised him was abruptly withdrawn two months later. They made up some reasons and said what needed to be said in order to keep him in his place.

He went to sea anyway. But not as Master and Commander and no longer as John Perkins. This time he sailed as Jack Punch, a pirate.

Caroline heard a voice behind her.

"Miss Sydney?" She clutched the rail for balance and turned slowly. The lieutenant frowned in sympathy. "I'm so sorry you are unwell, Miss Sydney. But all passengers are being called to their quarters. You must go below."

"I really prefer to stay on deck. I feel worse, if you can believe it, when I go below."

"I understand. But we anticipate a spot of trouble, you see. I assure you, you will be more comfortable below. It will not be safe out here."

"Is it a storm?"

He turned and pointed back toward the southwest. There, on the horizon. A schooner flying a black flag. The *Sapphire's* crew was already swiveling guns into place.

"You are not well. Allow me to assist you, Miss Sydney. Please."

Reluctantly she leaned on his arm. He tried to hurry her.

"Pirates?" she asked breathlessly.

"I'm afraid so. The schooner *Punch*, we believe."

She stopped and released his arm. "I think I'll stay out here. Yes, I will. I'm sure I can help. Just give me a pistol."

"Miss Sydney, the *Punch* is almost certainly on her way to Africa. A white woman, forgive me, but a beautiful young white woman cannot afford….my god, you would be sold for…."

"This is one pirate who would not dare to lay a finger on me. Get me a pistol."

As the *Punch* came closer, the captain of the *Sapphire* saw he was clearly outgunned. He surrendered without a fight. When Jack Punch and his pirates swung aboard, the captain had already ordered his crew to begin emptying the hold of sugar and tea.

"We don't want any trouble. We'll surrender our cargo," said the captain to Jack Punch, trying to sound gallant. "There are too many women and children aboard to risk a battle."

Jack Punch pushed a firm hand against the captain's shoulder. "Keep the passengers out of our way, Captain, and we won't bother them. I want all you and all your crew over there by the starboard rail. I want to see what else you are carrying," he insisted.

Caroline fumed silently. The pistol was hot in her hand. She burned with the urge to use it. Before she could be noticed, she ducked in among some crew who were heading back down to the hold.

The faster the captain could get Jack Punch off the *Sapphire,* the better he would feel. "My crew is bringing the rest of the barrels up," he said. "Start loading these to make room …."

Jack Punch feigned surprise. "Is there some question about who is in control here?" He thrust the captain aside as casually as a market woman would reject too-pricey bananas. "I'm going below."

"This is our entire cargo!" the captain squeaked.

Jack Punch looked at him for a moment, then burst out laughing. "You seem very eager to give up your sugar and tea. My guess is you're hiding something. Do you want to tell me about it, or should I find it without your help?" He smacked a small crowbar against his palm.

"The hold, we done cleared it out, Captain," assured one of the *Sapphire's* crew hurriedly. He dared, for one moment, to look Jack Punch in the face. "Empty, sir, completely empty."

"Bony! Where's Bony?" Jack Punch called. He gestured to a tall thin man with very black skin. "Bony, my man! Help me search below." He shoved the captain out of his way. None of the crew raised so much as an eyelid.

When Jack Punch ducked into the hold, he found Caroline Sydney sitting on a barrel directly in his path. She had her pistol pointed at him. He straightened and gave her a dazzling smile.

"Well, well. Look who finally turned up. I wondered what became of you, Princess."

"And I have been wondering what could possibly have happened to you. It's been five weeks since I've seen you."

"How sweet! You were keeping count. Did you miss me?"

Caroline leaned to one side so she could speak to his mate, standing behind. "Could we have a moment in private, please?"

Jack Punch didn't take his eyes off her trigger finger. But, airily over his shoulder he said "It's all right, Bony. She's harmless." He took a step closer to Caroline.

"Don't come near me!"

"You're angry, darling?" He spread his hands in appeal. She twitched the barrel of the pistol close to his face.

"Of course I'm angry, you piece of ...."

"Now don't, Caroline! Don't say something you'll regret."

"What I regret is that we will be tied together, you and I, for life. For life, Jack. What I most regret is that this can not be undone."

He widened his eyes and tipped his head to one side, blameless as a frolicking pup. "I can't imagine what you're talking about."

"Don't play stupid!"

His eyes were transparent green pools. "We made no promises to each other, Caroline."

"You still have responsibilities. We're tied together now, for good."

"What are you telling me? Are you are with child?"

"Yes, you're damn right I am with child! You're bloody well coming back to England with me, Jack, and we are bloody well getting married."

"Sorry, Princess. That can't happen. I've made other plans. I am sorry but that's the way it has to be." He shrugged and smiled.

"You're sorry? You're sorry! You can't possibly know the meaning of the word 'sorry'. I am the one who is sorry. You are the one who will have to make things right."

"Come on, Caroline!"

"I'm not going through this alone!"

"Really, do you think this is the first time I've heard this phony story? If I had a shilling for every girl who tells me I'm her baby's father, I'd be ...."

Caroline jumped up, her face crumpled in fury. Jack Punch lunged for her pistol and knocked her hand aside just as she fired. She screamed, dropped the gun and covered her face. Tears dripped through her fingers.

A trickle of golden liquid squirted from the hole the bullet had made in the hull. Jack Punch let out a howl of laughter. He bent to pick up the pistol. Then he put a finger to the liquid and tasted it.

"Hey, Bony!" he called.

The black man came running. "Trouble, Cap'n?"

"No," scoffed Jack Punch. "I told you. This one's harmless. The English! Pathetic, eh?" He gestured dismissively. "But look. She spared us the trouble of searching for the rum. See? Casks hidden inside the hull. Turns out she's some good to me, after all, my little Princess."

Bony grinned. "So who this doxy, Cap'n? You jilt this one, too?"

"They just keep adding up, don't they?" laughed Jack Punch.

"You want I should do somethin' with her?" Bony purred.

"Take her away. Unless you like her. What do you say, Princess? Bony's not bad looking. You won't mind the pox marks after a bit."

Caroline stood and collected herself. This man would never be her husband. She wished him eternal burning, itching and running sores deep in all his most sensitive regions.

But her effort at dignity was compromised the moment she threw up. It was fitting, though, that she found a worthy target. She hoped that Jack Punch's impressive double-breasted gold-braided brass-buttoned coat would stink of her vomit for a long time to come.


$T$he voyage back to Liverpool took eight long weeks. Caroline Sydney was now five months pregnant. She was certain her aunt would have written her parents from Jamaica, telling them Caroline was coming home, though her aunt could not have known the reason. Had a letter reached them yet?

She scanned the crowds on the Liverpool pier. No one from her family was there. She recognized no one at all. Much as she dreaded seeing her parents, still, she wished they had come. She felt a longing to see them that surprised her. She waited around at the dock until almost nightfall before deciding to take a room at an inn.

In her entire life, she had never been really lonely until now. How it sapped one's strength. And spirit. More than she had thought possible. Ever since she fired that pistol at Jack Punch, it was she, not he, who felt like a wounded animal, as though she had shot herself in the heart. And like a wounded animal, she only wanted to crawl home.

The next day she hired a cab to take her to London. When finally she stood outside her parents' house, her feet were leaden. Her stomach had knotted up so tightly she could hardly stand. To walk up their steps, to knock on their door seemed monumentally difficult. Caroline, who had never known cowardice, did not have the courage. She could not tell them what had happened to her. What she had done. The driver set her trunks down next to her.

"Front door, Miss?" he asked.

"No."

He looked at her and waited.

"No, put them back."

She, Caroline Sydney, simply could not go home. She would never have believed herself so weak-willed.

There was nowhere in the world she could go. Overwhelmed by emotions she had never before experienced, she turned and climbed back into the carriage.


*T*hree months later all her clothes had been sold. She had eaten her last chunk of stale bread and paid the slum lord the last of her money. She was so thin, she barely looked eight months pregnant, even in the raggedy piece of muslin that was her only gown.

It was February and night was coming on. On the street, she had to stop to lean against a pillar. Across the way, she stared at the door of the South London Hospital for Women and Children. It had become too difficult to take care of herself on the city streets. Tonight she simply did not have strength to fend off the beggars and pimps. She rubbed her thumb against the table knife in her sleeve. Her only friend, the table knife. She closed her eyes for a moment and thought again of going home. No, she must carry on alone. Wait until after the baby was born. Then she would go home. Another month. Maybe less, considering how she felt tonight. It would not be easy to go home. But to be warm, to be clean. No longer hungry. Someone caring about her. If they would have her.

She made an effort to move, lurching away from the building. She was hurting badly. Perhaps something would happen tonight to end it all. Perhaps childbirth would kill her. Oh lord, must she go through with this? She had figured on a couple more weeks of waiting. Now another wave of pain hit her. No, she must get help tonight. The door of the hospital was her goal. She looked at it again. It was a heavy door, solid, closed against her. She had to bend double until the cramp passed. She didn't realize this was no cramp, but a contraction. Her baby was on the way.

A man brushed against her backside and she flung around to face him.

"Get away from me!" She pointed the knife at him. He started to say something and she screamed and lunged at him.

"Crikey!" he said, throwing up his hands.

Hunched over with pain, she watched him shuffle away. She turned back toward the door and began again. A slow walk to the stone steps. Climbing them was another matter. She collapsed on the bottom step. Such pain.

The next contraction was a hot poker of agony. When it finally passed, she looked up the steps. That door, still closed. Cold, impassive. No one would answer her knock now. It was night. They were all warm in their beds, on clean sheets. Caroline got to her feet. She was shivering visibly. She could not stand up straight but she managed to get one foot to the first step. By the time she collapsed against the door another cramp had seized her. What was happening to her? She was dying, obviously. She was dying, and who would know?

She raised a fist and thudded it against the bottom of the door. She waited and tried it again. Again.

She heard a sound. A grate was opened, then closed. She banged her fist urgently and fell over the door sill when someone opened it a crack.

"Please. Help me, please."

A woman gasped. What wretched creature, filthy, with a knife in her hand, writhed at her feet?

Caroline's mouth opened in a soundless scream. Slumped on the floor, wracked with pain, she heard footsteps and voices.

"Help me!" she sobbed again.

"Are you hurt? What happened?"

She could not answer. Warm, a finger of warmth touched her.

"She just wants a bed and a free meal, that's all."

"No, I think she's in real pain."

"Sisters! Of course she is in pain. This woman is going to have a child. Get her upstairs. We'll have to keep her tonight."


*T*hey let her stay until she was stronger. Four days later she walked out of the hospital. She was clean. She had eaten. They had given her a gown, a clean, simple gown. She was thin again. She was strong enough, just barely, to shoulder her burden of despair. She had a baby daughter.

She had given birth to a baby daughter but she was afraid to keep her. Someone would take her away, and was this not better? Couldn't some married couple provide more than Caroline could give her? In a few days, they would send her to an orphanage. But where will you go from there, little baby? Where will you go? Caroline leaned over her baby's crib in the hour before dawn. She stroked the dark head and put her finger against the child's cheek.

"Good-bye, my little one," she whispered. She hadn't expected it would be so difficult to tear herself away. A little girl. It was wonderful how tiny her fingers were. Her hair lay so neatly along her head. Bundled inside her was a whole world waiting, waiting to unfold. Who would have thought she would be so perfect?

She must not allow herself to have second thoughts. "Good-bye," Caroline said again. But still she crouched there. "Will you be all right? You won't be alone for long, I hope." The tiny hand clutched her finger. "I'm very sorry. So sorry."

Caroline knew it was time for her to go. She slipped her finger from the infant's grasp and the little fingers sprang open, clawing the air, searching for a handhold. "Good-bye, my little one." No, that was wrong. "Good-bye, little baby."

Caroline Sydney slipped out. The hospital's great oaken door thudded closed behind her. She stood still for a time, head bowed, wondering why such a big closed door did not make everything feel more final. Nothing felt certain, everything felt wrong. In her heart she knew it was wrong, but where to find the strength to be a mother? She wavered for a long moment. Then she went slowly down the steps, sensing that the oaken door behind her sealed itself more tightly with every step. She left her child alone in an orphanage and traded her for a lifetime of regret.

Caroline walked every last mile of the way to her parents' house. She knocked. They were almost faint with the shock of seeing her. And wonderfully thrilled beyond imagining, never knowing what had become of their daughter. And for a long time, nearly fifteen years in fact, she did not tell them the truth.

*Clapper Bridge*

*A large slab of granite laid across the banks of a stream, it is an ancient form of bridge found on the moors of Cornwall. Being of very simple construction, when it becomes camouflaged with age it may even go unnoticed until trod upon.*

## ZEPHANIAH COBBS
## 1790

*P*eople say it never happens, but it does. Sometimes a spider rushes to defend itself and it gets caught in its own web. Zephaniah Cobbs was still a very young man when he became hopelessly tangled in a web of regrets, whether or not he recognized them as such. He spent the rest of his life trying to forget them. This begins a strand of his story. It takes us back a few more years, another twelve years earlier, to the Devon village of Dartmoor.

One of his worst regrets, one of the people Zephaniah Cobbs wanted most to forget, was a young lad back in Dartmoor. The reason was, well, the boy, Willie, this young boy had been hurt, badly hurt. Maybe even crippled for life. Cobbs also wished he could forget the boy's older brother. A brother, and the family bread-winner, too. He was barely alive after Cobbs beat him to the floor of the tavern. And Charlotte, Cobbs's fiancée. He finally blocked her from his mind completely. Not only did she break her promise to him. She called him a criminal. He shut her, and every memory of her, out of his life completely.

Growing up just outside of Dartmoor, Cobbs had been a promising young man and the pride of his mother's heart. Her Zephaniah! Who was chosen, she liked to remind people, when he was only fifteen, to fill the job of grass captain at the mine? Chosen over several older men. And who worked his way up to take the position of mine captain by the time he was seventeen? Her Zephaniah did. And he did his job very well. You had to discount the way he treated the men. He had no choice! They were to blame for the harsh choices he made, not he. They resented him and never even tried to hide it. And they always held it against him that he did not come from a mining family. It was very unfair of them to treat him the way they did. It was their complaining that lost Zephaniah that job.

The owner of the mine made the ridiculous claim that Zephaniah's violent temper was the reason he was fired. He said he could not entrust the safety of his men to someone who chopped up a ladder in a fit of fury. Men happened to be climbing that ladder, but still. He was a stupid old man, that owner. He provoked Zephaniah, that was all there was to it, jealous because Cobbs was young and smart and engaged to be married to a rich girl.

Cobbs liked his next job as schoolmaster well enough. He was especially fond of one of the boys, Willie Poldark. He was a bright eleven year old with the face of an angel. In the schoolyard at lunchtime, doe-eyed girls circled dangerously close to the boys' rowdy shenanigans, just to gape at Willie. Every morning, the sight of his radiant blue eyes was so cheering, it made Cobbs want to hum a tune. And Willie was smart. That was why Cobbs liked to find little projects for him to work on after school. The boy deserved this extra encouragement, and helping Willie made Cobbs feel warm-hearted, even generous.

So it hurt him unbearably when he heard boyish giggling in class late one afternoon. He tried to ignore it. He did try, but every time he turned his back, there was another eruption. They were laughing at him! Did they think him so ridiculous? Even Willie Poldark? Cobbs spun around and there he was, red-faced with smothered laughter. Willie, just as spiteful, just as malicious as all the rest of them. Cobbs stormed across the room and hauled Willie from his chair. He lifted Willie right off his feet and hurled him out the schoolroom window.

Three weeks later, the family was told there was no hope that Willie would ever walk normally again.

No one felt as badly as Cobbs did about that. Everyone loved Willie. Cobbs had loved him too, adored him, really. Hating himself, scorned by nearly everyone in the village, even his own fiancée, Cobbs stumbled into the tavern early one evening and drank until his head hit the table.

He was dragged from the bench sometime later that night by Willie's eldest brother. In spite of the drink, Cobbs was not too far gone to intercept the first punch, but the second punch landed right in his face.

The stupid lout should not have hit him. It was the punch in the face that did it. That punch made the violent rage boil up inside Cobbs. Even after he had beaten Willie's brother unconscious, it took three men to tear Cobbs away from him. They finally managed to fling him out the door, though he screamed obscenities and kicked at them like a crazed demon. They threw him so hard onto the cobblestones he thought his shoulder was broken. His nose was bleeding and his upper lip hung in tatters that never knit together properly. They carried Willie's brother away but Cobbs they ignored. They left him bleeding in the street as though he were nothing but garbage.

He had no idea how long he lay there before he was able to get up and stagger home. When he finally burst through the door of his house, he collapsed sobbing in his mother's arms. Two men, she cried, had already come looking for him. She thrust what money she had into his hand and begged him to run for his life. He just managed to slip out the back before an angry gang stomped up the path to their door. Cobbs was too terrified to run. He crouched at the edge of the woods, trembling in the shadows, listening to his mother's pleas as they tore the cottage apart looking for him. But he did not go back to help her.

He finally slithered away through the trees. He had no choice but to leave Dartmoor. But before he left, there was something he needed to do. He knew of a secret drawer where his fiancée's father kept his valuables. The hour was late, the big house was quiet. It wasn't all that difficult to slip through a window and make his way down the dark hall to the library. He considered himself too honest to take all the man's money, but Cobbs felt they owed him at least one bag of gold. Then he turned back and took one more. He stowed both bags in his sack, slipped back through the window and ran until he dropped. He kept on running for the next three nights, heading south. No help from anyone and going he knew not where.

On the fourth night, his path crossed a high moor. He had heard thunder rumbling in the distance all night and he was sure rain was coming. A powerful crack of lightning made his hair stand on end. He would have to find shelter quickly. There was a farm up ahead. He ran toward it and hid in the garden. He saw no signs of life. He worked round toward the barn and miraculously found the door open. He slipped in and waited just inside the door. He heard nothing, no dogs barking, no sheep restless in their pens. Cautiously he pulled some musty hay together to make a bed. When the rain came he had to move to avoid the leaks but he had shelter for the first time since he had left home.

In the night, a picture of his mother came unbidden to his mind. Until this moment, he had never given a thought as to how she was faring without money. What would she do for food, now that he was gone? Would she be turned out of her house? A pinprick of conscience, it troubled him briefly and then he fell fast asleep.

$A$ sharp jab to his leg wakened him the next morning. A small woman stood above him. Her long gray hair hung in tangles to her waist. She brandished a shovel. Cobbs looked at it warily, though she could barely lift it, it was so heavy for her.

"I knew there was somebody in here. Who are you?"

Cobbs sat up and raised his hands. "Don't worry! I mean you no harm! I, ah, only needed a place to get out of the storm."

"Eh? What?" His smiling blue eyes disarmed her. His poor upper lip! It was a wounded mess. Her shovel thudded to the floor and she wavered on her feet. "What's that you say? You better talk up … ooo."

Cobbs caught her when her knees crumpled beneath her. He laid her gently on the mound of moldy hay. She was nothing but a little bag of bones.

"Let me get you some water. Is there a well outside?"

"Eh?"

"Stay here," he said more loudly. "I'll find you some water." He found the well in the yard, drew up the bucket and filled the dipper.

She sucked noisily at the water, then fell back and looked at him in silent amazement.

"Maybe you should eat something." She was very frail.

She shook her head. "No food," she whispered. "No money."

"Come on. We'll get you inside." He helped her up and they swayed toward the tall stone house. "Tell me where I can buy some bread and cheese." He spoke loudly into her ear.

"Just follow this road down the hill."

Cobbs supported her through the door and stopped. "Have you no furniture?"

"They took everything. They left me here alone." He felt her tremble. "All alone."

"Is this your house?"

"No. It's theirs but they've been gone for months now. I don't think they're coming back."

Cobbs looked around the room, his eyes narrowing in thought. A lonely old woman and an empty house. A farm. There was a pile of dirty blankets in a corner. He led her there and helped her lie down.

"Will you wait for me?" He smiled and she studied him, silently taking his hand. He patted her. "What shall I call you?"

"Mrs. Pawley."

"All right, Mrs. Pawley. Don't worry. I'll, ah, be back soon."

The sign by the gate said Tregorna Farm. Zephaniah Cobbs would spend the next three decades here.

*T*wo days previously he had stolen a berry pie that had been left to cool on a windowsill. Except for that, he had eaten nothing since leaving Dartmoor. He hurried down the road. He had no idea where it would take him, but he prayed he was a long way from Dartmoor.

He passed a farmer working his field. The man looked up when Cobbs passed and watched him all the way down the road. The sign there read Polcoth Farm. Cobbs bent his head and kept walking. The road curved away from Polcoth and into the woods. It began a steep descent. At a crossroad, Cobbs followed the sign to Porthcoombe. Finally, down through the trees, he saw the ocean sparkling in the morning sun. How far had he come in four days? If only he could find out where he was, he would rest easier.

Morning was quiet in the hamlet of Porthcoombe. The fishermen had gone out long before. Cobbs passed the lofts where their wives mended nets or salted yesterday's catch. Some were packing fish into barrels. He waved an uncertain good-morning to them and received stony looks in response.

He heard hammering. He thought there might be a cooperage up there, up the hill near a little chapel. The scent of oakwood barrels warming over a cresset was just discernible over the heavy stink of fish down here in the harbor. There seemed to be very few other places of business in this village. Small children played unattended in the streets. They stopped when he passed, their eyes riveted on him. Cobbs looked around nervously. This was a small place indeed. He would not be anonymous here. He must try not to look like a fugitive. He covered his wounded mouth with his hand and scanned the waterfront.

This tiny hamlet rimmed a harbor that was beautifully protected from the sea by a horseshoe of headlands. However, some great earthly cataclysm had stabbed a very tall slab of rock right through the middle of the harbor, rendering it useless for any shipping except for the small fishing luggers. A few fishermen, a cooperage – there didn't seem to be much else going on in Porthcoombe. Above the harbor, a railing edged a narrow walkway, and along this walkway were jammed a couple of shops, the fishermen's lofts and a tavern called The Bell. In front of one shop, Cobbs saw a basket of sea urchins offered for sale. He went in and was met with a surprised look from the proprietor, Neddy Basko.

"Good morning," said Cobbs politely.

"Yuh." Neddy Basko was busy wrapping cheese and breathing audibly through his mouth.

"I need a few of those pilchards, some of that cheese and a dozen potatoes. Maybe a hunk of bacon. Please," Cobbs added, "if you have any."

Neddy Basko nodded. He tore a large piece of paper for the fish and carefully laid them out, one by one.

Both Neddy and Cobbs turned when two men burst into the shop. Their jaws dropped when they saw Cobbs. A stranger! They stopped in their tracks. They shut their mouths.

"Morning boys," said Neddy.

"Uh huh." They thrust their hands into their pockets.

Neddy Basko looked meaningfully toward Cobbs and back at the two men.

"Nice morning," offered Cobbs, trying to fill the awkward silence.

The men glanced up but could think of nothing to say. So they studied their feet.

"Zat everything then?" Neddy asked, waxing eloquent.

"Yes, thank you. What do I owe you?" Cobbs pulled a small gold coin from his purse. Three pairs of eyes widened dramatically. Neddy counted out the change, leaving his little dented cash box seriously depleted.

Cobbs left the shop with his bundles but hadn't gone ten paces when he heard running steps behind him.

The two men from Neddy Basko's grocery stopped short and gaped. Then they stepped closer, crowding him. Cobbs covered his torn lip with his hand.

One of the men pointed an accusing finger and leaned even closer. "You with the Revenuers?" he asked in a low voice.

"Why, ah, no. I've just come from, ah ...." Cobbs's eyes flicked sideways. "From Truro."

"You're nothin' to do with customs?" The man spoke right into Cobbs's face.

"No. Nothing," said Cobbs, backing away.

"Good." The men sighed with relief. "Well, we seen you got some gold."

"Ah?"

"We got a idea you could double your money. You interested?"

"I'm not really a betting man." Cobbs smiled and turned to go.

"This here ain't no bet. It's profit for sure. Positive sure." The man stepped so close, Cobbs felt his breath on his face. His hoarse whisper sent spittle flying. "We got a operation going to France tonight."

"France?"

"Shh! Bringin' back whiskey."

"Oh!" exclaimed Cobbs, finally understanding. "You want me to invest some money in a shipment of whiskey."

"Give us money to buy it and you can sell it for double your money. You won't be sorry."

"What happens to my money if you get caught by the Revenue men?"

The two men guffawed. "Them Revenuers," they looked quickly around and moved close again, "them Revenuers can't sail their way out of a flour bag! On the sea, we can outrun them with both hands spliced to the boom. They ain't nothin' to worry about, I can tell ya."

"You'll give me a receipt for my money?"

"Nope. You got our word. That's all. And our word's good."

"I'd like a receipt."

"Alls you gets is our word."

Then, in a flash, Cobbs realized! He had found in Porthcoombe exactly what he was looking for. He could buy into this smuggling business because he had gold. He could run the business eventually. He could invest in a boat and make his own trips to France, right across the Channel. Plus, Tregorna, the big farm he had found, was practically his for the taking. He would have an empire of his own. He pulled a large gold coin from his pocket and silently blessed his disloyal, unfaithful fiancée. Who needed a wife anyway, as long as there was gold coming in?

"Is this enough to get me started?"

The two grinned wolfishly. "Yeah! It's a start, pard! Where can we find you tomorrow?"

"There's an old farm, up the hill and around the bend."

"What, Tregorna?"

"An old lady, Mrs. Pawley, lives there. You know the place?"

"She's still there? She don't even own that farm."

"She was just the hired help," explained the other. "Since the family left, she's been squatting there. Nobody's seen her for ages though."

"Well, she is still there. That's where I'm staying for now."

They shrugged and finished their arrangements. Cobbs headed back up the hill to the old lady's farm, his head whirling with plans. He devoured a chunk of cheese as he went. Now he wished he had bought Mrs. Pawley one of the cakes he had seen in Basko's shop. He needed to make sure she liked him well enough to let him stay on. He could manage her farm, maybe raise some sheep and sell wool. Things were beginning to look promising once again. If he'd been a whistling man, he would have whistled. But he wasn't. Besides, he couldn't, with his mouth all smashed. He held his hand over his lip, even though he was alone.

When he got back to Tregorna, he started a fire. Mrs. Pawley nibbled at some cheese while he fried the bacon, then the potatoes and fish. He piled her plate high.

Food! It gave her such a sense of well-being. She hadn't felt this good in months.

"It's so kind of you to help an old lady," she told Cobbs. She saw sympathy in his poor wounded smile.

"You're not old, Mrs. Pawley," he said, speaking up so she could hear him. "I'll make sure you get plenty to eat from now on. Pretty soon you'll be dancing around this place and I won't even be able to keep up with you. Dancing, Mrs. Pawley, I promise."

Oh, he could be charming, that Zephaniah Cobbs.

Mrs. Pawley laughed a little and leaned back on her pile of dirty blankets. What angel had brought this young man to her? Nobody had cared for her like this in all her forty-two years.

*Arch bridge*

*One of the oldest types of bridges, in existence for thousands of years. Arch bridges have great natural strength.*

SANTINO MESOLA

Porthcoombe, Cornwall

June 1803, thirteen years later

$S$antino loved to tell the story. He had never known the mother of his daughter, never even laid eyes on her. It wasn't as though there was a scandal of any kind. He loved women, it's true. And women very often, possibly too often, loved him back. But he was still, at age thirty, a single man. Nor, to his knowledge, had he fathered any children. No, the girl he now called his daughter was acquired, not born to him.

He was a cooper, a builder of oak barrels. He owned a thriving business as well as a lovely piece of oakwood at the top of the coombe. In fact, his business was doing so well, he could hardly handle the work. So he had written to a London orphanage, asking for a boy who was willing to serve as an apprentice. The surgeon in Porthcoombe, his neighbor, had told him this was something that could be done, was often done. So he tried it. He asked for a boy of about twelve years of age, and eventually received a letter stating that a boat would be bringing a boy, Sydney, to Penzance in June. On the appointed day, he drove a cart to the harbor and watched the schooner sail in. Two other people were also waiting for children from the orphanage. So Santino Mesola waited with them.

It was a warm day. He took off his hat and fanned his face with it. He watched the other families collect their boys. He sat down on a pile of crates and waited some more. Whatever had become of this Sydney lad? Was he feeling reluctant at the last minute? Difficult, or troublesome?

Santino was suddenly seized with doubts of his own. This whole scheme was a gamble. He was having second thoughts.

The more he thought about it, the more worried he became. Maybe he should leave, and hire that dunce Ham Blewett to help him instead. He put on his hat and headed for his cart.

"Mr. Mel--Melo--?"

Santino turned with one foot on the wheel of his cart.

A very young woman was hurrying toward him. She was plump. She was jogging, sort of, in a halting sort of way, and that set several parts of her self a-jiggle. She was perspiring. It was too warm a day and the toddler she carried was heavy.

"Mr. Melosso!"

"Mesola. I'm Santino Mesola."

"Mr. Mesossa! It is you. Hello! How do you do? I am Rosemary Twirl, administrator in charge of, well, assistant administrator, really, in charge of placement for St. Jerome's. So! We don't often get requests for these wee ones. Here she is!" She plopped a five-month old girl into his arms.

*Una bambina?* His olive skin drained of color. Horror rendered him speechless. He held the child awkwardly, at arms length, like a dangerous animal. The little one smiled a very pretty smile and her feet went round and round in the air.

"Isn't she adorable?" gushed Rosemary. "Now, here are some nappies..."

"Nappies?"

"Well I thought you might not have ...."

"Nappies!" he roared.

"Well, Mr. Meposa, we aren't going to charge you for them. But obviously the child has to have ...."

"I didn't ask for a baby!"

"You don't have to shout, sir. I'm standing right next to you." She tried a tired, indulgent smile. She shifted her weight to get it off her sore foot. "I understand, Mr. Meposo. You're a bit nervous, are you? Worried, obviously. And it's to be expected! Don't fuss yourself. It will be fine."

"You've got the wrong child, Miss Twirl. Or the wrong man."

"No, no." She shook her head with an incredulous chuckle. "I hardly think so. The record book said. It clearly said: Sydney. For Melopa. In Penzance."

"Yes, Sydney. That was the name they gave me, but ...."

"Look! Look here, at this." It had been a long day for Rosemary Twirl but she held her temper. Always very patient, she was. "It tells here on their tags. Name, destination. Let's see." She grabbed the tag dangling on a string around the child's wrist. "How did this get ...? Well, she's ripped it." She shook the tag under the baby's nose. "You ripped this? You are a naughty little thing, you! We don't rip, do we! But see? The book said Sydney, this says (Baby) Sydney. This is definitely your child."

"No, this is wrong. Absolutely wrong. What are these parentheses for?" He struck the tag with his fingers. His olive complexion was now looking distinctly flushed.

"What are you going on about?" She snatched the torn tag back and looked at it again. "How should I know what those are for? This is nothing. It's their name for her. Baby. That's what they've been calling her because she had no given name. They explained it all to me but I forget what her story is. Are you going to make trouble over a couple of paralla--para--?"

"Parentheses. Look Miss Twirl, I was definitely told I was to get a boy!"

"Boy, girl. What is the difference? It's her color you are objecting to, isn't it? I mean, just because she's dark? A baby is a baby, in God's eyes, regardful of color."

"No, I did not ask for a baby. Of any color! I need a grown boy! Here, I'll show you! Where is my letter?" He began to scramble through his pockets. He had never, well, he had rarely had so much trouble with a woman.

"No, I'm very sorry, Mr. Messalo. You are wrong. This is a girl her tag says 'Sydney' the book said 'Sydney' that's who you ordered and you can't change your mind now, you can't, it's wrong, for heaven's sake be reasonable." She took a breath. "It's too late."

"I am not changing my mind!" he shouted. The baby waved her arms in distress. He shifted her to his other arm, found his handkerchief and wiped his brow. He closed his eyes and took a breath. "Listen! This is not what I asked for. Do you understand? I did not ask for a baby. Why would I? What I need is someone to work in my cooperage. Does that make sense?"

"Make sense? How should I know why people do the things they do? You probably don't remember what you asked for. Or else you have cold feet. I'll bet that's it. But you must take her now."

"I can't and I won't."

"No choice. All the other children are spoken for. And, I might remind you, I've come all this way to deliver her. All the way from London, and it hasn't been easy for me, I can tell you. Getting up at the crack of dawn, and me not fond of sea travel. I have enough troubles with my stomach as it is. And it's not as though I have the strength to cope with more worries. You are making it very difficult for me."

"Are you crazy? *Porca miseria*! Just -- you just – just take her back! Take her back! I don't want her." Sounding like a hot-headed Italian now. He was going to explode, surely. He mopped his face again.

Rosemary Twirl looked up at him through narrowed eyes. She spoke quietly, clenching her teeth, measuring her words. "You want me to take her back. You cruel, cruel man." She would contain her fury no longer. She bent forward, nearly unbalancing her mass of flesh. Shaking her finger at him, one hand on her hip, shouting, she refused to let him turn coward. "You are taking her, sir! How can you be so horrid? Be a man! Look! Now you're making her cry." By this time the woman was red-faced too. Shading to purple, actually, and panting heavily.

"I have explained all this, and I tell you again, this is not what I asked for!"

"She is not a 'what'. She is a who, a little girl. The book shows that you did ask for her. You take her. You care for her and that's that. By the grace! I thank God for my religion. If I were not so full of Christian chastity, I swear, you would drive me to commit murder."

"Full of what?" His English wasn't perfect, but still ....

Someone on the schooner blew a whistle, ready to depart.

"I am leaving now, sir. You are not my only concern, believe it or not. I do have other duties besides dealing with you. There are people waiting for me in Plymouth. By all the angels in heaven above, I have never had this kind of trouble in my entire life. I hope never to meet one of your irk again. Honestly, I am afraid you are the worst sort of man!"

People had gathered by now, to watch the screaming pair.

"Take this piece of baggage with you, you dreadful woman. I don't want her and that's final."

"Mis-ter Ma-las-so."

"ME-SO-LA!"

"Sir! You take this child and be happy we are giving you any child at all. You certainly don't deserve one! It's a wonder the Board approved such a nasty person as yourself in the first place! They might as well have given her to the devil! "

He stepped closer to her. He yelled right in her face. "Nasty? You bring me the wrong child and you call me nasty? *Cretina! Molto, molto stupida!*"

"I thank the Lord," Rosemary Twirl huffed, stabbing her finger at him as she backed away, "I will not have to deal with you ev-er a-gain. I shall pray for you, mister, believe you me! And I hope one day the error of your ways will come to rue you. Then we shall see what we shall see." She turned on her heel and flounced off.

Santino Mesola, dumbfounded, watched her rear end, left rightleft rightleft, jiggling off down the pier. She limped up the ramp.

He looked at the baby in his arms and she looked at him. How had this happened? How had he had lost his footing? Here he stood, his emotions a raging torrent, no way to get back onto solid ground.

Perils unimaginable. He, helpless with this --this burden, this plump little unexpected, golden-faced burden, looking at him so intently. Her big pale blue eyes were alight with joy.

$A$board the schooner departing Penzance, a twelve year old boy hung over the railing. He watched the harbor grow small in the distance and licked a candy stick the bosun's mate had given him. A woman appeared beside him. Rosemary Twirl, assistant administrator of the St. Jerome Emiliani Home for Motherless Children. She steadied her trembling body against the railing and stared back at Santino Mesola, still standing on the jetty with the baby in his arms. Rosemary Twirl was very glad to see the last of him. Horrid man! She knew his type. So obviously used to getting his own way with women. Not this time, Mr. Charming-Blue-Eyes Malasso! Her bosom churned with hate. Oh, she breathed, I really must compose myself. Such a detestable man. She sighed and turned to the boy beside her.

"Well." Miss Twirl tried to smile, but her face flatly refused. "Hello. You're off to live in Plymouth then, are you?"

He grinned easily and pulled the candy stick from his mouth with a loud sucking noise. "I guess."

"Don't you know where you're going?"

"Nope. Nobody said." He shrugged. "Can't read."

"Well, let's have a look." She turned over the tag on his wrist. Her heart dropped to her shoes.

Sydney Sack. To S. Mesola. Penzance.

Rosemary Twirl's heart flumped over. They would have to turn back! She would have to ask them, beg them to turn back to Penzance. To that beast of a man.

How could she do that? She couldn't. Face that man again? Could she tell him some tale? The office had made a mistake? A clerk copied wrong? She couldn't say that. Not to that Malpasso man. How could she confront him again?

Now wait a minute, Rosie, she told herself. Be calm. Don't go off half-cocked.

She began to settle down. She took a few deep breaths. This was not her fault. She couldn't, she just couldn't ask them to turn back to Penzance.

And she didn't.


$S$antino stared stupidly at the child in his arms. Her light-colored eyes searched his face. Such big, pale eyes, grey, no, more a very light blue. She reached a little hand to pat his cheek. The hair showing beneath her plain white bonnet was light brown and very curly, but her skin was dark. Not black, by any means, but certainly not white.

*Santa Maria*, he thought. Holy Mother Mary. If only he could just leave this child somewhere. Could he just set her down somewhere and walk away? Maybe he could give her to someone.

Surely, there was someone who wanted a baby? He looked helplessly around the busy harbor. Some village woman would love to add another mouth to the ever- expanding brood around her table, wouldn't she? Santino took out his handkerchief and wiped his brow again. The baby watched him with grave interest.

He climbed onto his cart and propped the child on the seat beside him. She promptly clutched at his arm and tried to crawl into his lap.

"Sit down!" he roared.

Her eyes, the most amazing eyes, filled with tears. Santino put his head in his hands, feeling like a heel. The baby began to blubber. He glanced at her and looked away with a groan. She opened her mouth wide and wailed. Two little pearl teeth gleamed in her wet pink mouth. He made helpless gestures with his hands but she continued to sob lustily, her fingers in her mouth and tears streaming down her cheeks.

*Mamma mia.* These little creatures were such a pile of trouble! Holy saints, what was he going to do?

A young woman had paused near his cart. She caught his eye. On one arm she carried a child and on the other, a market basket.

Santino fairly lunged across the seat of the cart toward her. He was desperate. "Oh! Oh, please, miss! Can you make it stop?"

"What's the problem?"

"I -- I don't know what to do with these."

She looked at him blankly. "These what?"

He spread his hands and gestured to the child.

The woman came closer, smiling knowingly. "What's happened? You've never had to care for the little one before?"

"Oh, *Dio mio*. Never!"

"Women's work is not as easy as you thought, eh?" She smiled playfully.

"I am completely humbled."

"I like the sound of that!" The woman considered for a moment. "How far you going?"

"Porthcoombe. Here, let me give you a ride. I'll take you wherever you want to go. Anywhere. I'll pay you, if you like, whatever you want. Climb up. Please! Just make it stop its noise."

The woman laughed. She sprang nimbly aboard his cart, set her basket in the back and gathered the crying child into her free arm. "There, there," she cooed. Baby Sydney snuffled and the woman dabbed at her cheeks with a hanky.

Santino was full of admiration. How did she manage that?

The woman crooned soothingly. "Dry your tears, my sweetie, dry your tears. Here, would you like a piece of bread? My, she's dark, ain't she?"

"Do you want her?" Santino asked eagerly. "You can have her."

"What?" She laughed and settled the two toddlers easily on her lap. "What kind of a papa are you? What would your wife say?"

"I have no wife. I'm not the papa. This is all a mistake."

The woman laughed. "Sure. They all say that."

"No, really. The orphanage was supposed to send a twelve year old boy. Instead I got this. What in the world am I going to do with it?" He shook his head and massaged his aching temples.

"Oh! I wondered what all the shouting was about, you and the woman. So that is what it was? Well." She threw back her head and laughed.

"I don't find this funny."

"There must be a childless couple somewhere who would take her, surely. Though such a color she is that ... it might ...."

Santino picked up the reins. "Do you think someone would want her? Do you know anyone who wants a child? We can visit them on the way."

"No, I can't think of anyone right off. There are those who wouldn't take a brown child, anyway. I'm sorry."

"I'll be scouring the countryside, believe me. I'll offer a reward! Any amount! Where did you say you are going?"

"Anywhere near Newlyn would be such a help."

"Newlyn Town?"

"We live in Street-an-Nowan."

"It's not far out of my way." He flicked the reins.

"Thank you. This is very kind of you." She nestled the two children close on her lap. "She's an awful pretty babe, ain't she? Even with the dark skin."

Santino spat and sighed deeply. "And to think I'd been looking forward to this day."

"You wouldn't think about keeping her? She's sweet."

"What am I going to do with an infant? I can barely take care of myself."

"You'll work something out. I'll bet you have a sweetheart who would be more than happy to help." She looked sideways at Santino.

"No, no sweetheart."

"What? A good-looking man like you?" Her eyes sparkled. She tried to tease a smile out of him. "You're joking."

"No. No one steady."

"Huh. I can hardly believe that, Mr. ...?"

"Oh, I'm sorry." He shook his head and poked his temple. "Santino Mesola."

"Go on with you! Don't tell me! You are Tino? Tino, from Porthcoombe? You know my friend Sophie. Yes! You were walking out with her a while back. Sophie, from Tolcarne?"

"Oh yeah. Sophie."

"You nearly broke her heart, as I'm sure you know."

"Well ...."

"You did." She laughed again. The two children in her arms looked up from the lumps of soggy bread mashed in their fists. "Wait 'til I tell her! She is going to like this story! You really were heartless to her, you know. But from what I hear tell, you break hearts pretty regular. Poor Sophie."

Santino shook his head again.

"Me, I'm called Mercy."

"Pleased to meet you, Mercy."

"Hmm. Tino. Now that's not a Cornish name that I ever heard."

"No. Italian."

"Oh! From It'ly? Sophie said you talk odd. How in the world did you come to be here then?"

"Well. You know. Long story. Some of my family came here. Cousins. They have a small business here in Penzance, packing fish to ship back home."

"You work with them?"

"I do. I bought a few acres of woodland above Porthcoombe. For my barrels. I make the barrels they pack the fish in."

"That's good work. You're lucky."

"Yes, that's so."

"There's lots here what don't have any work. My man, Johnnie, he has to hike off to the mines every day. Gets home after dark most times."

"Hard life, that."

"We're grateful for the money. It would be worse for us if the mine closed down. There's those what have closed already. And summer coming, they lay off the men when the water for the pumps dries up."

"So I hear."

"Look at this, now! Both babes asleep, or nearly so. Mind if I put them in the back?"

"No."

"Help me, could you?" She handed one child to Santino, spread her shawl and laid the two babies in the back. He marveled again at her deft ways. She opened her basket. "Want a bite of pasty?"

"I guess. Sure."

"So your family come all the way to Cornwall, Tino? What brought that about?"

"Oh, I don't know."

"No?"

"Things were heating up at home." He sighed wearily.

Mercy smiled and waited. The cart bumped along. "Are you always this talkative?"

"Sorry. I'm not usually this cranky. It's been a difficult day."

"What was your work in It'ly?"

"Well, my family lived up near the forest of Mesola. In the Emilia. Ever hear of it? That's where our name comes from, Mesola. We've been coopers there for ages. Back as far as anyone knows."

Mercy nodded.

"But then, we -- me and some of my cousins, we were getting into trouble with the priests, complaining they were sucking the life out of us."

"Oh, goodness. You're Catholic."

"They were always wanting handouts, from even the poorest of us. And they get pretty nasty when they don't get their tithes. And then, we got into really bad trouble with the police."

"Smuggling?"

"No, this was political business. Ever heard of the unification troubles?"

She shook her head.

He looked away abruptly. "Two of my cousins were shot, executed. Firing squad. I had a fiancée. She was killed, murdered in a raid."

"Oh dear," clucked Mercy.

"Not much reason to stay after that."

"I see, yes. I'm sorry for you. So how long have you been here?"

"It's been seven years. Seven good years. I've been lucky." Santino spread his arms. "And now this."

"You'll work something out, Tino. I know you will. Here, have an apple."

When the cart drew closer to Street-an-Nowan, Santino began to despair again.

"Please, Mercy. Are you sure you can't take one more child? I'll pay you."

"Thanks, but I've got my hands full as it is. I've got two more here at home. I thank you for the ride, Tino. It was nice to meet you."

"And you. Yes, thank you. Thanks for the help. I appreciate it. Have you thought of anyone who might want a child?"

"No one comes to mind."

"Some lonely simpleton? Some dessicated wife of a dried-up vicar?"

Mercy laughed. "You are a wicked one. Don't worry, Tino. Somebody will turn up."

S antino was relieved beyond imagining that the child, curled up on his coat in the back, slept all the way to Porthcoombe. He drew up in front of his cottage, left her sleeping in the cart and hurried across the lane. He knocked on his neighbor's door. Bess Campion had barely gotten the door open when he lunged through it.

"Bess, you're the only one I can turn to."

"It's lovely to see you, too, Tino. My word. It's nice to be needed, though. I take it something is wrong. Whatever has bitten you?" She looked out toward his cart standing in the lane. "Didn't you get your apprentice?"

"Just come here. Just come see what I got."

"What happened?" She followed him to the cart. "What in the world? My word! Oh, look at her! Who is this little one?"

"You don't have to act like this is some blessed event, Bess! This is just about the worst thing that could happen to me."

"But, Tino, how did you end up with a baby? There's a story here, isn't there? I can't wait to hear it. Oh, what a little sweetheart." Bess reached in and pulled the sleeping child into her arms.

"*Mi sento male.* Oh, what a tragedy."

Bess laughed at his long face. "It is not a tragedy. Look at her! She's so precious. Is she yours?"

"Don't be ridiculous! No, it is not mine! God, Bess, what am I going to do?"

"First, you should calm down and tell me what happened. What dark skin she has. Is she ...?" She looked at Tino questioningly.

He shrugged. "I have no idea what she is."

"Come inside. Tell me all about it while I cook. You'll stay for dinner?"

He put his hands together as if in prayer. "How I hoped you'd say that."

Bess Campion prided herself on the bounty of her table. Santino, their neighbor, was a frequent guest at it. Of all the vegetable gardens in the village, the only one that was more productive than hers was Santino's own. He had a larger variety of fruits and vegetables, but every year her two pigs were the fattest in town. Tonight, a crabmeat stew bubbled above her fire. Her family had taken up Santino's habit of eating out-of-doors in the summer, so she handed Santino a carafe of wine. She carried a bowl of peas that needed shelling and led him out to the table in the garden.

Bess's husband, Rafe, was a Scotsman by birth, educated in Edinburgh. Being the only surgeon within ten miles of Porthcoombe, he never lacked for work. The Campions were spared that worry, at least, unlike some folks in the village. His work wasn't seasonal, like the fishermen's. He didn't get laid off like the miners. He was obliged to invest in a light carriage and he kept a horse. But these investments did not compare to the amounts of money boat builders put into their business. And though, in his travels, Mr. Rafe Campion had to contend with weather, he could usually avoid doing battle with Nature at her most violent, unlike the men who put to sea. By Porthcoombe standards, the Campions and their two little girls lived very well.

In the entire village, Rafe and Bess Campion were the best neighbors Santino could wish for. But the Campions' good fortune was, to some folks in Porthcoombe, the source of a bit of ill feeling. The fact they had been born outside of Cornwall didn't help. And the villagers couldn't approve of Santino entirely, either. First of all, he was Eye-talian. Most maddening, he left town every week to spend the Sabbath with his Eye-talian relatives. He took a cartload of new barrels to Penzance every Saturday afternoon without exception. Mothers with marriageable daughters fumed. Obviously the local society was just not good enough for him. On top of that, even when he was in Porthcoombe, he was rarely seen down at The Bell, the local pub. Strange way for a bloke to act, growled the men. Those two cottages that faced each other at the top of Narrow Lane? They were both entirely too strange to suit anybody.

On this evening in June, Bess and Rafe Campion listened to Santino's tale of his altercation with Miss Rosemary Twirl.

"I wish," laughed Rafe, "oh, I wish I could have been there."

"Oh, thank you. You two give me so much comfort, giggling like a couple of maidens over my hideous problem."

"But Tino! You should know better than to argue with a woman."

"You should never have crossed her, Santino."

"That's the truth," Santino declared. "*Che pasticcio*! What am I going to do?"

"Why don't you get married?" asked Rafe.

"Now who am I going to marry, I ask you?"

"Tino, you of all people must know someone."

Bess interrupted. "This is where I leave the conversation. I'd better get the girls to bed. Your baby should stay here tonight, Tino, so you can get some sleep."

"Don't call it my baby. Are you sure, Bess? Will you be able to take care of it?"

She laughed. "I have had some dealings with children. Your little one will be fine here for a night or two. I have to get back in practice, you know. Before next fall." She patted her tummy.

Santino looked at her with sympathy. "*Povera* Bess. How do you ladies make motherhood seem so easy?"

*P*orthcoombe was a very small village. News traveled fast, but Santino never expected his news to travel as far as

Lamorna. He was amazed, two mornings later, when Zephaniah Cobbs opened the door to his workshop. Santino put down the iron hoop he was fitting and wiped his hands.

"Mr. Mesola. I hope I don't interrupt."

Santino shook the man's hand. "Mr. Cobbs. Good morning. How are things in Lamorna?"

"Quite well, thank you." He leaned on his cane and looked admiringly around the shop. You have a good supply of wood here. Will you really use all this?"

"Oh yes. Some of it has just been cut and will take time to season. Once it is aged, though, it gets used up very quickly."

"It's a nice tight grain," said Cobbs, sighting down a length of board.

Santino nodded and tapped his fingers impatiently on a barrel top.

Cobbs turned back to him and smiled. "We spoke once before about my purchasing some of these. I am still interested in buying some casks from you."

"I'm sorry, Mr. Cobbs. As I told you a couple of years ago, I have more work already than I can handle."

"Maybe a dozen firkin, and some tight-casks for, ah, certain liquids." Zephaniah Cobbs smiled again. "If you sold to me, you wouldn't have to drive to Penzance every week."

"Again, I'm sorry. But I have a commitment to people in Penzance." How did Mr. Cobbs know about his weekly trips? The man was a virtual stranger to him.

"I could give you a similar deal."

"My arrangement in Penzance is not a deal. It is a family obligation."

"Obligations can be broken."

"No. I thank you for your offer. But no."

"You could sell me part of your output. I would pay you five percent more than your Penzance relatives."

"Like I mentioned, I can hardly supply what they need as it is. I work alone here." Santino picked up the iron hoop again and began fiddling with it. He wanted to get back to work.

"Why don't you take an apprentice, Mr. Mesola? Perhaps I could find you someone?"

"Well, I have been searching for that very thing. But I have met with disappointment, so far. Which is why I must cut this conversation short. I need to …."

Cobbs interrupted. "I hear tell you have an addition to your family." He fingered his oversized moustache and watched Santino closely. "My congratulations, sir."

Santino paused. "Would you be interested in a child?"

"Oh good heavens no. Well, not a baby, anyway. No, I was going to propose arranging for someone to assist you with the care of your child. I act as an agent for several, ah, people in need of work. Foreigners. Like yourself."

Santino blinked. A nurse? Not quite the answer to his prayers. Still, this might offer a temporary way out of his dilemma. "You have someone in mind?"

"A very capable person. I could send her round to you tomorrow. Why don't you interview her and see if she fills your needs?"

"I'm interested, at least as a temporary measure. Strictly temporary." Santino paused again. "I can't pay you in barrels, if that is what you are going to propose."

"That is precisely what I would require."

"No. I'm sorry."

"Why don't you meet her and see what you think? Then we can negotiate."

"Well, maybe."

"I will send her to you tomorrow."

"This evening would not be too soon, actually."

Zephaniah Cobbs made a sound like laughter. "You sound desperate, Mr. Mesola. I do believe I have you over the proverbial barrel, do I not?"

Santino shrugged. He certainly could not deny that.

Cobbs twirled his cane and, only with effort, kept the smirk off his face.

$T$hat evening, Santino stopped at the house across the lane on his way home. When he walked in, Baby, as he had taken to calling the child, kicked happily from the arms of Bess's daughter. She reached for Santino with a big smile. He held her absent-mindedly, unresponsive as she beat her little hands joyfully against his chest.

Bess Campion was frowning. "The idea of getting involved with Zephaniah Cobbs?" She shuddered. "I don't know, Tino. It's a little worrisome."

"I have heard the odd remark about him. But he seemed very gentlemanly, well-dressed. He didn't act at all the way people make him sound." Santino shrugged. "As Cobbs pointed out, I am completely helpless. And I can't go on taking advantage of your good will, Bess."

"Better to be in my debt than his. You wouldn't be willing to search just a little longer for someone to take her?"

"Oh, I will keep searching. This woman he is sending will be strictly temporary, I assure you."


*O*nly temporary? A dangerous prediction. An hour later, when Santino Mesola opened his door to Miss Bianca LeFronde, a wave of shock hit him square in the chest and ran right down his spine. He took a step backwards.

"Mr. Mesola? Mr. Cobbs send me."

"*Si, buona sera...*" What a fool! Did people always revert to their native language in times of stress? He opened the door wide and gestured her in.

"*Merci,*" she answered, also reverting, and surprising herself as well.

They glanced at each other and looked quickly into opposite corners of the room. Santino pointed to a chair. Bianca LeFronde kept her eyes averted. They both sat down and tried to think of something to say.

What was happening, gasped Santino to himself? A fairy tale, a legend. Venus, Diana! A goddess!

A goddess had simply walked through his door. Walked through his door and pierced his heart clean through, without ever pulling a single arrow from her quiver.

*Drawbridge*

*A hinged bridge which keeps intruders from entering a castle. In the raised position the bridge would be flush against the gate, forming an additional barrier to entry.*

BIANCA LeFRONDE

"$M$r. Cobbs bring me here tonight. He –he will be back immediately," Bianca stuttered. She leaned towards Baby, who pulled away, a little shy in Santino's arms. "This is the little one? She look like… I'm sorry, my English. I don't know the word." She touched the baby's cheek.

"Mulatto. We think she must be a mulatto."

"Beautiful eyes," murmured Bianca. So big, the lightest blue eyes, and skin the color of *café au lait*. "What is she called?"

"Well, she has no name. Just Baby. I don't plan on keeping her so I never got around to calling her anything else. I just need someone to take care of her until I find parents for her."

"I see." Bianca was crestfallen. For the first time since she had come to Cornwall, she had found a job she might like. This cottage, with its lovely garden. Close to a village, instead of out on a lonely moor. This seemed to her like such a nice place to work. Such a pretty little baby. And, well, it must be admitted, such a lovely man. So gracious, courtly European manners, manners she had not seen since she left France. And so incredibly handsome.

"Shall we sit here?"

"*Merci.*"

Bianca noticed how the little girl clung to Mr. Mesola. This was a good sign, was it not? The baby liked him. Maybe he was gentle to her, and kind?

Mr. Mesola was sizing her up. Bianca sat straighter.

"So you have had experience with small children?"

"In Paris, a time ago, yes. I was in care for a small boy. Sébastien."

"You were his governess?"

"A little like a governess. But we, um, we came to Cornwall together. To Lamorna."

"That must have been quite a change, Paris to Lamorna."

"A very great change, yes. For both of us." Bianca dropped her eyes.

"Are you caring for children now?"

"Mr. Cobbs sends me to work in large houses. Cleaning, most times, but sometimes caring to children." She tucked her rough, red hands beneath her sleeves. "But I take care of Sébastien until he is old. I am working him, teaching him, after Mr. Cobbs brought us here. In evenings we study. He is like a son to me. When he is small, I make his education since Mr. Cobbs would not, um, find time for it." Bianca looked hopefully at Mr. Mesola. "I would work very hard on your little one."

"Would you mind being here alone every day? Except for the child, of course. And there is a nice neighbor lady across the way."

"Oh, I would like! Like very much." She glanced around the room. "It's very pretty here. I wasn't thinking such a nice place. Forgive me, I hope not to be rude. But I..." She would seem too eager, she knew, but oh! Was it foolish to betray how badly she wanted this job? "I could clean and cook for you, too. Unless someone else already do it. And teach the baby when she gets old. I teach Sébastien to read and write and do his numbers. He is old now, very smart." She stopped, flustered. She was talking too much.

"There is a room upstairs. I would have to clean it out for you. I have never used it so it's not very nice up there."

"Oh, I could do all that. I don't need anything so much." A room to herself? She thought of the bare, cold room she shared with the other girls in the attic at Tregorna Farm.

"Well then. It seems this would work very well."

"Yes?"

"Yes, if you're willing."

"Oh yes! Thank you, Mr. Mesola." Hope! This sensation, flooding over her for the first time in a very long time, was making her giddy. She had to hug herself to stop from quivering. "When you would like me to begin?"

"How soon could you leave your other job?"

She looked down, awkward. "Mr. Cobbs is taking care to all that."

"Mr. Cobbs makes these decisions for you?"

"Yes. He does. Um, I am ... he brings us from Paris, you see. When the Terror happens."

"Cobbs did that? He sounds like a very kind man. Is he a relation of yours?"

"Oh no, no." She laughed a little but was suddenly serious. "No. Sébastien's mother have such fear that we go to prison, so she give Mr. Cobbs money to get us out of Paris, to get her son and me out. She pay Cobbs a lot of money, all her money. So we work for him now, Sébastien and I. To pay him, you see."

"An interesting arrangement."

She nodded once.

"So I will pay him for your services, and he will pay you?"

"Well." She lowered her eyes. "You will pay him."

"And you are happy with this arrangement?"

She looked at him, dumb with confusion. Santino watched the light drain from her face. Had he said something wrong?

There was a knock on the door.

"That must be Cobbs now." Santino rose. "We'll see what we can work out."


*L*ater, Zephaniah Cobbs drove his carriage slowly down Narrow Lane. The street was dangerously steep. It was getting dark and he still had three miles to go to get to the farm. He was smoldering a bit over the deal he had just made. He would not be paid in barrels after all. He needed barrels badly. But he had managed to arrange a big fee for the girl. He would get decent compensation, at least. This is one French girl who would prove her worth, finally.

She sat silent and tense next to him, almost afraid to imagine her fortunes had finally turned. She would not have to live at

Tregorna Farm, for at least a little while. After nine years out there! It was too much to hope for. She sat very stiffly so Cobbs would not notice her trembling.

Cobbs interrupted her thoughts. "He will have to give you Thursday afternoons off so you can bring me his payment. Of course our arrangement will be the same as ever. I expect you to keep your eyes open and report back to me. Every Thursday."

"Yes sir," she replied.

"You will be in a different situation now. Living in a village, working for a tradesman. You'll be able to keep an eye on the harbor from there. Let me know if you hear about any activity here, anyone working the free trade. Say, ah, if someone brings in whiskey or tobacco, I want to hear about it. Anything like that, no matter how small. You understand?"

Bianca nodded.

"This will be a much easier situation for you. The work will be less taxing. I will not be making the same profit, unfortunately," he lied. "Therefore I expect a great deal from you in return. Keep your ears open, keep me informed about everything that happens in Porthcoombe. If you do well here, I will be able to promote you to a better household eventually. Working in a big house, possibly as governess for someone in shipping. A wealthy household, in Penzance, perhaps. That would be most useful to me. And much nicer for you."

They were passing through Lamorna, the village that had seemed so pitifully small when she first arrived from Paris. She had seen enough dirty, dreary farms on remote moors now to last a lifetime. She turned to look at the sights in the village.

"Are you listening, Miss LeFronde?"

"Yes, Mr. Cobbs."

"From time to time, I may require you to search out some special information. In such a case, I will send you word."

Bianca twitched in her seat. The carriage turned up the long hill to the farm. It was nine years since she had first been driven to Tregorna Farm. But this time, she hoped, oh, maybe this time would be her last. She couldn't believe it would actually happen.

Nine long years at Tregorna Farm.

September 1794, nine years earlier

Port du Bloscon, France

The *Serpent*

*B*ianca prodded the little boy awake.

"Look!" she cried in French. "See the boats, Sébastien?"

"Are we here?" He crawled over his mother's lap and hung out the window of the carriage as it drove to the docks. "Look, *Maman!*"

His mother, Marie Roland, put her hand on his back but she wasn't looking at the boats. She only had eyes for him. Watching her, Bianca could feel her own heart twisting. Marie would stay behind while she, Bianca, and the little boy escaped.

Sébastien looked back at his mother. "Are you crying, *Maman?*"

"No, no Sébastien. I need a handkerchief so I can wave good-bye to you."

"Why?"

"It's just a tradition when people are sailing away on big ships."

"I don't have a handkerchief. I need one too, *Maman*, and so does Bianca."

"I have hankies, Sébastien," Bianca assured him. "Here, this one will be yours."

The carriage came to a halt. Madame Roland stepped down. Erect, attractive, dressed to the hilt, she always commanded a second look. She knew everyone worth knowing in Paris and everyone wanted to know her. Or had wanted to, such a very short time ago. Everything had changed so swiftly. It numbed the mind. Now, even with all her contacts, she had little hope of escaping arrest. She dared not think what would happen to her after that.

Even with all the people she knew, it had still taken a small miracle to find someone who could put her in touch with a certain Cornish merchant. She scanned the groups of men gathered at the portside. She lived in terror thinking he might not show up.

Bianca, her friend and now her son's governess, began to panic as well. Would this turn out to be a wild goose chase? Certainly there was no one here she would care to follow onto a ship. Most gentlewomen would have been intimidated at the sight of gangs of such men, but Marie Roland was not put off. Especially now, when everything, absolutely everything, depended on her finding the man into whose care she would entrust her only child.

Sébastien hopped out of the carriage and Bianca chased him toward the docks.

"Wait, Sébastien. Let's make sure we are in the right place before you go running off."

Seeing a woman with a small boy, a young man stepped forward. Madame Roland was relieved to see that he looked much more approachable than the men around him.

"Madame Roland?" he asked in English.

"Yes. You must be Captain O'Brien."

"I am, and at your service, Madame." He touched his cap. "I trust you had a safe journey?"

"We had some trouble getting out of Paris, but here we are, thankfully. It has been a tiring journey." She wrung her handkerchief. "I hope, Captain O'Brien, I hope and trust you will keep my little boy safe?" She searched his face. He looked so young.

"I will take very good care of him, Madame."

"Forgive me for being frank, but I worry that the English animosity towards the French is so…what to call it?"

"Actually, I am not an Englishman," he said stiffly.

"*Vraiment?*" Truly?

"Absolutely not. I am Irish. You may put your mind at rest."

"Ah, I see. Well, I will feel better when I hear you have landed safely in Cornwall. You will send word to let me know you have arrived?"

"I will."

"Promise me that one favor, sir. It's very important to me."

"Certainly, Madame Roland. I do so promise. Of course I will let you know." He paused, awkward, groping for conversation. He could see what it was costing her to send her son into exile. "It certainly looks like we'll have fine weather for the crossing." Her face was buried in her handkerchief. He wanted to put his arm around her, as sympathetic to a teardrop as any Irishman, but he felt awkward. "There, now. This must be difficult. Let us hope the separation is only temporary."

"I have very little hope. If only my husband could be here, we would all be going with you. But he has been detained somewhere. I absolutely must find him, if I can." She put on a smile and waved to Sébastien, who gestured impatiently for her to come to look at a pile of lobster traps. "Oh, here, I mustn't forget. I will give you the money for Mr. Cobbs. I don't want Mademoiselle LeFronde to have to worry about it." Madame Roland handed the captain an envelope. "He is a worthy person, do you think, this Mr. Cobbs?" The way the captain quickly glanced away made her hand fly to her heart. "We are doing the right thing, Captain? Please assure me that my boy will be safe in Cornwall."

"He will be better off than in Paris, and I will give you my word, Madame, that I will do what I can for him. You can trust me on that."

Sébastien came bouncing back and pulled on his mother's hand. She bent and embraced him.

"*Maman*," he cried, struggling against her arms, "which boat is ours?"

"Let's ask the captain. This is Captain O'Brien, Sébastien. He will be taking you to Mr. Cobbs in Cornwall."

Sébastien looked up at the giant man. He made a small bow. "How do you do, sir," he said in English.

"Captain, may I also present his companion? This is my dear friend, Miss LeFronde."

"It's a pleasure, Miss. Are you ready to come aboard, Sébastien? We have a good stiff breeze this morning."

"Oh yes, I'm ready! May we go now, *Maman*? What? You are crying again, aren't you? Don't cry!" He reached up to put his arms around her. "You and Papa will soon be with us. Don't worry."

"Yes, my darling. Soon we will join you."

At this, Bianca could not stop her lips from trembling.

"Bianca, my dearest," said Marie Roland in French, "we said we would not do this today." She put her arms around the young woman. "If you break down," she whispered, "I shall be lost. You will write to me?"

"Without fail, Marie." Bianca didn't trust herself to say any more.

"All right. Let's say '*au revoir*' then."

Bianca was shaking. "I owe you so much, Marie."

"And you are repaying me, a hundredfold. Let us hope for the best. And now, my darling," she bent again to Sébastien, who was watching the women with a solemn face, "you must forgive us. We are foolish women and you are such a big, strong boy. We will have no tears from you. I am sure about that. Let me hug you one last time. Do as Bianca tells you, now, won't you? You have my rosary, and Papa's books?"

"*Maman*, don't be sad. We will have a wonderful time until you come. Won't we, Bianca?" His governess and his mother were both crying uncontrollably.

The captain took the little boy's hand. "Let me show you around the *Serpent*, Sébastien. Wave to your mother first. Now, have you ever done any sailing?"

Sébastien waved his handkerchief over his shoulder and followed the captain. The boy looked so small with his hand in the young Irishman's. Bianca stepped backwards, holding Madame Roland's hand until the last moment.

"May God be with you, Marie." She tore herself away and hurried to catch up with Sébastien.

Marie Roland watched until the *Serpent* disappeared over the horizon. Then she slowly turned and resumed her seat in the carriage, heading back to Paris, where she believed her husband was in hiding. Paris, where, instead of a king, an executioner reigned supreme.

*T*he *Serpent* made the crossing to Lamorna, in Cornwall, without event. The young captain asked Bianca if she would join them on a tour of the ship.

"Thank you, you are very kind." The last thing she wanted was a tour of the ship, but Sébastien was longing to explore and she didn't dare let him out of her sight. She dragged along behind them until Captain O'Brien insisted on putting a chair out on the deck for her. She dropped into it and closed her eyes. She was exhausted with the strain of the last few days but she knew she would not be able to sleep.

"I will take good care of Sébastien, Miss LeFronde," said Captain O'Brien. "Rest there until we get to Lamorna, if you like."

Somehow she felt she could trust this man. She really had no choice but to trust him, which worried her. He looked young to be a captain, eighteen years old at most, not much older than she was. The captain and Sébastien went off together and, by the end of the journey, Sébastien had explored every nook and cranny of the cutter.

Even the little boy's enthusiasm could not revive Bianca's spirits. But he insisted on pulling her to the rail as they approached the harbor.

"Miss LeFronde?" The captain was at her elbow. "When we arrive, there will be someone to take you and your luggage to Tregorna Farm. May I tell you something, in all sincerity? If you need help at any time, I will be happy to do what I can for you. Will you remember that, and call on me?"

Bianca hesitated. He seemed very serious. "Thank you, Captain. I appreciate this."

"Best of luck to you both."

"Thank you." Again, a pinprick of worry.

She was over-reacting, worn-down. She should be happy. They were in Cornwall! Paris and its bloody horrors were behind them. If only Marie and Jean-Pierre Roland were with them, everything would be perfect. She watched Sébastien carefully. He seemed ecstatic. He couldn't wait to swim off the slender sand beaches at the foot of huge granite cliffs. He wanted to climb the rocks, sit on the jetty. He waved to the fishing boats. Sébastien was sure that, when Papa arrived, he would get them a boat and the two of them would go exploring in and out of all those little coves. Did Bianca know how to sail? Would Captain O'Brien take them out in the *Serpent* again another day? When could he play on the beach?

For her part, the cliffs of Cornwall made Bianca uneasy. A Parisienne for her entire life, her only experiences with life outside the city were occasional lavish picnics on rolling green hillsides.

When they disembarked, she hobbled uncertainly down the short wooden jetty on her little city boots and stared up at the village in disbelief. Where were the shops? So few houses. And small, pitifully small, crowding the hillside above the harbor. All the people were dressed so poorly. Women with bare, muscular arms carried yards and yards of nets or heavy baskets of fish. Some were pitch-forking masses of seaweed from a cart into wheelbarrows. These were women! There was not one who was smartly dressed. She felt sure they were watching her covertly.

Looking around Lamorna cove, Bianca's spirits faltered. She and Sébastien's parents had had such high hopes. Cornwall, freedom! But all would soon be well, once they arrived at Tregorna House. She prayed all would be well. How many days until she could hope for the Rolands' arrival? If only Marie would be successful at making contact with her husband, if only they could escape Paris in time.

Bianca and Sébastien were handed into a crude wagon by Captain O'Brien and their luggage was loaded behind. He reminded her again that she could call on him at any time. Then, looking very solemn, he waved good-bye and the wagon groaned up the hill. Bianca sat in terror as the ox --an ox! -- strained to pull the cart up the treacherous road. They left the town behind almost before she could believe it. The narrow road continued to climb steeply. A tunnel of trees arched overhead. It was so completely quiet, all she could hear was the asthmatic old ox plodding along, huffing noisily through the twilight.

Now they were on a rough track through a forest. Still they climbed. They passed only a handful of stone houses, hidden among the trees. Candles glowed faintly in the windows. They turned to the left and finally the path ran out into the open, across a moor. Ahead was a little collection of houses. The signpost they passed said Polcoth. Was this their destination? No, the track ran on. Finally they rounded a curve that brought them to a slight rise, the highest point, such as it was, in the area.

The sun was setting in a glory of color and the moon, a big harvest moon, rose out of the sea below them. Silhouetted against it were the black shapes of barns and a house, Tregorna Farm at last. Everything seemed more hopeful now. Bianca felt her spirits lift a little.

The cart drove closer. She plunged into gloom again.

Probably once beautiful, the big square stone house and its barns brooded alone, an island adrift on the bare landscape. A wall surrounded the house and its overgrown garden. Not a glimmer of light showed anywhere. The silence seemed thick, forbidding. The stone barns were quiet when the ox, his step more lively now as he came closer to his barn, pulled them through the gate.

Even the ebullient Sébastien was subdued. No one came to meet them. The driver helped them down without a word and lifted their bags out. He set them on the stony ground and he and the ox retired for the night, probably, guessed Bianca uncharitably, sleeping in the same stall.

She hesitated on the edge of the drive. Sébastien was tired now. The trauma of leaving Paris this morning had been terrible for Bianca, even more so because they had to keep the real reason secret from Sébastien. She was worn out with worry. She waited, listening to the vespers sung by night creatures. The barn door creaked as the ox and cart were led inside. Sébastien took Bianca's hand and leaned against her, shifting from foot to foot. Still there was nobody about. Perhaps there was no one at home and they would both be sharing a stall with the ox.

"Where is everybody?" asked Sébastien in French.

"I don't know." It was almost dark. She could barely see the door. "I'll knock."

There was no door knocker. Bianca rapped lightly on the wood, then with more force. No one answered. She put her hand on the knob and it grated rustily. She opened the door and called out in English.

"Anyone is here?" She stepped inside and Sébastien shadowed her. A faint patch of light showed beneath a door. They crept toward it. "Hello?" Bianca called again. She pushed on the hall door. Its hinges were also creaky with rust. "Hello?"

A blade-thin woman stood with her back to them, peeling potatoes. Her shoulder blades stuck out like angel wings -- that was the first and last time this particular analogy would come to Bianca's mind. But for now Bianca straightened with relief at the sight. "Hello!" she said again, and walked into the room. One candle stood on the table. Shadows skulked in every corner.

She leaned closer to the woman. "Excuse me," she said more loudly. The woman threw up her arms and screamed, brandishing her knife.

"Who are you! What do you want?" she barked. She stuck the knife tip under Bianca's chin. Bianca backed away, her hands outstretched. Sébastien ducked quickly behind her and held her leg.

"We come to meet Mr. Cobbs."

"Eh? What?" The knife jabbed closer.

"Mr. Cobbs," Bianca said loudly. "We come to meet him here."

"He's busy." She gestured Bianca away. Too pretty, this one. Big trouble. Why don't she just leave us alone?

"You can tell him we are here?" She spoke as clearly as she could.

"What's that?"

A little harried now, Bianca repeated her request.

The woman banged her knife down on the table. "Stay here," she ordered. She limped through a dark doorway.

"What happened to her teeth?" Sébastien whispered, again in French. He looked like he was near tears.

"She doesn't have any, I guess."

"She should change her uniform. Did she spill her tea, do you think?"

"I'm not sure you could call it a uniform."

Sébastien looked around the room. "Do we have to stay here, Bianca?"

"I don't know where we are going to stay."

"I think I'd rather go back to Paris."

Bianca got down on one knee. "Listen, my darling. You must be brave for me, and for your mama and papa. We cannot go back to Paris for a long, long time."

"Why not?"

"There are people there who, well, do not like us very much."

"They don't like us?"

They heard the woman shuffling back into the kitchen. Bianca stood. She grasped Sébastien's hand and he pressed against her.

The woman scowled at them and jerked her head in the direction of the door. She made a swatting motion. They took that to mean they were to pass through.

"Thank you very much," Bianca said. She made a small nervous curtsy, not knowing why, as if the woman were nobility. When Bianca's back was turned, the woman stabbed the air behind her with her knife.

The hall was dark but once again, they saw the glimmer of a light beneath a door. Bianca opened it and urged Sébastien reluctantly through it.

Before them was a large desk. Behind the desk, a man leaned his elbows on a pile of open ledgers. His dark hair was tied behind his head. He had the largest moustache Bianca had ever seen. She couldn't help but wonder what was hiding beneath it. The robe he wore was shabby and frayed. Since he was busy writing, Bianca waited politely. Several times he dipped his pen in the inkwell. He shuffled through some notes. He didn't look up. The only sound was the scratch of his pen across the page of his book. Sébastien looked expectantly up at Bianca and she put her finger to her lips.

This room, like the kitchen, was full of shadow. Dark cabinets lurked in corners. The fireplace was full of cold ashes though the musty room would have benefited from a fire. There was no chair for visitors. Anyway, Bianca thought she would not care to sit down even if she were offered a seat. Finally Zephaniah Cobbs put his pen down and looked at them. He was not unpleasant to look at. His eyes were his best feature, intelligent, a deep blue, calculating. He offered no pleasantries.

"You brought my money, I presume?"

"Oh, *Monsieur*! I am so sorry, Mr. Cobbs. I think it is with Captain O'Brien. Madame Roland give it to the captain."

"She didn't do that! Ah, that is very unfortunate!" His palm struck his desk in disgust. "Now I'll have to wring the money out of him. That is so vexing." He covered his moustache with his hand and scrutinized Bianca's face. "It had better be the correct amount."

"Madame would never steal on you, Mr. Cobbs." Bianca's voice rose in panic. "She is so happy for your help."

He grunted. He looked them both up and down for a long time, tapping his finger against his moustache. If Bianca and Sébastien had been hoping for a warm welcome, it seemed they would not get one here. A razor of fear sawed at the top of Bianca's skull, already aching with the strain of the day.

"Everything will be fine, yes?" Bianca ventured.

"If there is money owing, you'll have to work it off."

"Pardon?" She did not know this English term, 'work it off'.

He ignored her. "Pawley will show you where to sleep. Tomorrow I'll drive you to Polcoth. After tomorrow, you'll, ah, walk back and forth. You," he pointed at Bianca, "will work in the kitchen there. You," he pointed to Sébastien, "will stay here and work in the fields."

"Work in fields?" cried Bianca. What was he talking about?

Cobbs flipped open his hands. "You protest? You thought I'd have you living here for free?"

"But Madame Roland pays you, and pays you well. She tells me this is cost her very much money."

"She paid me to help you escape a hostile country with your lives. She paid for your safe passage over here. Which I arranged, at my cost, in my ship. She paid so you would have a place to stay when you arrived." He pointed a long finger at her. "Now that you are here, you must pay for your upkeep."

"But she gives you more than enough! And Sébastien can not work! He is not yet five years old."

"He can make himself useful. His mother claims he is smart. For now my, ah, manager will put him to work digging vegetables, feeding the pigs. I don't know what I'll find for him come winter. He can pile firewood, I suppose. Next spring he'll be old enough to work at the mine."

"Mr.Cobbs! You are not serious!"

He picked up a large bell and nearly deafened them with its clamor. "Pawley!" he bellowed. Then he took up his pen and was absorbed in his books again. "Enough. You're bothering me. Pawley will take you to your room." He gestured at them to leave. The gray-haired woman stood in the doorway, waiting for them.

Bianca and Sébastien turned slowly and followed her back to the kitchen. On the table were two plates, each with a thin slab of dry bread. Pawley carried the plates to the stove and fished a few soggy greens from a pot. She slopped some onto each plate. Then she thrust one at Bianca and snapped her head toward the table. She stuck the other plate in Sébastien's face.

Sébastien looked at Pawley. She held his plate toward him and scowled. Tears filled his eyes.

"Take the plate, Sébastien, *cheri*," urged Bianca.

Slowly he reached for the plate. Pawley pulled it back, just out of reach. Twice he stretched farther and twice she pulled it away again. He dropped his hands, not knowing what was expected of him. Moving so fast, he hardly saw it coming, Pawley smacked his ear. He burst into a loud howl.

"Do not do this!" Bianca cried. She rushed to gather him in her arms. "*Cheri!*"

Pawley banged the plate onto the table. "We will have none of this temper!" she shouted.

Sébastien began to panic. "I want to go home!" he wailed. His face was flaming red.

Pawley grabbed Sébastien's arm and practically lifted him off his feet. She shook the little boy until his teeth rattled. "No crying!" she screeched. She glowered at Bianca. "You'd better make him stop or he'll get a whipping!"

"You can not do this to a child so! You hurt him."

Pawley dropped Sébastien's arm, turned swiftly and snatched up a broom. "Hurt him?" Like lightning, she struck Bianca's shoulder. Sébastien stopped crying abruptly. Bianca was struck dumb. They heard the door creak open.

Mr. Cobbs stood there. He spoke not a word.

Pawley arched an eyebrow and turned back to them with a leering smile. Her broom flew at Bianca again, knocking her to the floor. Sébastien began to scream.

"Shut him up! Shut him up!" Pawley cried with every thump of the broom on Bianca's body. "No crying!"

Mr. Cobbs said nothing.

Another man strode into the kitchen and seized Pawley by the wrist.

"What is the problem here, Mrs. Pawley? Put your broom down," he said, speaking close to Pawley's ear.

Mr. Cobbs turned away, closing the door behind him.

The man wiped his hand across his face. He leaned to help Bianca up from the floor. She stood up slowly, careful to stifle her sobs.

The man glared at Pawley, shaking his head. He put his hands on his hips. Finally he said loudly "I assume these are the new children from France?"

"Stupid French pigs!" spat Pawley.

The man turned to Bianca. "How do you do? I'm Ickes. I manage the farm for Mr. Cobbs. Mrs. Pawley, you may go on with your duties. I'll take care of these two."

With a hiss of anger, Pawley thrust her broom aside and went back to her stove.

"I'm sorry for this misunderstanding," he said, speaking softly. Pawley, half deaf, apparently could not hear him. "Mrs. Pawley gets carried away sometimes. Are you badly hurt?"

Trembling, Bianca shook her head. Sébastien wept silently and clung to her.

"Not a very nice welcome, is it? I'm sorry I was not on hand to meet you. Mr. Cobbs told me you were coming but I didn't catch your names."

Bianca stammered an answer.

"Sit down and try to eat something, Miss LeFronde." When Bianca shook her head, Ickes said "Try to eat. You'll need your strength. Sébastien, will you eat your supper?" Gently he nudged the little boy to a chair. "You eat just a little while I move your luggage to your room. I'll come back for you in a few minutes."

Bianca sat Sébastien at the bench near the table but she could not get him to eat the green slime on their plates. They were still sitting, heads down, plates untouched, when Ickes returned.

"At least take the bread to your room. You will be hungry before morning. Normally you would stay in the servants' rooms but they are full. Mr. Cobbs has brought several people from France in the last few weeks. I have cleaned out the attic in my house for you. Come with me. I'll show you where it is."

He lit a lantern and led them outside to a stone cottage. The parlor of Mr. Ickes's house opened to a bedroom on one side and an attic above. Ickes led them to the steep stairway.

"There are not many comforts at Tregorna, I'm afraid. Candles are in short supply so take care you use this one sparingly." He ran his hand back and forth across the top of his head, then spoke very softly. "We won't get much chance to talk. Life won't be easy here, I warn you. For now, there is not much I can do to change that. Try not to anger Mr. Cobbs. Don't contradict him or disobey him. Do you understand what I am saying, Sébastien? And just stay out of Mrs. Pawley's way as much as you can." He bent lower to talk to Sébastien. "You'll be working with me here on the farm until you are bigger. It will seem hard but I'm sure you can do it. Are you a strong boy? Yes? It will go badly for you if Mr. Cobbs sees any signs of weakness. I'm counting on you to be tough. Do you understand? Tough, strong?" Ickes turned to Bianca. "There will be times, Miss LeFronde, when you think the whole world is against you, even me. But be patient. I will do what I can for you."

Bianca did not know how to respond.

"Work starts early here. Try to get some rest. I won't see you most mornings, but I'll leave some bread on the table."

Dazed with exhaustion, Bianca took the candle he offered and led the way to the ladder. She dreaded to think what they would find up there. Two thin mattresses on the floor, a blanket on each, and nothing more. Only later would they realize how fortunate it was that they would be sharing a room. At least for a time they would be together.

"Good night, Mr. Ickes," she said, her face wet with tears. She started up and then turned back. "Thank you. You are kind."

Upstairs, Bianca collapsed onto the mattress. She and Sébastien looked at each other in disbelief. She pulled the little boy close. How had things come to this?

They fell asleep with their clothes on, curled up together like kittens.

*A*bout three weeks after they arrived in Cornwall, a letter made its way into Bianca's hands. Captain O'Brien, on his last trip to France, had been given an envelope for her. He dared not entrust it to Cobbs, his employer, but he had asked Ickes where

Bianca was working. He found her on her hands and knees, scrubbing stone floors in the big house at Polcoth.

Bianca thanked the captain profusely and tucked the letter into her apron. As soon as she finished work that evening, she hurried down the road toward Tregorna Farm. When she found a quiet place in a grove of trees along the roadside, she took out her letter. Her fingers trembled as she broke the seal and she held her breath as she read, and then, sick to her very core, re-read it.

It did not come from Marie Roland, but from a friend. It was devastating news, worse than she had ever imagined. She was immensely glad she had not waited for Sébastien to be with her before she opened it. How would she ever tell him? She would rather die. How to say that neither of his parents would be joining them in Cornwall?

The terrifying thing was that now, without the Rolands to support them financially, she and Sébastien were completely dependent on Zephaniah Cobbs. Who else in Cornwall would befriend a French person, much less give her work? There were too few jobs available as it was. She dragged herself back out to the road. Tregorna Farm huddled before her, dark and lonely on bare fields. This was to be her life now. The road before her was one of the most difficult she had ever walked.

$A$nd so began the long nine years. Sébastien did not thrive. She sorrowed to watch him grow ever thinner and more anxious, his spirit utterly broken. Nevertheless, she kept her promise to his mother and made sure he received a basic education. They read through his father's books many times together. She stole candle stubs so she could work with him at night. She made sure they said their prayers, he holding his mother's rosary, until the day it mysteriously disappeared. She tucked him into his bed each night, both of them dropping from exhaustion. But after he went into the mines at the age of seven, she could no longer be with him. She slept in the servants' rooms with the other girls then. He moved away from Tregorna Farm and they never saw each other. No longer there to hold him when the mine's poisons ravaged his lungs, when he shook from the chills and fevers. No longer there to soothe away his screaming night terrors.

Bianca did not flourish in Cornwall either. Her native country was hostile to England. War was a constant threat. To the people for whom she worked, she was the enemy. One of the kinder things they called her was "that Frenchie". Some of them took cruel pleasure in wringing from the stupid foreigner as much scrubbing and carrying as they could find. She had come to Cornwall at the height of her youth and beauty. Overwork, depression and loneliness in an unending cycle soon took their toll.

Back in France, waves of horrible killing sprees still inundated the countryside. Zephaniah Cobbs made a fortune taking full advantage of that chaos. He accepted money to bring other refugees to Tregorna Farm, mostly boys but women and girls too, all from upper class families. Like the Rolands, these people had also gotten caught on the wrong side of the struggle for power. These struggles were brutal, when some brand new revolutionary zealot felt compelled to murder the men who had been part of his brotherhood only the day before. Several desperate families paid Cobbs to sneak their children out of France. When they arrived in Cornwall, he put them to work in the mines at Botallack, near the Land's End, housing them in cottages a couple of miles from there. Bianca rarely saw them, except when they were sent back to Tregorna to die. Two or three of them tried to run away. When they were caught, as they almost always were, Cobbs made an example of them. They were no longer worth his time and effort. Accordingly, considering them now worthless, he did not care what happened to them. None of them lived.

Like the rest of Cobbs's immigrants, Bianca grew thin as a stick. Her good looks were gone. At age twenty-six, she was a gray version of her former self, her face listless, her skin without color, her shoulders stooped. She often asked herself why she bothered to carry on day after day, but somehow, for some reason, she did.

Then one day that baffling clockwork, the secret machinery that revolves the universe, slipped a cog. Or maybe this had been written all along, that gears were about to shift and springs to release. Perhaps it was just a long string of coincidences, uncoiling one by one. But something somewhere dictated that, on a warm evening in June of 1803, Bianca LeFronde would be standing in front of a cottage at the top of Narrow Lane.

She sighed. Here she stood, sent to take on another grueling job, the same grim routine. She would scrub her fingers to the bone, kneeling on bruised knees, earning money she would never see. Bending under the weight of heavy buckets. Being treated to the cold silence, or worse, that people inflict upon outsiders. That was the part she hated the most. Here she stood, by another gate, another job in a place where she did not belong.

Bianca, Bianca! Come into the garden. Why do you wait on the threshold? Open the gate. Come in, walk under this arbor, its roses all gilt with the soft light of evening. This is all for you Bianca, this time it is all for you. You hesitate? Go on up to Santino Mesola's cottage. Past his flower beds where the droning bees still tarry, gathering the last of the day's nectar for their magic potions. Past his fragrant herb garden and beneath his fruit trees. Come, knock on his door. And those nine long years, Bianca? They will blow away on the summer breeze.

$B$ianca had been caring for Baby for a month now. One afternoon, from the top of a ladder in Mr. Mesola's peach tree, Bianca heard the garden gate open. She took her basket of fruit and climbed down.

"*Regardes*! Look who already comes," she said to Baby, taking her hands. "*C'est Papa*. You're early tonight, Mr. Mesola." They met him on the path.

Santino held his arms out and Bianca helped Baby high-step to him as fast as she could go on her unsteady little legs.

"I came home a bit early so I could fix the water pump," he said, a bald-faced lie.

Bianca was about to mention that it was lucky dinner was already stewing away over the fire, when she noticed a young man wandering up the lane. He paused at the gate, craning his neck, looking for someone. She screamed. Baby and Santino both jumped. Bianca bolted down the path and out the gate. She literally threw herself into the man's arms. He swung her off her feet, and she, laughing and hugging him repeatedly, was so obviously overjoyed that Santino's heart froze in his chest. It crushed his good mood faster than a peeved Cornish wife can swing a rolling pin. Black despair engulfed him.

Chattering in French, Bianca pulled the stranger by the arm and led him into Santino's garden. "Mr. Mesola," she cried, oblivious to his sour face. "I'd please like you to meet Sébastien Roland."

Ridiculous! This was a boy, a mere boy she held so affectionately by the arm, this ... this whelp.

"So pleased," seethed Santino through his teeth, almost forgetting to extend his hand. This was absurd! How in the world could Miss LeFronde fall for a man so young? Ridiculously young! A woman her age? It was disgusting. He's barely out of boyhood. *Baccala!* Women cared nothing for character in a man. It was all looks. *Bello, bello.* They always fell for good looks.

"Sébastien is the boy that came together with me from Paris."

Santino's sulkiness was suffocating his powers of reasoning. He should have placed Sébastien then, but he didn't. "Hunh," was the most civil thing he could think of to say. His eyebrows clamped together across his forehead.

"You remember, I told you about Sébastien, Mr. Mesola. Remember I told you of a little boy? I was knowing him at home in France? Here he is, grown all up."

Santino frowned. "So he's ...."

"You are almost my little brother, aren't you, Sébastien?"

"Bianca is the closest thing I have to family." Sébastien put his ridiculously young arm around Miss LeFronde and beamed a ridiculously cheery smile.

"Family?" croaked Santino.

Miss LeFronde put her hand on Santino's arm. "Oh Mr. Mesola, would you so much mind if Sébastien stay for dinner? I have not seen him in so long time."

Santino looked down at her hand on his arm. He raised his eyes to her face. Her brown eyes begged him. He was mute.

"Please, I hardly see him, Mr. Mesola. We have so much to talk on."

"Dinner?"

"Oh, Sébastien," Bianca continued to gush, "you haven't met Baby. Look, isn't she adorable?"

Santino's frown was stuck. *Ridicolo*! Bianca -- Miss LeFronde was certainly in a lively mood tonight. *Cacchio*! *Stupido*!

Sébastien took Baby's hand and kissed it playfully. Baby was delighted and held out her arms to him.

"Look, she like you! Such a saucy little girl," said Bianca. "So, Sébastien, my darling," not noticing how Santino stared at the ground, his frown growing blacker, "you must have a sweetgirl by now?"

"A sweetheart? Are you kidding? I don't have any time for girls. Well, I do meet girls but I have no time for a special one." He laughed. "Anyway, there are so many girls in the world, I can't pick just one."

Santino lifted his face, his hopes. The corners of his mouth relaxed. His eyebrows sprang apart.

Sébastien continued. "I had to beg Captain O'Brien to give me time to come to see you today," he told Bianca. "Mr. Ickes told me you had a new job. He told me where I could find you. And look at you! This work must agree with you. You look wonderful, Bianca."

Miss LeFronde flashed a smile and turned to Mr. Mesola. Their eyes locked for a moment.

Santino was dazzled. She had smiled at him, Santino? Not at that outrageously, absurdly young *ragazzo*?

"You do, *cherie*, you do look beautiful. Doesn't she, Mr. Mesola?"

A world of confusion was swept from Santino's dim brain. Sébastien was a mere boy! Just a young boy! Sébastien was looking at him quizzically. He had asked Tino something. What was it? Santino spent another long moment gazing at Miss LeFronde. Finally he thought to say "It would be very nice to have you stay for dinner, Sébastien." Wait, was he repeating himself? "You must stay, really!"

$A$fter dinner, they lingered at the table in the garden.

"Would you hold Baby for one moment, Mr. Mesola? I will get a light for the table." Bianca rose to find a lantern.

Sébastien watched Santino playing with the little girl.

"I want to thank you, Mr. Mesola, for giving Bianca this position. You have brought her back to life. Like the Bianca I remember from long ago."

"She came along at just the right moment for me, too. I must remember to thank Mr. Cobbs one day."

"I wouldn't do that, if I were you. The less said to him about Bianca, the better. Cobbs doesn't need to be told anything, anyway. He keeps pretty close tabs on all of us."

"I have been wondering why Miss LeFronde still considers him her employer. It's a strange situation, it seems to me."

"It is. Worse than strange. If only you knew, you would understand why I am hoping to get her out of Cornwall. Maybe to London, if not Paris. If England and France were on better terms, it would be easier. But here she comes. We'll ruin her evening if we speak of it now. *Alors!* What's the matter? Are you all right, Mr. Mesola?"

Santino was choking on something. "Yes, sorry." He cleared his throat. "You're going back to France? What were you saying?"

Bianca returned with a lantern. Instead of answering, Sébastien grabbed at a safer topic of conversation. The baby, that would be safe. Talk about the baby. "I was just wondering what Baby's given name is?" he asked.

Santino and Bianca looked at each other blankly.

"Does she have a name, Mr. Mesola?" Bianca asked.

"No, she doesn't. My original plan, Sébastien, was to find parents for her. Proper parents. But then Miss LeFronde came along ...." He was running into murky territory here. How to explain that Bianca's coming had changed everything for him?

"Why don't you give her a name now?" suggested Sébastien.

"Yes, Mr. Mesola. That is a good idea. What do you want to call her?"

"Huh. I haven't thought about it."

"Is there someone you would like to name her from? Your mother or a sister?" Bianca asked. A lover?

Santino thought of his tribes of relatives. Italian women. *Dio mio*! Not a good idea to favor one over another. He thought of his homeland.

"Maybe I could name her after a part of my country, the place where I grew up. Emilia. Does that sound strange?"

Emilia. Both Bianca and Sébastien agreed instantly. Emilia, a beautiful name.

"And she will grow up to be a beautiful girl," predicted Sébastien.

*O*ne morning about a month after Sébastien's visit, as Mr. Mesola was going off to his workshop, Bianca reminded him what day it was.

"It's Thursday, *Monsieur*," Bianca told Santino. "I will have to go to Lamorna in the afternoon. Mr. Cobbs will want his pay."

"Sit down for a moment, Miss LeFronde, would you?" Santino pulled a chair away from the table for her. "First of all, it's a long way for you to go into Lamorna each week, carrying Emilia. She is not getting any lighter, are you, *mi'amaretta*? " He stopped to lift the little girl onto his lap. "Mrs. Campion said she would be happy to take her today, so you can be a little quicker getting there and back. It looks like rain. I don't want you two to get caught in a storm."

"Thank you. That will help a lot." Where would she ever find a man as considerate as this?

"Before you leave the village today, will you stop by the workshop? I am working on a little surprise for you. For you and Emilia."

Bianca smiled. "I would like to see where you work."

"Good. As you come down the lane, just before you get to the chapel, it's in a little alley to the left."

"I can find it."

"Now, about Mr. Cobbs." He cleared his throat. "I want to ask you about Mr. Cobbs."

She tensed as always when he mentioned that name. Even the word 'Thursday' could upset her. She shuddered. She was a wreck every Thursday.

Santino went on. "Do you mind if I ask you something? Does Mr. Cobbs take all your pay?" She gave a cautious nod. "He gives you nothing, sets no money aside for you?" She shook her head. "Not to be rude, Miss LeFronde, but what kind of arrangement is that?"

"Well, you see …." She hesitated. "Mr. Cobbs brought us to here when our lives were in much danger." She kept her eyes on the table.

"Ah. So he paid for your passage over here?"

"No, Sébastien's mother paid for that before we left France."

"What? So why does he now take everything you earn? You are not his slave."

"Slave?"

"He must pay you for your work."

"I…He says he must pay for my food and my bed."

"But you're eating and sleeping at my house now."

"Yes, but a French woman, when England has war with France, can not get work anywhere. Mr. Cobbs must always help me."

Santino, his head bent in thought, danced the baby idly on his knee. "You know, Miss LeFronde, the reason I'm asking all this is that I've been thinking about something."

"*Oui?*" A butterfly flapped about a thousand times in Bianca's heart.

Santino shifted in his chair. "I have been thinking about Baby Emilia. Maybe not... not giving her away. I wondered... maybe if... if I were to give up searching for parents for her, would you be willing to stay on here with me – or, *scusi*, with us? To take care of her?"

Bianca covered her mouth with her fingers. "*Oui, Monsieur.* Oh yes."

"You're sure? I don't want to pressure you into something you're not happy with."

She nodded, unable to speak.

"Then if you are willing to take this job and I am willing to hire you, why in the name of all the saints should I keep paying Cobbs?"

She shook her head. She looked at Mr. Mesola. She could only shrug.

"So. When you go to Lamorna today, would you be willing to tell him that this will be the last money he is getting from me? From now on, my money will go directly to you. He's gotten his fair share from you, and more, in nine years, I would say. Miss LeFronde?" He had upset her. "Miss LeFronde?"

She held herself very still. Two big tears splashed onto the tablecloth.

*T*hat afternoon, Bianca hummed along the lane until she came to the chapel. This was the first time she had been out walking by herself, without Baby, since she had come to Porthcoombe. She felt like a girl again! The alley she turned into was short. It ran along the side of the hill. At the end, stacks and stacks of neatly piled wood were stored in an open area that had a roof but no walls. She went cautiously past the fragrant wood piles.

There he was. She felt her whole body smile. Mr. Mesola. He was eating the lunch she had made for him. He jumped up as soon as she came in.

"Well, here's my surprise," he exclaimed. He pointed to what appeared to be a large bucket on wheels. "I have to put a better handle on it. I was hoping you could sew a cushion for it."

"*Oui?*"

"It's for Baby."

"Oh, I see," she said, finally understanding. "It's for when we walk. I push this and she can ride in it. This is wonderful!"

"Do you like it? It will look nicer when it's finished."

"It's very nice. You are such a clever man." Bianca wished she hadn't said that in quite those tones. She looked around the spacious workshop. "It smells so nice in here. All this wood! You need so much?"

"This pile over here is ready to be shaped. That pile has just been cut. I won't be able to use it until it's dried," Santino explained. "Fortunately this shop is in an ideal place. Feel the breeze coming from the sea? It blows right down this alley."

"So you need the air?"

"Circulation. That's right."

"And such lots of tools here!" She pointed to a long wall hung with row upon row of neatly arranged tools.

"Now if only I had a helper, I might be able to get caught up with my work."

"There's a boy at Tregorna Farm. He came from France just now. He seems very smart. He is a new boy for Mr. Cobbs's. You must pay Mr. Cobbs for him, though."

"Ah, I might look into that. Let's see how Cobbs responds when you tell him you are leaving him. Will he take it well, do you think?"

"Take it?"

"Will he allow you to leave?"

"No. I think no. I am afraid to tell him, actually. But when I say good-bye to him, I so much want to see his face."


*L*ater that afternoon, as she opened the door to Cobbs's office in Lamorna, Bianca smiled to herself. She sat down on one of his ornate wooden chairs to await her turn to see him. She would have the upper hand with Cobbs for the first time ever. And she had decided something else. She would tell him she would never go back to live at Tregorna Farm, no matter what.

However, Zephaniah Cobbs put a stop to that notion at once. An exceedingly definite stop. "You will do no such thing!" he sputtered, when she told him she would be keeping her pay from now on. His nostrils flared and he ground his teeth. He ran his finger over the bottom rim of his huge moustache, right then left. Then he stood so quickly, he knocked his chair over.

"Wait!" Bianca stood up. "Do not be angry! Mr. Mesola sends you this money!" She fumbled in her pocket. "Here, it's money for you, from Mr. Mesola. He pays you one more time!" Bianca held out an envelope, trying to placate him. "Here, take it."

"Chirgwin, get in here!" Cobbs shouted to his assistant. "Bring my carriage to the back!"

"Mr. Cobbs! Do not be angry! I give you everything for nine years!"

He rummaged through a drawer in his desk and pulled out a length of sturdy rope. Bianca's eyes widened in alarm.

"What are you doing?" she shrieked.

He came around his desk and took her arm. He kicked her chair out of the way.

"No! Let go of me! Get away!" Bianca fought against him but he was nearly twice her weight and very strong. He pulled her arms behind her and tied the rope tight about her wrists.

"If you don't shut up, I'll tie a gag over that mouth of yours."

He marched her out the back door, struggled her into the carriage and wrapped the end of the rope around his hand.

"One sound out of you …."

She flinched when he raised his hand as if to slap her.

"You can not do this! I am not your slave!" She screamed and tried to duck, but his open hand slammed her eye and then back, hard across her mouth.

"I warned you. Now shut up!" He pulled her back onto the seat. "Chirgwin, you drive! Out to Botallack. Fast!" Cobbs kept a tight hold of Bianca's arm. He twisted the rope that bound her wrists. It chafed until it drew blood.

Chirgwin snapped the reins and they sped off down the road.

$S$antino Mesola came home to an empty house that night. He walked over to inquire about Bianca at the Campions'. They had not seen her since early afternoon. He returned home to wait for her. When night fell and she still hadn't returned, he was seriously alarmed.

The next morning, leaving Baby Emilia with Bess Campion again, he drove to Lamorna. Cobbs's office was closed and no one could give him any information on Bianca's whereabouts. He drove to Tregorna Farm. In the yard, he found Ickes, the manager.

"I do know Miss LeFronde. Yes, indeed. But she has not been back here for a few weeks. Since she went to work for you."

"I sent her to Cobbs's office yesterday. She was to tell him I would be hiring her directly from now on, instead of giving Cobbs her pay."

Ickes looked worried. "Really? Mr. Cobbs would not have liked that." He shook his head. "That probably explains her disappearance."

Panic seized Santino. "Do you think he would do something drastic?"

"There is no telling what he'd do. He has a very bad temper, I know that for a fact."

He had doomed her! Santino had doomed Bianca to certain harm. "I don't know where to look for her," he told Ickes. "Where could she be? Can you give me some idea of where she could be?"

"I can't." Ickes thought for a minute. "She won't be anywhere around here, for certain. Probably he put her to work in some other town. You may never see her again."

"Are you serious?" What kind of a man was this Cobbs? "I must find her. This is all my fault."

"I'm warning you, Mr. Cobbs does not like to be crossed."

At that moment, a woman flung open a door of the house. "Ickes!" she shouted. "Ickes! Get in here this minute!"

"That's Mrs. Pawley. She thinks she runs this place." Ickes squinted at her without moving.

"Your ... wife?"

"No! Please! She's the housekeeper, of sorts."

"Would she know anything?"

"You wouldn't get it out of her if she does know anything. But I'd better humor her, go to her before she busts a puckering string. Saves a lot of trouble in the long run. Sorry I can't be more help."

"Ickes, get in here!" Pawley screamed.

Ickes turned back to Santino, his hands in his pockets. "You're better off not confronting Cobbs with this issue. He's like a snake. If you make him nervous, he'll strike."

"What shall I do then?" asked Santino in desperation.

"Let me look into this."

"Will you do it soon?"

"Right away. I'll send you word, if I find out anything. But don't come here again. I'll find you. Don't get your hopes up, though. Miss LeFronde could be anywhere. It's quite likely she is gone for good."

"Tom Ickes! Get in here this minute or I'll break your arm and hit you over the head with it!"

Mr. Ickes raised his eyebrows and smiled at Santino. He waved a finger and sauntered away.

Santino looked around the dilapidated farm. Maybe Bianca was being kept here somewhere. What a miserable place.

But that opinion was a matter of perspective. From Bianca's present place of employment, Tregorna Farm looked like a paradise.


$A$t the Ting Tong mine, out at Botallack, work began early every day except the Sabbath. Each morning the men filed into the boiler house to change into their rough flannel work clothes. They bought their candles and their gunpowder from the company store and before dawn's first light, they had already begun their long descent into the earth. Then, at dawn, the women and boys appeared. They were mostly young, unmarried women. They put on their gooks, white head-coverings with enormous stiff visors that circled their faces in a "U" shape. These long visors projected almost far enough to keep the dust and flying stone chips out of their faces while they pounded rocks. Their plain dresses were dark, long sleeved, their aprons snowy white in the morning, filthy by nightfall. With rough hands, they picked up their hammers and began to sort through rock piles.

The women weren't all young. Some of them were miners' widows. With children still at home, these women needed this job desperately. Some had been pounding rocks for so long, they had lost all feeling in their hands years before. Kneeling on the bare ground next to a rock pile, their job was to break the tin ore into smaller pieces, so the boys could load it onto a trolley and send it to the crushing machine. The way the women crushed the rock was simple: they held a rock in one hand and beat it with a hammer until it shattered. That was the work they did, morning 'til evening, rain or shine.

The pounding of huge pump engines, the earth-shaking stamping machines, the turning of the great water wheels, the rock hammering -- the noise was deafening and the air the women breathed was full of dust and poisoned with burning arsenic. Their job was very dirty, strenuous and boring, and their day long and tedious.

As soon as the workday was done, the men began coming back up to grass. The women had to endure their teasing, their endless ribald jokes. Work like this would literally kill some women, but not these ladies. These were the bal maidens, the mine maidens. Other women muttered that the bal maidens were rough as rats, and they were. They had to be. When the bell at Madron finally signaled the end of their shift, they had to walk miles back to their homes and their day was still not over. There was all the work that needed to be done at home before they could fall into bed. Then they rose in the dark the next morning and it started all over again.

Bianca had been a bal maiden for two weeks now. She boarded in the home of one of the less reputable mine captains. His wife, at Cobbs's insistence, made very sure Bianca got to work each day, when and where she was supposed to. Each grey dawn, Bianca followed the woman to the mine, a thin shadow hurrying behind her husky, sour-faced keeper.

Every evening, before they left work for the night, Bianca went with the women and boys to wash. She changed into clean clothes but took no part in the chatter going on around her. She watched the younger bal maidens pinning pieces of gaudy jewelry to their collars before they left for home. They tied colored ribbons in their hair. They flaunted their summer hats and maybe a fetching jacket, anything to make themselves feel feminine and pretty. The older women hurried on ahead but the younger ones flirted boldly and laughed with the miners as they went along. It made the miles of walking seem less dreary. Bianca dragged along behind them. She spoke to none of them and they were not the least bit interested in her. She was a foreigner and anyway, they thought she was strange, too strange to bother with.

She felt, if possible, even more lonely in this new life than she had when she had been a scullery maid. She was always the last to head home. It was not really her home after all. She felt like an intruder, even more out of place in that house than she did at the mine. Tonight, the other women were almost lost to sight when Bianca noticed one of the maidens hanging back by the edge of the woods. Probably hoping to meet a sweetheart, thought Bianca. Odd, though, that she hadn't taken off her big white gook. It shadowed her face and Bianca couldn't figure out who she was. She would have remembered one so tall.

The maiden came closer until she was actually walking beside her.

"Bianca? Don't walk so fast." In French? "Let the others go." Such a low voice? A Frenchman's voice, coming from within the depths of the enormous white hat.

She peered upwards to get a look at the bal maiden's face. She gasped. It was! "Sébastien!"

He looked over his shoulder. No one came behind them. "Come with me!"

Sébastien grasped her hand. They ran into the woods. He pulled off the big hat and worked his way out of the gown as he ran. A horse waited, tied to a tree. They were riding away before Bianca had time to think of the consequences, and running away from Zephaniah Cobbs would have serious consequences. They rode along the edges of the woods. As soon as it was dark, Sébastien thought it was safe to ride out on the road. They headed north. When they came to a fork they turned toward the coast and into the woods again. Sébastien pulled up beside an enormous tree and there, down on a little bridge over a brook, stood the one person Bianca most longed to see.

"Mr. Mesola." She slipped from the horse and Santino helped her to the ground.

"Miss LeFronde! Are you laughing or crying?"

"Both, a little. How did you find me?"

"Mr. Ickes finally found out where you were. He knew someone he could ask, though he couldn't tell us who it was," said Sébastien.

"Maybe he talked to the driver who took us there. I can't believe Mr. Ickes would do that for us."

"There may be a lot you don't know about Mr. Ickes," Sébastien replied.

Bianca turned to Santino again. "Mr. Mesola." She was giddy with emotion. "I missed you so much." Oh, now she had really gone too far. Her mouth had run away with her. Ah, *quelle bouche*!

Santino's knees felt a little weak. "You know, it feels odd when you call me 'Mister'. Can't you call me Tino?"

"Well," laughed Sébastien, "I guess it's time for me to be going." He remounted the horse.

"Wait! I am afraid of Mr. Cobbs! He comes again for me, do you think?" Bianca worried.

"If he does, we'll have him arrested for kidnapping. He has no document binding you to him," Santino explained. "I spoke with a solicitor in Penzance about this. Cobbs has kept you both for many years, laboring without pay. In this country, if someone forces you to work against your will, it's called involuntary servitude. In London, they are trying to pass a law to make that illegal."

"I don't care if it's legal or not," vowed Sébastien. "If he lays a finger on you, Bianca, he'll regret it. I hope to be done with him soon myself."

"Sébastien! What will you do without him? And where will I find you?"

"As soon as I figure that out, I'll let you know."

"Be careful, Sébastien! You know Mr. Cobbs is very bad!"

"Oh, trust me! That much I do know!" Sébastien said darkly.

"Thank you for coming to me! Both of you," cried Bianca.

"*Allez*! Go on, now, you two. *Au revoir, cherie*." Sébastien headed back up to the road.

"*Au revoir, mon petit.*"

Santino raised an eyebrow at that.

"*Oui.*" She laughed and ran her hands tentatively down Tino's arms. "He is my little Sébastien, don't you know."

"Little Sébastien?"

She fingered the buttons on his coat. "Yes, Mr. Tino. To me he is."

"Would you mind if I call you Bianca?"

"Oh yes."

"You have an Italian name."

"My... my mother's mother ...."

"Your grandmother?"

"Ah yes. She is Bianca too, from Italy."

"You're part Italian. No wonder I like you."

"You do?"

Santino pulled her close. "Shall we go home, my little Bianca? Where we can be alone?"

"We are alone here. These woods belong to someone?"

"These are my woods."

"Your woods? No one will come, then."

"But this old tree," he pointed, "is called the Passage Oak. People meet beneath this oak all the time."

"Really?"

"Yes, and have met here for decades. Probably centuries."

"Really?" She traced his collar with her fingertips. "A tree has a name?"

"This one does. It's a landmark, one of the last of the sessile oaks around here."

"What is it called again?"

"Some people call it the Tremen Oak. It means 'passage' in Cornish, or 'secret passage'. I forget. Something like that."

"If I can remember this name, it will be my favorite place."

"Will it? Why is that, I wonder?"

"Well, something good happens here. Now, today."

"Yes. I think so too. Something very good. But we had better be getting home. Baby will certainly be happy to see you. Will you take my arm, *mia bella signorina?*"

"*Avec plaisir, Monsieur.*"

They started down the path, hardly able to believe their good fortune.

Meanwhile, Sébastien Roland cantered along the road to Lamorna. He hoped he had convinced Santino of the threat Cobbs posed. As for himself, he was exceedingly tired of living with that fear.

*Suspension bridge*

*Light and strong, suspension bridges can span distances far longer than other kinds of bridges. Their flexibility, however, can cause oscillations dangerous to traffic and even to the bridge itself.*

## SÉBASTIEN ROLAND

*S*ébastien's young life had closed, not on that awful night when they arrived at Tregorna Farm, but one evening a few weeks later. He had just turned five years of age. He and Bianca had eaten their silent meal in Mrs. Pawley's kitchen. Plain boiled potatoes or stale bread and a slimy mass of greens, the same food every night. They were always hungry. These days at Tregorna Farm, they ate anything they were given. Though there were flitches of bacon hanging on the wall, and sometimes even the smell of roast pork in the kitchen, they were never given meat. Immediately after eating, they went as always to Mr. Ickes's cottage and climbed the stairs. Mr. Ickes would seldom be there. He spent most evenings in Cobbs's office, discussing plans for the following day, going over accounts. Bianca and Sébastien were always alone in the evening.

Their room was bare. Mrs. Pawley, on their very first day, had demanded to be given one of Bianca's trunks. She wanted it filled with all the clothes they had brought from France. They would no longer need such frumpery, she declared. Sébastien didn't care one way or another about his clothes but this nearly broke Bianca's heart.

So their two empty trunks were the only items of furniture other than the mattresses they slept on. They placed Sébastien's small trunk between their beds and in it they kept his mother's rosary and his father's books. They felt confident Mrs. Pawley would not regard those things as having any value. Why would she want them? A papist's rosary? And books? Books in French? What good would they be to her?

On this night, Bianca lit her stub of candle and knelt beside Sébastien's trunk. Sébastien thought she was praying until he saw her shoulders shaking. They had learned by now that, in Cornwall, weeping must be done in silence. He moved close and knelt beside her. Then Bianca opened the trunk and took out the garnet rosary and his father's copy of the *Méditations* of Marcus Aurelias. This was strange. She had mentioned before that this work was a little too difficult for Sébastien, though it was her favorite book.

She pulled him to sit next to her on the mattress. She no longer owned any handkerchiefs so she had to use a corner of her apron to dry her cheeks. She pressed the book and the rosary into Sébastien's hands and held them tight. They spoke in French.

"I received a letter from Paris today. It had some bad news, Sébastien. At first I was not going to tell you until you were older. Then I thought that, if I were your age, I would want to know."

"Is it about my parents?"

She nodded and looked away. When she turned to face him, her look was hard. "Your *maman*. She was executed. It was all arranged by Robespierre, once her friend, and now ...." She couldn't help sobbing.

"The guillotine? For *maman*?"

She nodded. "And your *papa*, you knew he was far out in the countryside. What you didn't know, my darling, was that he was in hiding. When he heard the news that your *maman* had been arrested, he immediately set out for Paris. He was hurrying to be with her when friends intercepted him on the road. They told him your *maman* was dead. Your *papa*, Sébastien," she stopped to take his hand, "he shot himself in the head."

Sébastien blinked. He looked at her, shocked, speechless.

*Maman, Papa*. After they had taken such care to send him to safety. *Maman et Papa*. This pain could not be borne.


*N*othing mattered anymore. Sébastien didn't care what happened to him. Mrs. Pawley hated him. She got her hackles up without fail every time she laid eyes on him. It was impossible to predict what would set her off. Sébastien gave up trying and just took the blows as they came.

But Mr. Cobbs did not hate him. Sébastien wished fervently that he did. Mr. Cobbs seemed to have an attraction for Sébastien that was mixed with anger in the most confusing way. He frightened Sébastien at first. When fright turned to terror, Sébastien discovered how to hate. Mr. Cobbs had a hideous temper and a very cruel streak. The boy trembled just at the sight of him. He did anything he could to keep away from him. He tried never to anger him, to no avail. Sébastien would look up from his chores, and there Cobbs would be. Waiting for Sébastien, beckoning him to come, come to him and take his punishment.

He didn't even remember Sébastien's name. Willie, he called him. Willie, Willie, he'd moan. Sébastien detested his fervent blue eyes, his eager face, his big ugly moustache. Cobbs always managed to send Ickes away on an errand. No one was ever around. Sébastien struggled, tried to get away. But there was no getting away. He screamed until his throat was raw, but no one came.

Most little boys, after a few weeks of this, might blame themselves, despising their own weaknesses or hating some fault in their own natures. Others might pine away, thinking life was too cruel, that they were its victims and had no recourse to a better situation. Sébastien did neither of these things. He dreamed of murdering Mr. Cobbs. The thought gave him strength. Until that opportunity arose, his only option was to endure. He would see Cobbs dead some day. That thought kept him going. His father's Marcus Aurelius book taught how to preserve equanimity in the midst of conflict. Sébastien learned self-control so he could survive to commit murder. Not quite what Marcus Aurelius had in mind, but it helped him get by.

The farm work did not bother Sébastien. He worked beside Mr. Ickes every morning and did whatever he was told. Mr. Ickes spoke to him in a way that was neither kind nor unkind. Yet, morning and afternoon, when they found themselves conveniently alone far out in the field, Mr. Ickes would call for a short rest and produce a sweet carrot, an apple or even a small cake for

Sébastien to share with him. Then it was back to work. "Sébastien, fetch this" or "Sébastien, hold that". He was worn out by the end of the day. But slowly, Mr. Ickes became a trusted center in his life. Mr. Ickes and of course Bianca. He had the two of them. He knew he should consider himself fortunate.

After a year, Sébastien had grown taller but he carried not an ounce of fat. He had dark circles under his eyes and a strained look that never relaxed.

He turned six. Mr. Ickes guessed what had developed the first time he found Sébastien, grey and shaking, crouched in a corner of the barn. He was desperate to help Sébastien get away from Tregorna Farm. He tried to suggest to Cobbs that the boy needed a change of scene.

"If I might suggest, Mr. Cobbs," Ickes said, "perhaps Sébastien would be useful to Captain O'Brien. He is not thriving here on the farm."

"Farm work is good for him."

"Certainly. But O'Brien has been saying he could use an apprentice. I think Sébastien would work out well."

"He is too small," argued Cobbs. "He would be no help at all on board a ship. Send that other boy, Robert, to O'Brien."

"Sébastien is a bright lad, though. He could start to learn navigation and be very useful to your shipping business by the time he is older. He reads and writes already. I think eventually he could even do some of the paperwork for O'Brien."

"It would cost me money to train him, Ickes. It is not my goal to lose money on these French brats. I wouldn't make a farthing off him for at least two years."

"But you could think of it as an investment. Once he was older ...."

"No. Enough! He stays here. I want him here, where I can keep an eye on him."

Ickes vowed to himself he too would keep an eye on Sébastien, insofar as that was possible. He wondered if Sébastien had spoken to Bianca about the things Cobbs did to him. Ickes considered speaking to her himself, but he knew, because she was away all day, it would only cause her an agony of worry. There was nothing she could do. He would only upset her.

The months went by. Ickes watched Sébastien sink into deep depression, plagued by Cobbs's madness. Ickes tried never to leave Sébastien by himself, but he simply could not be everywhere at once.

$B$y the year the boy turned seven, Cobbs gloated privately that he had molded Sébastien into exactly the sullen little weakling he needed him to be. Weak enough to suffer perpetual defeat. It was exhilarating. It thrilled him. Cobbs, the victor every time.

Meanwhile Ickes, desperate to do something to ease Sébastien's situation, decided a confrontation might change things. Or it might kill the boy. One way or the other, it was killing Ickes to see him diminishing month after month.

The next day, Ickes watched Cobbs drive his new rig down the road, on his way to his office in Lamorna. Then he told Sébastien they needed to bring the sheep in from the north pasture.

Walking through the fields together, Ickes asked casually "Have you ever learned to fight, Sébastien?"

Sébastien shook his head, silent as usual.

"You should know how to defend yourself. When we get out to the north meadow, I'll show you a few moves."

He showed Sébastien how to use his elbows, how to ram an elbow into an abdomen, or better yet, a solar plexus, just two of the sensitive spots on the male anatomy. In the weeks that followed, they tried out a few moves whenever they were out of sight of the house.

"You have to start building some strength in those arms." Ickes gave Sébastien a sledge hammer and made him lift it over his head twenty times. The same with the big axe, then the big pulleys in the barn.

"If ever someone, anyone, bothers you, Sébastien, or hurts you in any way, you shouldn't be afraid to hurt them back."

Sébastien said nothing.

"You understand what I am saying?"

The same brooding stare.

"It's not wrong to defend yourself, you know."

The next day, Sébastien had a black eye, puffed and swollen. Ickes waited for an explanation, but the boy's mood was so dark and morose, he didn't dare ask for one. The eye had barely healed when Sébastien came to his work unable to move his left arm.

"What happened?" asked Ickes, almost afraid to hear.

"Nothing," growled Sébastien.

However, when Ickes entered Cobbs's office that evening as usual, Cobbs immediately turned down the lamp. They went over the ledgers, Ickes peering closely at them in the dim light. When they finished, Ickes retrieved the cash box as Cobbs directed. Cobbs began to count the money, then dropped his head to his hand.

"Ickes, you'll have to finish this up. I'm not feeling well."

Ickes straightened, amazed. He had never heard Cobbs say he was unwell. Ickes had counted the money often, it was true. But in secret, never because Cobbs had asked him to count it. When Cobbs, holding his head, rose rather awkwardly from his chair, Ickes glimpsed something else he had never seen before.

One eye had swollen nearly closed. His nose was cut and bruised on that side. He limped out and stayed in his room for two days.

So Ickes counted the money, put most of it in the safe, and changed a few figures in the ledger. They all added up. He always made them add up.

$A$ few days later, Ickes asked to speak to Cobbs. He suggested the Ting Tong mines for Sébastien Roland.

Cobbs was in a very bad mood. But when Ickes brought up the subject of Sébastien working as a bal boy, Cobbs was surprisingly amenable. He tapped one finger against his moustache.

Yes, the mines. Deep and dark. The rock crushers pounding, the earth trembling. The sea roaring overhead in the deepest mines. Terror, total darkness, constant fears of a cave-in, a flood, an explosion. Even grown men broke down in the Ting Tong mines.

Sébastien deserved the mines, the little brute. He would send him into the deepest one, right along with the men. Cobbs looked at the long red scratches on the hand he kept hidden in his lap. Sébastien was turning into a hateful little demon. A hellcat. After all Cobbs had done for him. A most ungrateful boy.

He would break Sébastien. This measly, spineless child would buckle under his will. It was time the boy discovered what he was up against in the man, time he realized who it was that really controlled his entire life. Zephaniah Cobbs controlled him. Zephaniah Cobbs was not to be denied anything, ever.

He could destroy Sébastien Roland, if he wanted to. He was worthless. Besides, there was a new boy here now, much more promising. Cobbs knew what would happen. Tired and sick, Sébastien would beg to come back to Tregorna Farm. Then Cobbs would do whatever he wished with him. Whatever and whenever.

This, however, was not quite what happened.

$C$obbs sent Sébastien to board in a cottage at Crows-an-Wra, about four miles from the mine, with Susanna Gwennel's family. Susanna worked at the mine herself. She had to support her widowed mother, her two sisters and their little brother, Edmund. The Gwennels were happy to make a little extra money, taking Sébastien as a boarder. Cobbs visited them, made the arrangements, and also made it clear they needn't worry about giving the boy any special treatment. He certainly didn't want him to impose on the family. It wasn't necessary for him to eat with them or sleep in the house. He hoped that this was clear to Mrs. Gwennel.

After Cobbs left, Susanna and her mother, simple good-hearted women, puzzled over what he had said. What could he have meant by that?

Ickes knocked on their door the next day, bringing as sickly a boy as they had ever seen. The two women frowned with concern. What a sad-looking child. My goodness, their Edmund was only a year older than Sébastien. He was rosy-cheeked and twice Sébastien's girth. So at teatime, Mrs. Gwennel saw to it that Sébastien's plate had a good-size chunk of meat on it. But, unused to such rich fare, Sébastien was wretchedly ill soon after.

"I'm sorry," he told Mrs. Gwennel. "I think I ate too much."

"But good heavens," said the woman, "You need to eat, laddie. We need to put some fat on those bones of yours."

"Sébastien, tomorrow morning we'll have to leave early for Wheal Cock," Sue told him. "That's the mine you'll be working at. I'll introduce you to the grass captain. The boys your age work outdoors, on the floor alongside us bal maidens."

"I won't go down in the mine?"

"Not 'til you're older. Don't worry. It's not so bad there. Us maidens will help you get used to things."

"Will Mr. Cobbs be there?" asked Sébastien.

"Oh no. Mr. Cobbs? He's never there. Why?" She tilted her head and looked at Sébastien. "Do you miss him?"

"No."

"He seems like a nice man."

Sébastien bit his lip.

"Anyway, tonight you'll be sleeping in the attic with Edmund. At least it's nice and warm up there. Us girls and Mum are in the bedroom down here," Sue giggled. "Though with so many girls in one room, it gets pretty hot in there sometimes too."

Sébastien blushed. "The attic will be fine." At least he would be sleeping in the house. Mr. Cobbs could not get to him there.

In the morning, they were all given breakfast. Sébastien watched, amazed, as Edmund went off to school swinging a lunch bucket.

"Well sure he goes to school!" said Mrs. Gwennel. "We want our boy to have some education. If he does well, maybe he can be a mine captain one day, bring home some good money. Oh, don't forget your lunch," she added, handing Sébastien a covered bucket. "Mind you don't eat it aforetimes."

"For me?" he asked.

Mrs. Gwennel laughed. "We're getting paid for your keep. We don't want you to starve on us."

Sébastien could hardly remember what a full stomach felt like. He wished Bianca could live at Mrs. Gwennel's too.

He and Sue set out for Wheal Cock, passing a number of small whitewashed miners' cottages that were far from any road. It was when they came over the hill that Sébastien had to stop in his tracks. It was his first sight of Cape Cornwall.

Here the land ended in a crash and swirl of ocean. White foam spraying the feet of rocky cliffs, the sea heaving forever and forever beyond. Empty miles of ocean, moaning restlessly above the lost legendary islands that, according to old Cornish stories, had sunk off the cape. Far out to sea was the Longships light, marking some of the most treacherous rocks in Cornwall. And clinging precariously to the cliffside were the other-worldly engine houses of Botallack.

When he and Sue got near the mines, there was a lot to see, and so much noise, Sébastien could hardly hear Sue speak. Wheal Cock was a hive of activity. A large group of women and children was gathering from villages and farms all around. Great pumps rumbled and thudded, drawing water out of the tunnels. Water, the miners' most feared enemy, also turned the giant wheels that powered the deafeningly loud stamps. Sue Gwennel put her mouth to Sébastien's ear and explained that these were huge machines that crushed tin ore into powder. Pairs of horses plodded round and round the capstans or dragged wagons loaded with ore. Across the countryside, as far as Sébastien could see, were the lasting signs of deep mining, the heaps of poisonous slatey rubbish, scattered even in the midst of cow pastures.

"These are the deads," Sue explained, threading her way among them. "Rubbish thrown up from out of the mines. And watch for the holes. See? Shafts cut so the men down deep can get fresh air."

Sue found the mine manager in his white drill coat.

"You're late," he said.

"Late?"

"The men have all gone down already."

"I assumed Sébastien would be working at grass with us," she said.

"No. Mr. Cobbs says he's to be a lamp boy."

"But he's a little young to be below, isn't he?"

"Maybe, but Mr. Cobbs gave very specific orders."

"Well," she looked at Sébastien, her brow puckered with doubt. "I'll wait for you tonight at the end of the shift. We'll walk home together until you know the way." She had met this boy less than a day ago, but already she felt a motherly attachment to him. "We'll have us a couple of nice roast fowl for tea when we get home. Would you like that?"

Sébastien was overwhelmed by her kindness. "Yes. I thank you, Miss."

"Come along, boy," said the manager. "I'll get one of the captains to find you a lamp and show you what to do."

Sébastien followed him to a shed and was introduced to another captain.

"You're to go all the way down to the lowest level today," said the mine captain. "Mr. Cobbs's idea, not mine. They do need a lamp boy down there, so I guess that will be you. The men wear these flannel shirts. Put this one on and hang your clean clothes on this peg. Here's your tull." He handed Sébastien a hat with a leather brim. "It's really too big for you, ain't it? But it's the smallest we got, so hang on to it. Here's your candle. Hang on to it, too. Money for it comes out of your pay. Stick the candle in this wet clay." He put a blob of clay on the brim of Sébastien's hat and pushed the candle end down into it. "It's your only light. You want never to lose your candle. You'll see what I mean soon enough. Here's your loops. Hang 'em on your button here." Three more pairs of candles, each sharing a wick. He looped them from Sébastien's shirt button. "That's all the candles you get for the whole day. So don't eat them. Yeah, there's some what do. It's pig fat, what they're made of. Smelly, eh? But if you're hungry, they're tempting. So Mr. Cobbs has them put poison in the tallow. It'll make you good and sick if you eat them."

The mine captain showed Sébastien how to work the lamp. "The men are going to depend on you for extra light. Your job is to rotate this wheel as fast as you can. Then you hold this flint against it. And for the love o' mike, watch the sparks if you're near the gunpowder. We don't need no rogue explosions. Let's get going. Here's the lamp. Take your lunch bucket. It's a long way to the lowest level. It'll take you an hour and a half just to get there."

He led Sébastien to a dark hole and they started down a long ladder. It was so long, Sébastien's legs were tired when they reached the end. But another ladder was there to take them still lower.

"Watch this one at the bottom. Hey, careful! It's slippery. Step on that board unless you want to end up taking a flyer down the hole. It's a hundred feet deep down there. You'd never be seen again, if you slip."

Down they went, a thousand feet, and still there were more ladders to take them to the lowest galleries. It was becoming uncomfortably warm. Sébastien's face was wet with heat and exertion. Oxygen was sparse. He was panting for air.

"Okay, boy. This is as far as I go today. You gotta go the rest of the way by yourself, all the way down. Find Alfie and Dudley. That's who you're looking for. They're shooting the rocks down there and they're going to be waiting for your lamp. Go careful now."

Going down alone. A dark, narrow shaft. Only the candle on his hat to light the way. It was spooky down there. How far did these ladders go? Sébastien had been descending for over an hour, he felt certain. The surface, grass as they called it, seemed so very far away.

It was unbearably hot. He felt faint. He was almost sick with the thought that, if he ever did manage to reach the bottom and finish his work there, he'd have to climb all that way back to the top.

His hands were slippery with sweat. He concentrated on keeping a very firm grip on the ladder. His tin lunch bucket and the lamp banged against his back with every step. He tried to hurry but he was already worn out. It was exhausting, stepping down rung after rung. The same rhythm, step, step, step for what seemed like endless miles.

Step, step, empty air. Sébastien let out a yell. Terror jolted up his spine. He barely managed to replace one foot on the rung above. There was a rung missing! Maybe more than one. It was a bad scare. He wrapped his arms around the ladder, hugging it tight until he stopped shaking. But the brim of his big hat bumped against a rung. He fumbled, tried to catch it. He missed! Nooo! His hat, and the candle with it, went spinning to the floor far below. He gasped and listened until he heard it thud to the ground.

Then it was dark. Really dark. He could see nothing.

Total blackness.

It took a minute for him to realize the gravity of his situation. High on a ladder, the next rungs missing, far above the next rock shelf yet far, far below the surface of the earth. No light for his candles. He had last seen another person, when? An hour ago? How far to the next solid rung? Clinging tightly he stretched one foot as far as he could reach. He waved it around carefully. Nothing there.

Whimpering, he drew both feet under him again and squatted on one rung, hardly daring to turn his head for fear of dizziness, for fear of slipping and falling, falling into the deeps of the earth.

A sea of black nothingness. He had disappeared into emptiness. He clung to the ladder, his only solid point of contact. He was nothing but a tiny speck of life in all that black immensity.

For some time he had been aware of a soft knocking and a rhythmical shushing sound overhead. Now it began to bother him. What could that be? Was it growing louder? After a while he could hear sounds below him, too. Finally something! A low rumble. Then nothing. Total silence again.

He might be able to feel his way back up the ladder. But that was dangerous too. Even if he did manage to avoid falling into a hole, even if he did find the men up there, they would think him a coward, trying to get out of work on his first day. No, someone would surely come along soon. His hands were sore from clutching the ladder. His knees started to hurt from crouching there for so long. His feet, bent over the rung, were prickly from lack of circulation.

He waited, trying to keep his imagination from running away with him. Overhead, the knocking sounds, and the shushing, shushing. Nothing more from below, not a sound. Maybe there was no one down there at all.

Stupid! He should have swallowed his pride and begun the long climb to grass while he had the strength. His head began to swim. He was hot and dizzy. It was hard to breathe. The air was thin. He couldn't hang on much longer. He was afraid his hands would simply let go of the ladder at any moment and he would fall forever. He was so tired. Now he was hearing things, dangerous things lurking in the darkness. Or maybe it was people, miners. Maybe he should yell.

Just as he tried to call out for help, a mighty explosion rocked the ladder. The mine was caving in! The ladder would break, crash into the depths!

Sébastien heard running footsteps. He strained to look toward the sound below him but dared not turn his head too far. He was weak, afraid of losing his balance. Then way, way below him, he saw a faint light.

"Move it, Alfie!"

Voices! Sébastien almost wept.

"How much powder did you put in that straw anyway, Dud?"

"Enough, I guess. Haha! That were close, that one."

To Sébastien's everlasting joy, two men appeared far below him. Their candles were the most welcome sight in the world. Help, at last.

"Looks like you did one hell of a job, I'd say. Let's get back down there and see what's what."

"Hey, what's this? Someone lost his tull? Who's been down here but us? Now that's odd. Someone gone missing?" Dud leaned over and gingerly picked Sébastien's hat off a rock shelf.

Sébastien started to call to them when Alfie let out a yell.

"Ho-lee crap!" he bawled.

Dud followed his gaze up the ladder.

"What the…?" Both men froze.

"See what I told you?" whispered Alfie. "I told you they was down here."

"A knocker," Dud whispered back.

"An' you never believed me!" He and Alfie stared upwards into the dark, whispering with their heads close together, afraid to speak aloud, afraid even to move their lips.

"He's here to tell us something."

"What is it? It's probably something terrible."

"He's warning us. Something bad's gonna happen."

"Please!" Sébastien called weakly. That was the moment a long rumble came from below them. Then a deafening crash. Another fall of rocks! A cloud of dust billowed up out of the tunnel behind Alfie and Dud. Coughing, they looked down at the tunnel they had just come from, then up at Sébastien.

"Holy crap."

"He saved us," Dud whispered, awestruck.

"Told ya. I told ya. He was warning us. I told ya so."

"Do we say 'thank you'? Offer him a bite of pasty?"

"Gotta give him more than just a bite of pasty. What's he want, gold? Whiskey?"

"Can you help me?" called Sébastien. He couldn't hang on any longer.

Alfie and Dud jumped into each others' arms. They gaped, transfixed.

No one spoke.

"What did he say?" asked Dud through closed lips.

"Answer him! Say something to him! He wants to talk," Alfie whispered.

Dudley shook his head so hard his jowls shook.

"Yer a maid, Dud, if ever I knew one. I'll t-talk to him." Alf gathered his courage. "Thank you, little Master!" He gulped and stuttered and made a small stiff bow. "We very much appreciate your help."

"Please!" cried Sébastien. "I'm stuck."

Dud and Alfie looked at each other, mystified. They looked back up at Sébastien.

"Don't ask me to touch him!" whispered Dud.

"I'm going to fall!"

Alfie cocked his head. Then, at last, good old Alfie thought a thought. "Hey! What are you?" he asked, suspicious. "Are you our lamp boy?"

"He's the lamp boy! Yeah! Look, he's got the lamp on his back."

"He's stuck! Horseballs! A coupla rungs is missing, remember, Dud? That's what happened!" Alfie ran over to the ladder. "Hang on, lad. I'm coming! Grab my neck. C'mon, you can let go, little man. I'll catch you."

Sébastien's body was completely rigid by now. His legs wouldn't unbend, his movements were jerky. Alfie pried Sébastien's fingers off the ladder, took one of his arms and laid it across his shoulder. Then he put his own arm around the boy and, step by painful step, worked him to the bottom of the ladder. Dud reached up to lift Sébastien to the ground. His feet were so sore he could not even stand. They helped him lie down on the floor.

"Don't fret, young man. You're safe now."

"How long you been hanging there, lad?"

Sébastien could only shake his head.

"This your first day in the mine?"

Sébastien nodded. He fumbled a corner of his flannel work shirt and pressed it to his eyes. He finally managed a few words. "Thank you for helping me."

"Don't thank us!" roared Dud. "If it weren't for you, we woulda been squooshed flat as two pilchards in a press. Just take a peek at that rock fall."

"You saved us, lad!"

Sébastien looked up at them. They were grinning from ear to ear, white teeth gleaming in their filthy black faces. Their candles flickered on their hat brims. "Really?" Sébastien asked, disbelieving. They were pleased with him?

"We thought you was a spirit."

"We thought you was a knocker. We didn't know if you wished us well or harm."

"You thought I was a ghost?"

"Well, something near to like. Knockers, they're like half-size men. Like your size." Dud started to laugh. "Those eyes of yours! Big as plates. I was sure he were a knocker, eh? Wasn't you, Alf?"

"Yeah," laughed Alfie. "Face like a white-washed wall. And skinny, underfed! You look like a knocker, like you never seen the light of day, lad. Scared the pants off us, you did."

Finally, Sébastien started to laugh too.

Dudley swatted back-handed at Alfie's shoulder. "So this here's my pard, Alfie."

"Your pard?"

"Yup. Me, I'm Dud." Dudley extended a giant blackened paw.

Alf stuck his hand out. "Alfred. Pleased to meet ya."

"I'm Sébastien."

"C'mon then, S'bastien. We're done down here for today. It's a long way to grass. Wait til the men hear this story."

"Wait. If you tell George this lad was hanging on the ladder all the blessed day, he's not gonna pay him."

"Not a word to George. You and me, we owe Young S'bastien anyway. We owe him our lives."

"Up you go, then, little master. We're two skats behind you."

Sébastien was slow climbing back up all those ladders but at least he had company this time. Day was fading when they came out of the hole. The sky never looked so beautiful to Sébastien. They were the last to arrive at the engine house at the end of the shift. The other men were nearly finished washing up. Sébastien threw himself onto a bench and wolfed his lunch while Dud and Alfie told their story.

"You shoulda heard Alfie blatting when he saw the lad perched up on that ladder," laughed Dud.

"Dash my buttons! Don't listen to him! He's crazy! It was Dudley here was on top of me 'fore I had time to spit. This man jumped into my arms faster than a thirty year old bride, I tell ya. Yup, threw his arms right around my neck, shakin' and shiverin'."

"But Young Bastien, here," added Dud, all unperturbed, "he was brave as a Christmas Eve rooster." He laughed and banged Sébastien on the back.

So by the end of his first day, everyone at Wheal Cock had heard of Sébastien. They made him feel like a hero. The bal maidens made a fuss over him. The men tousled his hair and punched his shoulder. It had been a long time since Sébastien had smiled and even now he could not quite manage one. But his eyes glowed with pleasure at finding such kindness, and of all places, at the very bottom of a Cornish mine.

*T*he next morning, very early, as Sébastien came over the hill on his way to the mine, he could see there was a storm brewing. The wind tore at his clothes and clouds hid the stars. Sue wasn't with him this morning. She would come later, at dawn, with the bal maidens. But he had to go in early, so he could go deep with the men. He drank in the sight of the Land's End, the lead-colored waves dashing against the cliffs, and the dark sea running over the edge of the world. There was a raw beauty to it. And it was far, far from Tregorna Farm.

Rain spattered his shoulders as he hurried down to the engine house. The men roared a welcome to him as soon as he walked in the door. He stood still with surprise for a moment, blinking. He looked around at them, at their smiles, and didn't know what to say.

While he changed into his work shirt, the men relished the chance to pour their accumulated wisdom into his ear. This became almost a daily ritual. It was a fine thing for them to have a new and appreciative listener for their worn-out tales.

"Never whistle down a mine, my handsome. Nothing upsets the knockers more than that."

"Don't tell him that trash," bawled one of the younger men. "Don't let them old guys scare you, Young Bastien. All those hours in the dark, it addles their brains after a few years. They go all cakey."

"Giss on!" insisted Alfie. "I've seen 'em, them knockers, seen 'em twice. I know they're there. Don't eat the last bite of your lunch, Young Bastien. Always leave a bit for the knockers. They'll remember you."

"Maybe you and Dud should stop working the lowest galleries. The shortage of air down there is making you daft, Alf. Completely daft."

"How did they get them a lamp boy? It's more than we got."

"Yer damlucky," complained one old-timer. "Wish we had a lamp boy. I can't hardly see straight no more. Black as my old lady's heart, down there. Me, stuck flat on my back with my nose an inch from the rock. Nothin' worse. It drives my bad eye wild."

"Yeah I noticed, Zeke. Your one eye goes buzzing around like a bumblebee."

"Can't hold it still."

"Better watch your step down below, then. Find yourself a partner, why don't you, Zeke?"

"I could use a pard. The manager at Wheal Hearle hired Blind Sam over from Madron, did you hear? Yeah, their candles keep going out at Hearle because their ventilation, it's real bad. So if they lose their lights, Blind Sam can get them up to grass again. Yeah, he's had to take them out twice now in a month. He's accustomed to the dark, eh?"

And it was dark down there, as Sébastien could attest. As he began the descent that morning, he noticed the shushing sound he'd heard the day before, but now it grew louder as they went lower. When they finally arrived at the lowest level, it was a terrifying roar.

"Mr. Dud, what is that noise?"

"That? That's the ocean up there, my handsome. Big surf today. Storm at high tide. It's a wild one. And right over our heads, don't you know."

"It is? How close?"

"Don't really know. There's them what think it's too close for comfort. Forty feet maybe."

"We're actually under the ocean?"

"Yes sirree. We got lots of tunnels under the sea at Wheal Cock. Hear that crashing up there? That's underwater boulders, getting tossed around by the waves. Some men, when they hear that, are too scairt to work at this level. We've seen 'em go tearin' up that ladder and never come down again."

"We gotta be real careful," added Alfie. "One blow in the wrong place and in comes the sea. Boom! You're drown-ded for sure, 'fore you can say Pedn Vounder. Let's have a look at that rock fall from yesterday. I'd sure like to find the tools I lost under there. Can you get the lamp going, Young Bastien?"

*T*he weeks went by. Sébastien grew tired of his lampboy duties and bought himself a pick, a shovel, and a horn to hold the gunpowder for blasting rocks. The cost was taken out of his pay, which anyway went to Cobbs. He had expected Cobbs would complain of him buying tools, but Sébastien never heard he did. Mr. Ickes had told him Cobbs kept track of every cent. Perhaps Mr. Ickes had somehow hidden Sébastien's purchase?

Sébastien liked working with the miners. They taught him how to "shoot" the rocks. Soon, nobody could do a better job at it than Young Bastien. The men swore this was so. He could place the straws filled with just the right amount of gunpowder in just the right crevice and blow up an entire wall of rock. The men told him he should be paid more for working at the lowest levels. He assumed Cobbs was reaping the benefit.

He would always be Young Bastien to the men. By the time he turned nine years old, though, he was no longer the skinny weakling he had been. He had grown taller, and he was very strong.

Miners developed strong arms and broad chests. In fact, the sport of wrestling was a favorite hobby of many of these men. Unfortunately the incredibly long climb up and down the ladders was a terrible strain on their hearts and lungs, especially because there was so little oxygen at the lower depths. To make matters worse, they stressed themselves further by racing up the ladders at the end of the day, placing bets to see who would be fastest to the top. It was foolish of them, but after a long and dangerous day in the mines, no one would deny it felt good to be a little foolish.

Maybe the miners were a bit reckless, but, oh they were a stubborn lot. Tough too, and proud of it. Drive your donkey in the path of a Cornish miner if you must, they were fond of saying, but be prepared to ride home on a bullhorn snail.

A miner had the strength of an ox. Even so, few of the men lived past forty-five years of age, even if they did manage to avoid accidents. And the accidents happened regularly. Fuses might be mishandled or a crushing rock fall would take its toll. On one sober day, Sébastien saw two men above him fall off a ladder to their deaths. A rotted rung gave way. One man slipped off and slammed into the man below him. They fell hundreds of feet into a dark grave, never to be found again.

As time went on, the family that had taken Sébastien as a boarder, the Gwennels, were pleased to see significant changes in the boy. He had finally grown taller, and was even stronger than their son Edmund.

The boys got on well together, by the grace of kindness on the part of one and exceptionally wary trust on the part of the other. Sébastien never quite got over his dread that Edmund would reveal his shameful secret, that he had been startled awake more times that he could count by Sébastien's night terrors. It happened less often now, that he awoke screaming and sweating, that he only gradually became aware of Edmund comforting him, coaxing him back to safety. But he had no way to predict when a terrifying episode would recur, and it made him deeply ashamed.

Even so, Sébastien could not deny his good fortune. First, Bianca had become a trusted center of his existence, and gradually he came to be nearly certain that Mr. Ickes would do nothing to harm him. Now he hoped he had Edmund too, like a rock, a haven of safety. And so, with plenty of nourishing food, surrounded by good wholesome people, he began to flourish, that is until the headaches started.

At the Ting Tong mines, Sébastien was one of the youngest boys ever to work at such deep levels. Most boys stayed at grass and never went below until they were twelve years old. Even for them there were dangers. Many youngsters, and even adults, succumbed to the poisonous fumes. First there was the arsenic that was burned nearby to make an alloy with the tin. Arsenic was in the air all over Cape Cornwall. And down in the mines, the gases from detonated gunpowder were deadly. All this, combined with the atmospheric pressure that weighed heavily on them in the low galleries, and the shortage of oxygen, caused many men's lungs to give out. And the dust, the endless dust brought on the black lung. That disease took its toll too. When Sébastien started to complain of upset stomach and dizziness, the Gwennels recognized the symptoms right away.

"Can't you speak to Mr. Cobbs about Young Bastien?" Mrs. Gwennel asked her daughter Sue. "He looks like he's been drawn through a sick horse! They've got him working at the lowest levels. I mean, that's just criminal. Truly! What are they thinking? He's too young yet, much too young. I don't know whose idea that was. But Mr. Cobbs wouldn't want him there, if he knew."

"But Mama, how can I speak to Mr. Cobbs? I think his office is in Lamorna. The only day I could go there to talk to him would be on the Sabbath. And I'm sure he doesn't open his office on a Sunday."

"Then I'm going to have to speak to Tom Ickes at church tomorrow. Maybe he can talk to Mr. Cobbs and find Bastien a different position. Though I would be truly sorry for the lad to leave us. He and our Edmund have been so good for each other. Do you know, Susie, I actually found Edmund reading a book the other evening? No, I'm not joking."

Mrs. Gwennel did ask Tom Ickes to speak to Mr. Cobbs. Instead, Ickes went straight to Patrick O'Brien. Tom Ickes acted on the suspicion that Cobbs had found a new boy to interest him, and this might be as good a time as any to slip a change past him. He promised he would bear the brunt of Cobbs's anger if need be.

Patrick O'Brien was very curious to know how Ickes managed to manipulate Cobbs in this way and still keep life and limb together, but somehow he did. He wondered about the relationship between Cobbs and Ickes. O'Brien decided it was better not to think about it.

A week later, Sébastien said his good-byes to the miners and the Gwennel family of Crows-an-Wra and walked down to a cottage near the harbor in Lamorna, the new cabin boy for Captain Patrick O'Brien.

*Cantilever Bridge*

*One part of a cantilever bridge acts as an anchor for another part.
The ends of the bridge require firm support but the entire structure
relies on balance to achieve stability.*

## PATRICK O'BRIEN

$A$ few years before, back about 1792, Zephaniah Cobbs
had been looking for cheap labor. He heard the Irish needed jobs
and were willing to work for little pay. He made a trip to Dublin.
Down near the wharf, he was directed to a pub. Inside the door, he
hesitated. Then he crossed the dark room and spoke to the owner
behind the bar, saying he was looking for three or four sailors to
crew for him. He was given Patrick O'Brien's name. One of the
whiskery old bar flies overheard and, rhapsodizing in the Irish
manner, declared O'Brien to be a superior sailor.

"Aye, and don't Aeolus, god a' the winds, throw jealous fits at
the mere mention of Pat O'Brien's name? Aye, sure he do. I swear
to ya! The god a' the winds. Iss the abslute truth."

Cobbs finally tracked O'Brien down a couple of nights later. He
found him lying in a heap on a wharf, generously soaking it with
his blood. He had been ambushed by a gang of the Protestant Peep
o' Bay Boys and left for dead. He was fifteen years old, orphaned
since he was six. Cobbs hired an apothecary to see to his wounds.
After that, it was easy for Cobbs to lure him to Cornwall with

promises of working as a captain aboard the *Serpent*. Promises Cobbs had no intention of keeping.

Even at age fifteen, O'Brien was as broad-shouldered as a man. He reminded Cobbs of a big old turtle. Cobbs was certain he could manipulate him. Shrewd as he was, Cobbs should have known the languid snapping turtle takes but half a second to bite your finger off.

Perhaps O'Brien's steady, even temper made him seem lazy, even slow-witted. His gentle manner fooled Cobbs into thinking he would also be gratifyingly submissive. But in Dublin, on the docks at any rate, the Irish vocabulary has no word for 'submission'. A big-boned lad, already taller than most men, O'Brien had learned how to stand up for himself. He had no intention of either letting Cobbs go back on his promise, or dominate him in any way.

Consequently, the first time Cobbs tried to take advantage of Patrick O'Brien was also the last. After that encounter, Cobbs limped painfully for two months. He carried a cane in damp weather for the rest of his life. The mere recollection of the incident made Cobbs tremble with fury. He dreamed of responding in kind. There were so many ways he could hurt O'Brien. But how to really hurt him? He mulled for a long time over a suitable revenge, gloated over the possibilities, envisioned the humiliation. He himself was no match for a man of O'Brien's size and strength. Would he have to pay a couple of thugs? That irked him, the thought of having to pay good money for some everyday revenge. Then too, he wanted the personal satisfaction of seeing O'Brien suffer. Poison was a good option, perhaps the only viable one. But too quick, much too quick. He would have to bide his time.

By the time Cobbs had considered all these possibilities, however, O'Brien had managed to make himself indispensable. As captain of the *Serpent*, he was running down at least one enemy French ship every week and seizing their cargo in the name of the English king. That part of Cobbs's business, his privateering racket, had finally begun to thrive. O'Brien was bringing in more money than Cobbs made from all his French refugee workers combined. Best of all, it enabled Cobbs to sell expensive French products to some of the nobility in the area. Cobbs was gaining stature with the upper class, real respectability at last. Yes, O'Brien would be difficult to replace.

True, Cobbs was forced to pay Patrick O'Brien. The man had insisted upon it. But the rest of the crew were French refugees. He worked them devilishly hard and paid them nothing. When Cobbs sold the stolen goods, and because he rarely paid a single ha'penny of tax, his profits were enormous.

So all right, he would pay O'Brien a pittance, but he would reap a fortune. He decided to keep O'Brien for a while longer. But there would come a time, Cobbs promised himself, when he would show him what pain was. For a man with Cobbs's power, there was no end to the ways he could hurt someone.

After O'Brien had so clearly defined his relationship with Cobbs, they grew to be a little more cordial to each other, at least on the surface. This was quite a novelty for Cobbs, who was almost never forced to be cordial to anyone if it didn't suit him. And the young man turned out to be amazingly adept at manipulating customs officers. Cobbs gave him that much credit.

He was easy-going and clever of tongue. The customs men seemed almost fond of the lad.

Since Cobbs hardly ever set foot on a ship, he never personally ran afoul of the law. It was Patrick O'Brien, not Cobbs, that the English King George would have deemed a crook and a swindler. To the men O'Brien worked with, though, he was respected as an honest man. Not a trait Cobbs would strive for in himself, but so useful in others. Actually, Cobbs had secretly tested O'Brien's honesty on several occasions, leaving money or documents about, just to tempt him. Difficult as trust was for Cobbs, he finally conceded he could trust O'Brien more than he trusted most men. Since there were so many people who absolutely relished defrauding Zephaniah Cobbs, this made O'Brien doubly valuable to him.

In fact, on only one occasion did Cobbs suspect O'Brien of treachery. A few months after he had brought him to Cornwall, Cobbs sent him back to Ireland to sell a load of illegal tea. O'Brien docked at Dublin, sold the tea and used the money to buy tobacco from an East Indiaman. He loaded it aboard the *Serpent*. Then he disappeared.

Where was he? What had become of Cobbs's ship? Cobbs waited in Lamorna, fuming, more furious by the day. He paced up and down in his office. O'Brien, his crew and the *Serpent* had vanished, he was sure of it. He was spitting mad. That bloody O'Brien had cheated him out of a fortune!

Cobbs sent an agent to Dublin with orders to bring O'Brien back in chains. The agent disappeared too, and neither he nor the vessel Cobbs had lent him were ever seen again. But a month later, O'Brien sailed the *Serpent* back into Lamorna harbor. He brought a valuable cargo of tobacco that Cobbs sold illegally, tax-free. During the time O'Brien had been absent, the price of tobacco had gone up. So Cobbs was able to sell it for twice what it would have been worth four weeks earlier.

Cobbs made the mistake of insisting on knowing where O'Brien had gone and what he had been doing, since he was in Cobbs's pay. He found again, to his consternation, that it was useless to pressure O'Brien. This irked Cobbs to no end. Had O'Brien been visiting a woman? Settling an old score? Drinking himself into a stupor? If the man had a weakness, Cobbs needed to know about it. He could use that information.

Being the kind of man he was, Cobbs suspected every nefarious reason and never even came close to the truth: Patrick O'Brien had gone looking for his brother.

When O'Brien turned seventeen, he fell into a love affair with the daughter of a wealthy shipping magnate in Falmouth. The woman was six years his senior. They enjoyed each other's company until her parents married her off to a fifty-five year old man of her own class. But from her, O'Brien learned to appreciate good manners, fine food, and gentlemanly attire. He began to take an interest in shipping companies, their schemes and machinations. He gave no hint of any of this to Zephaniah Cobbs, who continued to regard O'Brien as a loafer and an Irish wharf rat. Cobbs only pretended to treat this rat with respect. A rat was still a rat. And some day, that rat would be trapped.

Was it foolish to disrespect a wharf rat, especially an Irish one? Cobbs never stopped to consider. He took advantage of people. He took advantage of situations. That is how he operated. He could see no reason to change his ways.

$T$hey say when the student is ready, the master will appear. Patrick O'Brien appeared again in Sébastien Roland's life just when he was most needed. When Sébastien came aboard the *Serpent*, he was sick and heavy-hearted, unable to stick it out in the mines, weighed down under a sense of failure. And, Patrick O'Brien was almost certain, he had a history of abuse. He had of course grown in stature from when O'Brien had first met him in France, but two years in the mines had nearly wrecked his lungs. If it weren't for the kindness of the men and women of Botallack, the boy would probably be dead by now.

O'Brien thought he understood Sébastien. He certainly understood what it was to be an orphan, pressed by the need to carve out a place for oneself. Trying to belong somewhere. Living with the realization that some things were granted automatically to other children, but for some inexplicable reason, not to oneself. And always, every day, wanting so badly to stop whatever it was that gnawed ceaselessly at an orphan's soul.

O'Brien remembered the lively little boy he had brought from France. He would not have connected this broken youth to that boy. Tom Ickes had come to him a few weeks ago, asking a favor. O'Brien seemed to have some influence with Cobbs, Ickes said. Would he take the boy under his wing?

Of course he would help. But it wasn't until he had worked with Sébastien for a few months that he realized that their relationship filled a need of his own.

*A*fter a year of apprenticeship with Captain O'Brien, Sébastien Roland had grown into a robust eleven year old. Fresh air had healed his body and a healthy relationship between apprentice and master helped to mask old wounds.

Most of the work O'Brien did for Zephaniah Cobbs involved smuggling and privateering. He found eager crews among the villagers along the coast. The fact that smuggling was illegal made little difference to them. Copper and tin mines were giving out. The fish were disappearing. What law proclaimed that people should live in grinding poverty? If they starved to death, what justice would be served? The opportunity was there and they so badly needed the work. They were happy to work for O'Brien.

If they were lucky, O'Brien hired them as privateers. The privateering racket was much less risky than smuggling. It meant that Cobbs had purchased documents from the king that allowed his crews to raid foreign ships the way any pirate would. What was it that made privateering more lawful than smuggling or pirating? Ah, there was a very simple answer. Privateers gave the king most of their profits. Pirates did not give him a farthing. Therefore, privateers were legal, pirates were outlaws. It made perfect sense to a cash-starved king.

The villagers considered smuggling almost a civic duty, since so many local people actually depended heavily on this income for their livelihood. Landed gentry, small fishermen, merchants, shopkeepers, shipbuilders -- maybe they were all cheating the king of his much-needed tax money. But who gave a pilchard's eyelash about the English king?

The king, they reasoned, wasn't even interested in Cornwall. Obliterating France from the map, that was the king's quest. This enmity had been going on for a long, long time, so long that English eyebrows raised in distaste at the mere mention of anything French. English lips sneered and shoulders froze. Not even an inch of French lace would be tolerated on English soil. No silks, laces, gloves, clocks, tea, coffee, chocolate, tobacco, whiskey, wine. No, the king wanted none of these. His customs officers would have apoplexies if a single ruddy French biscuit crossed the English Channel!

The French, meanwhile, were strangling British trade. Every French port on *La Manche* was closed to the British. So, to fill the void, an entire folk industry sprang into being, just to circumvent the foolishness of kings. *Voilá,* – smuggling!

Captain O'Brien had no trouble finding markets for French luxuries, and he managed to do so right under the noses of the customs officials. He put Sébastien in charge of distributing the goods they brought from Europe. If Sébastien found no ready customers for the merchandise, it was up to him to find a place to hide it until they could sell it.

It was a childishly simple arrangement. When Cornish smugglers docked at a port in France or Ireland, or the Isle of Guernsey, Belgium, or Holland, they sold their shipment and used the profits to buy more goods. Then they beat it back across the Channel to sell their contraband. Often O'Brien had the chance to buy things from distant ports: Spain, Italy, India, Africa. These exotic items sold very well in larger cities, even in London itself. O'Brien's ship ran by stealth into an English harbor at night, and the next day all the king's men, sipping way too much French *chocolat* from their Limoges china cups, burst their French silk waistcoats and popped their Parisian buttons right under the English king's nose. *Vive la France*, indeed.

$W$ith all the events of his new life, Sébastien was soon bartering with the cunning of a gypsy. He loved sailing and traveling to distant places. He appreciated the prosperity that the trade brought to so many poor Cornish families. He tried his hand at trading. He learned to keep track of finances, and to work out deals with all kinds of colorful personalities. He found hiding places for goods and for people. He was constantly inventing new ways to send signals, by day and by night from ship to shore, that the customs men would not recognize, and he learned to organize hordes of Cornishmen who could unload a ship the moment she touched the shore. He paid informers to watch the comings-and-goings of customs men, to find out when they took their days off, thus leaving a harbor unguarded. And to point out which officials would stoop to take a bribe.

One of Sébastien's favorite occupations was to imagine new ways to hide the goods on board the *Serpent*. They hollowed out the mast and made false bottoms for the drinking water tubs so they could conceal a cask of wine inside. They built false bulkheads and hollowed oars to hold embroidered goods. They roped barrels of whiskey together and towed them in the water behind the ship so nothing would be found on board. Tobacco was formed into every conceivable shape, from bricks to potatoes, in order to disguise it.

As he got older, Sébastien took over the task of accounting. Cobbs poured over every page of Sébastien's reports, making sure no one wasted or stole anything. There was only one task Sébastien would not accept. He refused to set foot in Cobbs's office for any reason. He would not go near the place. Even if something needed to be dropped off quickly, he would ask someone else to handle it. He knew Cobbs could not be trusted, but more to the point, he was certain he could not trust himself near that man.

By the end of their first year together, Patrick O'Brien began to regard Sébastien as a definite asset in their business dealings. Even the grown men would take orders from him. Early one evening, for example, as they were returning to Cornwall loaded with contraband, they spied a square-rigger plowing through the waves, heading straight toward them. Was this a customs ship? Every sailor watched its approach with bated breath. Apprehension narrowed every eye. Oh, they were almost home free! There was the coast of Cornwall, no more than three miles away! Not so near that they had a chance to make a run for it, but tantalizingly close. Cross your fingers, boys, and maybe that square rigger will pass by.

It wasn't long before they heard the warning shot, the obligatory signal from the customs officials. The crew of the *Serpent* groaned. They knew they were going to be boarded. They were carrying bolts and bolts of silk fabric hidden in the ceiling of the hold, and several pounds of tobacco, both illegal. Tea had been packed in oilskin bags which they could throw overboard and try to retrieve later, rather than have the customs officers find them. But there were also boxes of chocolates from Holland that were stuffed into corners. Who in their right mind could throw those overboard? They carried several barrels of wine too, but they did have papers for the wine, fortunately.

"They're coming for us, Captain," moaned Sébastien. "Should we man the guns?"

"I'd like to avoid a fight if we could," said O'Brien after a moment. "Just what we need tonight! A full load of silks on board, and here come the Revenue men."

"*Sacre bleu*! If they lay hands on Bianca's gift, I'll have to shoot them all!"

"There has to be a better way to deal with them."

"I know! We will give them beef!" suggested Sébastien.

"Beef?"

"The squire's beef. Cook them a beef dinner."

"Are you kidding?" One of the crew spat overboard. "That would be like feeding sugarplums to a goat!"

"The squire would raise ructions. That beef is for his daughter's wedding feast," declared the first mate.

"The squire can holler down a rain barrel, for all I care. I refuse to let them get Bianca's lace," said Sébastien.

"And I invested a fortune in that silk," declared O'Brien.

Sébastien had an idea. "Signal the fishing boats for help," he suggested.

"Now that is not a bad idea. While we're having dinner, the crew can pass the silks through the portholes. Johnnie, come here! Do you feel up to cooking a meal?"

"What? You dreamin'?"

"I think we should invite these fine officers to dinner. Sébastien, you will be in charge of off-loading the goods. Make sure to tell the men that the tobacco stays on board, though."

"And I'll tell the spotsman to signal for fishing boats to sail out to us."

"But they must use no lights. And no noise. Total silence, tell them."

"Right, Patrick."

"Johnnie, open a cask of wine. Pour it and keep pouring it. What else do we have to eat? Those vegetables from Belgium that the squire ordered? Cook a few of them, and set the table in my cabin. Use the linen cloth."

"If you're thinking of feeding them our chocolate, you will have to do so over my stinking dead and rotting body," declared little Johnnie, the cook.

"Absolutely right, Johnnie," Patrick agreed. "We will have to murder them if they touch the chocolates." He stopped to look around. "Pull us in very close to the customs ship, as close as you can get. Lower the ladder. Light the running lights on the starboard side only. And a lantern or two over here. No lights on the port side at all. Sébastien, did you speak to the spotsman?"

"He said it is just dark enough for him to use the signal lantern."

"But tell him to wait until the customs officers are in my cabin. We'll serve the King's weasels a dinner so splendid they'll want to board us every week."

"Uh, now that is worrisome. Are you sure you don't want to rethink this, Pat?"

"No time to rethink. It was your idea, Bastien, and I can't come up with any better plan on short notice. Meanwhile, direct the fishermen to our port side when they get here."

"The side opposite the customs vessel."

"Right. Here comes the English dinghy. Disappear, Sébastien, and don't show your face. They'll haul a young man like you into the Navy quicker than a seal can swallow a mackerel. Tell Danny the same."

"We're not invited to the dinner, then?"

"Not unless you have a hankering to scrub decks on a British square-rigger for the next couple of years."

Sébastien fled.

O'Brien greeted the customs men as they came up the ladder. He couldn't have been more amiable. The King's men were unused to such a smiling welcome. This was certainly not the treatment they usually received along the coast of Cornwall. It made their job so much easier.

They began their inspection. Harrumphing, consulting documents, peering suspiciously under tarps. But, by all that's holy! Was that ... my goodness, was that the smell of roasting beef and ... and frying onions? Going about the preliminaries of a search, the English noses furtively probed the air. Their attention wandered. Beef and onions. Can you smell that? It muddled the wits. It confused any sense of purpose. Ah me. If only duty could take second place to pleasure once in a while. But no! There were standards, sirrah, and standards must be upheld.

The English officers dutifully continued the task of inspection but their internal organs had other ideas. Those stomachs of theirs sang a veritable opera! Such an insistent organ, the stomach. One cannot nay-say hunger pains. An empty belly will not be ignored. These empty bellies played right into O'Brien's hands. He urged the Englishmen forward.

"There are coils of rope here, gentlemen. We wouldn't want you to trip." O'Brien snapped his fingers. "Mr. Brown, I want these ropes moved out of the way."

Mr. Brown did so, dutifully and with special care. Because these were not ropes at all, but tobacco, twisted and coiled to look like rope. A shop in Holland manufactured tobacco ropes and cables and string of many different sizes, and smugglers were their eager customers. Any one of these English inspectors might question the large amount of rope the *Serpent* was carrying, but, oh my, with that smell of roasting beef and onions, no one thought to do so.

For about the fifth time, yet another English stomach bellowed an aria so loud and lengthy, it would have inspired an entire oratorio from George Frederic Handel. O'Brien looked down at the English captain.

"Sir," O'Brien asked, "at the risk of being impolite, I must ask. Have you and your men dined this evening? No? But this is a travesty! Please consider gracing our table. My cook is just preparing a humble supper for our officers. And there are only three of you. Shall I tell him you'll join us? Are you willing to put your duties aside for an hour or so? You'll work better with some food under your belts, eh? Fine, then let us open some wine. Come, this way. We'll be more comfortable in my cabin. Leave the paperwork. We'll attend to it afterwards."

While O'Brien poured the wine and Johnnie, the little cook, sautéed onions and carrots in the galley, Sébastien crept out to the bow and peered into the darkness. The night was black and moonless. Heavy drifts of clouds sat unmoving over the land. No evening breeze rose to nudge them out to sea. It would have been a perfect night for their purpose, if they hadn't crossed the path of these customs agents. The breast of the sea, never completely still, heaved long slow sighs, rolling black and oily below him. Now Sébastien could just make out dark shapes on the water. Boats, coming their way.

"Can you signal them to make no noise?" he whispered to the spotsman.

"I did that. They'll see the king's ship and know something is afoot."

"I'll go below," said Sébastien. "Bring them over to the port side but don't let them bump up against the hull."

Below, the crew had gathered the bolts of silk. They quietly opened two portholes and handed the fabric down to the fishermen below. Once they found a rhythm, the work went smoothly.

"Will the boxes of chocolates fit through?"

"If they don't, I'll swim them ashore myself. Are we offloading the tobacco, Bastien?"

"Captain O'Brien said to leave the tobacco on board."

Johnnie came from the galley, lugging a large hunk of fresh, uncooked meat. "Get the rest of this beef out of here. It was meant for some wedding celebration. Too bad we had to waste some of it on the king's men."

"Not a total waste, Johnnie," grinned a member of the crew. "That there hunk of beef prolly saved us a fortune in merchandise!"

"You should charge the squire twice as much for it."

"But he'll be getting less meat."

"All the more reason. It's a rare commodity, all of a sudden."

In an hour the fishing boats had been loaded and the last of them was on its way back to shore.

"Spread the wine barrels out so it looks like they fill the hold," Sébastien suggested. "Danny, you and I have to hide in the lockers again. Quick, disappear. Here they come."

The *Serpent*, like many Cornish smuggling vessels, was outfitted with a small space in which to hide young sailors or older men considered too valuable to forfeit to the British. With a war on, the navy was desperate for sailors. It was constantly looking for men to impress into the service. They virtually kidnapped boys and forced them to become navy sailors. They considered it especially fortunate to get a Cornish sailor, even a smuggler, because they were the most skillful men on the sea. Quite suddenly, aboard the *Serpent,* every man seemed to acquire a limp, an eye patch or a hook hand.

Sébastien and Danny had just managed to cram themselves into their lockers when the customs officers came bumping and slipping down the companionway.

"Ow-ouch! Whoa! Oh dear me!" cried one, reeling unsteadily. "Wash out, Cappen! 'Sa big step."

"You really should get tha' … tha' thing there … tha', whaddya call it? … tha' ladder … *hiccup* … fished. Fixed!"

The captain didn't bother with any of the steps. He bumped down the rungs and landed hard on his ample butt. But, he didn't seem the least put out.

"Ho, iss a helluva rough sea t'night, innit? Now wha' we got here? Yep, wine. Les' get those cas ... cask-iz there counted. And you got your payspers, ermmm, your papers. Yep." The captain turned the documents upside down and right side up. He squinted closely at them. He eyeballed them at arm's length. He brought them back up to his nose. Then he thrust them aside. "Lessee, now. Where d'we sleep?"

Getting the three Englishmen back onto their own ship posed the biggest problem of the night.

"We could have wished them good-night and dropped them straight into the sea, they were so blootered."

"We could have had a whole flotilla of fishing boats out here," exclaimed Johnnie the cook. "They never would have known the difference in their condition."

"Their condition is all thanks to your good cooking, Johnnie."

"I think, Captain, there was another factor. The Liquid Effect."

"I fear they ain't fit to sail," commented a sailor, watching the ship pull away. "That ship's gonna to end up smashed on the Runnelstone by morning."

"Let them beach themselves on the rocks while they sleep it off. Then they can pay us to tow them back to London tomorrow."

"A doubly rich trip for us!"

"That," said Patrick O'Brien, "is what I call maximizing your profit."

*F*inally, in the year 1801, there was talk of peace with France. Peace at last! But that would leave hundreds of navy sailors with no jobs. This became a major concern until some bright light in government thought of clamping down on smuggling. Why not solve all their problems by expanding the Customs operations?

They put the older navy ships to use patrolling the coast, manned them with agents to catch the smugglers, and then hired agents to oversee the agents. And then, not a word of a lie, agents to oversee the agents who oversaw the agents. Soon the harbors all up and down the English coast were crawling with revenue men.

Did this call a halt to illegal operations in Cornwall? There were a few adjustments that had to be made, but the smugglers let nothing stand in their way for long. These were Cornishmen, tunnelers of unyielding rock and fishers of a hostile sea. Perseverance was not a trait they had to learn. It was an instinct born into them.

Indomitable, they believed it was an ill wind if it didn't blow someone some good. The French war that nearly ruined England had been good for the Cornish, who had taken full advantage of the opportunity to ply their "free trade". Wartime smuggling had honed their skills, too. No one could sail closer to the wind than a Cornishman. And they had developed a system. They could land cargo on a beach and bury it in the sand, or stow it in caves, or in wagons heaped with kelp, in no time flat. Or they could have the smuggled goods carted inland by fifty waiting compatriots, all before the clumsy Customs boat could navigate their treacherous, rocky little coves.

The revenuers were outmaneuvered, outmanned, and outsmarted, which made them zealously committed to seeing every last one of these Cornish thugs caught and hanged, or at least transported to the colonies.

They could have more easily captured a school of sharks in a sock.

But the people who govern nations seem to need enemies. So the English fashioned the smugglers into enemies, those bloody Cornishmen who did not even consider themselves English anyway.

If only they knew someone who could be persuaded to inform on these criminals. There was one man in Lamorna they might approach, apparently not Cornish born and bred. A very likely candidate, they were told, and smarmy as the day is long. Yes, that is what they needed. A spy, a good upstanding Englishman, tried and true.

*I*t was the fall of that same year, 1801. Sébastien shook hands with his old friend, Alfie. "All right, you've got the job, Alf. Our new lander, and we're very pleased to have you."

"Thank you, Young Bastien, thank you. I'm grateful. I really need the money now." Alfie patted his twisted leg. "I'm not the man I was before the accident."

"It won't be a very big haul this time, I'm afraid, but it will be a start. I told Captain O'Brien you are very reliable."

"I appreciate that. I'll do the best I can."

"I see you're getting around pretty well now, Alf."

"Pretty well, pretty well. It's a change, for certain, not going to Botallack every day. And a'course Dudley, my old pard, him going round the land like he did. That's been hard, that."

"Yeah. Poor Dudley. I bet you miss him. Not an easy way for someone to go."

"It was not, Bastien, it was not. So what is the first order of business here?"

"The captain wants to make sure you understand all the signals. From out in the Channel we'll be looking for either white horses on the edge of the cliff, or large white sheets spread out on rooftops, something big and white, to let us know where it's safe to land. Stay at your station all day to watch for the *Serpent* returning."

"I can arrange that. I'll do a good job, I promise, Bastien."

"And you'll get us some tubmen? Twenty men should be enough. Strong men. Those barrels are heavy and each man will have to carry two of them for several miles."

"I know lots of men who'd be more than willing."

"Let's meet again to make sure we're ready. Daytime landings are a new thing for us. So until we see how this works, we won't try any big loads."

"Just give me a couple of days, Bastien."

"A lot depends on the lander, Alf."

"Trust me. We'll keep a sharp eye on the Customs house. I'll see that you get back safe."

"I know you miss the income from the mine. But if all goes well for us, you should net a pretty good profit here."

"You must be getting rich yourself, Young Bastien."

"No, not me. I'm still working for Cobbs."

"No kidding? You can't go out on your own, lad?"

"No. Not yet, Alf."

"Well, you are just a boy. How old are you now?"

"I'll be twelve in the fall."

Alfie threw back his head and laughed. "Ten years from now, you'll be a force to be reckoned with, I'll bet. Ha! Not even twelve yet! Come on, tell old Alfie. You must have some plans in the back of your mind."

"I'm going to stay on with Captain O'Brien for now. He's been good to me."

"Well you deserve some luck. Working in the mines nearly killed us both."

"It's all behind us now, Alf."

"Well, I'd better get to work. See you in two days, my boy."

Sébastien watched Alfie limp slowly down the wharf. One night, a few months before, a violent storm had burst over Botallack out at the Land's End. In a hurry to get home ahead of the worsening weather, some miner had forgotten to lock the brakes on a newly-greased tram wagon. The gale caught the empty wagon and sent it rumbling down the slope. It picked up speed and ran over three people before it crashed into a storage shed. It had nearly severed Alfie's leg. The two others were less fortunate. The gruesome broken bodies of Alf's partner, Dudley, and a young bal maiden were carried home to their families.

The night this happened, the mine captain was expected to report the accident to the mine owners, but these worthies were busy spending the company's profits on one of the lavish feasts they held every three months. It took the mine captain some time to work up the nerve to interrupt them. Naturally, no one expected those sleek men in their white dress shirts to leave their bottles of port in order to aid Dudley's now-destitute widow, or to comfort to the bal maiden's young children. None of them offered to make sure Alfie received help from a surgeon. But the mining families flocked to help, as always, in whatever ways they could. And three young workers stepped forward to take the places of the fallen.

$N$ow that Patrick O'Brien had hired Alfie as their new lander, he asked a man named Phin to be their spotsman. Cornish smugglers had perfected an ingenious method for getting their cargo ashore undetected. No one knew in advance where their ship would land. They would wait offshore, watching for a signal from Alfie. Then Phin, their spotsman, who knew the south coast as well as his mother's face, would be responsible for getting them safely into whatever hidden cove or rocky harbor Alfie had chosen. By night, the lander might wave a lantern as soon as he saw a spark from a tinderbox on board the *Serpent*. By day, he might signal by raising and lowering a sail a certain number of times, or he might burn wet gorse to send up smoke. When the *Serpent* saw the agreed upon signal, she would put on all sail to reach the place where twenty, thirty, maybe fifty men waited to help unload her.

The *Serpent's* voyage was, as usual, financed by Zephaniah Cobbs. On this trip, Cobbs was exporting a legitimate shipment of tin and an illegitimate load of tea. He was greedy. He had purchased the tea two months ago from a Dutch ship and hoped to sell it abroad at a profit. To realize an even bigger profit, he had bulked up the tea with dried rose leaves. Zephaniah Cobbs never passed up an opportunity for gain.

As soon as they were away from Lamorna harbor, the *Serpent* raised a French flag, Patrick O'Brien's idea. The *Serpent* had been named by Cobbs, an Englishman, but the name worked in French as well. Customs officials cruising the Cornish coast had no right to stop a French ship. But it was Cobbs who thought of registering the boat in a Frenchman's name. Sébastien Roland's name was a practical choice. Of course, if they got into trouble with the Revenue men, Cobbs would always come to their aid, pay the fines and take the punishment himself. That went without saying. Using Sébastien's name was merely a formality.

*T*he *Serpent* crossed the Channel in high winds under a blue sky scudded with clouds. As soon as Cornwall disappeared over the western horizon, she raised the French flag and sailed into Port du Bloscon without incident. Patrick O'Brien sold the tin and the tea, and, as directed by Cobbs, bought three dozen half-ankers of whiskey. Half-ankers were the smallest barrels made, specially shaped so one strong man could carry two of them strapped together, one on his chest and another on his back. These were hidden aboard the *Serpent* in clever compartments, specially built on either side of the bilge.

When they had transacted all their business in France, they set sail. As Cornwall came in sight, down came the French flag. Phin, their spotsman, scanned the coast intently.

"There's Alf," he called, "up on the cliff near Mousehole, with a black horse. Not a good sign. We'd better not land."

"Prepare to come about!" called Patrick O'Brien.

"Wait. Look what's coming out of Lamorna."

"A square rigger. That's got to be a customs agent," said Patrick.

"Were they watching for us?"

They heard a gun shot. The customs agents were required to identify themselves by firing into the air and flying a special flag.

"That shot came right across our bow!" Sébastien jumped for cover behind the mast. "What's going on?"

"I don't know," said O'Brien. "But we're going to have to let them board. They're too close. Blast! How did they know we were coming?" He watched the ship through his glass. "It is British customs. The *Sydenham*. We could try to outrun them but I think it would be stupid. Besides, they'll never find the whiskey."

"Me, I'm praying for a storm to come up in the next ten minutes," said one of the crewmen. "The king's men are worse than useless in a storm."

"Let's co-operate with them. If there is a problem, we'll let Cobbs deal with it."

The English customs officers pulled alongside and came aboard. The Collector of Customs, Lieutenant Melvin Merton, peered down his snout at a document. He looked up at Patrick O'Brien.

"According to our records, this vessel is registered to Sébastien Roland," he announced. "Which is he?"

"I'm Roland."

"You are under arrest, sir."

"Arrest?" Patrick O'Brien demanded. "For what?"

"For smuggling. We're taking him in."

"On what evidence?"

"We will have all the evidence we need as soon as we inspect your cargo. Seize him."

"Wait! Why Roland? He's just a boy, a common sailor. Zephaniah Cobbs is the owner of this boat. He's the one you want. It's his operation."

"I was told Mr. Cobbs would not be aboard."

"Who gave you that information?"

Lieutenant Merton ignored the question. "Do not try to implicate Mr. Cobbs. He knows nothing of your illicit activities. You, on the other hand, have been caught red-handed in an illegal act."

"What illegal act would that be?"

"My men will answer that question in very short order. Mr. Roland, come with us."

"Wait a minute! I still haven't heard what crime Mr. Roland is accused of."

"You'll have to take that up with the Chief of the Waterguard. I am under orders to seize this vessel and take Roland into custody. He's coming with us. "

"Just hold on! Roland is an innocent crewman. If you're going to arrest anyone, take me instead. I'm the captain."

"Roland is the one accused. Roland is the one we want."

"There has been some mistake! You need to go see Mr. Zephaniah Cobbs. Better yet, let's go together."

An agent came up from the hold at that moment.

"We found it, Lieutenant," he said. "Just where they said it would be. Next to the bilge."

"Who? Who told you this?" O'Brien was beginning to lose his temper.

"You're surprised?" said Collector of Customs Merton. "We do have ways of finding things out, you must realize."

"From?"

"Don't be an idiot."

"I'm entitled to know."

"Obviously, I am not obligated to say. You're smugglers. You have no rights. Whereas, according to the law, we have the right to execute Mr. Roland."

"Come on! No Cornish judge would pass such a sentence on him."

"Nevertheless, I for one will press for it. We will also confiscate your merchandise. May we see some bills of lading?"

"Certainly."

"Mr. Richards will move any contraband items to our ship. Do not stand in our way, Captain O'Brien, or I will personally see to it that you are fully prosecuted. That includes having your ship's hull sawn into pieces. Now, we will load this merchandise and our First Mate will come aboard to steer the *Serpent* into port."

Where did they get all this information? fumed O'Brien to himself. He even knew my name. It was all bloody strange! He clenched his fists in frustration. But unless he and his men resorted to violence, they were powerless. His crew stood by, watching the proceedings with narrowed eyes, each man itching to be sighting down the barrel of a musket. O'Brien knew one word from him would set a fight in motion, but no, it would be better to let Cobbs straighten this out.

Helpless, they watched as the barrels of whiskey were loaded onto the English boat. Sébastien was not treated as gently as the merchandise. He was dragged down the ladder and pushed sprawling onto the deck of the square-rigger. The *Serpent*'s crew shouted their protests but Lieutenant Merton paid no attention.

The *Serpent* followed the square-rigger into Lamorna harbor. In a fury, O'Brien rowed himself ashore and ran immediately up to Cobbs's office. It was locked and no one, it seemed, had seen Cobbs at all that day.

Frustrated again, O'Brien watched the English sailors drag the confiscated goods up the cliff path to the customs house. A small crowd of Cornish villagers had begun to gather when Alfie and his accomplices came riding down onto the slipway.

"Patrick!" Alfie exclaimed, "Hey, I'm sorry, pard! I tried to warn you."

Patrick helped the crippled man dismount. "Alf, did you know about the *Sydenham*?"

"We knew something was afoot, just by accident. My boy overheard some talk last night. He was taking a shortcut home and heard two men talking about the *Serpent*. They moved on when they saw him coming though. Patrick, this is not the way it belongs to be! Somebody's ratted on you."

"Who were the men your son saw? Did he know them?"

"No, it was dark and he was scared. He never got a look at their faces. One of them used a cane. That's all he could say."

"Huh." O'Brien knew someone who used a cane. "Thanks, Alf. That is good to know."

A swelling crowd of villagers was making the Englishmen uneasy. Their officers barked at the crew to get that whiskey unloaded. As soon as the barrels were stowed in the customs house, the sailors beat it back to the *Sydenham*. Two of them stayed behind at the customs house. One kept a wary eye on the crowd while another hauled Sébastien into the building and tied him up. Snarling villagers immediately closed ranks. A couple of stones came hurtling out of nowhere. The Englishmen slammed the customs house door. They clanked a thick chain across it and buckled on a padlock the size of a dinner plate. Sébastien was inside, shut up like a criminal.

Making their way back to the *Sydenham*, the Englishmen had to run a gauntlet of fists and kicks, all the way down the path. When they finally climbed aboard their vessel, two guns on the deck of the *Sydenham* swiveled on their bases and were trained precisely on the door of the customs house up on the cliff. No one could go in or out without getting blown to pieces by the English. The crowd pulled back, out of firing range.

"Now ain't that a hell of a fix?"

"Look 'ere, can't we get in there, somehow, and get that boy out?"

"You miners know where to get some gunpowder, don't you? We could blast that place off the cliff."

"But the boy's in there, ya big dobeck!"

"Oh yeah."

"How 'bout tunneling in?"

"That's a pile of rock to get through."

"But what about all our whiskey? We invested good money in that, some of us did."

"We can't afford to lose that."

"Where is Cobbs, anyway?"

"Yeah, where is he? We paid him for a share of that cargo."

"They'll blow us to bits if we go near that door."

"Folks, let's gather at the inn," suggested Patrick O'Brien. "I have a plan."

A meeting at The Wink! Just the kind of suggestion the townspeople appreciated at one o'clock in the afternoon. This would give them a chance to drown their sorrows and rehash this issue. They could get themselves worked up good and proper, in true Cornish style. Just possibly, they would also get a few things straightened out.

When a crowd had collected inside, they huddled close and spoke in low voices.

"What do you have in mind, Pat?"

"Here's what I was thinking. The tide is high right now, correct? By evening it will have gone out."

Furtive eyes rolled sideways. The villagers shifted nervously.

"Well, Pat. That's pretty obvious."

"Uh, yes Pat. The tide will go out, like always."

The villagers squirmed and drained their glasses. Yi, these Irish! Was every one of 'em daft as a carrot half-scraped?

"All right Patrick, so what is your point? The tide will go out. But what will that aid?"

"Don't you see? The tide goes out, the water level goes down and the *Sydenham* will drop lower. Her guns will no longer be able to aim at the customs house. In fact, she will end up sitting on the bottom and just about helpless."

"That's when we shoot the lock off!"

"They'll see us, though."

"They'll pick us off with muskets."

"Yeah, Patrick. Who's going to stand there and shoot the lock off?"

"I think I've got that worked out," said Patrick. "First, we need someone to get a couple dozen tubmen down here tonight. Fast, strong men to carry those barrels out of here. And batsmen, a lot of them. After dark, they can hide behind the customs house and wait until we need them."

"Yeah! Yeah!" growled the villagers. "Fire their backsides off from the hill!"

"No, I don't think you'll have to shoot at them. They'll see they are outnumbered. I'll bet they back down. Can someone get John Trembath in here?"

"Sure, I'll go get him."

"Who's gonna have the guts to shoot that lock off, right in plain sight of customs?"

"I will," said Patrick.

Brows shot up and eyes rolled. Great hoddies, these Irishmen were.

$A$t two in the afternoon, Judge John Trembath came mincing down toward the wooden jetty, carefully avoiding piles of fish guts and ripe, smelly bait buckets.

"Permission to come aboard, sir," he said to the customs agent on board the *Sydenham*. "I wish to deliver a dinner invitation to your captain."

Another dinner invitation? Well, it had worked before.

Lord knows what they feed these Englishmen. Their own food must be dismal as dishwater because the invitation to dinner worked this time too. At five of the clock, a shiny red cabriolet transported the captain of the *Sydenham* to the home of Judge Trembath. They dined with Mrs. Trembath, John's little old mother. Two young, bright-eyed local ladies were also there, as was Patrick O'Brien.

Captain O'Brien was seated next to Mrs. Trembath. He was extremely affable. The English captain of the *Sydenham* was seated between the two young ladies who were as charming as any Englishman could desire. Judge Trembath helped smooth any hard feelings between Patrick O'Brien and the captain of the *Sydenham*, and thus the evening turned out to be quite pleasant. Entirely uneventful.

When the carriage returned the captain to his vessel at ten of the clock, he had some difficulty getting aboard because the *Sydenham* was barely afloat, her deck riding well below the jetty. The tide had indeed gone out and her mounted guns were now useless for protecting the customs house up on the cliff.

The men of his crew were shame-faced. They stuttered, they interrupted each other, trying to explain. There had been some developments, it seemed.

You should have seen, sir ... if you'd have been here ... it was really ... there were these big ... really big villagers... we tried, but ... um, nobody could ....

Well, here was the problem. The iron padlock on the door of the customs house was now hanging useless. Someone had walked right up to it and fired a pistol at it. They all heard it. Jonah had seen the scoundrel. It was that captain. Yes, Captain O'Brien. Jonah called to the crew for assistance. By the time they gathered on deck, there was a whole gang of men up at the customs house, led by Patrick O'Brien. Yes, they saw him. Sure, they all saw him, plain as day. He didn't even try to hide his face. It was O'Brien, all right.

The confiscated whiskey? Well, uh, you see, sir, they were carrying it off in six different directions, guarded by a whole regiment of men with clubs, very intimidating men. What could they have done? Some of those men had firearms. Another number of big, incredibly strong men simply heaved the tubs of whiskey over their shoulders and carried them away. Quicker than cockroaches. You never saw such strong men!

And, oh yes, one more thing. sir, about their prisoner, Sébastien Roland? Well, uh, he was, uh, set free. Yes sir, by that same outlaw. Who? Patrick O'Brien again? Yes, O'Brien!

All this before any of the dumbfounded Englishmen could fire a shot. No, nobody got off a shot. The muskets, they were all below. Well, no one had ordered them to get the muskets out.

*T*he next morning, when Judge Trembath drew up in front of his office in his red cabriolet, he got an earful of the whole fascinating tale from the English captain and his Collector of Customs, Lieutenant Merton. They were angry as a pair of vipers with their tails caught in the outhouse door on a sultry August day. They demanded restitution. They wanted someone's hide. They figured it should be Captain O'Brien's hide, and yet, that didn't make much sense.

"What?" cried the judge. "Who?"

"My dear Judge, I have never known this man to lie." The captain indicated Lieutenant Merton. "He says he is positive that before sunset last evening he saw Captain O'Brien up at that guard house with a pistol in his hand. The lock had been shot to pieces. Then Captain O'Brien stood there and watched while the people of your village stole confiscated goods. On top of that, O'Brien aided the criminal, Sébastien Roland, in his escape. I want to know how this happened. I insist on an explanation."

"You know very well it could not have been Captain O'Brien at that door."

"I'm absolutely sure it was, Judge Trembath," asserted Lieutenant Merton, huffing down his long nose. "We demand your cooperation."

"Gentlemen, I am as mystified as yourselves. Really, I am. I assure you that if I knew how Patrick O'Brien could be in two places at once, I would be happy to share that knowledge. Can you suggest how he could have done such a thing?"

"There has to be an explanation," cried the English captain. "My men saw what they saw!" The poor man was spitting in his anger.

"Sir," said Judge Trembath, turning to Lieutenant Merton, "may I ask you to repeat your version of events to my secretary? He will put down your entire story, word for word. In writing, on paper. We will get it all documented, all tickety-boo. We will get to the bottom of this and find out what's what. Come with me, if you please. His office is right this way." The judge tapped on an open door. "Mr. Ponk, would you please record this man's testimony of last night's proceedings down at the harbor? Give him all the time he needs. We don't want any inaccuracies." The judge ushered the Collector of Customs into Mr. Ponk's office, closed the door and returned to his desk.

"Now, Captain, I ask you. Did O'Brien sit across the table from you in my home all last evening, or did he not?"

"Well, he did but I ... I don't know what to say."

"May I make one little point, Captain? Might your crew have been deceived? Are you quite sure they were entirely sober last night? I was told that they made short work of an anonymous donation of a keg of ale."

"I don't ... Ale?"

"That raises a question, doesn't it? Their captain was gone, they were drinking, and one thing led to another. We can't rule out the possibility of, shall we say, confusion on the part of your crew." The judge stared at the captain from under his impressive eyebrows.

"Judge, there was no confusion. I can vouch for my men!"

"Can you really? But what was the talk I heard this morning? Something about carousing and tomfoolery going on down in the harbor last night. Some rather boisterous singing of English drinking songs. I would hate for word of that to get any farther."

"Whauhg, ahem, gauhg!" choked the English captain. "I don't need to tell you, Judge, that ... but, well, I am certain that they ... surely ...."

"My point is that you can hardly expect me to incarcerate a man who, we know for a fact, was not where your crew said he was. Now I say, Captain, is that reasonable?"

"But ...!"

"Captain O'Brien was with us. We know this for a fact, sir. Ir-re-futable."

"But Judge! How am I going to explain this to my superiors?"

"You will have to tell them the *Serpent* slipped your grasp. It is as simple as that. She slipped your grasp in spite of every effort to detain her." The judge rose and unlocked a small cabinet behind his desk. "Please, my dear Captain, trouble yourself no more about this. You'll ruin your digestion. And we can work everything out, I assure you. Let me set your mind at ease. May I offer you a tot of this quite superior whiskey? It's beautifully aged. I think you'll like it."

The judge poured a small glass for the captain and one for himself. Small glasses because it was only mid-morning and didn't they both still have a day's work ahead of them? Small glasses, too, because he was jealously guarding his supply of this excellent whiskey. He had received only part of a tub, just last night. Not as a gift, mind you. Nor a bribe. Nothing of the sort! It was payment for honest services rendered. Besides, Judge Trembath reminded himself, he had taken some risk, a significant measure of personal risk, and had earned this whiskey fairly. He chuckled silently, swirled his drink and sniffed appreciatively.

Yes, he thought as he sipped, last night's dinner had been most profitable. How Patrick O'Brien had managed to be in two places at once was completely mystifying. The less one pondered the imponderables, the better, but still, how had he pulled that off?

$S$ébastien Roland had only recently found the answer to this mystery himself. The previous evening, after the customs house raiders had seen the casks of whiskey off into the night, no one could figure out where Sébastien had gone. As a matter of fact, only two others knew he was sitting beside a fire in a comfortable home near Penzance. He was toasting his third slice bread and cheese, when he heard a rhythmic knock on the door.

"Yo, James?" said a quiet voice outside.

"Finish eating, Sébastien. I'll get the door. It's Pat."

"What about ye, James," said Patrick O'Brien.

"I'm grand, Brother!" replied James, hugging him in greeting. "All went well on your end?"

O'Brien strode swiftly through the door and closed it. "All went perfectly, so far. We'll get the full story from the local gossips by morning. Here is your share of the goods, and thank you for your help."

"Thank you. It was an easy night's work. You have had supper, have you, Pat? I'm glad because I don't have a lot to offer you. Sébastien is eating me out of house and home."

Sébastien grinned and chewed another bite. "Patrick!" he exclaimed. "You never told me!"

"About James? He is my best-kept secret. How long did it take you to figure it out?"

"We were half-way to Penzance before he finally set me straight."

"A twin comes in handy at times like this."

"I can hardly tell you two apart," said Sébastien. "I'm sure you've heard that before."

"Only for donkey's years," sighed James.

"If we had a French *sous* for every time," said Pat "we'd be rich as Croesus. We have deceived many an innocent soul and we're not a bit sorry."

"We'll deceive the Devil, too, when the time comes, I hope," James added.

"Keep this to yourself, though, will you Bastien, the fact that I have a twin? For now, at least."

"Aye, I may have to rescue Patrick again someday," said James.

"No one will hear of it from me. But Pat, I can't figure out how the Revenue men knew exactly where to look for that whiskey when they boarded us. Do you think we have a snitch?"

"There's a squealer somewhere." Patrick pulled a chair close to the fire. "We're going to have to smoke him out."

"You sold all the barrels?" asked James.

"Except for the one that you and Judge Trembath are sharing. I'll hear some nasty words from Cobbs about giving that one away."

"That plonker!"

"He'll claim we are stealing his profits."

"What can he expect? You had to do something to get your merchandise back, and he wasn't around to help."

"The thing that mystifies me is why they insisted on arresting Bastien. Did you insult someone's mother or something, laddie?"

"I've been wracking my brains, Pat." Sébastien shook his head. "I can't think why they wanted me. I was kind of scared there for a bit."

"I imagine you were. You know, I've been thinking, Bastien." Patrick put his elbows on his knees and stared at the fire for a moment. "We've both been working for Cobbs for a long time. What do you say we start making an exit plan?"

"Are you serious? We'll have to leave Cornwall. Cobbs will cause no end of trouble."

"Maybe not. If we settle in some place up the coast a ways, I don't think he'll bother us much. Why should he? I thought the Lizard Peninsula would suit us. We'd be far enough away from Cobbs and not too far from Penzance. James and I don't like to be separated."

"The Lizard?" Sébastien couldn't sit still. He got up to wander about the room. "Some nice little harbors there. But we have no money."

"I've saved some money. I've been doing some business for myself on the side now and again. You should join me. And James says he would give us a loan. He's one of these rich solicitors with pots of money, don't you know."

"Cobbs may try to make trouble," said James. "You've got to protect yourselves."

"He's gotten free labor from Bastien for years!" said Patrick.

"True, and legally speaking, he doesn't have a leg to stand on. As long as you keep yourselves financially sound, he might be a bit of a nuisance, but nothing more. Just don't borrow any money from him."

"A boat," mused Patrick. "We'll need our own boat."

$T$o the east of Penzance, the Lizard Peninsula juts out into the Channel and forms the edge of Mounts Bay. Patrick O'Brien borrowed a fishing boat one day and sailed out from Penzance, across the bay and toward the high, sheer cliffs of the Lizard. The coast here bristled with rocks, each one long known by name. The Nanchisick Rocks, the tall tower that was Steeple Rock, curiosities like the Post Office, where a piece of paper could disappear, sucked into a natural slit in the rock, and be forcefully blown back out a minute later. And everywhere along the coast of south Cornwall were the very dangerous submerged rocks, like The Manacles or the Runnelstone.

Cautiously O'Brien worked his boat around the bare island of Ennis Bronnow. He avoided the deadly Tregwyn rocks, where many a ship had foundered, and swung into Mullion Cove, guarded by tall black cliffs. The fierce sea burst endlessly over Ennis Bronnow but on the sheltered side, O'Brien watched a couple of carefree boys diving into the surf. He beached the small boat on the sand and stood looking speculatively at the hamlet of Mullion Cove. A river fell off the downs here and cut deeply into the rock, providing power for a small mill and forming a steep green valley where a handful of houses clung like barnacles. Crammed into the dark cliffs, so close to the sea that its windows were often sprayed with saltwater, was a small house known for two hundred years as the Net Loft. This was Patrick O'Brien's destination.

The Net Loft was a tiny gray stone cottage with its back turned to the sea. Its two front windows faced across the cove toward the houses scattered on the hillside. It had weathered intact more storms than any jetty or dock that had ever been built in Mullion Cove. Indeed, wedged against the rocks, it was almost part of the cliff itself.

Patrick O'Brien side-stepped the old lobster traps that had been left lying on the stone steps. He stood at the front door and looked back towards the heath, all a-bloom on this warm July afternoon. He pulled the tangy salt air deep into his lungs. He didn't even have to go inside to know he had finally found himself a home. As boys, he and his twin brother had been passed from one relative to another after their mother died, never in one place for long. The Net Loft would be his anchorage, a place of his own, his first since he and James were six years old. He would bring Sébastien here, if he wanted to come. He would buy a big table and some chairs. Maybe they could find a sheltered spot to grow a few vegetables. They would moor their own boat, when they found one, in the cove.

A house by the sea and a boat. All that was needed to make any Irishman happy.

The *Prelude*

*I*t took them only a few months to find her. A cutter, she sat demurely in the river while they admired her beautiful lines, her long bowsprit. With a shape like that, she could almost take flight. All you had to do was wish it. She was all they could want. She rode serenely at her mooring and promised them everything. Unfortunately it was a fairly inopportune moment for them to be looking at boats. They had just been chased clear across the Channel by the king's men and were now running the *Serpent* up the Helford River. The king's men were still in hot pursuit.

"Those ruddy Englishmen still back there?" asked Patrick.

"They are," replied Sébastien, "but they should be scraping bottom soon."

"We'll have plenty of time to unload up the river farther. They'll have to wait hours before both the tide and the wind change so they can get themselves turned around."

"Why haven't they figured out that their square-riggers don't have a chance in these rivers?"

The small fore-and-aft rigged boats that smugglers favored could sail in almost any wind, in almost any direction. The big square-riggers had to have the wind behind them, so had little choice of direction.

Sébastien and Patrick took a last look at their new love before they passed her.

"She's a fine-looking vessel, don't you think, Pat?"

"I think that's our boat!"

"But no fisherman in his right mind would part with her."

"That particular fisherman has already parted with her. It's Tom Tior's cutter. As it happens, he himself has departed. They found him dead off the Manacles this past winter, frozen to the seat of a fishing dory."

"Terrible."

"I say, Pat! How far are you going?" called the spotsman. "The Revenue boat ran aground a mile back."

"Sorry, Phin. We got distracted," Patrick called. He took one more backward look at the cutter and spoke softly to Sébastien. "After we finish unloading, let's go talk to his widow."

"I forgot, for a minute, that we have business here."

"Important business. Part of this cargo is the start of our down payment on a boat."

"You're getting my hopes up, Pat."

"Not a word to anyone about our venture, though. Trust no one, Sébastien. Ha! I can't believe I'm saying that to you, of all people."

$W$idow Tior had a brood of five children. She held a bouncing toddler on her lap while she snapped beans into a bowl. She badly needed the money the cutter might bring, but hadn't yet had an offer she could consider. She had to demand a high price for Tom's boat. She simply had no choice. She had rent to pay. The cutter was the only thing she owned that she could sell and she meant to make the most of it.

Patrick shook his head when she told him the price.

"We don't have that kind of money, Mrs. Tior," Patrick told her. "But if you are willing to let us pay in installments, over time we'll promise to give you more than you're asking."

She frowned and chewed her lip. "How much more?"

Patrick named a figure. She wanted twice that. He scratched his head and looked at Sébastien.

"Tell you what. We'll meet you halfway between your price and ours, Mrs. Tior. We'll give you a down payment and we'll also hire your boy there when he's old enough. That will give you a small income. Will that help?"

"You would hire Timmy?" Her son looked up at the mention of his name. "You wouldn't be sorry. He can sail rings around most men already and he's only thirteen years old. He knows the whole coast of the Lizard, east and west."

"Can he take us out for a trial run?"

Timmy's dark eyes were troubled. He looked hard at his mother. She was sending him away? How could she do this to him? No, he knew why she did it. He knew precisely why she did it. She couldn't stand to look at him anymore.

"You'll give Tim a fair wage?"

"A good wage for good work."

"You'll find none better than my Timmy." She wiped her cheeks with her handkerchief. "I don't want you to take my husband's cutter nor my boy, but it must be done. So I think, Mr. O'Brien, we are close to a deal."

"You drive a hard bargain, Mrs. Tior. Your husband would be proud."

Timmy said not a word. He had earned this punishment, deserved even worse.

Tim Tior was indeed well-acquainted with the coast of the Lizard. He took no pride in his knowledge. He had grown up under the influence of his father's passion for sailing and fishing, for reading the clouds and winds, for predicting the smallest changes in a moody sea. The man felt the tides in his bones. The slightest breeze along the back of his neck forewarned him of changes in the weather, though ironically his knowledge did not save him in the end. He had been caught by a southwesterly with snow on its back and never made it to shore alive.

But Timmy was a creature of the earth, not the sea. To be in the woods in sunshine or rain, that was his idea of contentment. The smells of the forest, the heavy scent of damp wood, the sensations of trees reaching deep down into the moist soil for nourishment. Tim's fascination was with the land, not the sky and sea. He loved to build. He had built little forts and towns out of sticks and wood chips since childhood. In his father's eyes, he had been a grave disappointment. Tim knew that. Now that his father was gone, it was a judgment Tim could do nothing to change.

He lived with another guilt, a worse guilt. It haunted him, sleeping and waking. His father had been angry at him that last day, too angry to ask Tim to go out with him in the dory. He was going to fish the Stag Rocks off the Lizard and he could have used Timmy's help. But Tim would not yield, not unless his father gave him an outright order. So his father sailed alone. Tim could shelter under the excuse that maybe he and his father both would have died that day, but that thought brought him no comfort. Tim knew he would feel this pain forever. It would have been better for everyone if they had both died.

*I*n October, Patrick O'Brien took possession of the Tior's cutter and they brought her into Mullion Cove. They could work on her here from time to time. It wasn't too far from Lamorna, but hopefully far enough that Cobbs would not bother them. They winched her ashore and set to work on her. Patrick O'Brien handed Tim a bucket of paint.

"Black?" So far, Tim had been rather sullen with them so far. But he had to ask about the black paint.

"She'll have a black hull and two sets of sails, black and white both."

"That will cost you some."

"We'll order them as we can afford them. Black for night raids, white for day."

"You'll be working the free trade then?"

"That's the plan, Tim. Does that bother you, the smuggling?"

"My pa was dead against it. Said it harmed the local merchants."

"That it does, somewhat. He was right. On the other hand, many of the locals rely on the merchandise we bring them."

"Always seemed to me that we Tiors were the poorest people on the river. Other men made lots of money doing the odd smuggling job."

"What did your mother think?"

"Some days, in winter, she couldn't even put food on the table. It didn't seem right to her, to make us go without. But Pa was stubborn."

"Your mother has been through a lot. She's a good woman. We'll have to make sure that she is well taken care of."

Tim stopped painting and looked at Patrick, his dark eyes somber. His voice was husky when he answered. "I'd appreciate that, sir."

"Pat. Call me Pat."

## 1804

*I*t was to be several months before the black hulled boat was launched. Patrick and Sébastien continued to invest in night raids on other ships, unbeknownst to Cobbs. In the meantime, Tim Tior made a proposal.

He and Sébastien were kneeling on the deck of the boat one afternoon, installing new brass cleats. Tim's dark, curly head nearly bumped Sébastien's fair one. Sébastien wished he could get the boy to open up, to talk a little. He never spoke to them, except to answer a question.

Sébastien sat back and brushed his hair out of his face. "Do you think your father would be proud to see his cutter in new paint?" he asked Tim.

"He wasn't much into looks," replied Tim. "But it's a shame, if you ask me, how he let her go."

"Well, she was a working boat."

"Still, it wouldn't go amiss to fix her combing."

"Here, around the cockpit?"

"Yes. And around the lights. See here? It's leaking bad, all around this porthole. The deck fastenings need to be tightened down, and the hatches don't close properly."

"Yes, you're right."

"She'd be all right for coasting but if you're going to cross the Channel, all that should be taken care of."

"I guess we'd better tell Patrick."

"I could work on her, repair her real nice."

"It's tedious work."

"No, I'd really like it. I've got some ideas for hidden cubbyholes too, in case there is cargo you don't want the king's men to know about."

"If you're willing, Tim, it would be a fine thing to have you do some of that work. You must like carpentry."

"I've been wanting to mention these things, but I didn't know how you'd take it."

"I'm glad that you spoke up, finally. You've hardly said two words together since I've known you. And Tim!" Sébastien pretended to study Tim's face. "What's happened?"

Tim ran his hand over his jaw. "What?"

"You're smiling!"


*F*inally the cutter's launch day was coming near. Tim, Sébastien and Patrick were sitting on the deck sharing a lunch of bread and smoked fish.

"She's a proud-looking ship," said Patrick. "You've done great work on her, Tim. All she needs now is a name. One that spells the same in French and English, like the *Serpent*."

"Actually," said Tim, "she's not quite finished. I want to reinforce that rib that got damaged a couple of years ago. I need to find a long piece of oak."

"I know where you can get oak," said Sébastien. "I know someone who owns an entire forest of oak."

Tim stood up. "Let's go. Can we?"

*T*he three of them left their cart on Narrow Lane and turned down the alley by the little chapel in Porthcoombe. They threaded their way through the piles of carefully stacked wood.

"This looks more like a lumber yard than a cooperage," said Pat.

"But smell!" exclaimed Tim, enchanted. He sniffed at the sweet, smoky scent of heating oak.

They entered Santino Mesola's shop. Santino pulled a barrel off the fire and stretched a hand to Sébastien.

"I'm so pleased to see you again!"

"Santino, these are my friends Patrick O'Brien and … where's Tim?"

Tim Tior stood across the room, gazing raptly at the orderly procession of tools all along one wall of Santino's shop. He turned, hearing his name.

"Tim?"

"Oh, I … sorry," Tim stammered. He hurried over to shake Santino's hand, then turned to Patrick. "I was just thinking."

"I wondered what you were doing," said Patrick.

"I'm thinking about barrels."

"I see. I wonder what put you in mind of barrels in a cooperage?"

"Well, I was thinking about tubs, really." They waited while Tim's eyes came back into focus. "Slimmer tubs. To fit into those cubby holes. I could learn to make them." He turned quickly to Santino. "Maybe."

Patrick and Sébastien smiled.

Sébastien explained to Santino. "Tim gets a little cakey when he gets too close to a piece of raw wood."

Santino turned to Tim, his eyes eager. "You are a cooper?" he asked him.

"Me? Oh no. I wish I could do this. But no."

"I could certainly use help here, if you were interested."

Tim stepped closer. "I could help you."

"No! Tino, please! You're not going to steal our spotsman!" cried Sébastien.

Tim's brow furrowed. He looked from Sébastien to Patrick, his mouth hanging open.

They stared back at him, alarmed.

"Oh no, Tim. Don't be playin' the maggot, please, I beg ye!" Patrick threw up his hands in mock despair. "Look at him. We've lost him, Bastien."

"Say good-bye to our spotsman," said Sébastien.

Tim was still speechless. Was this happening? He didn't deserve this kind of luck.

Patrick turned to Tino with false belligerence. "Are you going to pay him as much as we give him?" he asked Tino.

Tino shrugged. "He'll have to take apprentice's wages for at least a couple of years."

"You hear that, Tim? You'll earn next to nothing. You still want to work for this cheapskate?"

A slow grin spread across Tim's face. "You'll take me on, Mr. Tino?"

"I have been desperate for help." Santino Mesola clapped his hands. He raised his arms over his head and danced in a circle. "When I wished for an apprentice, I ended up with a baby. Then a fiancée."

"It's true then? You and Bianca are going to be married?" asked Patrick.

"Yes we are."

"Very good!"

"But now I finally get my first wish! An apprentice! How many blessings is a man allowed?"

"You have probably about reached your limit, Tino."

Santino broke into an exuberant bellow of Italian song. Sébastien and Patrick laughed.

"You're having second thoughts about working with this madman, aren't you, Tim?" Sébastien asked. "Are you sure you aren't better off with us?"

Tim shuffled his feet, turned a half-circle and cleared his throat nervously. "Maybe he looks the madman to you." He grinned crookedly. "To me, it's kind of the other way round."

Patrick and Sébastien looked at each other.

"Is he calling us madmen?" asked Patrick.

"Us? Naw. Did you ever hear me singing Italian songs?"

"Not on your nelly."

"Do you even know any Italian songs?"

"Nary a one. Now if it's an Irish lullaby you're wanting, maybe I could manage one."

"Singing in Italian," Sébastien shook his head, "that's the first sign of madness, they say."

"There you go, then. That proves it. There's nothing remotely wrong with us."


*O*n a Saturday in the spring, Santino loaded his cart with barrels as he did every Saturday afternoon, but this time several of them were full instead of empty. Bianca took the seat next to Tino as she always did now, with Emilia on her lap. Every week they delivered barrels to Santino's relatives near Market Jew Street in Penzance. They always spent Saturday night there. On Sunday mornings the whole family attended mass. Tino's relatives had built a small private Catholic chapel, since there were no other Catholics near Porthcoombe. They enjoyed a big family dinner after mass and were back home by Sunday evening. On this trip, however, they took Tim Tior with them, dressed in his new Sunday clothes. He squeezed in between barrels at the back of the cart. Some of those barrels were packed with sausages and cheeses, smoked fish, large boxes of pasties, three loaves of Tino's special bread and four spice cakes. And this time they didn't stop in Penzance. They drove past and went on around the bay to Mullion Cove.

The roads that crossed the downs on the Lizard peninsula were little more than rough tracks through farmland, used mostly for getting livestock to market in Penzance. The ruts and bumps were so large, it was easier to walk beside the wagon. It was pleasant, though, a mild day in spring. They could almost hear the tinkle of fairy music from the pink and lilac bells of Cornish heath, and the air was full of the dancing flight of stone chats. The flat sea was a-glitter beyond Old Lizard Head, reflecting the blue that arched from one horizon to the other. As they neared the edge of the cliff above Mullion Cove, the wail of Patrick O'Brien's Irish bagpipes welcomed them.

From the steep cliff path, they had their first view of Patrick's ancient stone cottage. In his front garden, he had set up a long make-shift table and readied it for a feast. He had invited what few neighbors there were in Mullion Cove, as well as friends from Lamorna. Mrs. Tior came, and all Tim's brothers and sisters. Sébastien had sent a note to Edmund Gwennel, the first friend he had made when he went to work in the mines. When Sébastien caught sight of Edmund picking his way down the cliff path, he ran to greet him like a long-lost brother.

This was to be an important day, a very important day, and Patrick and Sébastien were as frenzied as new parents. It was to be the launch of the *Prelude*. For them, the day also marked the end of their years with Zephaniah Cobbs.

The *Prelude* had spent months in the cradle. Her decks had been refurbished and her brightwork polished. She had two new sets of sails. In the eyes of her owners, she was the most magnificent vessel afloat. She was their new beginning, their freedom and, hopefully, their prosperity. Seeing her elegant black hull slide smoothly into the waters of the cove, there was no question in anyone's mind that she would fulfill their every hope.

*A* few days after the launching celebration they sailed her into Lamorna. Sébastien was tense.

"Let's not sail the *Prelude* to Lamorna, Patrick. I can't face having Cobbs find out about her. I don't want him even looking at her."

"We have nothing to fear from Cobbs. We will deal honestly with him and we'll expect him to do the same with us now."

When Patrick walked up to Mr. Cobbs's office to give notice that they were working for themselves now, Sébastien could not bring himself to go along. He hung around the harbor, hands in pockets. He was actually trembling. He paced up and down the wooden jetty, anxiously watching for Patrick's return. It seemed like forever, but it was only a matter of minutes before he saw Patrick come out and close the office door.

"You got away with life and limb?"

"He seemed to take it in stride."

"Really?"

"I expected much worse."

"He didn't threaten you or …?"

"Don't worry about him. Relax, Bastien."

"He'll get some kind of revenge on us. He won't go away, Pat."

"Maybe he won't. But we'll deal with him, whatever happens."

Up in his office above the harbor, Cobbs pulled away from the window before he could be seen. He snatched up an oil lamp but at the last second he came to his senses and thought better of throwing it. He stalked around his desk, quivering like a twanging bowstring. His fists clenched, his face convulsed, he let out a soundless scream of rage, then collapsed against a cabinet, massaging his oversize moustache with a shaking finger.

He hadn't been paying close enough attention. He had let things slide. Now they were taking advantage of him. Always, everybody trying to be better than him, not one single person offering him a shred of loyalty. Someone forever trying to stab him in the gut.

Good. He should be glad, really. This was a warning. He should have been more vigilant. From now on, he would be on his guard.

Yes, he would turn this to his benefit. He would make them pay. Besides, he hadn't had a really nasty fight in ages. He was ready. Yes, he was.

$S$ ébastien had given Bianca a wedding gift earlier that spring.

"Sébastien, what is this? It's heavy."

"Well, sit down and open it."

She did, with eager fingers. Yards of French lace cascaded to the floor.

"Sébastien!"

"It's for a gown to wear on your wedding day."

"It's too much! Oh, *merci, merci! Comme je t'adore!*" She stretched her arms and he bent to hug her.

"*C'est rien, cherie.* You deserve it. Where would I have been without you?"

Bianca sewed every day for weeks before her wedding. She had enough lace left over to put a bit of trim on a new dress for Emilia, and on the dress worn by their neighbor's daughter, pretty little Elizabeth Campion. Since there was no Catholic church in Porthcoombe, Santino's large, jolly cousin, Father Giacomo, would marry them in Santino's garden beneath the fruit trees. This allowed Santino the liberty of asking the entire village to attend, in true Italian style.

Not one family stayed away. That foreigner, Mesola, they sputtered, he's finally getting married. 'Course, he could have found a nice girl in the village a long time ago, but no, no one here would do for him. You'd never see him join the men for a pint, neither. But he had all kinds of time, notice you, to visit his Eye-talian relatives every Sabbath. Them foreigners, everyone knows how they shut good people out. And as for that snooty Frenchwoman he was throwing himself away on, that Bianca, well! Never would a body get more than a word or two out of that one.

But turn down the invitation to the wedding? They weren't daft! How could they stay away?

When the ceremony began and little Elizabeth Campion led the way between the trees, with her lace-trimmed dress and her basket of rose petals, the Cornish ladies stared. Their mouths were little flower buds, squeezed so tightly closed that no reluctant "Oh!" could escape. But their jaws dropped at the sight of the radiant Bianca. She took their collective breaths away, as did her pale blue gown peeking beneath a French lace overdress.

Merciful heavens. They all agreed later it was a bit overdone. I mean you had to admit it was too much, didn't you? Yes, everyone thought so. Would you have worn something like that to your wedding? Even to your funeral? Well I should think not. And you could trust the French, couldn't you just, to get carried away like that? Fancy fancy fancy! What was she thinking, all that lace? That she was the Queen of England or someone?

But on the other hand, that tall, handsome Sébastien standing beside Santino, he was a picture now, wasn't he? Several of the village mothers were only pretending to heed the priest droning on and on with his Roman Catholic mumbo jumbo. They were too busy struggling with arithmetic.

Thumbs surreptitiously tapped fingers, assisting the tallying of years. How close in age was her eldest daughter to that French boy? Actually, her second daughter was by far their prettiest. Looked like her mother, she did. Like her mother used to, before the six children. Ah yes, her second daughter might win Sébastien's heart. And borrow that lace overdress herself in a year or so. Two years at most. By the end of the ceremony, each mother very privately discovered something a little disconcerting. Private because, heaven forbid, it was hardly a thing a body could admit out loud. SHH! It might not be impossible to tolerate one Frenchman in the family. Just the one, mind you. Especially such a good-looking Frenchman. And they say he owns his own boat already. Fifteen years old and he owns a boat! Yes, he'd be good for our daughter. That Mary Trembath only thinks she has gotten her claws into him. Look how he stares at our girl! Just think, a wedding in our church. A year from now, two at the most.

*T*hat fall, Patrick O'Brien answered a knock at the door of the Net Loft, his cottage in Mullion Cove.

"Tom! Come in! What brings you here?"

Tom Ickes ducked over the threshold. "Is Sébastien around, Pat? I have a rather strange request for him."

"Yes, he's out in the back. He is determined to get an old weathervane working for the roof. Go on out. He'll be pleased to see you."

"Perhaps not, when he hears what I have to say."

Outside, Sébastien jumped up and extended a hand to Tom Ickes. "Mr. Ickes!"

"You were going to call me Tom, remember? How are you, Sébastien? I haven't seen you since Miss LeFronde's wedding."

"I'm doing well, thanks. And you?"

"Well, things are changing at Tregorna Farm. I was telling Pat that I have a rather strange favor to ask of you."

"Anything, Mr. — Tom."

"It seems that Mrs. Pawley is dying, Sébastien. I know that is hardly sad news for you. But, believe it or not, she is asking to see you."

"Me?"

"It is strange, isn't it? But she is a strange woman. She wants to redeem herself, I think, before she goes to her Maker."

"How she goes to her Maker is entirely her problem, not mine. She can go to the devil for all I care."

"She is pretty upset, Sébastien. If you saw how tortured she is, you would take pity."

"Never."

"She was a demon, I'll grant you that. I know she caused you a lot of pain in the past."

"When I think of how much misery she ...."

"Those memories can haunt you forever. Believe me, I know," Tom Ickes interrupted.

"She and Cobbs ruined our lives, Bianca's and mine."

Tom Ickes looked around. He gazed out at the harbor, turquoise blue in the fall sunshine. Fat vegetables sunned themselves in the garden and geraniums overflowed their pots. He scratched his head. "I don't know. It doesn't look to me like your life is completely ruined."

"No thanks to her!" Sébastien turned his back on Tom Ickes.

"The hurts will stream away like a river, Sébastien, if you let them go."

A sudden breeze from the sea spilled into the garden. For some reason, it made Sébastien think of his long-dead father and mother. A breeze, a garden in Paris. He turned, frowning, looking at Tom but lost in a tangle of black thoughts.

Tom bit his lip, hesitating. "Miss LeFronde is waiting in my carriage."

"Don't tell me Bianca is going to Tregorna."

"Yes, she is." Tom waited for Sébastien to wrestle with that idea. Then he added "Mr. Cobbs won't be there. He left for France as soon as he saw how it was with Mrs. Pawley."

"What a prince."

The back door of the cottage opened and Bianca stepped into the garden. Her face was drawn and grave. The three of them stood silent, Sébastien's stomach tightening into a knot. Bianca gestured and, with a sigh, he slumped toward her.

$A$s Tregorna Farm rose across the moor, Bianca and Sébastien gripped each other's hands. Ten years had passed since they had first come up this road in an ox cart. Little had changed about the place, except that the building that had been used as a dormitory had finally fallen down. Tom Ickes pulled into Tregorna's lane and sat for a minute. They stared at the kitchen door. Then he turned to them.

"You won't be sorry you came. Mrs. Pawley did some unkind things …."

"Many," interrupted Sébastien. "Many unkind things."

"But she wants to feel, at the end, that some one or two of you can forgive her. At least a couple, of all the people who passed through here. It was wrong of her, doing the things she did. But for you to ignore her now, to leave this undone," he shook his head, "you would regret it."

Bianca lifted her face. "You know, there is a philosopher, Marcus Aurelius, …."

Tom Ickes looked surprised. "That's right. You've heard of him?"

"*Meditations* is one of my favorites."

"Until I came across that book, I was … well, it changed a lot of things for me." Tom Ickes got out of the carriage and offered Bianca his hand. She hesitated, wondering about this man who had been such a quiet influence in their lives.

Tom Ickes led the way and held the creaky old kitchen door.

They entered. Like a blow to the midriff, the smell of that room instantly brought back memories for them.

"Mrs. Pawley's room is upstairs."

He led them up a dirty staircase. The treads squawked with every step. They paused nervously at the top. Mrs. Pawley was in a tiny bare room at the back of the house, servants' quarters with no hint of comfort.

She lay on a narrow cot. Bianca drew an involuntary breath when she saw the woman. She was stretched out on top of the covers, wearing a light blue suit of very fine material. Not only was it much too big for her. It was also so much more elegant than anything they had ever seen her wear, that Sébastien could only describe it as grotesque. He didn't recognize the clothes. Bianca did. She had worn that suit when they arrived in Cornwall. Mrs. Pawley had taken away all her beautiful clothes and Bianca had never seen them again. Why did she want to wear these clothes now? What possessed her? Did she feel so desperately unprepared for her next journey that she could not travel as herself, Mrs. Pawley from Tregorna Farm? Now, at the end, was she wishing she had been someone or something else?

What fixed Sébastien's stare were the old woman's hands. She clutched his mother's garnet rosary.

Tom Ickes went to the bedside, bent low and spoke in a very loud voice. "Did the priest come today, Mrs. Pawley?"

She nodded slightly and looked at him uneasily. Cornwall was almost entirely Protestant. Now, at the last, she had been forced to tell Tom Ickes something she had never had the courage to admit, that she was different from everyone else. She was

Catholic. It was Tom that had arranged for a priest to come, the first she had seen in thirty years.

"You remember Miss LeFronde and Sébastien Roland?"

Slowly she turned her head. Her troubled eyes sought theirs. She nodded again, her face pinched with pain. Had she asked to see them because they too were Catholic? They would understand, or feel a bond? Or forgive?

Bianca drew closer to the bed. "You look very pretty, Mrs. Pawley," she said loudly. She brushed a lock of white hair from the woman's face. Mrs. Pawley grasped her hand and held it to her cheek, her eyes closed, her head shaking no, no. Bianca looked up at Tom, distressed and confused.

"Mrs. Pawley," Tom Ickes raised his voice and leaned over the bed. "Aren't you glad to have these nice visitors?" He hesitated. "We don't know when Mr. Cobbs will be able to visit you. He is far away."

Mrs. Pawley began to weep. Then she stretched her hand like an old claw toward Sébastien. He looked at that hand in horror.

"Sébastien," Bianca whispered.

He was paralyzed.

"Sébastien. Everything is only for a day," said Bianca, softly.

Damn Marcus Aurelius. Sébastien took a step toward the bed. His hand came up awkwardly to his chest. He could not bring himself to reach out.

Mrs. Pawley dropped her hand. He stood stiffly, making no move. With difficulty, she untangled her fingers from his mother's rosary and lifted it toward him. Did she remember it had been his?

Something broke inside him and his eyes filled with tears. He moved closer to the bed and touched her hand with his fingertips. He touched his mother's rosary. He fingered the garnets, set in gold. Then he laid her hand and the rosary back on her breast. He patted her arm and nodded. He could not get any words out. His throat was too tight. Mrs. Pawley sighed and closed her eyes.

After a time, Tom Ickes leaned down and kissed the old lady's forehead. They turned quietly and went out.

They got into the carriage in heavy silence. Tom Ickes turned the horse and stopped. They sat looking at the old house again.

"Thank you, Sébastien, Miss LeFronde."

"I'm Mrs. Mesola now, Tom."

"Yes of course. Sorry. Thank you both for coming today." He paused. "She was in love with him. Did you know?"

"Who?"

"Mrs. Pawley was entirely devoted to Cobbs. I think she was jealous of you, Sébastien. You got more attention from him than she did."

Jealous of him? Warm feelings for that monster? No, he had never realized. The thought would never have occurred to him. What a strange world this was.

Bianca was thinking the same. She wondered, too, what peculiar force held Tom Ickes to Tregorna Farm and its bizarre occupants. What a strange world indeed.

The next day they each received a note from Tom Ickes, saying Mrs. Pawley had died last evening.

"*O*h?" said Zephaniah Cobbs when he returned from France. He was busy with the evening paperwork. Tom Ickes was trying to tell him about Mrs. Pawley passing away. "Ah. That is most inconvenient."

"You'll miss her, I know, Mr. Cobbs."

"You are going to have to take over her laundry chores, Ickes, until one of the girls is free. I must have clean shirts. You will have to brush my wool clothing each day. Polish my boots."

"I'm sorry, Mr. Cobbs. I can barely take care of my own laundry. You will have to hire someone."

"What? You expect me to pay someone?"

Tom Ickes chuckled. "Mrs. Pawley saved you a lot of money over the years."

"That's right. Mrs. Pawley was not greedy. She never asked for a farthing. Of course I supplied her with everything she needed."

"You were most fortunate to have her."

"This is most inconvenient," Cobbs said again. He put his pen on the inkstand and frowned at Tom Ickes. "Honestly, Ickes. I don't understand why you can't take care of this for me. After all I have done for you."

"One more thing, Mr. Cobbs. I took some money out of the account for Mrs. Pawley's burial plot and the grave-digger. Also the ...."

"You what?" Cobbs exploded. "I did not authorize you to charge me for any of that."

"Mrs. Pawley had no money."

"You should have had her buried in a pauper's grave. Ickes! What the devil were you thinking, man? You have completely over-stepped here." Cobbs reached his cane across his desk and tried to whack Tom Ickes.

Tom side-stepped it. "You don't think you owed her at least that much, after she served you for all those years?"

"That is not the point! You are out of line, Ickes. I am going to take these expenses out of your pay. With interest! That will teach you to be so free with my money. I ought to have you horse-whipped. That's what I ought to do. A cemetery plot?"

"And a coffin and a small stone. And the priest."

"You are dangerously close to losing your job, sirrah!"

Ickes looked at Cobbs without a trace of concern.

"Do you understand what I am saying, Ickes? One more misstep and you will leave my employ."

"I understand, Mr. Cobbs."

"You bloody well better understand. I mean what I say." Cobbs stared at Tom Ickes. His stare turned murderous when he saw that Tom Ickes neither flinched nor looked away.

1806

*T*wo years went by. Bianca Mesola gave birth to a little girl, Violetta. Napoleon was storming through Europe and free-traders in Cornwall were taking full and very profitable advantage of the turmoil. Tim Tior and Santino had doubled the output of the cooperage, supplying his cousins with enough barrels to ship gunpowder to the Italians who were battling Napoleon's troops.

And Sébastien Roland had made enough money to buy a run-down shipyard in Cawsands.

"I'm going to live above the office until I can buy a decent house, a big house. A mansion," Sébastien told Patrick. "I'll make sure there is plenty of room for you too."

"I prefer my little cottage here. But thanks. Why do you want a big house?"

"I don't know. Maybe I'll buy a title for myself."

"You're serious?"

"Yes, and if I do, I'd like you to call me 'sir'."

Patrick snorted.

"Or 'my lord'."

"Oh aye, to be sure I will." Patrick shook his head. "And they say it's only the Irish who chase rainbows."


1808


*A*nother couple of years passed and local folks might have noticed a woman lumbering along the Uphill Road on her way out of Porthcoombe. It was Ham Blewett's mother, Mabel.

She turned in at the gate to her sister's house. Her hair was falling out of its pins and there was blood on her forehead where she had tried to push the hair from her eyes with a soiled hand. The skirt of her gown wore a spray of blood and the apron wadded in her hands was heavily smeared with it. It was the blood of Bianca Mesola, Santino's wife.

"Well?" queried her sister, Myrna. "Did she deliver?"

"It took us two full days, Sister. But yes, she had a boy." Mabel threw herself onto one of the hard wooden chairs at her sister's table. She chewed her finger reflectively, then took it quickly from her mouth and stared at it critically. "So listen 'ere. This neighbor of theirs, Mr. Campion, a surgeon mind you, he comes over when the poor woman's fit to perish and tells me I am supposed to wash my hands before touching her."

"What? That's malarkey! Wash your hands? Lord! As if you had nothing else pressing that needed doing."

"He made me scrub my fingernails even! Look 'ere." She showed Myrna her clean nails. "And he made me wash again 'fore I left."

"Mercy, Mabel."

"With this smelly stuff he had." She held her hand to her nose and snuffed loudly. "'Ere. Smell that. And I am supposed to go straight home, he tells me, and put on clean clothes and wash these'uns today, this afternoon. 'Can't just leave soiled clothes lying about!' he says to me. The man's so full of blather, it's running out his ears, so it is."

"What a finicky fanicky."

"I know. Do you believe it? A little blood and he's all up on his high horse."

"Have a dish of tea, Mabe. Been a long day for you, I guess." Myrna handed her a cup.

"You ain't heard nothing yet, Sister. This baby was giving me a lot of trouble. Obviously! Since I been up there working my backside off since Tuesday. It was his bottom showing, you know? Not his head."

"Oh mercy me."

"The poor woman was in agony. 'Course I had my various simples with me."

"The shepherd's purse, I hope, what Mother used to use?"

"'Xactly so, and yarrow and so forth. I had everything. I always do. I keep it all with me."

"'Course you do."

"And I was keeping a close eye on everything, too, checking her constantly." Mabel slapped the table soundly. "Heee told me not to do that!"

"Fer pity sake."

"Yep! Said that freek-wint 'xaminations is bad!" She rolled her head side to side. "I was starting to get really lathered up with this gobdaw!"

"Well, he's a foreigner, don'cha know."

" Yep. 'Course, he is. He is a foreigner, so whaddya 'xpect?"

"A Scot, as I hear told."

"Yep." Mabel slapped the table again. "And why didn't he stay in Scotland, I ask ya? What's he come here for?"

"And what is a man, a foreign man to boot, doing in the birthing chamber anyway? That poor woman wasn't suffering enough? Then having a man poking at her? It's criminal!"

"Oh, you ain't heard it all, Sister! First off, he has the gumption to tell me I shouldn't pay any attention to old women's widdles. He studied in Eddinburra, don't ya know, and that's where he picked up these notions." The head rolling again. "Grand stuff, eh? And just when I'm thinking he's off his nut, then …!"

"What?"

"You'll never believe it."

"What?"

"Then comes the real clincher."

"Yeah?"

"Oh, Sister!" Mabel's hands shaped the air in front of her. "He goes and pulls this thing outa his bag."

"What thing?" Myrna's eyes were saucers.

"He's got this fancy-type bag, you know? Leather! And he pulls out this thing. I nearly dropped."

"Mercy, Mabe. What?" Myrna leaned closer.

"He pulls out this instrument."

"What was it?"

"He said it was for ceps."

"For ceps? What're ceps?"

"I haven't a clue. Mother never mentioned any such of a thing. Not to me. You ever hear her say anything about ceps? But wait til you hear. He used it, this instrument thing, see? And he stuck it in and pulled the child from its mother."

"What?" Myrna screeched.

"I am not flittering ya. He actually did. Made me stay and watch, though it give me such a case of the colly-wobbles, I almost lost my creamed codfish what they give me for lunch. I was dying to sit down but he wouldna let me. He said I had to 'ssist him. That means I had to help."

"Well what happened? The child? Gone dead?"

"No! He's alive and kicking! Come through just fine."

"The woman?"

"She's fine too!" Mabel leaned heavily on the table and rose with difficulty. "Ugh, my aching back. I gotta get home, Myrna."

"You must be plum tuckered out, Mabel. Two days of hard labor?"

"Yeah and putting up with a lot of horse poop besides. What I had to listen to. And I gotta go back! First I gotta wash," another roll of the head, "and find a clean gown, then I gotta go back. And wash again!"

"Mercy."

"I'm like to dry up and blow away with all this washing."

"I should say. Just leave that cup there, Mabel. Obediah'll be home soon and be wanting his tea. One less cup I have to put away."

"But Mryna, you mustn't mention to no one that there was a surgeon in my birthing chamber. Don't tell nobody. Y'hear?"

"Well, I hardly would. The shame!"

"Word gets out that I seen what I seen, or let him tell me what to do, not another woman never will call on me."

"Thank goodness Mother didn't live to see this, Mabel. Mercy sakes. Men in the birthing chamber!"

"I know." Mabel studied her hands again. "And all this talk about washing." She shook her head. "What a farce. Don't know what this world's coming to."

$M$rs. Mabel Blewett, now spotlessly clean, puffed her way back up Narrow Lane and stopped to catch her breath at the Mesola's gate. Then she steeled herself for the ordeal ahead and waddled through the garden. Near the house, Sébastien Roland sat on a bench with a book and the little brown girl, Emilia, on his lap.

Sébastien looked up. "Mrs. Blewett! You're back! We are so grateful for your help these last couple of days. You must be exhausted."

Mrs. Blewett thudded heavily onto the bench. "That I am, Mr. Roland. I'm nearly done in, what with this back of mine giving me such pains. And that neighbor of yours giving me pain in a different place!"

"Mr. Campion?"

"Aye, he's a queer hawk if ever I seen one. Don't you think? Ain't he just?"

"Did he ...?"

"Oh lordy, after all the guff he give me about washing my hands, I'm drying out like an old cat turd."

"Well, washing probably can't hurt."

"But then, Mr. Roland, some of the other stuff he done, let me tell ya, I can't even repeat. I never seen such a thing in all my livelong years. It's not for men's ears, but I can tell you that man in there don't have a baldy notion about childbirth. And how can he? A man in the birthing chamber? It's not the way it belongs to be. The things he done to Mrs. Mesola would give ya goosebumps the size of anthills. No man woulda put up with it, if he was bearing a child. Which a course can't be done. But still. It's a wonder the poor woman is alive and breathing at all today." The flow of her conversation hit a snag. She paused for a moment while she considered what she had just said. "She ain't gone dead, are she?"

"No, she is still with us, thanks to you and the surgeon."

"And the child?"

"He's doing well. Mr. Mesola is on his way to St. Buryan's right now, to register the birth. Mrs. Mesola does have a bit of fever. But Mr. Campion ...."

"Oh I'm certain sure he's got somethin' to say about the matter, that man. He really cheeses me off with all his uppity notions. Now, I brung along some things here, brewed from my old mother's recipes. Good remedies, tried and true. You can't let a man take care of these things, Mr. Roland. It takes a woman to know what a woman needs. I don't care what they say up in Eddinburra. Ruddy Scotsmen."

"Mrs. Mesola said she could never have gotten through the last couple of days without you."

"Did she so? Well. What do you know." Mrs. Blewett shifted her weight on the bench. Her bottles of secret remedies tinkled in their bag. "Say, Mr. Roland. Whilst I think on it, we do thank you for giving our Ham that job on your sheep farm. What with his trick hand and all, he never could get nothing elsewheres." Swiftly she segued into the real heart of her concern. "Ham tells us you're not walking out with that Anne Marie no more. What happened? You got another new girl now?"

"Well, kind of new."

"And what's this one's name? You gonna ask for her hand ever?"

"Her name is Laura, Mrs. Blewett, but I don't know. I don't have any plans to marry right away."

"There's lots of nice girls right here near to Porthcoombe, you know. I got a daughter myself. You don't have to go all the way to Penzance to find someone proper. And our girls can cook and clean so good. Our little Bertha ...."

Sébastien interrupted. "I haven't made up my mind what I'll do just yet."

"Well." Another new girl, oh my. Mrs. Blewett paused briefly. She probably had enough news to pass on to her gossips for now. Mustn't appear to be butting in to other people's business. "I better go gitten along in and see what I can do for Mrs. Mesola. Before that surgeon neighbor of yours starts getting in my way." She heaved herself off the bench.

"Well, I hardly think, Mrs. Blewett ...."

But Mabel Blewett had paused to look down at Emilia. "She sure is a funny looking little thing, ain't she?" she commented, as though the child were not even there.

Sébastien tried to cover her rudeness with a laugh. "She's only joking, Emilia."

"Well she ain't no Cornish flower, you gotta say that much. Where in the world she come from? Did they ever find out? Never saw skin that color in all my days. And those eyes!"

"Aren't they beautiful?"

"Humph. I seen prettier eyes on a spud."

"And she's learning to read, Mrs. Blewett," Sébastien said hastily.

"Reading? A little piece of work that size can read?" Mrs. Blewett gave a snort and humped off for the cottage door. She herself couldn't read her own name, no great handicap in her estimation, and this attitude informed her opinions on the subject.

As Mrs. Blewett walked away, Emilia spoke softly in French to Sébastien. "The big lady does not like me."

Also in French, Sébastien said "The big lady has a brain made of goose fat."

Emilia giggled. "She's a cat turd."

"Emilia!"

"Cat turd, cat turd!" she chanted.

Mabel Blewett turned around and glared at her. What was all this Frenchie babbling? She shook herself and trundled on. That girl's eyes gave her the willies. She'd seen pee holes in the snow that were nicer to look at. What a strange child, scary strange.

"Shall we go see what Violetta is doing?" Sébastien asked Emilia, closing the book.

"No."

"You don't want to see Violetta?"

"No no no. Don't want to."

"Why not?"

"She's a cat turd."

"Hey!"

"I want to stay here with you, Bastien."

"We can't ignore Violetta. That would be unkind, Emilia."

"Nope. No Violetta. No no no."

*M*r. Campion turned from the fire as Mabel Blewett came in. "Mrs. Blewett! I'm glad you're back!"

"Woulda been here sooner, but Mr. Roland caught me on the way in. That man talks the hind leg off a donkey."

"I just heated some water for you." Mr. Campion poured hot water into a small basin and handed Mabel Blewett a bottle of soap.

"I washed …."

"Would you mind washing again, Mrs. Blewett? Your hands and your forearms, if you please."

Mrs. Blewett snatched the bottle and didn't bother to stifle her groan.

"Mrs. Mesola has a touch of infection, I'm afraid. We don't want to spread it around."

We don't want to spread what around? Whatever was this man blathering about? Spreading infection? What in the name of heaven did that mean?

"We can't be too careful, Mrs. Blewett."

Mabel snorted her opinion once more.

"I was wondering if you could stay with Mrs. Mesola for the next week or so. I don't think she is quite up to taking care of her two girls and the baby. It will ease her mind greatly to know she has you to depend on. Do you think that would be possible?"

"A week?"

"By then, the infection should be cleared up. Don't worry. Mr. Mesola said he is willing to pay you."

"Hmph."

"I'll feel better, too, if you're here. I know you midwives have your own special herbal concoctions."

"Herbal what?"

"Concoctions. Recipes? Simples? What do you usually recommend for a new mother?"

Mabel frowned at the surgeon. "Well, I do got some cures what my mum used, back along."

"I won't ask you to reveal your secrets. But I have seen that some of these concoct...these remedies are quite effective."

"There's this one I like." She took a bottle from her jealously-guarded cloth bag. Ancient secrets, these were, here in this bag. Glancing at the surgeon, she waited until he looked away to open her secret remedy.

All was revealed the moment she removed the cork. Whewf!

The surgeon stifled a cough. "Would you brew her some of that after I'm gone?" The scent of garlic was potent. Probably mixed with honey and vinegar, he guessed.

"Well, maybe." Mrs. Blewett could have been knocked over with a pilchard fin. "Maybe I could. All right. If you need me to."

"Thank you, Mrs. Blewett. Shall I bring Baby Rafe out while you get that ready? You should see him. He's a sturdy little man."

"Rafe?"

"Yes," laughed Mr. Campion. "She named him after me. I'm very honored. And his middle name is Blewett, after you."

Mabel Blewett's little mind braked in mid-thought. Then, like a pot of live eels just set over a fire, it began to writhe and boil. She gripped her secret potion and stared blankly.

From faraway they heard the bells of St. Buryan's announcing that little Rafe Mesola had come into the light.

*Beam Bridge*

*In its most basic form, a beam bridge consists of a horizontal beam supported at each end by piers. It needs to be stiff. It needs to resist twisting and bending under load.*

## TOM ICKES

*T*om Ickes was loitering along the harbor front in Lamorna. When he saw the last client of the afternoon leave Zephaniah Cobbs's office, he ran up the stairs. He paused for a moment, then turned the knob without knocking and stepped inside. He closed the door carefully. He couldn't keep a smile off his face.

Cobbs had spent the afternoon pandering to rich clients, yes-sirring and no-sirring until he was ready to scream. He glanced up from the document he was holding and then went back to his reading. No need to bother with niceties now. "Ickes, what are you doing here?"

"Good afternoon, Mr. Cobbs. Yes, this is a first, isn't it? I've never actually done more than just poke my head through your office door. You have some very nice paintings here. These are some of the ships of your line, I take it? Yes, I recognize these names." He turned and locked the door behind him. Cobbs looked up and frowned. Tom Ickes took off his hat and sat down, not waiting to be invited. He leaned back and crossed one ankle over the other knee, as relaxed as if he were visiting an old friend, and ready to chew the fat.

This was too much for Cobbs. "What the hell are you doing?"

"I thought we should have a chat in private, Mr. Cobbs."

"Concerning?"

"Concerning the future."

"The future? That is, ah, not something I feel any need or desire to discuss with you, Ickes."

"However, I'm hoping you'll bear with me for a moment." He went on, blithely ignoring the black frown that would have made another man choke on his own words. "I promised myself, Mr. Cobbs, when I first came to work for you over twenty years ago, that I would stay at Tregorna until my mother passed away. When that happened, I would need to return home to care for my younger brother. He was an invalid, you see."

"What is this? Your roundabout way of telling me your mother has died?"

"She died two years ago, actually."

"Hnh."

"Yes."

"What am I to do with this information?"

"When she passed away, my invalid brother was taken in by an aunt."

"I couldn't be more pleased for you." Cobbs looked ready to spit. "So there is no problem then. You can, ah, return to your duties. I'll see you at the farm."

"Actually, you won't. The purpose of my visit today is to inform you that I am finally leaving your employ."

Cobbs took up his document again. "Not possible, Ickes. I don't see how that can be arranged."

"Nevertheless, it has been."

Cobbs slammed the document down on his desk and sighed impatiently. "Perhaps in six months we can discuss this again. It will take me that long to tidy up my records and find a replacement."

"I'm leaving this afternoon."

"Ickes, I see no need for you to be elsewhere. Your ... your brother, was it? Yes? He is being looked after." A dismissive wave of the hand. "Or whatever you said he needed."

"My brother is dead, Mr. Cobbs. I received word that he died yesterday."

"Ah. So? What is it then? You expect a day off?"

"Well, with my brother gone, my situation changes. So I am going back to Dartmoor."

Cobbs shifted in his seat. "Dartmoor?"

"Yes." Tom Ickes smiled. "You weren't aware that you and I came from the same town?"

Cobbs stared. Tom Ickes watched his wariness unfold like a shield.

"Yes, Mr. Cobbs. We both come from Dartmoor. And, while you may not realize it, you knew my younger brother. The one who just passed away."

"I, ah, know of no one by the name of Ickes," Cobbs shot back.

"The name isn't Ickes, actually. I assumed that name when I came here. My family name is Poldark."

"P-P ...."

"Poldark. You remember Willie Poldark? The little schoolboy you threw out the window in a fit of anger? He was my younger brother."

Cobbs's fingers were shaking as they brushed back and forth over his enormous moustache. The heavy scars beneath the moustache shot a sting of pain through his upper lip. "I ...."

"You must remember Willie."

"No. All right, I do. You ... you can't blame me for his death. I ... I ...."

"You didn't kill him directly, no. But if you had taken the trouble to visit him these last few years, you would realize that his days were a living hell because of you."

Cobbs fell back in his chair, bowed his head and pressed his shaking hands to his mouth. His face was grey.

Tom crossed one leg over the other, casually. "Speaking of the old days in Dartmoor, you probably remember my other brother, too. Robert Poldark. He was a year older than I. Nineteen years old when you killed him. He did die by your hand, Cobbs. Which makes you a murderer, wouldn't you agree?"

A small sound escaped from the back of Cobbs's throat.

"You knew that Robert died, didn't you?"

"I never ... when I left Dartmoor, I, ah ..."

"Yes, you left in a great hurry. And never came back. Everyone wondered what had become of you. Even your own mother didn't know. It took me a long time to find you."

"All right." Cobbs put his elbows on his desk and pressed his fingers to his temples. His worst nightmare had just exploded into reality. "What is it, exactly, that you want?"

"I don't want anything from you, Cobbs. I have taken all I wanted."

Cobbs's mouth dropped open. "You what?" His voice shook.

"I have been taking what I needed from your accounts for the last, let me see, twenty-three years."

Cobbs, his eyes popping, smashed his fist on the table. "You have been stealing from me!"

"I became quite adept at changing the numerals in your accounts. Changing a three to an eight, or a one to a four. A mere flick of the pen."

"You'll go to prison for this!"

"I never took a lot of money, only a fraction of your fortune. I took so little, you never even missed it, in all these years. I had to force myself not to be greedy, though. That part was difficult. My original plan was to strip you of every penny."

Cobbs roared one incomprehensible syllable.

"But I did no such thing. You must understand, Mr. Cobbs, I wasn't taking it for myself. I sent my mother a stipend every month. How can you object? She had no way to earn a living. Not with Robert dead and Willie at home, in need of constant care. I knew you would want to do something for her, if you could."

Cobbs rose and leaned over his desk. "I am summoning the authorities right this minute. Chirgwin!" he hollered. "Chirgwin, get in here!"

"Oh, Mr. Chirgwin is over at the inn, having a pint or two. Another expense I knew you would be willing to cover."

"This is intolerable." Mr. Cobbs almost tripped over himself as he came around the desk. "You will pay for this! You cannot steal from Zephaniah Cobbs and get away with it!"

"Sit down, Mr. Cobbs, while I explain. First of all, I am certain you do not want your wealthy clients to hear about what went on in Dartmoor. I could also report on your heinous activities at Tregorna. And you can be sure I would find plenty of witnesses to substantiate those claims."

Cobbs had to support himself on his desk. "I didn't drag those French people over here. They begged me to get them out of France, every one of them."

"I am not speaking so much about bringing in refugees. I'm referring to another issue. The young boys. You know what I am talking about."

Cobbs sucked in a sharp breath. He was speechless. He put a hand to his abdomen, as though he had been punched. His legs gave out and he slumped onto the edge of his desk.

"And you must know, too, that Judge Trembath is a particular friend of mine, Mr. Cobbs. I have a feeling he would believe my story over any version you could concoct. And if he didn't believe me, no matter. He owes me many favors and I would not hesitate to call them in."

Cobbs shook his head. "No! You can't frighten me with this rot. This is blackmail! I have the judge in my pocket. And I wield a lot more power around here than you do."

"You'd better sit down, Cobbs. Let me set you straight. You know the judge's penchant for whiskey. I have been hiding barrels of his smuggled spirits for years. Yes, more times than I can count."

Cobbs made a sound of derision. "Phff!"

"More interesting still is where I hid them. Do you know what we did with a good many of them? We hid them at Tregorna."

Cobbs looked apoplectic.

Tom laughed. "We hid them in your barns, in your dormitories, even in your cellars, Mr. Cobbs. Right under your nose. That way, if the revenuers found them, you would be the one to go to jail."

"I will kill you!" Cobbs jerked open a drawer and fumbled madly inside.

"Looking for your pistol, are you? You might try asking Mr. Chirgwin where it is. I believe he borrowed it. By the way, Chirgwin's name is false also."

"You will die for this, Ickes!" Cobbs yelled, wiping saliva from his chin. "You will die!"

"Are you threatening me? That would not be wise. It would force me to discuss all these issues with Judge Trembath." Tom glanced at the clock. "I arranged to have him nearby. He could be here in one moment if you think we need him."

Cobbs dropped onto his chair like a sack of wet flour.

"Not interested?" said Tom. "Well then, it looks as though we have reached an understanding. I think that about covers everything I wanted to say. So unless you would like to add something, I'll say 'good-bye', Mr. Cobbs."

"Get the hell out of here, Ickes!" Cobbs's voice was quivering.

"It's Poldark. I'm Tom Poldark again." Tom stood up and extended his hand. "In spite of everything, I do wish you well, sir."

Cobbs pressed his palms to his head, disregarding Tom's outstretched hand.

"All right." With a smile, Tom eased his hat onto his head. "Well, good luck, then."

Tom left the office and strode up the walk toward the inn. He greeted Judge Trembath, who was sitting at a table with Chirgwin. Tom handed the judge a large brass house key.

"No need to visit Mr. Cobbs at his office after all, Judge. Everything is all arranged. Mr. Cobbs assured me you are welcome to store your shipment in his pantry. Just go in tomorrow during the day while he is at his office. If the revenue men do find your goods, well, Cobbs should be able to bribe them to keep quiet."

The judge stood up. "Thanks, Tom. I wish you both good luck. You'll be missed around these parts. I don't know how Zephaniah will ever replace either of you."

"Frankly, at the moment, I don't believe he shares that sentiment. Good-bye, Judge." They shook hands warmly. "Shall we go, Chirgwin? It's a long way to Dartmoor."

As the two men left the inn and struck the road, the one formerly known as Chirgwin asked "Cobbs agreed to storing the stolen whiskey?"

"No, I confess I made that up. My final act of defiance."

"Good old respectable Tom Ickes would do such a thing?"

"Who would have thought?"

*B*ack in Lamorna, Zephaniah Cobbs was still reeling with shock. He had supported Tom Ickes for how many years? At top pay! And Chirgwin? He had bent over backward for both of them, time and again. And now they just waltz off, not a smidgen of loyalty from either of them. Leaving him marooned. No housekeeper, no manager, no office assistant.

Cobbs got up and paced the room. He was still trying to get it through his head that Willie Poldark's brother had been here, right on his doorstep all these years. Invading his privacy, watching him. Stealing from him! And aaagh, knowing his deepest secrets.

His records! He must examine all his ledgers, go over them in minute detail. He must do that immediately. The man must have cheated him out of a fortune! Tom Ickes had surely taken far more than just a pension for his dratted old mother, Cobbs was certain of that.

He hit his palm against his forehead. My god, something else just occurred to him. Did Ickes squeal on him? In all this time he must have told someone that Cobbs had accidentally killed a young man. He must have! Who could keep that to himself? And here Cobbs had given Ickes his complete trust, only to be horribly, horribly deceived. The world was a very cruel place indeed.

Cobbs leaned on his desk in physical pain. His stomach was killing him. So who in the village knew about his crimes? Oh God, he was vulnerable now, in terrible danger. Years of deception, misplaced trust. Years! Cobbs threw back his head and gave a long howl. Tom Ickes had stolen his money! What could he do? He was powerless. It was impossible to go to the police.

Cobbs sat down again and beat his head with both hands. He must do something. But what? Should he move away? Should he go to London, a big city where he could start all over? Where no one would know him? Oh God. Start all over? This was so cruelly difficult. A sob wracked his body. What should he do?

He sat in his office until dark. He lit no lamp. He brooded, deeply depressed.

He was finally brought to a conclusion. Everyone hated him. That was clear. And he returned that hatred a hundredfold. A thousandfold! There was only one way for him to get any satisfaction. He would do exactly what Tom Ickes had done to him. From now on he would take anything he could, from anyone, wherever he could get it. If innocent people got hurt, too bad. He had been hurt! Let other people find out how that feels. He would get as much as he could for himself and when he had an enormous pile of riches, he too would leave Lamorna. He would go … he would go to … wherever he felt like going. He would take everything he could get his hands on. This town would be reeling when he left. He would claw their hearts out. They would suffer the way he suffered. And they, not he, would be left poor and alone!

*Stepping Stone Bridge*

*Stepping stones are the most ancient design for crossing a watercourse. If a large amount of baggage is being transported, they could be an impediment to passage. But just a small amount of dexterity and courage transforms ordinary stones into an invisible bridge.*

EMILIA MESOLA

1817

St. Peter's Eve

*E*very year, on the afternoon of the summer solstice, a gang of little boys sits out on the headland, waiting, watching. Looking up and down the coast. Where are they? Don't you wish they'd come? Finally, one boy leaps to his feet. There they are! They have spotted the fishing boats coming down from the Lizard. Run and tell Mother! She'll never believe they are coming in so early.

The fishermen haul their vessels as far up the slipway as they can this afternoon, and well away from the walkways. Their wives and daughters meet them as always, and help them spread the nets to dry. Then the catch must be cleaned and salted, and put away in the cool cellar.

Today the fishing was lousy. They didn't catch many. For once, the children are secretly glad. The work will be finished all the sooner. They hover round, wondering how this can possibly take any longer. On this day of all days! Then, when the oars and sails and nets are safely stowed, then and only then can they drag their parents home. They push, they pull, they nip at the adults' heels all the way.

On this saint's day, it is even more trying for the children in the mining communities. Their parents have employers to satisfy. Any celebrating will have to wait until the shift is over. Those children mill about, hating that it will be nearly dark before their parents get home. They will miss the lighting of the fires! But the farmers come in from their fields early. Pigs and sheep are locked in their pens. The grocer closes his store, the twine spinner and the blacksmith lock their shops. The excitement mounts. It is St. Peter's Eve!

$T$im Tior, now a full partner in the cooperage in Porthcoombe, hurried to tidy up their shop. His fiancée, Elizabeth Campion, would be waiting so they could walk down to the harbor together. He could not bear to keep Elizabeth waiting. How could he ever say her nay?

Santino moved more slowly, a little less eager to leave his work, until Emilia came storming in to announce that dinner was ready and would he please hurry? Tim shook his head. It wouldn't hurt Emilia to be told "no" once in a while, but Santino never denied that girl anything. They put double padlocks on the shop and headed for home.

All up and down the Cornish coast, work clothes are cast aside. Girls have been getting ready since lunchtime but boys must have their clothes peeled from their skinny white bodies under threat of a caning. Then there is the bathing to endure. They must all take turns getting washed. If you don't have a bath, no festivities! The girls bring tubs of hot water, and ugh, soap. The men put on clean shirts and the women their prettiest summer frocks, ironed since yesterday.

And still no one is allowed to leave the house. Don't make such a fuss, dinner is all ready. A nice fish chowder. It must be gulped down, but before it even hits bottom, the boys are watching eagerly for their mother's nod. She barely lowers her eyelids when, like a school of spooked mullet, they are out the door and gone. The girls, anxious to follow, clamor to have Mother pin wreaths of flowers in their hair. It's Saint Peter's Eve and they have worked on their daisy crowns all afternoon.

$A$bbie Campion and her two younger brothers ran across the lane to see if Emilia was ready. Abbie, at sixteen, was a full two years older than Emilia but they had always been close. Abbie was a kind-hearted girl and she remained a loyal comrade through thick and thin. She would be hard put to say which extreme prevailed with Emilia, whether there had been more thick or more thin. Because when it came to extremes, Emilia seemed to have an ample supply.

The girls balanced each other, though, and Abbie found a kind of satisfaction in taking Emilia under her wing. Emilia, for her part, knew she should be grateful for Abbie's patience.

Tonight Abbie planned to stay especially close to Emilia, for reasons of her own.

"Are you ready, Emilia? Where are your flowers? Aren't you wearing flowers in your hair?"

"This hair!" Emilia slammed her hairbrush down. "I need you to fix it, Abbie. Will you?" Even Bianca's clever fingers could not tame Emilia's corkscrew curls.

"Let's pin it up like we did the other day. It was so pretty."

"You're the only one that thought so."

"Your mama liked it that way. Sit down. It won't take long." She paid no attention to the boys' furious complaints. The girls were taking their younger siblings down to the village celebrations tonight, Abbie's two brothers and Emilia's sister and brother.

"Oh come on, Abbie!" bawled William Campion. "We're already missing the concert."

"I think Emilia's hair looks nice the way it is," his brother Roddy said quietly.

Emilia rolled her eyes. "You'd say that if I had twigs for hair, Roddy."

"Rafe Mesola," scolded Abbie. "Give me back that hairbrush. Just be patient! It won't take me but a minute to do her hair."

But by the time they stepped out of the house and into the fragrant summer twilight, the evening had turned to dusky indigo. Rosy-edged clouds were darkening to the color of plums and a diamond winked above the slate-colored sea. Lanterns glowed here and there in the village below and other eager children were running pell-mell toward the harbor.

Abbie Campion led the way down Narrow Lane. She held one of Violetta Mesola's hands and Emilia held the other. Abbie's brothers, Roddy and William Campion, cavorted behind, and nine year old Rafe Mesola, the youngest, looked for any opportunity to outdo their high jinks. The excitement on this solstice night made him a high-spirited menace if ever there was one.

"Let's run!" cried Abbie. "They're lighting the fires." She was beyond the age when the Golowan Festival meant crowds, flaming torches and show-off boys jumping over fires. For sixteen year old girls, the festival gained the added frisson of romance and flirtation. Who was Abbie looking for? Emilia noticed her scanning the faces of passers-by intently.

Whoever she was looking for had better beware. It would be impossible to resist her charms, especially the way she looked tonight. Emilia forever envied her clear white skin and pink cheeks, and if it were possible to hate Abbie, which it was not, she could despise her just for her luxuriant hair.

Crowds had gathered along High Street to hear the magnificent fishermen's choir. With voices rich and lusty, their pure, uninhibited joy in song transfixed every soul within hearing. Until their last note died away, not a person moved, neither man, woman nor child. Then the crowd erupted and the festivities began.

In every town along the coast tonight, barrels of tar were set aflame on the walkways in front of the shops. As darkness came on, bonfires would be lit along the clifftops and down on the beaches, from the Land's End all the way round the Lizard peninsula. Tomorrow was St. Peter's Day, patron saint of fishermen, and this was the turning of the year. Tonight's festival was the official beginning of summer. Tomorrow, the street fairs!

In Porthcoombe, parents thought nothing of letting their children run wild. The older children were accustomed to keeping an eye on the younger ones and besides, independence was prized as the highest virtue in Cornwall. The children needed to learn to get along on their own. As an added benefit, it gave the parents the chance to socialize amongst themselves.

"Oh, it's so nice to have a minute for a comfortable old cousse," one wife would say to another. "Did you hear tell about Mariah Jerrard's daughter? Oh my! I tell you, that business is a quite the crum-a-grackle."

Such gossips, these biddy hens! The gents, on the other hand, were wise enough not to stray into rumor mongering. Their concerns were for strictly artistic matters. Truth and beauty, those were the major topics, transmitted via a sharp poke to the next fellow on the bench. This not only woke the old geezer. Wordlessly, eloquently, it was also a signal: a pretty girl was passing, or at least a girl with some very worthy attributes. Which, as it turned out, applied to just about every female under the age of twenty-nine.

"Arrr. Lookee, Dick. That'un's eyeable."

"Yer blind as a dumbledory, Cousin. She's a punick, that'un. Not enough there to bounce a tin penny on."

"It's sweet meat, close to the bone. So said me old pa. Harharhar."

"Now that man, yer pa, I knows he liked them plump and bouncy. Never could account for him marrying such a skinny woman as your mother. Begging yer pardon."

"Yer a cussed old scroggin, y'know that, Cuz?"

"Yar, well, here's what I know. What's fish pie to one is stinking cat food to another. Can't argue with that. Nope."

But St. Peter's Eve was not to be wasted in idle chitchat for the younger generations.

"Go on, boys. Run along," Abbie said to her little brothers. "Keep an eye on Rafe. Have a good time, but no shenanigans or you won't go to the fair tomorrow. Here, Violetta. Climb up on the railing. We'll get a good view here."

They elbowed their way to the crowded railing and found perches where they could see over the harbor front.

"Sébastien said he brought a surprise from France for tonight," said Emilia.

Suddenly she had Abbie's full attention. "A surprise? What is it?"

"He wouldn't tell me."

"So he is here tonight?"

"Well ...," Emilia had turned to her with a questioning frown when a loud boom came from out on the headland. Everyone ducked, crouching low in defensive postures. They threw up their arms for protection. Oh! Ahh! The sky had exploded, a dazzling display of sparks! Colored stars burst over the entire harbor. Terrified, people stared open-mouthed. Thousands of green lights rained down upon them in brilliant arcs. Screams erupted from the crowd. Parents reached for their children and tried to cover their heads. Old people tottered and gaped. The end of the world! Another explosion, red stars this time. What was happening? It was terrifying. It was beautiful. The children laughed in delight. When the next great boom sounded, it was met with an expectant hush. All eyes were on the heavens. What would burst out of the sky this time? Embers of colored fire, fountains, starbursts, rockets and rainbows, shooting across the night. More screams and applause. Amazing! Magical! They were all children again. What a flay-gerry this night had turned out to be! A fine frolic! The best ever!

Bianca and Santino Mesola came down a bit later, sauntering along arm in arm until they found Emilia and Violetta.

"Was that Sébastien's surprise?" Abbie asked Bianca.

"Is that what he brought from France, Bianca?"

"Yes," Bianca replied. "Fireworks, I guess they're called. Weren't they beautiful?"

"Is Sébastien coming to your party tonight, Mrs. Mesola?"

"I don't know, Abbie. We never know for sure what he is doing. Or who will be with him."

"The man is getting quite the reputation along this coast," said Santino. "A real ladies' man."

"Why, Tino, I think you are a bit envious," teased Bianca.

"I should say not. I never carried on like that, in my day."

"That's not what I've heard." Bianca looked at him from the corner of her eye and smiled. "Besides, he's only a young man."

"And how many fiancées has this young man had now?"

"Only one. The rest of the girls were just ...."

"Just what?"

"*Amoreuses,*" replied Bianca.

Santino snorted.

Abbie, looking concerned, was following every word they said.

A suspicion bloomed in Emilia's mind. Was it Sébastien that Abbie was looking for, standing on tiptoe and craning her neck?

Suddenly the crowd was moving again.

"Look 'ere!" everyone cried. "The torches!"

The traditional torches were being lit. Runners carried them along the street, up the hill, lighting more fires along the cliff edge, and meeting fire carriers from other towns and villages along the path. The entire coastline was necklaced with flaming beacons. The bravest young men of all carried poles nearly as tall as themselves, with huge canvas flags attached. These they dipped into barrels of tar until they were completely saturated. Then, parading along the street, they set them afire and swung them over their heads in great smoking sheets of flame. All the young people lined up to follow them, oblivious to the fiery peril and the stink of burning tar.

Tambourines, horns, Irish pipes and fiddles! A parade, the Serpent Dance! Everyone joined the line, hooting and clapping and dancing through the village. The most fool-hardy of the boys leapt over the flaming tar barrels. It was a custom that had begun in pagan days and was too intoxicating to give up. Good Methodist mothers might scold about the scorched trouser seats, but they were badges worn proudly by their sons.

Two boys ran out of the dancing crowd. They grabbed Abbie's hands and pulled her into the parade.

"Don't forget my friend! Someone bring Emilia!"

But no one heeded and Emilia stood alone, watching Abbie dance down the street. The Serpent Dance grew ever longer.

Everyone she had known from school frolicked past her. She was trying her best to look bored when Sébastien came along.

"Here she is! Look at you, Emilia! How nice you look." Sébastien left the line of dancers and introduced the girl leaning giddily on his arm.

"This is Joan from Newlyn."

Emilia gave her a rather curt greeting.

"Why aren't you dancing, Emilia?"

"I don't know. I don't, usually."

"Don't be ridiculous! Come on. Take my hand." Sébastien pulled her into the line and tugged Joan along behind. The Serpent writhed and wriggled through the short streets of the village and out along the cliff. From out here they could see twinkles of fire all up and down the coast. Young couples began to drop off. They circled round to the dark side of the rocks and tried to hide from the unmerciful teasing of little boys. Some couples picked their way down to the slender sand beach. Joan tugged suggestively on Sébastien's arm and Emilia kept a tight hold on his other hand. She was surprised to suddenly find Abbie at her elbow. Her flushed cheeks and merry eyes caught Sébastien's attention immediately. Abbie didn't seem to notice Joan at all, or Emilia either, for that matter.

"This can't be little Abbie Campion, can it?"

"Yes! Hello, Sébastien!"

"You've certainly grown. I remember you as, well…a little crumb of a child." He gestured with his hand to show how small she was the last time he remembered seeing her. What he remembered was a scraggly-haired, sickly little thing. She was scraggly no longer.

"Are you coming back to Emilia's house later, Sébastien? They're having a big party."

"Of course he's coming. I have already asked him," said Emilia. She was getting impatient with Abbie and Bastien, getting all googly over each other. She noticed Joan looking a bit grumpy as well. "Wait!" she cried, as Sébastien swept Abbie in among the dancers. "We're going to miss the Hobby Horse!" But she and Joan were left on the side. They gave each other mean looks, tossed their heads and ignored each other.

"Dance, Emilia?" It was Roddy Campion. Of course it was Roddy. Who else? He was always hanging about. She nodded, pretending to be enthusiastic. Roddy was shorter than she was. He was almost a year younger, and he had been madly, tiresomely in love with her for a year now. But he was a dance partner, and, except for two dances with Sébastien, he was her only partner all evening.

$G$uests poured through the Mesola's door later, eager for food and drink. Santino Mesola had prepared plenty of both. A generous host, he was in his element here.

Abbie squeezed Emilia's arm and pulled her into a corner.

"You'll never guess what! Sébastien said we could meet at the fair tomorrow."

Emilia scowled. "Really."

"I had the best time with him tonight. Oh, here he is! Sébastien!" She fairly danced across the floor to him.

Bianca appeared at Emilia's side. "I saw you were dancing with Roddy tonight, Emilia."

"Yes."

"You don't like him?"

"He's all right. Will you look at that Abbie? What is she doing? She has been monopolizing Bastien all night."

"She's a lot nicer than some of the girls he has been chasing."

"He hardly needs to chase her. She's practically throwing herself at him." Frowning, Emilia leaned forward so she could observe Abbie's transgressions more closely.

"Abbie is much too shy to throw herself at anyone."

"Abbie is not shy, Bianca."

"Bastien could do worse."

"But look at her. She's shameless!"

Bianca turned suddenly to smile at Emilia. "You're not jealous, are you?"

"Of Abbie? Of course not."

"She is close to his age, at least."

"She is not! She's only sixteen. And how old is he? Twenty something?"

"Twenty-six."

"He is way too old for her!"

Bianca nodded. "And he's too old for you. You're only a schoolgirl."

"I am not! I'm finished with school. Miss Wickwire said I could probably get a job if I wanted." She looked nervously at Bianca from the corners of her eyes. She had been looking for a chance to bring up this very subject.

"Did she? Well, Papa needs you to do his paperwork. That is job enough for now."

"No, she meant a real job. Plenty of girls my age are going into service."

"Believe me, Emilia. I know you would hate being in service. I've never seen any —what's the word?—sign. I haven't seen any sign that you care for cooking or cleaning."

Emilia didn't answer. She was no longer a schoolgirl, but what exactly was she? She was only sure of one thing. She needed something that would get her out of Porthcoombe.

There was a disturbance at the door.

"Father! Where's Father?" It was Roddy Campion. He was half-carrying Emilia's little brother, Rafe.

Dr. Campion put down the cake he was eating and stood. "What's the problem, Roderick?"

"Look at Rafe's arm!"

"Rafe!" cried Bianca. "What happened?"

"I jumped the fire, *Maman!*" He cradled a limp arm.

"What?" Bianca shrieked. "Oh, Rafe! I've told you and told you! Now look at you!"

Dr. Campion put his hand on Bianca's shoulder. "Let me have a look. Come into the other room, Rafe." A howl of pain was heard over all the party noise, followed by a scream from Bianca. When they emerged a little later, young Rafe was green around the gills, but smiling. His arm was in a sling. Bianca was just as green, and not smiling.

"I jumped the fire, Emilia," Rafe bragged.

"You're a brainless idiot, Rafe. You could have broken your neck. Or fallen into the barrel. A nice dunking in flaming tar would have been fun, wouldn't it?"

Rafe ignored her question. "I jumped as high as Johnny Jerrard, and he's fourteen."

Emilia watched Rafe move on through the room, boasting of the only item that had any resonance for him: he had jumped as high as Johnny Jerrard and he, Rafe, was only nine.

"Cake, Emilia?" Roddy Campion, at her elbow again.


*A* couple of days later, Bianca dropped a bowl of vegetables onto the table with a loud bang. "Emilia! You can't be serious!"

"Yes, I am. He came into the shop to talk to me again today. He said he needs a new clerk and I could start whenever I was ready."

"But you have a job, working in the shop for Papa."

"Papa doesn't pay me! And I need the money."

"What do you need money for?"

"For when I leave. When I go to Penzance."

"What?"

"I'm going to Penzance. Mr. Davies said I should think about studying with him someday."

"Who? That ... that scientist?"

"He's a brilliant inventor. He's famous. You remember. The one Bastien took me to see."

"This is ridiculous!"

"I'm not staying in Porthcoombe, Bianca, that is for sure."

"Was this Miss Wickwire's idea?"

"She said I might even be better off in London than …."

"London?" Bianca screeched. "Why does she put these ideas in your head?"

"We were just talking. She said I could come and live with her, if I wanted to."

"Impossible!" Bianca began rattling in French. "This is impossible! Here comes Papa. Tino! Will you talk some sense into this girl?"

"What's for dinner?" Santino threw himself into the chair by the fire.

"Tino! This is serious. Emilia has a ridiculous idea that she wants to work for Zephaniah Cobbs."

Santino sat up. "What? Emilia, why would you ever think of doing such a thing? Tell me you're joking."

"I am going to work for him. I've already told him so. He needs someone to help with his record-keeping and Miss Wickwire told him I was her best student. It's all arranged."

"Emilia," Bianca nearly yelled in frustration. "You do not know what you'd be getting yourself into. I can't even begin to tell you what an evil man he is."

"He is not evil! He behaved like a gentleman to me, Bianca. Much more polite than a lot of men around here. I liked him."

Tino was on his feet now, glaring down at Emilia. "Bianca is right, Emilia. Cobbs puts on a good face but he is not someone you could ever trust."

"I am fourteen years old. I think I can judge for myself whether a person is trustworthy."

"Fourteen years old but no common sense!" cried Bianca.

"I have enough sense to make my own decisions!"

"No, this is out of the question, Emilia." Santino glared down at her. "You will not work for that man!"

"Yes, I will, Papa! Other girls my age have already gotten jobs."

"Jobs in service, in respectable homes. There is nothing respectable about Zephaniah Cobbs." Bianca was shouting now, almost crying.

"How can you say he is not respectable? His business must be doing very well. Look at the number of ships he owns."

"That does not make him an honorable man!"

"I don't care if he's honorable. I just want to make some money and I think I can choose for myself how to earn it!"

The door opened and Sébastien Roland poked his head inside. "Do I come at a bad time?"

"Sébastien! No, this is perfect timing. Come in. Please tell Emilia she is crazy!"

Sébastien came in and put an arm across Emilia's shoulders. Playfully, he shook his finger under her nose. "What have you done now, *Cocotte?*"

"She thinks she is going to work for Zephaniah Cobbs. Please tell her we know him far better than she does."

Sébastien stood away from Emilia, staring.

"Tell her, Bastien!"

"*Cocotte!* Surely this is a joke of some kind."

"No, it is not. I am going to work for him. I need the money."

"Emilia, your parents are right, unquestionably. I mean it. You must not have anything to do with this man."

"You are all against me! You think I cannot take care of myself?"

"We are not against you, *ma petite*. Just the opposite. You must believe us. Bianca and I know this man very well. There is nothing good about him. You have no idea what kind ...."

"How do you know him? I never once heard you mention him, either of you."

"When we came from France, Sébastien and I worked for him for several years. Believe me, it was not pleasant."

"So if you worked for him, why can't I?"

"It's different. We did not have a choice. You do."

"And this is what I choose."

"You can't possibly know what you'd be getting into."

"I'm not entirely stupid, Bastien."

"I know you're not ...."

"I don't care what any of you say! I'll do what I want." Emilia stomped out and was through the garden gate before they could say a word to stop her.

S he ran to the end of Narrow Lane and took the path along the cliffs, away from the village. When she had gone half a mile she clambered down through the rocks to Old Man Jeremiah's hut. The hermit had built a shack into the side of the cliff two decades ago, using driftwood and lumber he had dragged from various shipwrecks. It had been abandoned now, ever since Old Jeremiah had gone round the land, and it suffered from a number of structural problems. Sooner or later it would probably collapse and get washed back into the sea. The village children were all forbidden to go there. So of course it was a favorite spot, as it had been for their parents before them.

The front door of the shack had blown off a long time ago. Emilia sat on the doorstep. She hugged her knees to her chest. The narrow sand beach was deserted. It was chilly for June. The waves rose above her, like walls of green glass, only to shatter on the sand not far from where she sat. She watched them rise high against a sky of lead, their tops breaking into shards of white.

Waves, pulled up by the moon, the most mysterious thing she had ever heard. The scientist Humphrey Davies had told them about the tides, on that night she and Bastien had heard him lecture in Penzance. The unfeeling moon beckoned to the waves, then changed its mind and dropped them indifferently on the beach. Indifferent, that is what Emilia wished to be. Why couldn't she make herself be that way? Indifferent, more easy-going, less defiant.

She sat brooding, watching the sea. It was a long time before she heard the rattle and crunch of stones. Behind her, someone scrambled down the side of the cliff. It was probably children, sneaking down to Jeremiah's hut, but just before she turned to look, she caught herself hoping it would be someone else.

She looked back. Strands of Sébastien's dark blonde hair had pulled loose and blew across his face. He came and sat beside her.

"I looked everywhere for you."

She was in too bad a mood to answer. She turned away and hugged her arms to her body.

"Emilia, I hope you'll understand why I did not take your side in that argument." He paused, waiting for her to answer. "You have to realize there are people in this world who enjoy hurting others. I would hate for you to be a victim of one of them."

"Don't you think I know that, Bastien? I put up with people like that every day of my life."

"I don't think we are talking about the same thing. It's not just ugly words I'm talking about. If you wanted to work for anyone else, Bianca and Tino would probably get used to that idea. But Cobbs? You couldn't have picked a worse person."

"Maybe I got along with him better than you did. He was perfectly polite, when I was talking to him."

"Did you ask him for a job, or did he come looking for you?"

"He came to the workshop one day."

"That scoundrel!"

"It was nothing he had planned."

"Don't be so sure."

"He came on business and saw me there. We started to talk and he told me to come to his office if I wanted a job. There is nothing wrong with that."

"You don't know this man. You don't know how he operates."

"You're just overly-suspicious, that's all," she cried.

"I know what I'm talking about, Emilia."

"Just because you hate someone, it doesn't mean I have to."

"I'm saying you do not know …."

"Stop telling me that I don't know anything!" They were yelling now.

"You can't possibly know anyone like this man."

"He is only a man, Bastien," she shouted. "He runs an office and he needs a clerk. It's very simple."

"You're being naive, Emilia! Do you want to hear what he is capable of?" He hurled his words like spears. "Do you? Because I can tell you things about him that will give you nightmares."

"Nightmares?" Emilia looked at him, her eyes narrowed. "Go ahead," she challenged. "Tell me."

Sébastien lowered his head, suddenly quiet.

"Yes. Just as I thought," Emilia sneered. "You are exaggerating the whole problem."

"And you," cried Sébastien, very angry now, "are a stupid, ignorant child!" He got up and walked to the water's edge. He had called her a child, but he was suddenly acutely, uncomfortably aware she was not.

He turned suddenly and stormed back to where she sat. "Do you want to know what Cobbs is like? You think you can handle hearing it? You have the stomach for this? I surely don't! But if you really want to know, I'll tell you some of the things he's done. I'll tell you, but you'll be sorry you ever heard them."

"Go ahead. I'm listening."

He didn't answer right away. Shaking her head, Emilia turned away from him again.

He sat down once more. When he did start to speak, his voice was trembling. "I've never told anyone this." He rubbed his forehead. "No one, even Bianca."

Emilia looked at him over her shoulder. There were tears on his face.

He began, painfully wrenching out old memories he wished he could forget. He told her some of the things Cobbs had done to him. He told her of the screaming nightmares that still sometimes plagued him. By the time he was finished, he was crying openly in her arms.

Bastien had been right. She had never imagined anything so brutal in her entire life.

"You were a little child," she whispered. "Nothing but a child."

"And I'm trying to tell you that you are still a child." He wiped his face quickly with his handkerchief and sat up. He looked at her for a long moment. "You are just an innocent little girl. You could never survive Zephaniah Cobbs. Never, Emilia!"

"You don't have to be mean."

"I'm not being mean!"

"You don't have to shout, either!"

"You are the most stubborn person in the world! All right. Do you know what you should do? If that's what you want, you should go ahead. Go right ahead and take that job. I've warned you. Your parents have tried to warn you. If you think you can handle working for Zephaniah Cobbs, just take the damn job."

"Fine. I will."

He made a sudden decision. "I won't be around to pick up the pieces when he shatters your life."

"What? Why? What do you mean?"

"I have to go away."

"Away?"

"For, I don't know, a couple of years."

"No! Why? No, please Bastien. Don't leave!"

Now he turned away. He mustn't listen to her.

"Bastien, please. Stay here. I don't want you to go away."

He didn't answer.

She took his arm in both her hands. She could feel him shaking. "Please. I couldn't bear it. " She tugged him gently. "Look at me, Bastien." He didn't move. "You'll break my heart."

"Don't break your heart over me," he growled. He must not give in. He closed his eyes.

"You're breaking it already. I'll die if you go away."

"No you won't!"

"Please stay. You're the only person who makes me happy. You know how much I care for you."

He was almost vicious now. "No! Don't ever! You can't ever care for me! I've been wrecked," he cried. "Wounded beyond repair!"

"I don't believe you. You've had thousands of women."

"Don't you understand? I can't love anyone!" His voice rose again. "I'm garbage! You must realize that now."

"No. Not to me! You're not!"

"I've just told you how ruined I am. I'm no good for you. For anybody."

"I don't care. I still --"

He suddenly pulled his arm from her grasp. It was too dangerous, sitting next to her. Only yesterday she had been a child. She was still a child. He had to keep that in mind. A child in woman's clothing. He must take care. "I've got to get out of here. I'm sorry."

"Go then! Don't say you're sorry. Go, if you want. Go ahead! What do I care? I can see there is nothing here for you!" Her blood pounded in her ears. "Get away! Just get out of here!"

He took a deep breath and finally turned to look at her, her smooth brown skin, those eyes of the lightest blue. It would be so easy ... no, he mustn't make a wrong move. "You're young, *Cocotte*. Someday you'll understand." Bastien rose abruptly. "You don't even realize ... you think you are tough, but you are really quite fragile." He scuffed his boot across the sand. "I hope you never lose that." He strode away, bounding up the cliff as if pursued by demons.

Now Emilia was shaking. She sat huddled on the shack's doorstep, rocking back and forth. Finally she turned and scanned the cliff side. Had he really gone? She couldn't see him anywhere. She stood up.

"Bastien!" she screamed. "Bastien!"

She was alone on the beach. The waves roared and pounded and the mischievous wind snatched her words and blew them out to sea.

Zephaniah Cobbs looked very pleased as he greeted his new accountant. "Good morning, Mr. Pendolthick." He thought Peter Pendolthick seemed like a pliable young man. He liked men who were young and pliable. And Cobbs had scored such a political triumph in hiring him away from a rival. Perhaps it was a good thing after all that Tom Ickes had deserted him. "Welcome to Lamorna. I'll show you to your office. I hope it pleases you."

Peter Pendolthick's eyes swept over the small room and he swelled with pride. His own office. Not bad for a man of nineteen years. "It's very nice. Thank you, Mr. Cobbs."

"Next week we will be joined by a new clerk. A young woman. Quite capable, I think. I hope you will work well together."

"I'm sure we will."

"Now, before we begin our day, I'd like to have a word with you. Please, have a seat. First, I have found you a comfortable place to live. I couldn't find anything appropriate in Lamorna. So I thought perhaps a rented room in a cottage in Porthcoombe would suit. It will be a bit of a walk for you every day, but it will allow me, allow us, to extend our reach into the various communities nearby. You could be a sort of ambassador for me, perhaps supply me with information from time to time. I hope that will be suitable?"

"It sounds very good, Mr. Cobbs."

"Excellent. We'll go down to Porthcoombe this afternoon so you can meet your landlady and get yourself settled."

"I hope the room is not too expensive?"

"No, not at all. Very reasonable, well within your means, I should think. I trust you will find it to your satisfaction. Now, another little matter we should discuss. I am paying you a great deal of money, wouldn't you agree, Mr. Pendolthick?" Cobbs smiled and waved his hand in a suave gesture.

Peter Pendolthick leaned in his chair and chewed on his thumb. Mr. Cobbs was staring intently, waiting for a response. Peter nodded.

"I'm just reminding you that I expect a good return on my investment. Which means some of your duties might be beyond what is normally required of an accountant. Perhaps some deliveries, perhaps ferreting out some information for me. I will rely on you to assist me in certain matters. Nothing too difficult, fairly routine. Actually, I am offering you a broader range of experience than you would acquire in other accounting positions. Is that disagreeable to you?"

Peter Pendolthick paused a moment before answering. "I can't think of any reason that should be a problem. Whatever you need, Mr. Cobbs, I will try my hardest to do."

"Splendid. So tell me this. In strictest confidence, of course. I was wondering about some of the methods that your former employer uses to evade customs. Can you enlighten me? For example, what plans had he put in motion when you left?"

"He is away right now. But I'm not sure I should be talking about his business affairs, Mr. Cobbs. He was very fair with me."

"Indeed? Do we speak of the same person?"

"You mean the owner?"

"Yes. The owner of the shipyard in Cawsands."

"And the new gunpowder mill in Ponsanooth," added Peter Pendolthick.

"Ah? A gunpowder mill? I hadn't heard about that. Now, you see? Already you have been helpful to me."

"Mr. Roland owns several enterprises. He is a very clever businessman. His home is beautiful too. Last year he gave a party there for all of us. He roasted a ...."

"Well!" Cobbs interrupted. "He certainly seems to have pulled the wool over your eyes, my dear boy."

"What do you mean?"

"You must have heard about some of the dirty deals he has pulled. Oh, yes! It's the truth! He is ruthless. He'll stoop to anything. He'll try to steal our business, Mr. Pendolthick, steal our business right out from under our noses. Yes, it's happened to me already. He's a very nasty competitor. Very underhanded, take my word for it."

"I guess I did not realize that, Mr. Cobbs."

"I don't think I exaggerate when I call him a snake-in-the-grass."

"Mr. Roland?"

"You don't want to turn your back on him, my good man. Never turn your back on Sébastien Roland."

"It never occurred to me to doubt him." Peter Pendolthick blushed and squirmed in his chair. "My mum always says I am too gullible."

"Oh my. I'm afraid your mother is right, my boy. Now, let's put our heads together and see what we can do about the problem of Mr. Roland."

*I*t was Emilia's first day in her new job, working for Mr. Cobbs. She had hardly slept the night before. She had dressed her hair carefully, pulling it back into a tight bun to make it look like normal peoples' hair. And she wore a new gown. Bianca, as a kind of peace offering, had trimmed it with some of the new gimp she had ordered from Paris.

Emilia was harboring a secret dread that she tried to ignore, a dread that there would be troublesome problems in this job, problems with Mr. Cobbs that she was unequipped for. She must be very wary, try not to be naive. She admitted she had accepted the job out of foolish pride. Still, she was determined to handle any situation in as mature a fashion as she was able. She wanted to prove herself to her parents. To herself. To Bastien, if he ever came back.

She had pretended to be as surprised as her mother when Bianca received an abrupt note from him. He was going away for a while, a long while, going perhaps as far as Turkey.

She would never admit how much that hurt her. Sébastien was trying to get away from her, going away because of her. She was desolate. No, not desolate. She was very disappointed. But she had no control over him, or over anything, it seemed. She must try hard to be indifferent. Still, she felt she had lost something. Whatever it was, that something, it cast a long shadow.

She knew she was early getting to Mr. Cobbs's office in Lamorna, but she was not the first to arrive. A young red-haired man was also waiting, leaning on the railing.

"You must be Mr. Pendolthick," she said.

His reaction was the usual. A look of astonishment, then, trying not to stare, looking at his feet.

That's right, she thought. The person you see before you, sir, really does have brown skin. She stifled her impulse to comment.

He stammered a greeting. "Oh! Yes. Are you the …?"

"Emilia Mesola, Mr. Cobbs's new clerk."

"Miss Meslo …."

"Mesola." Her name. It didn't make meeting people any easier. The Cornish had no end of trouble wrapping their tongues around her name.

"Mr. Cobbs told me you were starting today. He should be along very soon."

"You're fairly new as well, aren't you?"

"Yes, I used to work for Roland Shipping in Cawsands."

"Did you? Mr. Roland is a family friend. You didn't like working for him?"

"I loved working for him. I learned so much in that office. But Mr. Cobbs has given me much more responsibility. And he made me an offer I could not resist." He smiled. "He pays very well, doesn't he?" Then, awkwardly he added "Or, at least, to me it seems …."

"Oh, here he is now. Good morning, Mr. Cobbs."

"I see you two have met. Splendid. Shall we go in?"

*E*very morning Emilia left their cottage by the back door and walked up the steep path through the oak wood. She liked going this way. It took longer to get to Lamorna but she met few people at that early hour of the day, and that suited her just fine. She had finally, she thought, gotten used to being alone. An outsider. She was resigned to it, indifferent. So she took the path up through the coombe, and once she reached the high road, it was almost two and a half miles to Lamorna. Mr. Cobbs's office was at the bottom of another steep hill and overlooked the harbor.

She liked her job as clerk very much. She had taken over the office of a Mr. Chirgwin and, after some industrious cleaning and rearranging, she was quite satisfied with it. She kept her one little window polished so she could enjoy a narrow view of the harbor. Her job, at first, involved writing out certificates, bills of lading and permits to satisfy English customs requirements. When Mr. Cobbs discovered she could read and write French, and even translate Italian passably well, her responsibilities grew.

On this August morning, Mr. Cobbs was there to greet her when she came in.

"Good morning, my dear. What is this lovely flower you bring today?"

"This is called broom, Mr. Cobbs. Would you like some for your desk?"

"How lovely. Thank you, I would."

"Shall I put it in this blue vase?"

He sat on the edge of his desk, absorbed in watching her arrange the bouquets. "Oh, yes. That blue one is very cheerful. I feel the office has such a breath of fresh air since you've come, Miss Mesola."

"Why, thank you. That is nice of you to say." She carried a vase into her office and placed it on the broad windowsill. "There is nothing like a bouquet to brighten a room. Don't you think?"

"I do." He smiled and leaned casually in the doorway. "And how is your dear family? Did you go to Penzance for the Sabbath?"

"Oh yes. Every week."

"I suppose it is a good way for your father to sell his barrels. What do they fill them with, anyway?"

"My mother filled one with food this time. We had some relatives from Italy visiting in Penzance."

"Is that so?" Mr. Cobbs waited, looking at her encouragingly. "And ... ah, and how is your family?"

"They are pretty well, thank you."

"Now, did I not hear that Sébastien Roland is a friend of yours? I seem to remember he mentioned that to me at some point," said Mr. Cobbs. "I haven't seen him in some months. How is he?"

"We have not seen him either." Emilia's smile faded. She looked away. But her antennae came out. She was wary. "He is traveling. To Turkey, I think."

"Now isn't that clever of him. He'll undoubtedly bring back all sorts of wonderful things. You must let me know, the minute he gets back." He paused expectantly. "You'll do that, won't you? It would be such a treat to see him again."

She must answer carefully. "Certainly, Mr. Cobbs. If you wish."

"Well, we have quite a bit to do today. This is payday at the mine."

"Yes, I have everything ready."

"I wondered if I could ask you to go out to the counting house later this afternoon and dispense the pay for me this week. I have business in Penzance this evening. I am able to drive you out to Botallack. I couldn't let you walk alone, carrying all that cash. But I would have to ask you to walk home."

"I see. Well, I don't think that would be a problem."

"It's quite a long way back to Porthcoombe."

"As long as I'm home at my usual time. I don't want my family to worry."

"Shall we send them a note? I'll get that boy, who is he? Donny Dart. He can take a note to your father's workshop." Cobbs was anxious to appear considerate, though he had no intention of bothering with a note.

"I would appreciate that, Mr. Cobbs."

Cobbs was anxious to appear considerate, though he had no intention of bothering with a note.

$S$he had lived in Cornwall all her life, but Emilia had never seen the mines. Even from a distance, the place pulsed with energy. The screech of the enormous overshot water wheels was ear-splitting, but the pumps and stamps were worse, shaking the earth, relentlessly smashing the ore from the rocks. How could the workers stand the din? Tall chimneys were perched above the sea along the face of the cliffs, rising high above weather-beaten sheds and huge winding machines. Mules and riders trotted on cliffside trails that were terrifyingly steep and narrow. Emilia pointed to some men who were trying to handle a small herd of screaming ponies.

"What are they doing to them, Mr. Cobbs?" Emilia demanded.

"Those young ponies? The men will tie their legs to their bodies and lower them down a mine shaft. They're not very happy about going down there, are they?"

"How dreadful! The poor creatures! Do they have to go down there every day?"

"Oh no. Only today."

"That's good."

"They'll never come up again, you see. They will work down there until they die."

"Oh." Sobering thought.

Mr. Cobbs drove her to the counting house, a battered building on a sagging wooden platform. The noise here was not quite as deafening but the place was right opposite the arsenic works. Men, looking like mummies with their faces wrapped with cotton, slaved in the poisonous fumes.

"Why do they wrap their faces up?" Emilia asked Mr. Cobbs.

"Oh, they have some ridiculous notion that the arsenic fumes are harmful. Or that is what they claim to believe. They'll say anything to get out of a little work. Here we are now. I have the cash box. Bring the ledger inside for me, would you please, Miss Mesola?"

Cobbs helped her set up a table with her ledger in front of her. Weeks ago, he had given her the task of reorganizing the accounts. She had noticed women's names in the list, though she couldn't imagine what work they did here. But children? Seeing that some of the workers were children was quite unexpected. She called a name and a mere slip of a boy stepped up to take his few coins. She stared. His clothes were filthy. A young boy, already working in the mines.

"Thank 'ee, Mum," they all said with a smile, as though she had given them a bag of gold. The men touched their caps with a forefinger. A week of work for a few coins. How did they feed their families on such small wages?

She began to call the women's names. She dropped coins into their calloused palms. Their hands were as hard as the men's. Some were badly misshapen by injury.

When the last woman had been paid and left, Emilia closed her book and stood beside the window, buttoning her jacket. Outside, a few of the women had gathered to laugh about something before beginning the long walk to their homes. When she stepped out of the door, the group broke up. A couple of the younger women were going her way.

"Where are you headed?" one of the bal maidens asked her politely.

"I'm going to Porthcoombe."

"I thought so. Walking, are you?"

"Yes. As long as it is light out, I don't mind."

"We can go along together, if you'd like the company."

Emilia was a bit taken aback. This was an unexpected offer. "All right. That would be nice."

"I live in Porthcoombe, too. I seen you there many times."

Emilia readied herself for the barbed comment. Or the probing question.

"My name's Katie, by the way."

"I'm Emilia." That usually provoked a criticism. Odd name, foreigner, outsider.

"Yes, I know who you are. You used to pass my house on your way to school, back along when we was kids."

"I never saw you at school."

"No, I never went. I just seen you pass by."

"You never went to school at all?"

"No, me dad doesn't hold with it. He's a fisherman, eh? Couldn't never see the point of schooling. Wish I coulda gone. I was watching you write in your book this afternoon. So clever with the pen, you are."

"You can't write?"

"No. Nor read. I wanted to teach my own self once, but I couldn't figure out how to do it. How does that all work?"

"You mean, reading?"

"Yeah, how do you figure what all those words are?"

"Well, each letter makes its own sound. Here, give me your hand." Emilia took Katie's hand and traced a letter on her palm.

"Here is a K. It makes a 'kk' sound. It is the first letter of your name."

"Then what?"

"Then the A. Kay." She wrote again on Katie's palm. "The T sound. Kate."

"Oh my gosh. That is wonderful. Couldn't I learn to do that?"

"Of course you could."

"Are there many letters to learn?"

"There are twenty-six."

"Ooh, such a lot." Katie went along silently for a moment. "I wish you could teach me. But I know you're busy." She glanced up at Emilia and quickly looked away.

"I don't think it would work out, Katie. I'm sorry."

"Oh, that's all right. I didn't think … Eh, what's this? Look 'ere. Some lady on a donkey. Is she waving?"

Emilia stared. "That's my mother." She ran ahead. "Bianca, what's the matter?"

"Emilia! Are you all right? Where have you been? I was so worried."

"Didn't you get my note?"

"Stop, Giovanni, *arrêtez*, you stupid animal!" Bianca swatted the donkey with the reins. "No, I didn't get a note. Make this creature stop, will you, Emilia? I went to your father's workshop. He didn't know where you were. Then I went to Mr. Cobbs's office. A boy said he saw you get into a carriage with Mr. Cobbs, and that he goes to Botallack on Fridays. I nearly died. Giovanni, *arrêtez*! How do you make this demented animal hold still?"

"Whoa, Giovanni! Why were you worried, Bianca? Mr. Cobbs asked me to go to the counting house, that's all. He sent you a note this morning, or he said he would. Maybe he forgot. What did you think happened?"

"I thought the very worst. You can't imagine. I wish this jackass would hold steady. Help me down, will you?" Bianca dismounted. "Oh, Emilia! What a relief to find you! I was so worried. You sent me a note?"

"Yes! Well, Mr. Cobbs took care of it. Bianca, let me introduce you. Katie, this is my mother, Mrs. Mesola."

"I'm sorry to be so upset, Katie. I was frantic when Emilia didn't come home on time. I'm happy to meet you."

"Yes'm. I … Katie Gummer." She gave a small curtsey. Her hands gripped each other tightly. She tried not to stare at this stylish little woman.

"You work at the mine?"

"Yes, mum."

"Well Katie, Emilia and I have to get home. I hope we meet again some day. Give me a hand here, Emilia. Help me get back up on this wretched beast."

"Steady, Giovanni, steady boy." Emilia held the donkey's head while her mother mounted. "He won't like taking both of us."

"He'll do what he's told, horrid creature. I would put him in the stockpot, but why bother? I'd get more flavor out of an old work boot." She took hold of one of the donkey's ears. " Do you hear that? The stockpot, that's where you belong! *Sale bête!*"

"He's not a dirty beast. Poor Giovanni!" Emilia climbed up behind Bianca. "Good-bye, Katie."

Bianca called back over her shoulder. "It was nice to meet you, Katie. Oh! Oh, *mon Dieu*. He's off! Slow down, Giovanni! Make him slow down, Emilia!"

The donkey set a smart pace for home with a bone-rattling trot.

*E*milia went to Botallack every Friday now, and walked back to Porthcoombe at the end of the afternoon. Oddly enough, Katie Gummer, the bal maiden, seemed to like her company. They always walked home together.

The season turned. They had to hurry across the open moor now, holding their cloaks tight around themselves. Blue skies turned to lead and bitter winds whipped off the sea. Emilia found herself looking forward to their walks, and Katie, naturally inquisitive, thought Emilia was the most interesting person she knew.

It was Katie's warmth and evident admiration that probably won Emilia over. She finally agreed to teach Katie to read.

"It will have to be in the evenings, Katie."

Katie's face fell to her boot tops. "Oh. I can't. I have to help my mum in the evenings. She has a hard time keeping up with all the housework, what with me and five brothers." Then she brightened. "Why not Sunday afternoons, after church?"

"I can't. My family spends Sundays in Penzance."

"Oh yes. I guess you told me that."

"But maybe I could take one of the donkeys and ride back to Porthcoombe early."

"You wouldn't miss anything important in Penzance?"

"Listening to my aunts sniping at each other? And my cousins fretting about their friends' marriage offers? No, I'd be glad to miss all that."

"You could come to our house. Oh, that would be wonderful, Emilia!"

"We probably should put it off until the weather is better, though."

"Well, all right. If you think so. March, maybe? Could we start in March?"

"That would be fine with me."

"Oh, you can't imagine how happy you've made me, Emilia!"

At home, Emilia mentioned to Bianca how pleased she was to finally find a friend.

"You didn't find a friend, Emilia. You made a friend."


*A*utumn rains came and went, rinsing the color out of the world. Across the moor and out to sea, the husk of the landscape was rendered in greys and browns. The oak wood rattled dry leaves on bony branches and the wind whistled cold and damp. Schools of fish had moved on and would not be sited from Cornish cliff tops again until next summer. The pig that the family had fattened so lovingly since last spring was dispatched and every juicy bit of him smoked, roasted, salted or pickled. Choice tidbits were shared with neighbors in return for past favors, and the old widow down the way looked forward to the portions her neighbors always saved for her. Emilia walked on the beach in front of Old Jeremiah's shack and watched the iron grey ocean. Endlessly, endlessly, she scanned the watery horizon.

Winter gales blew up and kept fishing boats close to the harbors. On many late afternoons, Emilia walked to the end of the lane and crossed the brown meadow to stand on the edge of the cliff. Some days, the wind battered snow from the clouds in curtains so thick she could hardly see. On such days, she prayed that ships everywhere were safe in harbors, not battling the fierce sea, not risking the rocky treacheries of the Cornish coast. Were they working their way home, though, those ships? Coming home, every one? Soon to appear on the horizon, soon to be safe in the home port? Emilia gathered her cloak closer and watched and searched.

The sun, if seen at all, crawled across the sky as if tethered to the horizon. These short winter days gave the fishermen time to mend their nets and clean their lofts, and didn't this mean there would be room for holiday dancing?

Come along then, Charlie! Bring Nancy and Nell! Parties, games and tables loaded with food on frozen winter nights. Blind mackerel staring from stargazy pies. Apple pasties with the initials of the proud baker in one corner. Songs of the fishermen's choirs, carried on wintery winds away down to the ends of the dark, narrow streets. Henry, the local fiddler, quite gone in the head by now, but still able to saw out all the old jigs and three-hand reels. Candlelight catching the glow that shone on the warm faces of the dancers. Nights growing longer, until, on the winter solstice, the night of all nights, the merry-making dancing-in-the-street time, St. Thomas's eve. Men wore their cocked hats and women the most elaborate costumes and masks, permitting every imaginable kind of flirting and foolery. Then Christmas plays and guise dancing and festivities galore until Twelfth Night.

And Emilia stood and sipped punch while her friend Abbie danced holes in her shoes and Roddy Campion danced every dance with Katie Gummer and partiers whirled madly around her. Emilia stood and sipped. Over-heated, multicolored, boisterous, dancers swirled around and about her. A whirlwind of festivity, and she the still, vacant center.

*F*inally the wicked wind skulked off to northern realms and took its mischief with it. It was a gentler hand, the soft breezes of spring, that managed to coax open the buds in the oak forest above Porthcoombe. The air lost its steely scent and long catkins swayed from the trees. And color! Color came back to the meadow above the village, and the near sea turned to turquoise and the far sea to ultramarine. Emilia picked her way down to Old Jeremiah's hut, only to find it had finally been washed away. Lost, not a trace remained.

Fishermen took to the sea again. White sails plied the ocean up and down the coast. Up and down went the white sails on cobalt waves. But none turned in to harbor. None at all. Or none that made a difference.

*O*n a March Sunday, Emilia tied Giovanni the donkey to Katie Gummer's gate. Katie, the bal maiden, ran out to meet her. She was still wearing her Sunday gown, her hair neatly braided and pinned up, a ribbon woven into the plaits. She held the front door while Emilia ducked into the Gummer's spotlessly clean cottage.

Sunlight poured through the parlor window and lit the white curtains. Though they were but simple cotton, they had been draped in graceful folds. Three young women were seated at the polished table, looking at Emilia with eager eyes. Katie's mother, red-haired Mrs. Gummer, was also there, as was her orange-haired freckle-faced youngest son, Dickie. All five people waited, hands folded on the table, beaming with expectation. Katie had promised them Miss Mesola could give them the key to a new world of wonder. They could hardly wait to begin.

Emilia looked at them all uncertainly.

"I hope you don't mind, Emilia," Katie said apprehensively. "These are friends who work at the mine with me. They would also like to learn the twenty-six letters."

"Me too!" said Dickie, pulling on his sister's arm. "Don't forget to tell her me too."

"Oh. Well, that's fine," said Emilia. "Very good. I brought my school slate for you to write on. I'm sorry, I only have the one."

"We can share!" said Katie. "We'll take turns."

Emilia looked at their expectant faces. She braced herself. They were aware, they must be, of how the villagers usually spoke of her? Or had they come just to make fun of her?

"There is only one thing, Emilia. This here is Jeanne-Marie. Mr. Cobbs brung her over from France a coupla years ago and she still can hardly speak the English. But she wants to try to learn her letters. Will that be all right?"

Emilia spoke to Jeanne-Marie in French. "I would be happy to help you. Just tell me if you don't understand something, or if you get confused."

Jeanne-Marie's face lit up at the sound of her native language. "Oh, thank you, Mademoiselle! I would be so grateful."

"Let's get started then."

*T*hree weeks later, the group had expanded to six women. Word had gotten out, among the bal maidens, that someone was willing to teach them to read. Emilia had never met so many people who were agreeable, even eager to spend time with her. Mrs. Gummer and little Dickie were as enthusiastic as any of them. They had all purchased slates and clustered around the table. Emilia used an oak board and a piece of charcoal to demonstrate for the group.

"We're going to learn to put letters together to make words today."

"Finally!" exclaimed Dickie, wriggling on his chair. The women laughed.

"If I write this letter, do you know its sound?"

"Ddd."

"Add this sound. Good. And this. Do you know what word those sounds make?"

While the women puzzled over this, Dickie bolted from his chair. He ran forward and touched the letters on Emilia's board.

"Ddd. Oh. Guh. Dd-oh-guh. Dog! It says dog!" He leapt into the air in triumph. "Don't it, Miss? It is dog, ain't it?"

"That's right, Dickie." Emilia bent down to him. "Very good!"

Dickie threw his arms around her neck. "Dog! Give us another one, Miss! Another word." He kissed her cheek and ran back to his seat.

The women were laughing and teasing Dickie and didn't hear the door open behind them. Emilia, facing that way, saw a large man enter, dark-haired and burly. She watched him. He was smiling, looking at all the women around his dining table, feigning alarm. But when his eyes met hers, his expression soured.

Emilia froze. The women noticed her look and turned to see that Mr. Gummer had come in.

"What's going on here, Anna? What's she doing here?" His finger stabbed in Emilia's direction.

"Shush, Rufus! She's a friend of Katie's."

"No she ain't."

"She certainly is. We're just... we thought we'd... Why, we're about to have tea." Mrs. Gummer hurried to a dresser and brought back a platter of sweet cakes. She placed it on the table. Not a word was spoken. Emilia stood awkwardly next to her board. Katie Gummer jumped up to help her mother serve the tea.

Dickie was the only one not bothered by Mr. Gummer's dark frown. "Pa, I figured out 'dog' all by myself."

"What're you talking about?"

"Miss is helping us."

"Helping you? What? What's going on here?"

"She learnt us all the letters real good, Pa, all of them. And there's twenty-six! Now we're learning words."

"Words? What words?"

"All the words. Reading words. And writing them."

"Is that what you're doing here?" Mr. Gummer advanced on Emilia. "Are you trying to learn them reading behind my back? Is that what you're up to?" He came as close to her as he dared, given the rumors.

She lifted her head and stared back at him. "I'm teaching them to read and write, Mr. Gummer. There's no harm in that."

"You get out of this house! Get out right now! I don't want the likes of you in my parlor!"

"No, Pa!" cried Dickie. "She's nice! She's not a brown witch, honest. We like her!"

Brown witch. Emilia had heard that more than once. She gathered her things.

Mrs. Gummer wrung her apron. "Just a minute, there, Rufus!" She planted herself between Emilia and her husband, a red-head with her ire up. Being only a head taller than Dickie, she must have wielded some mysterious power because her husband was suddenly rendered immobile. She put one hand on her hip and jabbed her finger under her husband's chin. "You embarrass us, Rufus. You embarrass us dreadfully. We're so sorry for this, Miss Mesola. Rufus, I may as well tell you. It was us what asked Miss Mesola to come here and teach us. And we … Rufus, you keep your mouth shut! Don't you butt in when I'm talking! Now you got no call to carry on against her like this. We want her to stay."

"The devil she will! I'll not have her in this house another minute."

"You're not telling me who I can have in my house!"

Katie Gummer came to stand beside her mother. "We'll just go somewheres else, Pa. You ain't going to stop us learning to read this time. We never got a chance like this before, did we, girls?"

"We all like it, Mr. Gummer."

"It's wonderful."

"We think it's fine to be learning reading."

"No! You'll not do this! Women got no need to know this, none of yous. Reading! You, of all people, Anna. What're you needing to do this for anyhow? You got plenty of work keeping this house without all that. It ain't right for a God-fearing woman and it ain't going to happen."

"If you're going to bring God into this, Rufus Gummer, you would do well to use the brains He gave you. You should be thanking that girl. She is doing us a favor. She's giving up her Sunday afternoons just for us. I ain't going to stop having her here. I ain't stopping this, now that we got such a fine start on it. Nor is Katie. Am I right, Katie?"

"That's right, Mama."

"Nor is Dickie." Mrs. Gummer crossed her arms and glared up at her husband. Emilia swore she saw the man shrink an inch in height.

Dickie took hold of the fingers of one of his father's huge hands. "You gotta let us, Pa. Cuz, see, before this, I didn't know I was smart. But I are. Miss said that I are."

That got Rufus Gummer's attention. "You are?"

"I want her to keep teaching us. Please, Pa. We can't stop now that I just learnt 'D-O-G dog'."

Mr. Gummer looked at Emilia. "That true? Dickie here is smart?"

"He's very bright, Mr. Gummer. He should be in school. Shame on you for not sending him."

Mr. Gummer looked at his youngest son.

"Please, Pa. Let her stay. She's real good."

"Eeiyaah." Mr. Gummer scratched his jaw. "You think," he asked, squinting at Emilia, "you think Dickie could make something of himself? If he learnt reading?"

"I know he could, Mr. Gummer. He's a very good student. I think he's a wonderful boy."

Rufus Gummer heard those words and melted. He looked at Dickie again with the light of hope in his eyes.

Anna Gummer saw that her husband's mood had turned, but he was stalled. He could hardly back down now, not without losing face. "Look 'ere," she pulled his arm close to her. "Look 'ere at all the sweets the girls have brought us for tea. Sit down and have some with us, Rufus dear."

Mr. Gummer scratched his head. He scratched his chest and scratched his way to his belly. Fortunately, standing there in a house full of females, he left off scratching body parts and shook his head. "No. No Anna," he finally decided. "I'll not sit down, not today." He sighed. "I'm going to head over to The Bell. Even though it's Sunday. I'm that bad in need of a pint, I am."

"Now that is the best idea you've had in a fortnight. Here. Here's money left from my shopping. Have two pints, dear. We'll save some sweets for when you get back."

Mr. Gummer was writhing and scratching again. He rolled his shoulders and grunted, his body still sending distress signals. "I hates to think what the boys'll say about all this, Anna," he confessed.

"Do the boys live here, Rufus? No, they don't. But you do, and if you want to keep on living here, and keep eating the food I cook and wearing the clothes I wash for you, you won't worry about what those dodgy great glunterpecks down at The Bell say about anything."

"Anna!"

"Oh go on. I'm just yanking your fish hook. Go on, Rufie dear. Go along and enjoy a bit of cabbaging with your mates." She turned him in the right direction.

So Mr. Gummer, a perplexed black frown knotting his face, shuffled out the door, as distressed as a horse staring into a gluepot.

Mrs. Gummer watched him go. "Look at him! Feet as big as a pair of half-crown shovels, and he has to go and put one of 'em in his mouth." She shook her head.

The mood in the parlor relaxed immediately.

Mrs. Gummer took her place at the table again. "Sit down, girls. I'm sorry for the disturbance. Now, where was we, Miss Mesola?"

"D-O-G, Mama," said Dickie, impatient. "D-O-G!"

*L*ittle Dickie Gummer, even though he had never had a day of formal schooling, had always been one of those supremely confident people who assumed he could master any situation.

Among the other boys his age, he tended to have followers but no one he called a friend, until the day he met his match in the intrepid Rafe Mesola. It happened late one afternoon.

"Rafe, *mon petit*," Bianca called from the kitchen sink.

"What do you want?"

"Come in here, please."

"Just a minute."

"I need you now, Rafe. Would you go down to Mr. Basko's and see if the fishermen have come in yet? Get me whatever is fresh."

"*Maman*! I am working on my trap right now."

"No, you're not. Right now you are going to get me something for dinner. And anyway, I don't want you trapping my birds. *Jamais, jamais*! How could you, Rafe? It's so cruel."

"You're a sissy, *Maman*."

"Stop that! You're being rude! Now go."

Rafe Mesola groaned and ran out the door, ran all the way down to the village and barreled into Neddy Basko's shop.

"My mum wants a fish, Mr. Basko. Did they come in yet?"

"Nope."

"Are they coming in soon, do you think?"

"Yup."

"All right, I'll come back. Thank you, Mr. Basko."

Rafe banged the door shut behind him and went to hang on the railing above the harbor. Two fishing boats were just coming through the opening between the headlands, and down on the slipway, a boy of Rafe's age was stepping the mast on a small, homemade sailboat. Rafe sauntered down to have a closer look. The boy had carrot-orange hair and front teeth that really belonged in a much larger face. He had more freckles scattered across his snub nose than a speckled trout has speckles, but it was extremely dangerous to refer to them in his presence.

"Whatcha doing?" Rafe asked him.

"Going for a sail."

"By yourself?"

"Sure. I always do."

"How old are you?"

"Ten. Near enough."

"Me too."

"Ten in September."

"I'm already ten." Rafe paused to let that make a suitable impression. "Going far?"

"I can go pretty much anywheres I want. Can't you?"

"Well, no. Not anywhere. Your pa a fisherman?"

"Sure. Your's?"

"No. He's the cooper." Rafe gestured up the hill towards Santino's workshop.

"Oh yeah, him."

"He never takes me sailing."

"You go to school though, doncha?"

"Sure I do. But I've never seen you there."

"Pa says I'm going next fall." The boy smiled proudly. "I already know how to read though. And write."

"Good."

"Miss Emilia learns us. It's a special class she gives us."

"Hey, that's my sister."

"You kidding me? Wow! You're lucky! She's smart."

"Emilia? She's not what I'd call smart."

"You wanna come for a sail with me?"

"I ... I don't really know how to sail."

"Just come for the ride. I can handle the boat all by myself."

"Whoa." It was Rafe's turn to be impressed. "You gonna be gone long?"

"No. Just out to Cribba Head."

Rafe thought for a half-minute, or maybe not half that long. "All right. As long as we don't get back too late. I'm Rafe, by the way."

"Dickie Gummer. Let's go, pard."


*T*wenty minutes later, Rafe's mother dispatched Violetta to go down to the village to find her brother. And the fish. Violetta returned with a very nice fish and the rather alarming news that Mr. Basko had spoken with Rafe, but he had never come back to make a purchase.

Bianca sighed. "You'll have to go look for him, Violetta. I still have the potatoes to do. He'd better have that money I gave him."

Down in Porthcoombe again, Violetta dawdled by the railing, wondering where to start looking for the errant Rafe. She saw two fishermen on their way to Neddy Basko's store.

"Excuse me, please. I'm looking for my little brother and I wondered if you've seen him. He's ten years old, dark hair, blue eyes..."

"Is he that Eye-talian kid we saw, Orrin? You know, the cooper's kid. I misremember his name."

"Oh yeah. Good lookin' kid. The one named after the doc. I seen him."

"Yes, that's him. Rafe. You have seen him?"

"Well." The man pinched his lips between his fingers. "I misremember the name of the other kid he was with."

"Oh, you mean the Gummer boy," said Orrin. "Yeah, they was both heading out, about half an hour ago."

"Heading out? To sea?" squeaked Violetta.

"Oh sure. Don't worry. That Gummer boy's a born sailor."

"I don't think that will hold much weight with my mother," Violetta said doubtfully.

"Oh, boys is just boys. Tell her not to give herself fits."

But Bianca, as expected, did have a fit. "That boy will be the death of me. When will he learn he can't just go tearing off on a lark any time he chooses?"

Once in the grip of motherly rage, Bianca was fuming. Violetta, the soul of obedience, could offer neither explanation nor comfort to her mother.

When Rafe finally showed up it was almost dark. Mr. Basko had closed his shop. Rafe came home empty-handed. No fish. Violetta was mortally afraid for him, their mother was that angry. Bianca tore up one side of him and down the other, all in French. He was sent to bed with no dinner. And though this was the gravest of punishments for a growing boy, Rafe lived to lark another day. He and Dickie became fast friends and, as Mrs. Gummer put it, there never was such a pair of rapscallions in all of Cornwall.

*A*ll these months, Sébastien Roland had been baking in the Mediterranean sun. And all this time, trying not to think of Cornwall. Or miss his shipyard and his businesses. Not even longing for his big, elaborate house. Trying not to think at all. He roamed the sea, the *Prelude* sailing ever farther east, drifting from port to port. He traded wines and fruit from Porto and Barcelona, and studied the shipyards in Marseille and Genoa. He became interested in a rather exotic Frenchwoman he met in Madrid, and she sailed to Turkey with him. She apparently enjoyed his companionship and was never inquisitive about personal matters, which suited him very well.

Spring had surely come to Cornwall by now and he could not, would not let himself picture the bluebells in the woodlands at home. Nor yellow celandine, nor squill, whole carpets of it, bluer than blue it must be by now. And the rosy sand beaches hidden in secret coves, awash with peridot waves. Shining white gulls wheeling along the dark faces of the cliffs. He wasn't thinking of any of that.

Still, somehow, a restlessness sneaked up on him. It had nothing to do with homesickness, he was sure, but it urged him out of his lethargy. By the end of April he was back in France, but he went no further north than St. Nazaire. He refused to allow himself the sight of Cornwall.

And then June danced across the land and that was his undoing. Even at sea, he swore he could smell blooming things, and a great longing swept over him for the sight of Cornish cliffs carpeted with flowers. Pink thrift, white sea campion, yellow and orange vetch, fanning their subtly alluring perfumes into the warm salt air.

Bastien made a decision. He talked his to French lady friend, Renée, about it and they turned the *Prelude* toward Cornwall.

Going back to Cornwall, come what may, come what may.

The invisible wind rippled and eddied about him. The river of time shoaled up at his passing. He was going back, crossing back over to before, to what he had before. Back to whatever he had run away from. Later, he might have had a reason to wish he hadn't. If only he hadn't tried to go back. He should have known you can only cross over. You cannot cross back.

*I*t was June when Emilia overheard a disturbing conversation in Cobbs's office. She had been sitting on a rock above the harbor, eating her lunch, enjoying the sun, watching to see what came sailing over the sea. She noticed Peter Pendolthick run up the steps and back into the office. It must be time to get back to work. By the time she entered the office, he had gone into his room and closed his door. Mr. Cobbs was obviously in there with him. She could hear them both talking. She wasn't sure what it was about. Was someone, somewhere in trouble? She stood by the outer door, transfixed.

"I felt kind of badly, Mr. Cobbs," Peter Pendolthick was saying. "He was real angry."

"Did he see you?"

"No, thank goodness. It's just – he never did me any harm, see."

"All's fair in love and war, Peter."

"I know. But still, I didn't feel quite right."

"I need you to keep your connection with the man you spoke with, the one who works for him. Even if it costs me more money, I need his information. Did the customs officials do as I instructed with the vessel?"

"Oh yes. That ship is going nowhere. They ripped a piece right out of the hull and they won't allow him to make repairs. Not until he pays the fine, and it's a lot of money they want from him. They confiscated his entire shipment. But what really made him furious, I hear tell, was when they tore into that hull. Right at the waterline. So if a storm comes up, it could cause quite a bit of damage. I felt real bad. They say he loves that boat."

"Does he, now? Well, that's the punishment for smuggling. He can just cool his heels in jail for a while. And that's good for us, don't you see? Remember what I told you? If we want to get into that market, we have got to fight our way in. You think rich scoundrels like him want to see us succeed?"

"He wasn't always rich, Mr. Cobbs. He had to work his way up, just like you and me."

"Nonsense. He comes from money."

"That's not what I heard."

"His parents were nobility. Put in prison in France during the Terror. And he ran away and left them there."

"No. I can't believe that."

"It's true. The man has no conscience, Peter. He sold his own mother to the rabble and they executed her."

"I don't believe it!"

"Well, believe it. He did. You see? I told you he was a liar. But listen! Don't pity him. He's a dirty rat. You just keep your anger hot, good and hot, like I do. If our anger is deep and strong enough, we can find the strength to whip these big bullies. Now, let's get to work and put together an offer to buy some of those silks he brought back. We should be able to get them at a very decent price. Go get the green ledger off my desk, if you would."

Peter opened his door and was surprised to see Emilia. "Miss Mesola. Did you just come in?"

"Yes, I had to … I went for a rather long walk after I ate." Emilia went into her office, troubled. She wasn't sure what was wrong, but she had a strong feeling that not everything was right.

*W*hen Emilia was leaving for home that night, Peter Pendolthick caught her at the door.

"Miss Mesola, we're nearly neighbors, you know. We should walk together once in a while."

"Well, all right."

"It's funny I never see you walking home, me living right across from your father's workshop and all."

"I take the long way round to Porthcoombe. You probably take the coast path. And I usually leave before you're finished."

"Let's go along the coast today, shall we?"

The coast path was sunk deep between high Cornish hedges. In their shade, the last of the hellebores drooped their spotted faces and long canes of wild rose were sagging with fat buds. Fritillary butterflies fluttered against the feet of passers-by and far below, the cerulean sea washed the cliffs in long, gentle rolls.

"It's nice to have someone to talk to for a change. I still hardly know anyone here," Peter Pendolthick admitted to Emilia.

"I don't know many people myself."

"You haven't lived here for long?"

"All my life. But, oh, you know. I guess I just don't fit in all that well here."

"I don't imagine you try very hard, do you?"

"Why? Why do you say that?"

"Well, just looking at you."

"You mean, my coloring? You can say it, Mr. Pendolthick. I know I'm odd-looking."

"Not at all. I meant you don't dress like the women here. Look at you, so stylish! Where's your shawl? Where are your clogs? Your baggy old skirt?"

They both laughed.

"My mother is from Paris and she is a wonderful seamstress. She makes all my clothes."

"And you are different in other ways. A little more, oh, independent. Scratchy, I guess I would say. I don't mean to insult you, Emilia. Can I call you Emilia?"

"Of course." She paused. "I know I put people off."

"But you must have some friends after all these years."

"Actually, my neighbor, Abbie. She's a friend. She's your neighbor too, I guess. You're welcome to come to tea at my house this afternoon. You can meet her."

As they came to the top of Narrow Lane, Emilia saw a carriage outside their cottage.

She gasped. "Bastien is home!" A froth of emotion made her hesitate, then she quickened her pace. "Why don't you come along?"

Peter Pendolthick had stopped in his tracks. His face turned grey. Emilia was about to ask him what was wrong when she heard her name called. Abbie Campion ran through her gate and joined them in the lane. Ha, bristled Emilia, as soon as Bastien shows up, Abbie is here.

"It looks like Sébastien is home!" Abbie cried. "Oh, hello." When she finally took notice of Peter, she couldn't help looking him up and down. A tall, handsome red-head. How nice. "I'm sorry for being rude. I didn't mean to ignore you. I'm Abbie Campion."

He had noticed her, out and about. Finally he was getting to meet her. "Peter Pendolthick," was all he could think of to say.

"Peter is the accountant for Mr. Cobbs," Emilia explained. "He has rooms at Widow Anthony's."

"Oh, right down the lane from us! How convenient," said Abbie. "I'm going there just now, to deliver some medicine from my father."

"I'd be happy to accompany you," Peter offered quickly.

"That would be lovely." She waved over her shoulder. "Maybe I'll drop in later, Emilia."

"Good-bye." So much for Abbie's crush on Bastien.

Emilia ran into the house. How should she greet Sébastien? They had not parted as friends last June, and she hadn't seen him since. A whole year had gone by. She had been so horrible to him. Would he still be angry? Why was she running?

He wasn't in the room, but there was a woman she had never seen before, draped in Santino's chair beside the fire. She wore a traveling suit of brilliant red and some kind of small turban on her head. She was very beautiful. And, how very odd. She was smoking! She held a thin cigar in her long white fingers. Bianca came forward to introduce the lady, speaking in French.

"I'd like you to meet our daughter, Emilia. And this is Renée, Bastien's fiancée."

Fiancée.

"How do you do," Emilia managed to croak. She was used to being the one that was gawked at. It was a new sensation, being the one doing the gawking.

Fiancée! Well, she no longer had to worry about how Sébastien would act toward her. She hardly knew what to think. Sébastien? Sébastien Roland, finally engaged to be married?

"It seems Renée and Bastien have been back in Cawsands for quite some time."

"Yes, and I'm sorry we were unable to visit," drawled Renée.

"Emilia, Renée tells us that Bastien is in jail for smuggling!" said Bianca.

"Jail?"

"The poor man. We must take him some nourishing food. They confiscated his entire shipment. He no sooner touched land when they clapped him in a jail cell. And we never knew. Sit here, Emilia." Bianca nearly pushed her into a chair. "Renée will tell you all about it. I'll go finish the vegetables."

Emilia had to force herself to stop staring.

Renée took a long drag on her cigar. She tipped her head back and blew smoke toward the ceiling. "I hope this does not offend you," she said, holding up the cigar. "I can put it out, if you like."

"No." Emilia smothered a cough and waved her hands. "No, no. Go right ahead." She wanted to see that done again, smoke coming out a person's nose. Smoke coming out the nose belonging to Bastien's ... fiancée.

$B$y the next day, Patrick O'Brien had appeared at the jail with enough money to pay Sébastien's fine. But another three weeks went by before Sébastien came to visit Porthcoombe. Finally he drove Renée up to the Mesola's, and before dinner he and Tino wandered into the garden. Tino leaned on the fence, admiring the evening, and Bastien paced up and down in front of him.

"Anything wrong, Bastien?"

"Now that you mention it, I could use your help with something."

"What's that?"

"I'm going to need a dozen half-anker barrels."

"That's easy. I have at least that many sitting on the floor of my shop. What else?"

"I need you to help me sink them in the pond at Polcoth Farm."

"That's a great hiding place. Then you'll run them inland, sometime when the Revenuers aren't paying attention?"

"I want them to pay attention. Somebody is spying on me and I want to catch him red-handed."

"Spying on you?"

Bastien hooked his thumbs into his waistcoat. "In the last year, the ships in my company have run afoul of the customs agents twice as often as anyone else on this entire coast. All right, I was used to that. But in the last four months, even before I came back, they tell me it's gotten much worse."

"But why do you suspect a spy?"

"First of all, none of my ships can even approach the coast of Cornwall without getting boarded. Not one! Customs seems to know exactly what to look for when they board us and they have figured out all our onboard hiding places. At best, they take two-thirds of my cargo. At worst, they take all of it and put me in jail again. I was in overnight again last night. And I am not treated politely." He pointed to his bandaged forehead. "Lately I'm either in jail or they refuse to give me permission to leave the harbor. Or they fine me for some little misdemeanor. Always something."

"What are you going to do?"

"I don't know. Is someone following me? I think so, but I'm not sure. I'm going to hide those whiskey barrels and not tell a soul. Then wait to see who turns up to claim them. Will you help me?"

"Sure. Just say when."

"Thanks, Tino."

"Any time, Bastien. Let's go inside. Bianca is probably ready to serve dinner."

*E*milia and Bianca were relieved when the men rejoined them. They had been listening to Renée talk about herself for the last half hour. To her consternation, Emilia could hardly take her eyes off Bastien. He looked so healthy and strong. The southern sun had bleached his hair and tanned him deeply. When she caught him regarding her with his frank brown eyes, she had to look away.

After an absence of a whole year, he greeted her with none of his usual banter. He gave her a quick, light hug and she knew she deserved no better. Still, it made her indescribably sad. She knew what the others did not, that it wasn't only jail that had kept him from visiting them.

Tonight, she heard Bastien and Santino continuing a conversation they must have been having in the garden.

"When shall we do this?" Santino asked Bastien.

"I want to do it soon."

"There will be no moon tomorrow night."

"So tomorrow night is all right with you? Can you borrow a horse? I'll meet you at your workshop." Bastien turned to his fiancée. "Renée, my love, you'll have to go to the concert without me tomorrow night. Tino and I have a little job to do."

"I'm to go to the concert alone? You're deserting me?"

"I'm sorry. There's no help for it. Shall I ask Squire Etchcock to escort you?

"Squire Etchcock?" She put on a pout. Sébastien had a lot of nerve. He had neglected her enough. He deserved an insult in return. "Actually I don't really mind. At least Etchcock has a title. And he's rich, isn't he?"

Rafe Mesola jumped up and hung on Bastien's arm. "Can I come with you and Papa?"

"Not this time, Rafe."

"Why not?"

"There might be trouble. It's a little risky and it's heavy work."

"I'm very strong."

"We're going to be moving heavy barrels. It would be too much for a boy your age, though I appreciate your offer."

"Are they half-anker barrels? They're the smallest ones! I can handle them."

"Not when they are full of whiskey. I seriously doubt, Rafe, that even your strong arms could handle these."

"Aww! You never let me go with you!"

"Don't say that. I'll be happy to take you sailing with me one day. Would you like that?"

"Well ...."

"Wouldn't that be a good compromise? I'd even let you take the helm of my new boat."

"The *Formidable*? Can Dickie Gummer come too?"

Bastien rolled his eyes. "Sure. Dickie too."

"But we won't let him take the helm, will we? He's a little too young, Bastien."

"You'll be the captain for the whole day."

Rafe punched the air in victory.


"*I* know a fun thing we can do tonight," said Rafe, very secretively, to Dickie the next day.

"Yeah? What?"

"My father and Uncle Bastien are hiding some barrels of whiskey. Want to spy on them?"

"Sure. How?"

"I know a secret place where we can watch them. Then maybe we'll follow them."

"Better be really secret. If they catch us, they'll murder us."

"Oh it's secret all right. Meet me at the Passage Oak. Better bring a lantern."

*B*ianca was pleasantly surprised when her son Rafe went willingly off to bed at her first suggestion that night. He was out the window five minutes later, and down the cherry tree. The lump in his bed looked convincingly like a boy. He ran up through the night woods and waited for Dickie at the appointed place.

He wished his friend would hurry. The longer he sat there, the louder the ghost whispering became. Or was it just Gwill Brook, gushing down to the sea? The woods were dark, the trees were haunted with wind and Rafe was rapidly losing his courage.

But Dickie, never one to miss an adventure, came galloping down the path before Rafe came completely unraveled. Much relieved, Rafe gathered his bravado. So far, all was going well.

"You swear not to tell anything you will see tonight?" he asked Dickie.

"Why should I swear? Who am I going to tell?"

"You're just supposed to swear these things. It makes it more exciting. Look." Rafe led Dickie to a pile of rocks lying against the hillside.

"See this rock?" Rafe asked. "See these pick marks?" He moved some brush aside.

Dickie raised his lantern. "Hey, a date carved here. 1703."

"That's when this was built. It's a tunnel."

Dickie whistled, suitably awed. "That's why they call this the Passage Oak. I always wondered."

"The oak marks the secret passage."

They pulled more bushes aside. Dickie bent down to peer into the hole. "Where's it go?"

"To a fake well, right behind my father's workshop."

"No kidding! How'd you find out about it?"

"I hear things. They think I don't, but I soak it all up. Then I go investigate on my own. See that bridge down there? It was built with the rock that came out of the tunnel. They had to pretend they were building a bridge because they needed some excuse for ex-vacating."

"What's exva... what is that?"

"Digging up tunnels. So, ready?"

"Let's go."

Two small boys could move through the tunnel quite quickly. It was high enough that they hardly had to bend over. It was creepy too, oh deliciously creepy now that there were two of them, and what with the dark twists and turns and having to go by lantern light in the dark of night when they should have been in bed. Their boyish faces were flushed with excitement.

When they got to the end, they both squeezed up to the top of the ladder. Together they lifted the lid over the well, just a crack, and peered out. Santino and Sébastien were already at work, loading small barrels onto a cart. It was the easiest thing in the world for the boys to douse the lanterns, hang them on the ladder for their return and slither out of the well. They moved around the outside of the workshop.

The men had just finished loading the cart, working in silence. They climbed aboard and flicked the reins.

"That's not your Giovanni," whispered Dickie.

"Giovanni's too small to pull that load. They had to get a horse."

"Want to follow them?"

Rafe was suddenly unsure about that dangerous option. "Well, I guess we could. They won't be going very fast."

They scampered down the alley after the disappearing cart.

"Hold it!" Rafe whispered.

"Who's that?" A man hurried out of the cottage across the way and stood quietly in the shadows along the lane.

"What's he doing here?"

"I think he's spying on your pa. Look, he's following them."

The boys shrank back under cover of a shrub.

"Look at that, Dickie. He is following them."

"Should we follow him?"

The man had paused and the light from a cottage window illuminated him for a moment.

"Hey! Red hair."

"Yeah, really red," gloated the orange-haired Dickie.

"It's that Peter Pender-stick or something, that works with Emilia!"

"Looks like he has a pistol."

"I can't tell. We better get out of here. Bastien said there might be trouble."

"But your pa might need our help."

"If we get caught, though …."

"Oh boy. Instant death. Your pa will tell my pa. And then my ma will find out." Dickie made a slicing motion across his throat and gagged.

"Let's get out of here."

The two brave adventurers, hearts pounding, slid back into the dark tunnel, out into the oak woods and home to their beds. Now that was an adventure! They bragged about it for months, but only to each other, of course.

$T$here was no moon late that night when Santino's wagon pulled away from his shop. It was blacker than your hat on Narrow Lane. Tino owned two donkeys but for this it was easier to borrow Farmer Bagwell's nag. They had muffled her hooves. They had greased the wagon wheels so they wouldn't squeak. They wanted their quarry to follow them, but they didn't need the whole village to hear them. Santino and Bastien spoke, if they spoke at all, in whispers. They kept their eyes peeled at all times.

Down through the village they went, then up the hill toward Lamorna. They veered off onto the road to Polcoth Farm. They expected they would be followed. Maybe customs agents were watching them, maybe they would be ambushed. That would ruin their plans, but they would surrender rather than risk bloodshed. Or maybe whoever followed them had wisely decided he would find their hiding place and then seize the barrels after they left. They only hoped they wouldn't be caught in the very trap they were setting.

*T*hat night, they saw no one. But the following night, when it got dark, Tino and Sébastien hid again near the pond at Polcoth Farm. They could see that the whiskey barrels were still submerged, just as they had left them. The hour turned late, the time when pirates and smugglers do their best work. The road was empty, though. Insects, frogs, toads and a choir of night-chanting Cornish snakes all croaked their hymns to the night. But otherwise, nothing happened. Still, both men were wound tight as harp strings.

Then they heard something. The cart that came down the lane used no lantern. Its horse also had muffled hooves. The cart's wheels made only the smallest rhythmic squeaks as it pulled up to the pond and stopped. Tino and Bastien watched. A man searched the shore of the pond using a closely shuttered lantern, soon found the rope they had hidden under some rocks, and began to pull. He tugged hard until he dislodged the weight that had served to anchor something below the surface of the pond. Twelve small barrels floated into view, roped together. He pulled them ashore and strained to heave them one by one into the back of the cart. Then he turned the cart around and headed back toward Lamorna.

Bastien and Tino followed on foot, catching up with the cart as it slowed to make its careful descent of the steep hill. They had predicted the cart would head up the coast. Instead, it drove into Lamorna and turned into a shed near the harbor. Bastien crept forward and came up behind the driver. He grabbed him and held a knife against the man's throat. He also held one large silver coin, right in front of the man's face. That was all that was needed to find out the name of the person who had hired him.

Zephaniah Cobbs, none other. How unlucky that tomorrow Cobbs would find himself the owner of a dozen small barrels of water.

But how had he found out about their scheme?

How had Cobbs found out? Bastien pushed his hair off his forehead.

"There is only one possible connection," he said, after a pause.

"What is it?"

"I hate to say it Tino. It's got to be Emilia."

"That is ridiculous!" Santino snapped.

"I know it sounds incredible, but she was right there the night we talked about this."

"No, Bastien. You're wrong. Emilia would never do …."

"Maybe she wouldn't do it on purpose …."

"Maybe? Of course she wouldn't!"

"You've got to ask her, Tino. I need to know who is behind this."

Exasperated and tired, Santino squeezed the back of his neck. "I can't do that, Bastien."

"She is the obvious connection to Cobbs. If you don't want to confront her, I will." Bastien thrust his hands into his pockets. "It's no problem for me to bring this up with her. She is angry at me anyway."

"Angry at you? For what?"

"I said some things to her. A long time ago, before she went to work for Cobbs. She probably wants to punish me for that."

"I think you are imagining things. She would not want to hurt you."

"Just ask her for me, will you, Tino?"

$S$antino looked up from his work the next morning when Bastien came in. He took the iron brand he was heating out of the fire and set it aside. He told Tim Tior he'd be right back.

"Good morning, Tim," said Bastien, hardly looking at him. He hurried through the shop and followed Tino outside.

Tim tried to think of what he had said to offend Bastien. He hadn't seen the man in months. Why was he getting the cold shoulder this morning?

"What did she say?" Bastien asked Tino immediately, when they had gotten outside.

Tino crossed his arms tight across his chest. "Emilia swears she told no one of our conversation. She was very upset."

"She was?"

Tino nodded. "Practically hysterical. She couldn't even go to work this morning. I had to send a note to Cobbs, excusing her for the day. She was in bed when I left."

"Oh *mon Dieu*." Sébastien paced in a circle. "You believe what she says?"

"I do, Bastien. I don't think she was lying. She's not your spy. It just isn't possible. I mean, she has heard us talking occasionally, but all those other times your ships have been intercepted? How could she have known about those?"

Bastien dropped his head into his hands. He still didn't know who was passing information about him, but he felt relieved to think it wasn't Emilia. But if he had accused her wrongly, how could he face her now? That dismaying thought, even more than the issue of an informer, nearly swamped him.

Why had he been so quick to blame her? She must hate him. How much damage had he done?

*E*milia finally dragged herself out of bed. Her head ached from crying. She was alone in the house. Bianca had hitched Giovanni the donkey to his cart and had ridden out to the flour mill. Violetta and Rafe had just started back to school.

Emilia went downstairs, built up the fire and threw herself into Tino's big chair. The wind whistled at the corners of the stone cottage. The morning sky was dark and heavy, an unseasonably cold day on the coat tails of August.

Someone rapped lightly at the door.

Emilia ignored it. Whoever was there would have to come back later. Again someone knocked. The knob turned and she sat up. She didn't want to see anyone. She rose quietly and hurried out of the room.

"Emilia."

It was Sébastien. She half-turned, then marched for the stairs. He ran across the room and caught her arm.

"Let me go!"

"Emilia! Let me explain, please. Let me talk to you! Just give me one minute."

She wrenched her arm away and ran up the steps but he caught her again part way up. She tried to wriggle free. "Get away from me! Get away! Leave me alone!"

"I'm so sorry this happened. Please, I'm begging you. Please listen to me."

She turned her back. She did not want him to see her face, all crumpled and teary.

"I was the one to blame you, Emilia. Tino just went along with me. You can't possibly know how sorry I am that we accused you."

"I don't want to hear your stupid excuses."

He gave her arm a little tug. "Will you come down and talk to me? I can't stand it when you're angry with me."

"I have nothing to say to you."

"I was afraid that you and Cobbs …."

"You thought I would be that hypocritical? To go behind your back?"

"Well, I did, because I thought …."

"Just because Cobbs was evil to you, Bastien, you paint the whole world with the same brush." She turned to glare at him. "Don't you?"

He let go of her arm, stunned. Did he do that? "I – I was stupid."

"Do you think you are the only upright, moral person in the world? You could trust other people to have decent values too, you know."

"I feel terrible. I've made you unhappy …." He stopped. Had he ever said that before, to any woman, in his entire life?

"But you don't trust me. Me," she cried, her fist on her chest. "Me, of all people? I would have done anything for you, Bastien."

He stared, mouth hanging open.

"Let me rephrase that. There was a time I would have done anything for you."

Well, look at that, she fumed. He has absolutely nothing to say. Crushed, she walked on up the stairs without another word.

And, like a seizure, the realization hit home for Sébastien. That's what was bothering him. He was devastated because he had made Emilia unhappy. That is what had eaten at him all night.

How could he ever get back in her good graces? And Renée. What would he do about Renée?

*I*n Lamorna, that same day, Zephaniah Cobbs sat fuming alone in his office. Mr. Pendolthick was down at the harbor. Miss Mesola had taken ill.

He was glad to be alone. He had to think.

He groaned, loud and agonized. He had been made a fool of by Sébastien Roland. Twelve barrels of water? It was a direct challenge! He knew of only one way to settle this, once and for all. He hadn't wanted it to come to this, because Zephaniah Cobbs was a gentleman now, he was. Violence was below him. But when one is slapped in the face, taunted like an inferior, one has no choice.

That gang from Coverack, they would solve his problem. The Hawkhurst gang was notorious. They would do anything, it was said, for a price. He took his hat from its hook and went out the back door.

The *Formidable*

*T*here are some days in a child's life that stand out forever. Today was turning out to be one of those days for Rafe Mesola and Dickie Gummer. A perfect September afternoon. At this time of year, there would be few days as fine as this. They were riding the sea on a beautiful sailing vessel, brand new, belonging to Sébastien, their hero.

Bastien gave Rafe the helm, while Dickie, with cat-like grace, prowled all over the boat from stem to stern. They were bringing the *Formidable* around Lizard Head, past Landewednack, to Dolor Hugo. Dolor Hugo was the Cornish name for a certain smugglers' cave. It was only accessible when the sea was perfectly flat. For almost all the days of the year, waves like wild beasts made it unapproachable.

"There's the Balk, boys," said Sébastien, pointing to a sheer cliff. "Another mile now to Dolor Hugo. You can't possibly grow up in Cornwall without seeing this place."

And when they came upon it, Sébastien had to take the helm again. The boys forgot everything else, hanging awe-struck over the side.

"It's gloomy. Kind of scary," said Rafe.

"Look at the colors!" exclaimed Dickie.

At the opening, the cave was high and quite wide. The entrance formed a magnificent portal of serpentine rock, shading from rose pink to deep brown, splotched with green and purple. The water at its mouth was very deep and remarkably clear. The boys could see all the way to the bottom. A school of jade-colored fish hung suspended in its olive green deeps. Sébastien was able to get them close enough to hear the endlessly reverberating splashes of water from very far inside the cave.

"Listen to that! It's spooky."

"I wish we could go inside."

"If we had a rowing boat we might, but only on a very calm day. They say that no one has ever seen the end of that cave. Even the entrance is almost always inaccessible."

"Do they hide stuff in there?"

"Sometimes, if they're desperate. Ravens Hugo, a cave just up the coast, is used more often. I was hoping to show you the Devil's Frying Pan today, too, but I don't like the looks of those clouds massing on the horizon. Let's come about and beat that weather back to Mullion Cove. We'll visit Captain O'Brien. Maybe he'll give us tea."

"Is your, uh, lady going to be there?" Dickie asked.

"Renée? Oh no. No, Renée has left me, boys. Gone and left me."

"She's not your finnancy any more?"

"She is not. She ran off with Squire Etchcock two or three weeks ago."

"That fancy-pants? Pee-ooo!" Dickie held his nose. "He wears perfume like a girl."

"Are you sad, Bastien?" asked Rafe.

"Me? No, not very."

"I didn't like her much myself," confided Rafe. He turned to Dickie. "You ever see smoke come out somebody's nose? Yeah, it came out of hers, honest! All the time! Yeah, it did!"

"Yeah? Why did she run off with old Scratchcock?" Dickie grinned wickedly.

"What did you call him?" asked Sébastien.

"Scratch—" Dickie giggled so hard he couldn't speak. That got Rafe started.

"Boys! Are we out here to sail or to abuse the squire?"

"We're abusing old Scratchycock!" yelled Dickie hilariously, infecting all three of them with sick humor.


*E*milia answered Dickie's knock one afternoon a couple of weeks later.

"Hello, Dickie. How are you?"

"Good. Is Rafe home yet?"

"He's running an errand but come in. He'll be right back. Would you like some tea?"

"Is there cake?"

"I think there is a little left."

"Sure, I'll have some." Dickie instantly lost his appetite when he saw who was sitting in the parlor.

"You know Miss Campion, don't you, Dickie? And this is her fiancé, Mr. Pendolthick."

"How do," Dickie said and quietly sat down. He stared for a full minute. Then and only then could he bring himself to reach for a cake.

"We should be going, Peter," said Abbie Campion. "I have to help my mother with dinner."

They left, and none too soon for Dickie.

"What's the big sigh for?" Emilia asked him, coming back to sit beside him.

"That man! You shouldn't invite him here, Miss Emilia."

"Why not? He works in the same office I do."

"I know. But Miss Emilia! I have a sus-ticion he's a bad one."

"A suspicion? Why ever do you say that?"

Dickie squirmed and tried to remember if he had actually sworn an oath of secrecy or not. No, he was pretty sure he had never actually sworn that night. He hedged. "I'm afeared to say."

"Is it a secret?"

"If I tell you, you promise not to tell my sister? Or especially my ma?"

"Well, all right."

"I'll get such a whupping if my ma finds out."

"I won't tell."

Dickie moved to sit nearer Emilia, speaking low. "We was out late one night, uh, this friend and me. And we saw that man," he pointed to where Peter had been sitting, "sneaking around, following your pa and Mr. Bastien. I wouldna said anything, but he looked real evil, like he was trying to be secret."

"What were my papa and Mr. Bastien doing?" Emilia asked, controlling the quaver in her voice.

"They was moving barrels of whiskey."

Her heart started to pound. "When would this have been?"

"Oh, 'bout a week or two or three ago, I guess. A while ago."

"And Mr. Pendolthick was watching them?"

"He followed them. Came out of his house and hid til they went by, then followed them. We saw his red hair and Rafe said --- UH!" He panicked.

"That's fine, Dickie. I assumed it could be no one but Rafe with you. Rafe said what?"

"Rafe said he knew it was him, the man what worked with you."

"I see."

"He's Miss Campion's finnancy?"

"Yes, they're to be married at Christmas."

"Eww, yuck." Dickie pondered for a moment, looking worried. He cocked his head. "You got a finnancy, Miss Emilia?"

"No, I don't, Dickie."

"Why not?"

"No one has ever asked me to marry him."

"Huh." This was hard for Dickie to believe. Miss Emilia was such a beautiful creature, and smart too.

She nudged his elbow. "I could wait for you to grow up and marry me."

"BLGHKKaaaggg!" Dickie made it fairly plain he was not remotely interested in matrimony, but he noticed her hurt little smile. "Sorry, Miss Emilia. But I ain't never marrying nobody." He paused before confiding. "When I was little though, I used to want to marry Lump. He's my dog." He was relieved that made her laugh. "Why don't you ask Mr. Bastien to marry you?"

"He already has a fiancée, Dickie."

"No he don't. She ran off and left him."

Emilia looked up sharply. "What?"

"Sure. The fire-breather? She ran off with the smelly squire. Yup, ages ago."

"With who?"

"Squire Scratchcock." That sent Dickie into gales of laughter.

"Dickie!"

"I mean Etchcock."

"Where did you hear that?"

"From Mr. Bastien himself. But he didn't say Scratch--" He couldn't speak again for giggling.

Emilia's shoulders started to shake and tears of laughter ran down her cheeks. She would have claimed it was only because Dickie was such a joker. Yes, that was what had lifted her mood. Dickie! He really made her laugh. When Rafe came in, he couldn't get a straight word out of either of them.

*I*t took a couple of days before Emilia could calm down enough to piece everything together. First and foremost was the news that Sébastien's fiancée was gone. Emilia would never have attributed her sudden light-heartedness to this news. If it was accurate. A big 'if', considering the source. But that was the major reason she never got around to thinking about Peter Pendolthick again until Monday, the next work day.

She met him in the office and that triggered the recollection of something ... something momentous. Then it dawned upon her. Dickie Gummer's claim that Peter had followed her father and Bastien, right around the time they had blamed her for spying on them. She had almost forgotten about that.

Why was he following them? Had Bastien ever found his spy? Could she ask him? No, it took all her courage to bring up such a sore subject with her father.

She stopped by Tino's workshop on her way home that day, and asked to speak privately with him.

"Papa, there is something I need to know and it is only right that you answer me."

Tino frowned and tilted his head, expecting her to bring up one of any number of subjects.

She continued. "Did you ever find out who told Mr. Cobbs about those whiskey barrels?"

"No. We never did."

"If I suspected someone, how could I prove it?"

"Do you suspect someone?"

She bit her lip and stared at him. "Yes, I do. Peter Pendolthick. The other person who works in Cobbs's office."

"That red-headed man who's going to marry Abbie Campion?"

She nodded.

"Why do you suspect him?"

"I am not really at liberty to say. I was told he followed you that night."

"Followed us?"

"But how could I prove such a thing?"

Santino rubbed his jaw. "That's a tough question." He thought for a minute. "You said Cobbs was pretty obsessive about keeping records. Maybe you can look through his books and see if he paid Pendolthick for extra services."

"Mr. Cobbs keeps all the records pertaining to the running of his business in his office. I've never had so much as a peek at those. The only records I see relate to shipping."

"Could you sneak a look at the others?"

"I don't know. Is that the only way I can find out?"

"I can't think of another, unless you happen to overhear something."

"I did hear something odd, one time. Nothing I really understood."

"You know, the best idea would be to stay out of the whole thing, Emilia. In fact, I insist you stay out of it."

"It was my honesty that was called into question."

"I believed you when you said you were innocent. I still believe you, *amaretta*."

"Sébastien doesn't believe me."

Santino put his hands on her shoulders. "I'm the only man who matters in your life. Don't you know that?"

Emilia had to laugh. "That's right, Papa. That is one reason I'm still single. I'll never find another like you."

*A* few days later, a rare opportunity presented itself. Both Mr. Cobbs and Peter were out of the office. Emilia went to Cobbs's door to see if he had taken his ledgers. There they sat, on his desk. It was the green one that he kept close. She had never had a look into that green one.

She went into his office. She stood beside his desk, memorizing the position of all the objects. She slipped the green ledger from the pile. A red ribbon marked the most recent entry. She made a note of that and opened to that page. She flipped back a couple of pages. There! Here was an entry that was strange, and involved a very large amount of money.

Hawkhurst. She knew that name. Quickly she closed the book, put it back and fled to her own office. She would have to speak to her papa about this.

"*H*awkhurst!" Santino was clearly upset. "We all know who they are."

"Maybe there are other Hawkhursts in Cornwall?"

"There are too many Hawkhursts in Cornwall and one is worse than the other. I shudder to think why Cobbs would connect himself with that gang. I don't even want to tell you how cruel they are."

"I've heard the stories, Papa. Every kid has been terrified by Hawkhurst stories since infancy." She leaned against a table and folded her arms.

"We've said all along, haven't we Emilia, that Cobbs is not to be trusted?" Santino paced an aimless path through the workshop. "Does this mean that gang is lurking around our own parish now?"

"But Peter Pendolthick? What if he is involved with this? Poor Abbie!"

"Did you see his name in that ledger?"

"No, but I only looked for a few seconds. I was too afraid to look further." They both bent their heads in thought.

"Maybe Peter was just being nosy the night he followed you," suggested Emilia. "Maybe he wondered what the noise was in the middle of the night, and followed you for a lark."

"Hmm," was all Santino said. No, he and Sébastien had been very quiet. And if Peter Pendolthick hadn't passed the information on to Cobbs, who had? They had no other suspects.

$T$hat question had taken hold in Emilia's mind too. And to answer it, she watched for another chance to look at the green ledger. She tried to stop herself from acting nervous and worried when she was around Cobbs and Peter. But the suspicion that Cobbs had hired the Hawkhurst gang to do some job for him made her almost sick with worry. What were they planning to do?

She had been dreading being alone in the office again, for fear she would be compelled to sneak another look at that green ledger. She didn't want to look. But she had to find out if Peter Pendolthick was involved, for Abbie's sake, for everyone's sake. It was another week before she had both the opportunity and the courage to take advantage of it.

Again she stood before the desk, trying to remember how everything was arranged. She opened the green ledger and held its red ribbon in one hand while she scanned down the page. Good! Nothing there. She turned back to a page at random. Oh no. Her legs gave out from under her. She sat down. Under expenditures:

Oct 5, P. Pendolthick. Delivered 40 pounds in bank notes. James Hawkhurst (Delivery refused and returned)

Oct 6, P. Pendolthick. Delivered 40 guineas to James Hawkhurst. No receipt.

Evidently Hawkhurst demanded cash for some job and did not trust Cobbs's bank notes. Peter must have had to take back forty pounds worth of notes and exchange them for gold guineas. And

Cobbs paid a premium for that mistake. Forty gold guineas were worth even more than forty pounds. What was the money for? Was Peter part of some deal between them? Did he know what he was doing?

Emilia sensed a disturbance and looked up quickly. Cobbs was standing in the doorway.

He spoke very slowly. "I came back for my umbrella. And look what I find. What are you doing in here, Miss Mesola?"

Emilia was frozen to the chair. She opened her mouth but nothing came out.

Like a bolt of lightning, Cobbs came striding across the office and that got her moving. His face was a terror of anger and she bumped around to the other side of the desk. She dared not take her eyes off him. He looked at the page she had opened and then lifted his eyes to her, snarling.

"You evil little witch!" he screamed. "You lying, conniving nigger!" He pushed the chair aside and came round to her side of the desk. She fled towards the door. He caught her by the hair, holding it tight, and began whipping her with his cane. She kicked back at him and caught him in the knee. Little did she know it was the same knee that Patrick O'Brien had injured years ago.

Cobbs went down in a heap, screaming in pain. She watched him, horrified at what she had done, before she gathered her wits, ran for her cloak and then the door.

As soon as she turned the knob, the door blew open. A gale of wind was blowing, pouring freezing rain so heavily that she could hardly see her way. She slipped and fell to one knee on the icy street. She got up, kept running, leaning into the wind, fleeing, heart pumping. Her arm shielding her eyes, her cloak billowing. Should she take the more commonly-used coast path? If Cobbs caught her, there might be some passerby who would help. No, the woods. She wanted the safety of the woods. He might not guess she had taken the long road. Hurry! She could hardly get a breath. Panic had her by the throat.

She stumbled through the rain for two miles. It wasn't until she got to her father's oak wood that she paused, her lungs pumping air. She leaned heavily against the mighty tree, the Passage Oak. Panting to get her breath, she looked back. No one came behind her.

She jumped violently at the sound of lightning. No, not lightning. It was a cannon boom. Shipwreck! She ran across the bridge and slipped and slid down through the woods, through their garden and out into Narrow Lane.

There she saw the *Crocodile's* smashed and broken hull riding up and down against the great slab of rock, Karrek Fekyl. A dying ship, groaning piteously, thrown against the rock on wave after wave, and sinking, sinking. All her crew except one, broken and smashed too.

$A$nd later that afternoon, that one survivor gone also. Emilia closed the Campions' front door and went out through their gate. A dead woman was in the house behind her. The wind moaned in the trees as Emilia crossed the lane to her own home. It rained still, she realized. She went in and stood by the cold fireplace. Bianca and the children must have gone down to the harbor, or perhaps were taking tea with someone. She leaned against the mantel and that is where her father found her when he came home.

Santino Mesola had thought about going down to the harbor to see the shipwreck when his work was finished. His partner, Tim Tior, had left when they heard the cannon, but came back shortly after, saying the disaster was tragically beyond need of his help. At the end of the afternoon, Tino decided to go home for a cup of hot tea instead of standing about in the driving wind and rain with the rest of the villagers.

He found only Emilia at home. She stood before the fireplace, staring at dying coals. She buried her face in his chest, shaking uncontrollably. She sobbed out the story of the woman she had hoped to save. And there was more. Zephaniah Cobbs had caught her prying through his books. They had struggled. She had kicked him. She would never be able to go back to that office. And Peter Pendolthick was involved in terrible dealings with the Hawkhurst gang. And Sébastien had said mean things to her down at the harbor today or maybe it was she that had been mean to him, she couldn't remember.

Tino made her a pot of tea. He poured himself a cup and sat with her. Her cup rattled a little on the saucer but she was beginning to calm down. She showed him the dainty little gold cross that had belonged to the dead woman, the only thing she had had left behind. Or so they thought.

*E*milia came down with a wretched cold but insisted on returning to Porthcoombe on Sunday, to teach her little class of bal maidens. When she knocked on the Gummers' door, Mrs.

Gummer answered with a grave face. It was quiet in the house. The women were nowhere to be seen. No sign of Dickie, or their slates or their chatter, no array of cakes that had appeared every week without fail.

The bal maidens had been threatened with being fired, Mrs. Gummer explained, if they so much as spoke to Emilia Mesola again. Zephaniah Cobbs had gone in person out to the mine and made that very clear. There would be no more schooling for them if they wished to continue working at Botallack, or indeed, if they wished to work anywhere in Cornwall ever again. Mrs. Gummer was so sorry to be the bearer of that news. She was even more distressed to see tears in Miss Mesola's eyes when she told her. Apparently these classes meant as much to her as they did to her students. Who would have thought?

Later that week

*I*t was evening, the end of the working day, and Peter Pendolthick was turning down his lamp, getting ready to leave his office. Mr. Cobbs came in quietly and shut the door. His eyes glittered with a ruthless drive. He was in terrible need.

"I'm finished for today, Mr. Cobbs," said Peter, rising from his desk.

"No, you're not quite finished, Peter."

Peter, startled at Cobbs's tone, turned toward him but was stopped by the point of a letter opener in his neck. Cobbs stood very close behind him.

"Mr. Co—"

"Quiet, Peter. Not another word." Cobbs was fumbling in Peter's clothing.

Peter panicked. He tried to wrench free but gasped when the letter opener against his throat showed Cobbs meant business. He could not believe this was happening.

"I will kill you if you give me trouble of any kind, Peter. Never doubt that I mean what I say. Just be quiet now."

Peter could not stifle a cry pain. The letter opener pressed harder.

Anguish tore a great sob from deep inside him.

His spirit, all that he had been, was desecrated.

Buttoning his pants later, Cobbs's manner was insolent. "You'll discuss this with no one. Do you understand? And don't think for one minute you can go elsewhere to hide from me. You are mine now."

Somehow Peter remained standing, leaning against his desk. After Cobbs left he collapsed, weeping, on the floor.

Abbie Campion had expected him at their house for dinner that night but he never appeared.

*T*he next morning, Cobbs summoned his accountant. "Mr. Pendolthick," he roared.

Peter stood in sullen silence at Cobbs's door.

"This note came here by mistake. Will you find that boy we hire and get him to deliver it to the proper address?" Far better, thought Cobbs, to have this note pass through several hands so it could not be easily traced. "Anyone can see where it should have gone in the first place. Find that Donny Dart boy to take it there. But bargain him down on the price. He tries to charge me too much."

A letter for Sébastien Roland. Peter turned it in his hand. It had not been sealed.

"Someone forgot to seal it," Cobbs explained. "But just deliver it the way it is." Cobbs certainly did not want his seal on that note. He looked at Peter with snake eyes.

Peter Pendolthick turned away. But an unsealed letter seemed like an open invitation. He read it and was relieved it was nothing momentous. He had already made enough trouble for Mr. Roland and he desperately regretted every bit of it.

He went down the steps, looking for the usual messenger boy. His eye was caught by another boy, a boy with hair the color of carrots. He was just leaving the blacksmith's, leading a donkey. Peter watched him for a moment, heart-sick. Such a carefree boy. Red-haired, so like himself at that age. Peter would have done anything, anything to be that boy again. Could not his most desperate wish make it so?

He cleared his throat and called to the boy in a cracking voice.

The lad looked up. Peter recognized him. He had met him at Emilia Mesola's house. He seemed like a reliable kid.

"Would you like to make some money?" Peter asked him.

Make some money? Dickie Gummer immediately put aside his prejudice against this man. Sure, he was more than willing to ride out to Penlee, Mr. Roland's estate. Mr. Tior had lent him the Mesola's donkey today and asked him to pick up some iron hoops from the blacksmith. But the hoops wouldn't be ready until afternoon. He could double his earnings today if he rode to Penlee.

"I'll pay you, but not until you get back. Come to my office." In days before, Peter had been proud to refer to his office. It no longer sounded at all impressive. With a stab of longing, he watched Dickie scramble onto Giovanni the donkey's back.

No one should ever ask a donkey what he thinks of his rider, but it was obvious that Giovanni responded to Dickie's slightest touch. Peter stood watching them until they disappeared, not realizing what evil he had helped put in motion.

As he rode along, Dickie also considered an unsealed note to be an invitation. He could read very well now, and before he handed the note to Sébastien Roland, that is what he did.

$B$y the time Dickie Gummer climbed the steps to Cobbs's office later that day, Mr. Cobbs had left. Peter Pendolthick paid him and Dickie rode the coast path back to Porthcoombe. He would return this noble donkey, the handsome, the lovable Giovanni, and get paid again. Later, when he tried to figure out if he was responsible for what happened, he remembered thinking it was a lucky day.

"Dickie! What are you doing here?" Miss Emilia was coming down the lane, on her way to her father's workshop.

Dickie's too-large teeth flashed in a crooked smile. "Mr. Tior paid me to ride Giovanni to Lamorna. He and your pa needed these here hoops. Then that Mr. Peter, you know, the man with the red hair? I'm talking about really red hair. He paid me to take a note to Mr. Bastien."

"Mr. Bastien? You went all that way to deliver a note from Mr. Pendolthick?"

"Sure I did. But it wasn't from Mr. Pentho-- him. It was from your pa."

"My father?"

"I read it," claimed Dickie, completely innocent of a sense of wrong-doing. "He wants Mr. Bastien to meet him this afternoon at four o'clock. They are supposed to meet at the Passage Oak."

"Now that is odd," said Emilia. "Meeting out in the woods? That makes no sense."

"That's what it said, Miss Emilia. I'm certain sure it said that, and you know how good I can read."

The more Emilia thought about it, the weirder the circumstances seemed. "When is this supposed to happen?"

"This afternoon, four o'clock, like I said."

"I wish I could have seen that note." Emilia gestured for Dickie to bring Giovanni and follow her down the alley to the shop. "It's almost four o'clock and it looks like Papa has already left. I'm going up to the woods. This is too strange."

"You want I should come with you, Miss Emilia? In case you need per-tection?"

"No thank you, Dickie. I'll be fine on my own."

"All right," said Dickie, crestfallen. He never should have told her that he wanted to marry his dog instead of her. She probably would have let him come along, otherwise.


*W*hen Sébastien Roland received the note that Dickie brought him, he too was puzzled by it. Why would Santino insist on meeting under an oak tree? He had just saddled his horse so, before Dickie had even turned his donkey around, Sébastien rode off to find Santino in his workshop in Porthcoombe. As always, he dreaded seeing Zephaniah Cobbs in Lamorna, so he went round by the high road.

Santino greeted him heartily. "Bastien! What brings you here this afternoon?"

"I thought you did."

"Well, I'm glad you have come. We're roasting pork tonight. Stay and dine with us."

"Is that what this is about?"

Santino looked puzzled.

Bastien tapped the note on his fingertips. "You said to meet you at four o'clock."

"I? No. I'm happy to see you but …."

"You didn't send me a note, asking me to meet you at the Passage Oak?"

Santino frowned. "I did not." He thought for a minute. "Is that the note?"

Sébastien gave it to him. "Does this look like your handwriting?"

"It is not my writing. *Mama mia.* What is this about?" He tore off his apron. "Who is planning to meet us? I want to see who it is. Let's go up there."

"It's only half after three."

"That's good. We can have a look around. By the way, Emilia discovered some interesting things in Cobbs's books the other day. I'll tell you about them on the way."

"Should we use the tunnel?"

"Sure. Go ahead. I'm right behind you."

"This whole thing feels wrong. You don't have a gun, do you?"

"No, I don't, Bastien. But let's not get hasty. We'll hide in the tunnel and see who turns up. We don't have to confront anyone."

When they got to the mouth of the tunnel, they knelt behind its covering of shrubbery and peered out into the woods.

"I don't see anyone," Sébastien whispered.

Half an hour went by.

"What time is it?"

"My watch says it's after four."

They scanned the wooded slope up and down.

"Someone's coming!" Santino crept forward so he could see. Yes, someone was coming up the path. He crawled out of the tunnel and stood up. "Emilia!"

She looked up, surprised, and started toward him.

The gunshot was deafening. Santino's face registered shock. He looked at his daughter. Then he fell to the ground.

"Papa!" Emilia screamed. She ran to crouch beside him. "Papa, Papa!" She heard someone run off through the woods.

"Tino!" Sébastien was by her side. He looked wildly around. "Did you see who that was?"

"No," she cried. "Someone went that way." She scrambled to her feet. "I'll see if I can find Mr. Campion. Will you stay with him?"

"Yes. Hurry! Hurry, oh God, hurry Emilia!"

*T*he funeral procession was long. It wound clear down the hill from St. Buryan's churchyard, even though this man had been a foreigner and not really one of them. Well, anyone from east of the Tamar River was a foreigner to the Cornish, and this man was from farther away than that. He was a Catholic too, but he was a Christian and one had to make allowances. Pretty nearly everyone in the village had come to say good-bye to Santino Mesola, the Eye-talian. His body would forever be a part of Cornwall now. Funny, how Death smoothed over even the most enormous differences.

His widow, draped in veils, leaned heavily on Sébastien Roland's arm. The three children held fast to the remnants of their family, gripping each other's hands so tightly that their knuckles were white. The tall brown one in the middle was not really born a Mesola, but Santino had raised her as his own. Some said she blamed herself for his death. Those eyes of hers, full of the question they all had. Why this man?

Just behind the widow were the Italian relatives from Penzance. Look at the crowd of them! The villagers could not help gawking. How these Eye-talians carried on! Even the men crying shamelessly, supporting women bent with grief. Every one in deep black mourning. How did they afford that?

Once more the villagers got to listen to the fat papist priest saying strange things is some other language. The last time the priest had come it had been a happy occasion. Santino's own wedding, a dozen or so years ago. A much happier occasion. That had been quite the celebration.

Well, the Lord giveth and the Lord taketh away. One more widow in the village who would need looking after. A fairly young widow she was too. Death must have struggled mightily with Santino Mesola, to get him to leave her behind.

*I*n Lamorna, one early morning a few days later, Zephaniah Cobbs was alone in his well-appointed office. His desk was nicely separated from the waiting area by a carved wooden banister. The walls were lined with large paintings of the ships that Cobbs had owned over the years and a map showing the various shipping routes. All symbols of his success. Yes, he wanted his fat rich clients to dwell on his success. He wanted to rub their noses in it. From his desk he could look through a large window to the harbor below. His world, his kingdom.

He had hoped by this time he would have been sitting on top of that world, his affairs nicely tied up, his demons laid to rest. But those Hawkhurst brothers had made a complete mess of things. He had paid them half a fortune and he still owed them more, but they were not going to get it. They were supposed to be so clever. If that were so, Sébastien Roland would be dead by now. Cobbs should have done the job himself. No, Hawkhurst was not going to get the rest of his money, that was for sure. The idiot! Shooting the wrong man!

But actually, Cobbs considered, things had worked out rather well after all. The shooting was a final parting blow to his former clerk, that evil nigger witch. He was well rid of her. His other employee, Peter Pendolthick, had been brought to heel now, under his thumb, completely at his beck and call. Yes, when he reconsidered, his affairs were beginning to take on the sheen of success.

A visitor called, unannounced. The man was well-dressed, elegant. All the way from Plymouth, or so he claimed.

Cobbs was pleased that his office attracted such upper-crust clientele. He rose, immediately at his oily best. "How may I be of service to you?" he asked. He offered a glass of his best contraband whiskey but the man waved it away.

"I bring bad news, I am afraid. I regret to inform you that I have a Notice of Eviction for you, sir," the man said. He passed the document across the desk.

Cobbs sat abruptly. The blood left his face. He took the papers with an unsteady hand. "Eviction? But how can that be? This is my building, bought and paid for."

"I am talking about Tregorna Farm. It has been purchased from the owners and the new owner does not wish to continue your tenancy."

"Tregorna?" Cobbs almost shrieked. "I have lived there for over a decade. Two decades! Why was I not informed the house was for sale?"

"An agreement to sell was reached privately. My client searched out the owners and initiated the process. He has now procured it officially. It was an option you could have pursued years ago, Mr. Cobbs, had you so desired. Therefore the previous owners felt no obligation to inform you of their plans. Especially since you have not paid a ha'penny of rent during all the time you were there. Given these circumstances, you can hardly expect to receive special consideration, from them or from my client."

Cobbs snatched up his letter opener and clutched it in a predatory claw. "This client of yours. I need a name." He stabbed the desktop. "Who would have the nerve to do this to Zephaniah Cobbs?" He punctuated each word with a stab of the letter opener. He couldn't stop his voice from shaking.

"I am not at liberty to say, sir. But it is necessary for you to vacate the premises almost immediately."

"This cannot be!" Cobbs jumped from his chair so suddenly that he stumbled against it. "It cannot be! This is not only unfair. There is something rotten going on here." He banged his fist against the wall behind him. He stalked back and forth. "You can't throw a man out of his house like this. And I have tenants living there as well."

"So we are informed. We are also informed that you are employing them without their consent, which is illegal, Mr. Cobbs. You really don't have a leg to stand on."

"What are you talking about? My tenants came here by choice. They are working off the cost of their voyage."

"We can go into the legality of it. And we certainly will, if you fail to comply with this notice. My client is being most considerate, in my estimation. He is giving you two weeks, Mr. Cobbs, to tie up your affairs and get out." The visitor rose. "I trust you will make the necessary arrangements before that time. I wish you a good day, sir."

He had to show himself out.

Cobbs was shaking with rage. He kicked the coat tree over. He wiped his mouth against his sleeve and staggered backwards. He tripped on the overturned chair behind him and fell against the wall. His head hit the large frame of a painting behind him, knocking it askew. Howling, he swept it savagely from the wall and threw it across the room.

Who could have pulled this hideous trick on him? Tregorna belonged to him! He had lived there, taken care of it, maintained it at his own cost. For years! He would find out who was behind this diabolical deal. Someone would pay for this! The more he thought about it, the more certain he became. He knew exactly who had done this.

$A$t Tregorna, a man climbed down from his cart and began fumbling with the rope on the gate.

Zephaniah Cobbs heard the bleating of sheep and came out of the barn. He had just ridden in, ridden hard to get home, and barely had time to unsaddle his horse, much less a chance to catch his breath. He was expecting someone, Richard Hawkhurst, looking for his pay. But he was not expecting sheep.

Now what? He was getting too old for all this. What was Ham Blewett doing here? Ham Blewett, that dunderhead? Herding sheep into his, Zephaniah's, farmyard? Cobbs strode across the yard.

"You! What are you doing?"

"Afternoon, Mr. Cobbs," said Ham affably. "Just getting the livestock moved in. I'll be bringing my wife and children and our bits of furniture tomorrow. We'll be in the cottage so don't worry. We won't be getting in your way." Quite a long speech for the taciturn Ham Blewett.

"You bought this place?" How could this poor farmer buy Tregorna Farm? Granted, the place was a bit run-down, but the big stone house alone was worth a lot of money.

"Oh, no!" laughed Ham, unruffled by Cobbs's rudeness. "I couldn't buy this in a month of Sundays. Wish I could, but I can't."

"Then what the hell are you doing here?"

"Well," Ham squashed his felt hat in his one good hand and grinned widely. "I'm not the new owner, Mr. Cobbs, only the tenant. And the new manager. I'll be managing the farm." Ham shifted from foot to foot, delighted with his good fortune and his new position.

"So who is this new owner, would you mind telling me?"

"Why, it's Mr. Roland."

"Mr. Roland. Sébastien Roland."

"Yessir. We'll be raising sheep and exporting fleeces to Flanders. He says them'll buy near to all we can raise."

Cobbs reached into his pocket and clutched his pistol, swearing like a maniac.

"Sébastien Roland?"

Ham Blewett looked sideways at Cobbs. "Yessir, that's him. Sébastien Roland." Hadn't he just said that? "What's the matter, Mr. Cobbs?" Ham was worried now. The man's face was nearly purple. Then Ham flinched in terror. "What you need the pistol for, Mr. Cobbs? Ain't no reason to shoot a man."

Cobbs turned away, stiff with fury, and limped into the house. Heaven have mercy! How much bad luck could a man have in his life? This boy Sébastien, this pathetic boy thought he was going to ruin Zephaniah Cobbs? Ha! Well that won't be happening now, will it, Mr. Roland? I'll take care of you once and for all, and I'll do it myself and do it right this time! He patted his pocket to make sure the ammunition was still there.

Cobbs had just reached the kitchen door when he heard Richard Hawkhurst ride into the yard. Cobbs gestured him into the house. They stood in the kitchen, arguing. Hawkhurst said he deserved the rest of his money. He had done what he was told. There was a man in the woods and he had shot him. Cobbs, towering over him, shouted that the man he wanted dead was still walking around. Well, Richard Hawkhurst screamed up at him, how was he supposed to know there were two men out there in those woods? Nobody ever said a word about two men.

Again the sound of hoof beats. Who was it this time? Cobbs peered through the grimy kitchen window. Roland? That heap of putrid pig patoots? What was he doing here? Roland was heading to the kitchen door! Cobbs jumped to ram his shoulder against it and lock and bolt it. He looked frantically around the kitchen. That loathsome devil would not get his farm! He grabbed a lamp and smashed the chimney on the floor. With a shaking hand, he lit the wick and then hurled the lamp against the wall. The puddle of oil burst into flames. Haha!

"Cobbs! What the hell are you doing?" screamed Hawkhurst. Outside, Roland had heard the noise and, alarmed, had gone back toward the barn, calling to Ham Blewett. Hawkhurst saw his chance and ran for the kitchen door, but Cobbs intercepted him. They struggled. Cobbs had his pistol out. He shot the stupid little brute dead.

Cobbs seized a sliver of wood from the hearth and held it in the flames. Then, holding the burning stick aloft, he ran to the window and touched it to the curtain. The greasy old cloth exploded into flame. Cobbs laughed madly, reloaded and fired his pistol into the ceiling. He went to the next window and set its curtain alight. Haha! Watch this, Sébastien Roland! Look what is happening to the house you thought you owned! Cobbs rammed a ball down the barrel, fired his pistol at the burning curtain and danced with glee.

He heard someone pounding on the door but he paid no attention. He had to get this fire going. He wanted a big blaze! Flaming bits of curtain fell onto an untidy pile of dishtowels. They began to smoke. A basket smoldered, Mrs. Pawley's old apron caught and went up in flames. He fired at the apron and threw the pistol aside, out of ammunition. Cobbs began to cough. He grabbed a pan of bacon fat he had left on the table the week before and flung it into the flames. He backed away, covering his face to protect it from the wall of fire that erupted.

The animals outside were stamping and screaming with fear. Later, the authorities looked for the saddled horse that Sébastien Roland claimed was standing by the gate when he rode in. If there had been a horse there, it must have bolted because it was never found.

Sébastien and Ham battered and kicked the immense old door. By the time they managed to break it down, the kitchen was a roaring blaze. Ham saw the body lying half under the table and ducked in to try to reach it. He couldn't get close enough. It was too hot.

It was two days before they could approach the smoking ruins. The stone walls were all that remained of Tregorna House. The walls and the memories. They dug a skeleton out of the ashes. So Zephaniah Cobbs was dead. His remains seemed so much smaller than he had appeared in life. They put that down to the influence of a powerful personality.

*T*here had been yet another death in Porthcoombe earlier the same week. Poor Abbie Campion's fiancé met his end. Of course, she was such a pretty thing, it was certain she wouldn't be grieving and alone for long. But it was too bad about the red-haired boy.

Someone from Lamorna finally came forward days later, when the sheriff from Penzance came to investigate the death. He said he knew the young man, Peter Pendolthick. He wasn't going to name names, absolutely not, but he knew a few things, he did. He had heard that Pendolthick had been sent by someone, one dark night, to haul in a raft of whiskey barrels and several oilcloth bags of tea that had been hidden in the sea near Cadgwith. Who had Peter met there? Had he been threatened? Had someone chased him? Was it fear or was it despair that had driven the boy to mount a horse and flee into the darkness? No one knew for sure. But it was assumed that his animal had stopped very suddenly at the edge of the Devil's Frying Pan and sent the boy flying over the side. A two hundred foot drop, straight down.

Of course, anyone who lived on the Lizard Peninsula would have known to ride carefully near that coast. The horse knew better than the young man, apparently. In the long ago, the roof of a giant cave had collapsed but the arched entrance from the sea remained. Now the water poured in through the hole, hissing and rattling through the opening, reminding someone of a sizzling frying pan. Up on the moor, the huge crater, foaming with seawater and over a hundred feet wide, gave little warning of its presence. Apparently, in the dark, it had caught Peter Pendolthick completely unawares. They spotted his body floating down there the next day but by the time the sea was calm enough for a boat to get through the entrance to the Devil's Frying Pan, it had disappeared.

Bad luck comes in threes and that was the third death in the last month. Not counting the shipwrecked sailors, of course.


December 1818


$S$ tanding out on the wind-raked headland in Porthcoombe one cold afternoon about a month later, Rafe Mesola and Dickie Gummer were sure they had spotted Sébastien's black-hulled cutter, the *Formidable*, putting in to Lamorna.

"Sure, I know it's him!" exclaimed Rafe. "His sheep farm is nearby. He's probably here to load stuff. Let's go see him!"

They ran along the coast path and down the road into Lamorna. There sat the *Formidable*, riding proudly beside the wooden jetty.

"Uncle Bastien!" Rafe called, hoping for permission to come aboard. He called again but no one answered.

"Nobody's here."

"Well, let's go aboard and wait. He won't mind."

"Sure, he'll never care. Let's hide. We'll surprise him."

$S$ébastien had, meanwhile, ridden to Tregorna. The cottage that Tom Ickes had lived in was still intact and they were still able to work the farm, though the main house was a ruin. He was pleased to see that Ham Blewett was doing a surprisingly good job of running the place. Then he rode on to Porthcoombe and up to Bianca's house. He had worried a lot about her and the children since Santino's death. And he worried about Emilia. Emilia, on his mind all the time.

"It's pretty quiet here. Where is everyone?" he asked Bianca.

"Well, Rafe went out with Dickie, as you might have guessed. Emilia is in her room, reading. Here comes Violetta."

She bounced into the room. "Uncle Bastien!" She was thrilled to see him and he was very relieved to see her looking cheerful.

He thought he noticed a little liveliness returning to Bianca's face, too. After all, it had only been a month since the funeral. But he didn't like her sitting at home day after day.

"Why don't we ride to Lamorna and you can inspect my new cutter?"

"I'll go with you, Uncle Bastien."

"There! Violetta will go with me." He put his arm around her shoulders. "Come with us, Bianca!"

"Oh, I don't know, Bastien. Take Violetta. I'll do just as well staying here by the fire."

"But it's a lovely day and there won't be many more sunny days for a while. Come on! You need some fresh air. I'll hitch up your cart. We can have tea at the Wink afterwards."

"Come on, *Maman*. It will be fun!"

"Oh ...."

"Yes, you're going. I insist." Sébastien pulled Bianca from her chair.

"You were a lot less bossy, Bastien, when you were a little boy," she complained. But she and Violetta went to get their wraps.

"Get that other daughter of yours down here too. We'll all go."

He heard a bit of discussion upstairs. He paced the room. He watched the stairs. He turned and paced some more. Ah, finally. Emilia descended, a pout on her face.

"Hello, Sébastien," she mumbled.

"Hello, Emilia." Awkward, he stuck his hands in his pockets. "You look like you could use an outing too."

"So I've been informed."

"Will you help me hitch up those beasts of yours?"

"I'll help you with the donkeys, Uncle Bastien!" Violetta would do anything for a diversion. Everyone been so glum lately, but she knew for certain that black despair would have been the last thing Papa wanted for them.


*T*heir cart bumped down the hill and in Lamorna they left it near the slipway, next to a couple of hard-ridden horses that no one recognized.

"Look at her!" Sébastien exclaimed, gazing fondly at the *Formidable*. "Isn't she beautiful? May I escort you ladies aboard?"

He handed them from the dock into the cockpit.

"Come below. I'll show you all our secret hiding places." He climbed down the companionway and turned to offer the ladies a hand. A rough arm encircled his neck and a pistol was jabbed into his back.

"Get them down here too," a man commanded. He pushed the pistol tighter against Sébastien's ribs. "Get 'em down here!"

"Oho!" cackled another man. "Ladies! This looks like fun!"

Sébastien beckoned to Violetta who was standing uncertainly, looking down at him. The three women descended, silent with shock, staring wide-eyed at the strange men.

"Get over there, all of ya. Tie 'em up, Bobby."

Grinning broadly, the odiferous Bobby tied their hands behind their backs.

"Throw them in the hold while I chain this one up."

Bobby forced the women through a door and into the hold. He pushed Bianca and Emilia to the floor but he kept a tight grip on Violetta's arm.

"I like this little one! She's purty." He pulled the ribbon from her hair and spread her long dark locks over her shoulders. She was trembling. Her blue eyes brimmed with tears.

"Don't you dare lay a finger on her!" A tigress, Bianca lashed out at him from the floor.

"You jealous, sugar plum? Don't worry. There's enough of me to go around. And around and around." His black teeth gleamed with saliva.

"Bobby! Get out here!" the other man called.

Bobby pushed Violetta down beside her sister. "I'll be back, my little sweet," he told her. He leaned down and tried to kiss her. Emilia kicked him hard in the ankle. Swiftly, his hand landed a loud slap on her cheek. "You little ---!"

"Robert!"

Bobby groaned and went out to the main cabin.

"Be quick! Go take the helm. Let's pull out of here. I don't want anybody to hear his screams." He drew a knife from its scabbard and pressed its point against Sébastien's cheekbone.

Bobby climbed up to the cockpit and pushed the boat away from the dock. He swung it into the wind and headed out to sea.

When they had left the harbor behind, the other man moved close and put his mouth next to Sébastien's ear. He spoke quietly.

"I'm going to ask you just one question," he told Sébastien. "I want a straight answer and I want it now. Where's my brother?"

"I don't know your brother." The man landed a vicious kick to Sébastien's midriff.

"You were the last to see him."

"I don't know who you're talking about."

The next kick cracked a rib.

Bobby scrambled down from the cockpit. "We're at least a mile out. Ooo! Let me help with this."

"Then hold him still while I carve him up. We'll start with his face. He doesn't seem to think we're serious."

"I'll show him serious." Bobby landed a punch to Sébastien's eye. He grabbed Sébastien's chin and pulled it upright again. "Word is, you were the last to see our brother."

"I told you. I have never heard of your brother." Another punch. The eye was bleeding now.

"Oh yes you done! It were your farm he were going to, last anyone knowed."

"I have no idea …." Bobby punched him in the stomach. Sébastien's body sagged. The chains cut into his bruised flesh.

"That's enough slapping him around, Bobby. My knife'll be quicker." He grabbed a handful of hair, pulled Sébastien upright and sliced the tip of his blade across Sébastien's chin. Blood ran down his shirt. "Richard Hawkhurst. What become of him?"

"I don't know any Richard Hawkhurst."

Another cut of the blade.

"Richard Hawkhurst. Where is he?"


*I*n the hold, the three women were in tears, terrified for Bastien's life.

Violetta was shaking violently. "Make them stop, *Maman*," she whimpered. "Can't we do something?"

There was a scraping sound above them. They looked up. A tiny opening had appeared.

"Watch out! Rats!" They squirmed backwards. A pair of eyes glittered in the darkness above them. Then a nose appeared, a snub nose. A snub nose covered with freckles and teeth that belonged in a larger face. And another pair of eyes, as blue as his father's had been, blue as the sky.

The women gasped. Dickie Gummer grinned and Rafe Mesola put a finger to his lips. The boys slid down and sliced the bonds on the women's wrists.

Silently, Emilia gestured an idea. The boys nodded, very enthusiastic. Back up through the top of the hold they went. They pulled Violetta after them and exited through a hatch to the empty deck.

Bianca opened the door to the main cabin, just a crack. Bobby stood with his back to them while his brother dragged a bloody and unconscious Sébastien into the captain's quarters, apparently to make room for dealing with the three women.

"Ssst!" hissed Bianca.

Bobby turned in surprise. His eyes popped like two boiled cranberries. Bianca leaned in the doorway to the hold, alone, her chemise completely undone. She smiled and beckoned provocatively.

His knees turned to water. He stumbled into the hold.

As soon as he was through the door, Emilia clubbed him as hard as she could with a belaying pin. He hit the floor. They dragged him into the hold and shut the door.

Another minute went by before his brother, mystified, came looking for him and made an acquaintance with the same belaying pin. Lying there like two sacks of rotted kelp, the Hawkhurst brothers were rank enough to attract buzzards. Trussing them up was not a pleasant task but the women managed it.

"That takes care of them!" exclaimed Bianca, wiping her hands on her gown.

"Bianca! You were obscene!"

"What must be done, must, *cherie*. Come on, let's find Bastien and head back home. *Mon Dieu*! I could have been sitting with my girls beside a nice fire all afternoon!"

They exited the hold.

"Does this door lock? Here, help me move these chests in front of it."

"What did they do with Bastien?"

"He's in here, Bianca."

"Is he all right?"

"He's unconscious but he's breathing. I think."

"You attend to him and I'll see what those children are up to." Bianca started up to the cockpit. "*Sacré bleu*! We're miles out to sea! How will we get back? Children? Where are you? What are you up to?" A small scream. "Rafe! What are you doing?"

Emilia was sickened at the sight of Bastien sagging against a post, heavy chains tight across his chest, a puddle of blood spreading across the floor. He was unconscious. She knelt beside him. Yes, he was breathing. Oh, thank goodness.

Frantically, she rifled through cabinets. The only liquid she could find was rum. She soaked a cloth and began to dab some of the cuts around his eyes. He gasped and rolled his head.

"Crap!"

She sat up. "You're alive."

"Well, lord have mercy, OUCH! Are you trying to kill me? OW, that stings."

"Be quiet. I couldn't find any water."

"All of you are unhurt?"

"Everyone's fine."

"Who –" He closed his eyes to make his head stop spinning. "Who – who is sailing this boat?"

She stopped dabbing for a moment, and listened. They were sailing. She could hear the water rushing past the hull. Then she shook her head. "You would never believe me if I told you."

He attempted to sit up but leaned woozily and fell back. "Bloody hell! Will you stop torturing me?"

"I'm just trying to clean your face so you can see, at least."

"Get these chains off me! They're heavy."

"Just lie still while I finish."

"Stop torturing me and find the key to this damn lock!"

"You needn't be quite so rude! I don't think I care to unchain you, you big bully. You're not even grateful we saved your life?"

He groaned. "Come on. The key, damn it! I've got to get ...."

"I've got the key."

"Well have pity on me and use the bloody thing, you little witch!"

Emilia jumped up. "Don't you ever call me that again!"

"Emilia, just come down here and help me."

She tossed the key from hand to hand. "No."

"Listen, do you want me dead before the wedding?" He struggled against the thick iron chains, trying again to prop himself up on his elbows.

"I have no idea what you are talking about."

"The damn wedding!"

"Why ever are we talking of weddings at a time like this?"

"Not weddings. My wedding, blast you!"

"Lie back and rest a bit, Sébastien. You're hallucinating. Remember your fiancée? Renée? Remember she left you? Your bride is gone, not at all surprisingly."

"I'm not marrying her. She is a witch."

"Well. At least your mind is clearing."

"Look, I'll throw in a bribe. I'll bring more of that French lace if you will just unlock this."

"Save the lace for your next fiancée."

"Emilia! These hurt!"

"You'll definitely need to bribe someone, such a ghastly old scarred thing you are now."

"You've never seen my scars."

"Your face will be covered with them." Standing over him, she pointed to her chin and with a finger she traced a long line down the side of her face. "You are going to look such a wreck. Hardly marriageable material."

He hooked one foot around the back of her knee and pulled. She fell to her hands and knees on the floor beside him.

"Are you aware that if you don't unchain the father of your children, Emilia Mesola, you will die a horrid old maid?"

She blinked.

"That shut you up, didn't it? Come here. Come on, closer."

A minute later he said "Don't! Don't touch my ribs. About fifty of them are broken."


March 1819


Sébastien stood with Patrick O'Brien on a slight rise at the gate to Penlee, his country home. They watched the people gathering on the lawn below. There was still no Catholic church in the area but his terraces and lawns were beautiful settings for a church service on this mild March day. Bianca was down there, chatting with Patrick's new wife, Margaret. From the Land's End to the Lizard, people had come in wagons and carts of every description.

"Nice day for a wedding. So you're finally going to be a married man," marveled Patrick.

"It appears that way," answered Sébastien.

"Well it is about bloody time."

"You haven't done much better yourself, old man."

"I know. It took me a long time to find Margaret."

"And you're older than I am, O'Brien."

"You don't need to remind me. Ah, there's your bride. She looks beautiful. Time to go down and do this, my friend."

"I guess so."

"Are you nervous?"

"Not a bit. She will make a good wife, I can feel it."

"She's young. Will she be able to keep you in line?"

"Oh, not a doubt about that. Not a doubt in the world. Shall we go?"

"I have to get my satchel from the carriage. You go on ahead."

"You don't need it, Pat."

"I left your bride's ring in it."

"Ah. Then you'd better get it. She won't marry me without the jewelry."

Sébastien headed down the drive. Patrick O'Brien started to cross the road, but stopped. A very handsome rig was tearing along the road, pulled by two horses and driven by a liveried servant. Not wishing to get run over on the most important day in his friend's life, O'Brien waited to let it pass.

His mouth fell open. Seated alone in the open carriage, his arms spread wide on its luxurious upholstery, was Zephaniah Cobbs. Cobbs leaned forward and met O'Brien's stare with a grin so wide it showed every long, stained tooth. He waved arrogantly, threw his head back in laughter and went on his way in a cloud of dust. O'Brien stood frozen to the spot.

"O'Brien!" Sébastien called. "Hey, O'Brien! What are you doing? Are you coming?"

"Sure."

"Who was that in the fancy rig?"

"I don't know," O'Brien lied. "I do not have a clue."

*Spider Silk Bridge*

*Every spiderweb begins with a single thread released into the wind to form a bridge. When that thread finds an anchor, the rest of the web can be built. The tensile strength of spider silk is greater than steel of the same weight, and has much greater elasticity.*

William Sydney
April 1819

*I*t was one of those cold wet days that are welcomed just because it is April and anything everything is fine in April. Heavy clouds enrobed the world in thick damp mist and a chill took hold of the bones. But it was April and that meant life and hope. Things were growing where before there was nothing, little things that had been forgotten, hidden away in darkness.

In the churchyard at St. Buryan's, Emilia stood at a nameless grave marked only with a rock and the budded thorns of a rosebush. She plucked a Lenten rose blossom from her bouquet and laid it in a shallow pool of rainwater trapped on the rock's surface. Then she forced herself to turn her eyes to her father's stone. Cruel, so cruel that a man of his sunny, generous nature, was forced to lie alone in the cold rain. She stood over him and wept bitterly.

And while she did, the wind changed. The rain stopped and for just a moment, the sky cleared. Clouds were pulled away, thrown back like a big thick blanket. Emilia looked up, transfixed. There was a patch of blue sky above her and when she looked down again, the churchyard sparkled clean and bright. Two big yellow cats had come from nowhere and were lounging against Santino's stone, flicking their tails provocatively. Then the clouds billowed out to cover the sky again and the moment was gone. Emilia laid her bouquet on Santino's stone. The cats meowed cryptically and Emilia forced herself to turn away.

She had stolen the time to come here. Today, this one last time, she and Bianca were cleaning the cottage on Narrow Lane, getting ready to move to Penlee. Emilia knew she should hurry back to help. But her feet were leaden. Walking amongst the gravestones, she lost her sense of purpose. There seemed to be nowhere else she wanted to be, but here.

$A$bbie Campion was, at the same time, coming out of Neddy Basko's grocery when she was approached by a very well-dressed gentleman. He asked her a question and got her immediate attention. She stood beside him in quiet sympathy, her mouth a little "O" of sorrow. They looked together at Karrek Fekyl, the huge slab of rock in the middle of Porthcoombe cove. He had come out from London and was staying at the inn, he said. Then he asked for directions. No, Abbie said, it wasn't a difficult walk. She was going the same way, she offered. They could walk together.

Abbie chatted and pointed, the man listening with rapt attention. Up the lane, she showed him Santino's workshop, where Tim Tior worked alone now. Tim and her sister Elizabeth were expecting their first baby any day. They turned at the top of the lane and looked back toward the harbor, speaking low, Abbie shaking her head, the man shrinking into himself. Then she waited at her gate, watched him limp through Santino's garden. Saw him knock on the Mesola's door. Watched as he spoke to Bianca, and saw her hand fly suddenly to her lips. Watched her nodding, pointing through the garden, up the path to the oakwood. The gentleman bowing, swinging his walking stick resolutely, wishing her good-day and heading up the hill. Bianca beginning to follow, then stopping uncertainly under the pergola, watching after him.

$T$he path was steep and muddy, though the rain had stopped. He was glad enough to rest near the huge oak tree that the lady had mentioned. There was a pretty little arched bridge below it. He paused there to catch his breath, his heart pounding with anticipation, as much as from exertion. Gwill Brook was full of rainwater. It tumbled and sang down through the coombe. He looked up the hill and waited.

When she appeared on the path above he simply dissolved in tears. He hadn't expected her to be so exactly the image of his daughter. The same trim shape, the thoughtful set of the head. As she came closer he recognized the light brown skin he had expected. What he did not expect were the eyes, a blue so pale they seemed alight. He mopped his face with a handkerchief and tried to regain some composure before she saw him.

Emilia came down through her father's oakwood one last time. She had walked here all her life and she wondered when she would see it again. Her thoughts were deep in the past and she didn't notice the man on the bridge until she was close above him.

She would have been disturbed at seeing a man lurking there, obviously watching her intently, seeming almost to wait for her. The fine cut of his clothing, though, was curious, not what she would have expected to see in the middle of the woods here. And there was something else, something she felt inexplicably drawn toward, as though hypnotized. Something would not allow her to pass him by with only a greeting. She stepped onto the bridge and wished him a good afternoon.

"Mrs. Roland?"

"Yes?" He knew her name?

"My name is William Sydney. I was told you were with my daughter when she died in the wreck of the *Crocodile* last fall."

"Oh yes!" She felt the shock of that memory. "I was with a woman, yes. She was your daughter?"

"I believe it was she. My daughter, Caroline. She sailed on the last voyage of the *Crocodile*."

"I'm so sorry for your loss, Mr. Sydney. She was a beautiful woman."

"I wanted to come, to see this place and to, well …. I would have come sooner," he hurried on, "but my wife was ill. She also passed away last fall. Truth be told, it actually took me a while to get up the courage to come." He tried to keep the tremor out of his voice. You're a foolish old man, he said to himself. Just say what you have to say. "I had a reason to come, you see."

"Oh?"

"We had been speaking with an orphanage in London since last fall." He explained everything to her as gently as he could. His daughter had decided to go to Penzance last November, he said, looking for a brown-skinned girl.

Emilia put a hand out to feel for somewhere to sit. He sat there on the bridge with her for a time.

Finally, they rose. They started down the hill together, Emilia slipping her hand into the crook of his arm, he covering her hand with his. Both wrestling with more emotion than either could express.

What chance that, in the unnoticed breeze, over measureless oceans of space and time, a thread so thin would have caught? Somehow, a gossamer thread had caught and anchored, and a bridge was formed. A bridge that was needed was formed. And two souls made their passage, crossing together into that vacant vast surrounding from which there was no return.

## ACKNOWLEDGEMENTS

I am glad that my late mother was able to read at least part of this book and know that her life inspired the story. Her work as a foster and adoptive mother was her effort, I think, to lay to rest her feelings of abandonment. If David Campion of Stratford, Ontario had not told me about his grandfather, a Barnardo boy, I might never have heard of over 100,000 young children that were sent from England to labor on Canadian farms. Though well-intentioned, the plight of these children was often heart-breaking. The photographer Baz Richardson was so kind to allow me to transform his image of Portloe, Cornwall into the fictional Porthcoombe. Thank you to my favorite beta readers, Dorian Kincaid, Nancy Dilmore, Heidi Weimer and Lori Rivers Dilmore. Your early encouragement was heartening and your critiques invaluable. And once again and as always, thanks to Henry for, well, all the rest.

And thank you for reading *Passage Oak*. If you enjoyed it, an online review would be much appreciated. You may also be interested in *Whitebeam* and *Willow Oak,* two other books in the 'Silent Grove' series.

Proof

49908369R00193

Made in the USA
Charleston, SC
05 December 2015